WAR PARTY!

It was no more than a hunch that made Leander decide to check his back trail. He was within a few miles of Luther Ferris's farm, far from the heavy forest and into rolling lands, but an uneasy feeling came over him and made his scalp crawl beneath his coonskin cap. He halted his horse, stepped down, and tied its reins in good cover, then crept back to the trail, searching with his eyes until he spotted a narrow peephole in the brush.

Then he saw them, tall copper figures ghosting up the rise, and he counted them as they passed. He had been wrong. This was a large party—and not a hunting party. This was a war party hot on the scent. He lay still until they had passed, counting his breaths and the beating of his heart.

Then from the direction of Luther's place not far away, he heard the clanging of a bell . . .

DAN PARKINSON

SUMMER LAND

ZEBRA BOOKS

KENSINGTON PUBLISHING CORP.

ZEBRA BOOKS

are published by

Kensington Publishing Corp.
475 Park Avenue South
New York, NY 10016

First printing: June 1989

Printed in the United States of America

To Carol . . .

*An' th' two of us know
that there's no lookin' back
when a man's found his lady fair.*

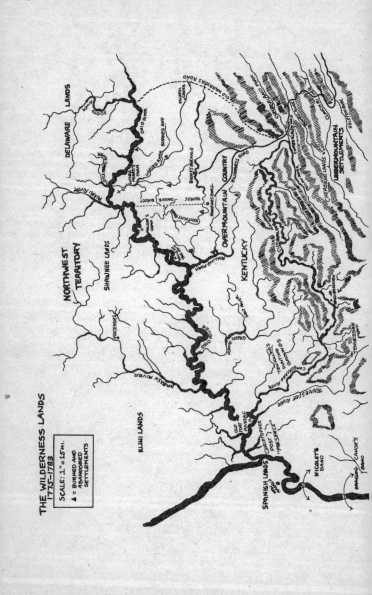

THE WILDERNESS LANDS
1775-1783

SCALE: 1" = 15 MI.

▲ = BURNED AND ABANDONED SETTLEMENTS

The White Horn

I

Autumn-Winter 1775

It had been a poor old ox with a broken horn. The bleached skull of it lay shrouded in leaf mold. Luther Ferris kicked at the porous gray bone and the one good horn rattled on its upright stump. Weather and insects had been at work on it. The soft inside, the adhesive body of the horn, was gone. He stooped to pick it up.

"That isn't any good," his sister said. "It's nigh white."

He turned it before his eyes. "That doesn't matter," he decided. "I like it."

It was a short horn, just ten inches long, but it had a subtle curve and recurve, and the lines of it pleased him. The wide body of it was bone-white, the tip black. It was hollowed deep into the tip end.

"It's a good horn," he said.

She wrinkled her nose. "Plain old white horn." Then with the sudden interest of a child, she asked, "Can you make a callin' horn of it, Luther?"

He shrugged. "I guess it's too little for that. About right for powder, though." He dropped it into the sack he carried. "Come on, Ellie. There's another tree over there."

She skipped ahead of him across a narrow meadow,

chiding over her shoulder, "Come on yourself, slowpoke. I always pick up more than you, anyway."

Sack over his shoulder, the old long gun in his hand, he ignored her. He judged they had ten pounds of walnuts already and would have fifteen by chore time. Luther was fond of his little sister. He didn't mind her teasing him for being slow. It was clumsy gathering nuts when he had to tend the sack and tote the gun at the same time. He would set down the gun long enough to clear an arm's reach of ground, but he always picked it up again before he moved. Pa had taught him that. In this country a man didn't leave his gun out of reach.

The Ferris claim lay far afield from neighbors, and the woods about were deep. They had seen Shawnee more than once, and one time they had found a fresh campsite that Pa said might have been Kickapoo.

Pa dealt fairly with the Indians that came to their gate, and he had learned a little of their language. But he cautioned the family always: "Because we trade, some will take to us. This bunch might let us be, but the next might not. Their ways aren't ours."

Luther kept an eye on the sun as they clattered nuts into the sack. When it was midway into the western sky, he picked up the gun and slung the sack over his shoulder. "Let's go home, Ellie. There'll be milkin' to do."

They crossed the creek, climbed the low bluff that bounded the high field, and started down the slope, walking between gold stalks left from the harvest. "Ellie," he said, "would you do a thing for me?"

She glanced up at him, bright and suspicious. "What is it?"

"That white horn I picked up . . . don't say anything about it. I been thinkin' about Pa's rifle. He needs a good horn for it and never made himself one. I want to fix this'un up for him. It can be a surprise."

"Can I help fix it?"

10

"You can. It'll be a surprise from both of us. How's that?"

"All right. I won't say anything. But I get to help."

The horn lay on a beam in the shed for a month. There was wood to split for winter, frost squash to gather, meal to grind, and milk to churn. There were a hundred chores to do and the cold months to prepare for. Ellie had forgotten the horn by the time Luther got around to it, but he called her nevertheless. "Do you still want to help with this?"

Her bright eyes danced. "Can we give it to Pa for Christmas?"

"I expect we can. Now you sit down here and you can shape the funnel. I'll show you how."

With a curved rasp he incised a ring around the horn, a finger-length from its tip, just below where the black color began. "You make it neat, now. Go just deep enough to cut to black, but not any deeper."

"You're doing it all!" she protested. "Let me."

He left her with it, and when he returned the ring was cut. Its edge shouldered cleanly into white keratin and its depth was midnight-black, as was the rest of the tip. "You did that just right, Ellie. It looks real pretty. Now we need another ring just here. . . ."

"You can do that one if you want to, Luther. I better help Ma." And off she went, satisfied but tired of the task. Luther grinned. She had done more and better than he expected.

When he had time, he cut the rough bottom off with a saw, filed a second strap-ring, and bored a pour-hole through the tip end. Then from a walnutwood bat, he cut a bottom plug and shaped it with chisel and file. Boiling the horn to soften it, he drove the plug into place, then heated glue and coated the seam. He sucked at the bored top to draw glue into any leaks or cracks there might have been.

He was fine-filing the edges when the bell sounded

11

from the house. He tossed the horn up on a beam, grabbed the long gun, and ran. He saw Ellie ahead of him, scurrying through the door. Pa stood there, his Pennsylvania rifle cradled in his arm. Out on the high field beyond, a file of Indians came over the rise. The leaders were already halfway down the field. Luther sprinted and hauled up beside his father, who only glanced at him.

"Stand here, Son. Your mother and sister are inside."

Luther took his father's place at the door. The older man stepped out away from the house and waited. The Indians carried bows and clubs but wore no paint. At his back, Luther heard the door open and his mother's voice.

"Jonathan?" She would have come out, but Luther extended an arm to stop her.

"Stay inside, Nora," his father said. "It's all right. I know that one there. That's Kitsicum."

The warriors were all past the crest now, and Luther saw squaws coming behind them with children. He took a deep breath and expelled it slowly. Kitsicum had been to their gate before. He and Pa had smoked and traded. Kitsicum spoke a little English as well.

At the gate the leaders stopped, and Kitsicum raised a hand. "Hasana Ferris . . . make talk."

Pa raised his hand and went to the gate. Luther stayed where he was, shielding his mother. Kitsicum had never threatened them, but one never knew about Indians. Luther heard a scuffing in the doorway behind him and knew Ellie was there, peering past Nora's skirts.

At the gate Kitsicum spoke. "We go," he told Jonathan Ferris. "Popos come, too many. Hatasi go."

Pa said something Luther couldn't hear. Kitsicum raised his arm, pointing toward the northeast. "Popos. Redcoat chief say give Popos knife. Popos come. Two, three sun. Hatasi go. Hasana Ferris go."

Luther saw his father's head shake and heard the murmur of his voice. His breath steamed in the cold air.

12

The Indian's face remained impassive, but he said again, "Popos come. Go."

Pa turned. "Luther," he called, "go to the shed. Get a sack of meal and that hindquarter hanging there."

Handing the long gun to his mother, Luther hurried out to the shed and came back lugging a fifty-pound sack and a quarter of venison. His father took them one at a time and handed them across the gate to Kitsicum, who passed them to his warriors.

"Where will the Hatasi go?" Pa asked.

Kitsicum struggled for words. He pointed to the west. "Hatasi go . . . hai, two river. Maybe Hatasi-koti two river. Maybe so. Then Hatasi plenty."

Snow had begun to fall as they talked, sodden flakes sprinkling from a leaden sky. Pa reached into his pouch and pulled out a wrap of tobacco. He extended it. "Kitsicum friend, Merry Christmas."

The Indian took it, impassive. "Merry Christmas," he repeated. Then he walked away, flanking the line of Indians still passing. There were twenty warriors, no more. But there were twice that number of women, children, and old people.

Back at the house, Luther asked, "Pa, what are Popos?"

"I don't know, Son. Another tribe, I expect. Someone Kitsicum and his people don't like."

"He said something about a redcoat chief. Does he mean British? Out here?"

Nora's eyes were large with concern. "Jonathan, do you think we should leave? Is there danger?"

Jonathan smiled. He walked to her and kissed her. Then he went to hang his rifle on its pegs. "There are no British out here. We've left all that a long way behind us. And as to the Indians . . . well, we've got along with them so far. They know we mean them no harm."

*   *   *

13

The first snow of winter was wet but not deep. Within three days it had retreated before a sky bright with frosty sun and the high field was mud beneath it. Winter's provisions were in and they stayed close for the time. Yet on the fourth morning, Pa had the need to be out. He got his rifle down. "I'll get us another deer. We can use the meat." He slung his old powder flask from his shoulder and it banged against his belt, rattling its bung loose. He replaced it. "Get me another one some day," he muttered.

As the door closed behind him, Ellie and Luther looked at each other and Ellie grinned.

At the shed, Luther got down the horn. He cleaned its glued seam with a fine rasp. Using a turn-bore, he angled a hole through the wood plug, starting at its side, and another shallow hole at the bottom to meet it. Then he turned a thong from a piece of tanned hide and fed it through the hole, drawing its end from the bottom. He tied a knot and pulled the thong back, setting the knot in the hole. The strap's other end he tied in a slipknot and fixed it around the second ring below the funnel. Finally, he trimmed the funnel mouth and whittled a bung from hickory wood. With flannel and sand he worked the horn to a fine, soft luster and took it out to see it in the light. It was a handsome horn. The ivory whiteness between black tip and dark wood plug held the eye.

At the dugout he took powder from its safe. He filled the horn and capped it, then went on to the house. Ellie's eyes danced. "Oh, Luther, it is pretty! Ma, look. We made this for Pa. For Christmas."

Nora turned it over in her hands, admiring it. "Hang it there on the peg," she said. "He can find it when he comes home."

It was late afternoon when the heard the shot. Luther came from the pole barn, gun in hand, to look up the field. At first he saw nothing, then suddenly his father was there at the crest, running hard. Directly behind him

14

were four Indians, fierce faces bright with yellow and black stripes, their heads shaved up to tall crests of feathered hair. Luther heard his mother ringing the bell, and he ran for the house.

When he gained the front corner his father was halfway down the muddy high field, slipping and weaving in the treacherous rows, and the Indians were closer behind him. Their yelping, yipping cries were a hideous din. Luther reached the stoop and glanced inside. His mother and Ellie were there, white-faced. He turned, bringing the long gun to his shoulder. He saw his father go down then, the Indians atop him. Hatchets swung and glinted red in the sun. Luther squinted along the barrel of the old musket and fired. One of the warriors spun away, then looked toward him. Blood welled from a dark arm. The old long gun was of little use at such a distance.

The Indians ran toward the house. There were more coming over the crest now, behind them. Luther dodged through the door, slammed it, and dropped the bar into place. Nora's eyes were huge. "Luther . . . your father. Jonathan!"

He gritted his teeth. "Ma, get down that fowler and stand beside the window. Ellie, you get yourself down the hidey-hole." They were standing there, staring at him, "Now!" he roared.

As fast as he could, he reloaded the musket. He poured powder from his flinthide flask, dropped and tamped an unpatched ball, dabbed powder into the frizzen pan. There was a loud thump at the door, then another.

Luther stepped to the shuttered window. He pushed his mother aside, took a deep breath, then swung open the shutter. A painted face was there and he fired full into it. He thrust the long gun at his mother and grabbed the fowler from her hand. "Load," he said.

Another Indian was in view and Luther touched off the fowler's right barrel. Its blast rattled the room and smoke

15

obscured his vision. From outside the window, stabbing from one side, a red hand grabbed the fowler's barrel and wrenched at it. Luther clung to it, twisting. The savage whirled into view, his axe raised to throw. Luther pushed the fowler forward and touched off its left barrel an inch from the Indian's chest. Then he slammed the shutter closed. There were more thumps at the door and he heard leather hinges giving way at the back window.

His mother handed him the long gun. It was now his only loaded weapon.

The door gave way first, and Nora screamed. Luther triggered the musket and saw a warrior stagger and fall, but another came in over him and Luther reversed the gun to swing it like a club. The Indian went down. Outside there more more. He saw six at a glance, then more . . . coming in.

He steeled himself, the long gun swung wide. Behind him, Nora had snugged the table atop the hidey-hole and she stood there now, holding an axe. The Indians were at the door.

There were howls outside, and the painted savages stopped. They looked to the right and began to edge away. Some of them broke and ran. Others followed. Hard on their heels, streaming past the broken door, came buckskinned warriors of the Hatasi.

Luther Ferris stood for a time, letting the shakes go through him. When he walked out the door the Popos were gone, except the ones who lay dead in the dooryard.

There were Hatasi warriors everywhere, more than he had ever seen. They stared at him curiously. He walked past them, stiff-legged, out past the ruined gate and up the muddy field to where a cluster of them stood. Pa—what was left of him—lay facedown in the mud. His fine rifle was beside him.

Kitsicum was there, and he turned impassive dark eyes to Luther. "We go . . . find Hatasi-koti two suns. We come." The Indian looked down at the body of Jonathan Ferris. "Hasana Ferris friend. Merry Christmas."

Luther buried his father in soft ground at the crest of the field. "Popo Sahawani," Kitsicum told him. "Many more. Redcoat chief give knife. Warrior come. Many, many. Bad moon time. Hatasi go. Leni-Lanape go. You go. Many bad moon."

When they were gone, Luther went down to the shed. With cold hands, he laid out tools and built a wooden cross, and inscribed it with a hot iron: *Jonathan Ferris, 1733–1775.*

When he set it at the grave, they knelt there.

"I'll load the cart," he said. "We will go in to Sulley's Fort. But I'll come back." He looked around him, at the cleared fields, the wooded lands, the lonely cabin, and barn, and shed. "I will come back." Snow was falling again, and it was Christmas Day. Some in these lands did not keep the Christ Mass, but Pa had had a feeling for it.

In the house, on the peg wall, hung a white powder horn. Before beginning to load the cart, Luther cleaned the Pennsylvania rifle. He loaded it from the new horn, then set them both aside to wait.

Time of the Red Knives

II

Summer 1778

In the evening, Kate McCarthy climbed the parapet to cross her arms on the stockade wall and let the cool breeze play in her hair. She had tended the ovens alone this day, because Julie was late delivering the bread.

Men came armed from the fields, driving cattle ahead of them. Beyond, at the forest's edge, a bend of creek caught cloud-light. How nice it would be, she thought, to slip off down there and let that cool water flow around her until the heat of day was washed away. Cool water could bathe her, cool breezes could dry her, and cool, sun-sweet gowns would await her. She sighed. Her gaze lifted across the evening distances and she caught her breath. Out there, a long way off, a ribbon of smoke rose from the darkening forest. At its base, she knew, a cabin or barn was burning.

"You shouldn't be here, miss."

She turned, startled. She had not heard his approach. He was a young man, one of the new arrivals. He cradled a long rifle in his arm, and his eyes were dark and cool.

"I came up to get some air. It's hot down there . . . and smelly."

"It is that," he nodded. "But it's near dark now. You should go down."

Not wanting to leave the coolness so soon, she pointed at the distant smoke. "I was looking at that."

"Yes. So was I." He leaned against the wall. "I was thinking it could be our place. Except our place is way past there." He leaned his rifle against the uprights and rested his arms there, next to her. "I expect it's gone now. They say they're burning all the places from here up to the river."

The distant smoke danced and dissolved as breezes found it. It was gone among the darkening hills. "When did you come in?" she asked.

"The past week. I brought my ma and my sister. Some militia came to Sulley's Fort and told us to leave. There weren't enough of us there to hold out. So we came here."

"Sulley's Fort? That's a long way, isn't it?"

"There was a settlement between, at Cherry Creek, but it's gone now. They all went upriver."

She was aware of the warm, smoky odor of him, the deep sadness in his voice. "Do you think they'll come here? The Indians?"

He shook his head. "I don't know. A place like this would be hard to take. I don't think those are big war parties out there . . . mostly just small bands lookin' for a few easy . . . ah . . ."

"A few easy scalps? That's what you started to say."

"Yes."

They stood silent, watching the night descend. Then with hard bitterness, she said, "I think they are vile!"

He thought about it, then shook his head again. "No, they're not vile, miss. It's just their way. The vile ones are them that buy the scalps."

She shuddered. Everyone now had heard rumors of the "hair buyer" at Detroit, the "Redcoat Chief" who traded trinkets for death. "You sound as though you know them . . . the Indians."

"I've known some. They aren't all bad. They're just not like us."

19

"Would you feel that way if you'd lost someone to them?"

She heard the soft intake of breath, sensed the tightening of his shoulders, and regretted saying that. He had lost someone. "I'm sorry," she said. "I'm thoughtless."

Footsteps approached in the compound below. A voice said, "Sentry there, name yourself."

He turned, picking up his rifle. "Luther Ferris, sir."

"Who is that with you?"

"It's me, Captain," she answered. "Kate McCarthy. I came up to get some air."

"You'd best come down, Miss Kate. Your pa will be lookin' for you." They heard him move away along the wall.

"Kate is a pretty name," Luther said. "And you smell like fresh baked bread."

She started and felt a flush creep up her neck. At sixteen, she was aware of the awareness of young men. But there was nothing suggestive in his tone. He had simply stated a fact. "I'd best go down now," she said.

As she started down the ladder, his voice came from above. "It will be cool up here tomorrow evening, too."

Across the crowded compound, McCarthy was doing his ledger by lamplight when Kate came in. He glanced up at her. "Ovens need to be cleaned before morning, Katie."

She glanced sharply at her sister, who sat by the open window gazing out into the night. "Julie? You were going to do that."

Julie looked around, her eyes distant. "Next time, Kate. Please? It's important."

McCarthy paid no attention, buried in his ledger, tallying supplies and sales, costs and profits. With all the extra people down from the outlands to crowd the fort at Harrodsburg, his business was doubled and more. They all needed bread and had no way to make their own. Kate wrinkled her nose, got pail and scoop, and went out to the ovens. A few moments later she heard the scuff of feet near the house, then a young man's voice and her sister's bright laughter. When she came back in, Julie was gone off someplace and her father was still at his ledger.

In early morning, as she carried meal from the shed, she saw Luther Ferris across the way and let her eyes follow him. It puzzled her that she did. He was not particularly striking, neither as tall nor as handsome as some. But there was a steadiness about him, a sureness that caught the eye. Like a sturdy young tree, she thought. He might lean from the wind, but he would stand firm and rooted and would be there when the wind had passed away.

She chided herself at such thoughts. There was work awaiting and baking to do.

But that evening when the sun was down, she went again to the stockade wall to find the cool air. And again they stood and talked and watched the night settle across a haunted land.

The beds they'd found for Nora and Ellie were bunks in a shed that would hold grain in the fall. They shared the space with a dozen other women and girls, as well as several small children. They were refugees and they took what shelter they could get. For a time Nora was withdrawn and uncertain. But at the same time she was fascinated. Rarely in late years—so many years—had she seen so many people in one place, all at once.

Jonathan had loved the distances. He had been a man of learning and a man of lore. He had gathered the old songs and the old stories, and had loved to share them when he could. But he had loved the distances more. Their piece of land near the river had been remote and often lonely, but he had loved it. Nora had seldom complained. She had him and she had her children, and

21

she immersed herself in them. The rare visits to settlements at Cherry Creek and Long Point, as well as the occasional harvest socials, had been marvelous moments that she cherished. But each had passed and they had returned to their claim. And each time she was satisfied just to be home.

She was lonely at times. It was miles to the nearest neighbor, and the occasions to call were rare. And there was always the fear of the Indians. Though Jonathan had got on well with many of them, still there were stories of others and of attacks on isolated farms.

But mostly it had been a full life, busy and cheerful, tending the corn—and later the rye and sorghum as Jonathan and Luther cleared fields of their stumps— pounding meal for johnnycake, soaking hides, spinning and weaving. And always there had been an hour each evening when they gathered by lamplight for quiet talk, sharing the things of the day. Often on those occasions Jonathan would tell them of the "wanderin' times" of his youth, reciting verses he had learned—or made up; sometimes she didn't know which—and spinning tall stories to enthrall them.

Nora loved those times. They were more than enough, she had felt, to repay for the toil and worry of each day in the wilderness.

And how he had loved to sing, her sturdy man! Old ballads, strange bits of jingle from here and there, funny songs and sad songs and songs that could make the heart swell and ache. All these he sang, strumming on a dulcimer while his rich male voice filled the cozy cabin with wonder. He taught the children his songs, and Nora marvelled at the harmonies they could produce— Jonathan's voice carrying the strong lead, Luther's changing voice more and more a match for his father's, Ellie's sweet child-angel voice stumbling over the words sometimes to delight them all.

Of it all, those lost times, she missed the singing most. She had come to accept, eventually, that Jonathan was gone. She was a widow now, and one of many in this land. But the singing was gone, and with it the sense of home that the cabin above the river had once held. Luther, she knew, still had the feeling. In the seasons at Sulley's Fort sometimes he would slip away, alone in the hostile woods, to go back there and tend the place, and she feared for him. Always they could see the distant smokes. Yet he was his father's son, with his father's love of land. Sometimes he had to go.

Gradually, Nora's hurts began to heal. She worked beside other women as lonely as she, and the stored-up talk flowed among them. The day came when a stranger, a tall, homely man visiting Harrodsburg, smiled at her and tipped his hat, and she blushed and ducked her head. That had been some time ago and meant nothing, but later she had found a piece of mirror and looked at herself and was not displeased. She was still an attractive woman, and the sorrows had not hardened her. Only her eyes, she thought, seemed wiser now than she remembered. She combed and tied her hair, and that evening she traded one of their two milk cows for some coins and a bolt of bright linen. Luther would be furious. She had smiled to herself. It wouldn't hurt Luther to be furious. She would make new things for herself and Ellie, along with a new shirt for him, and if he wanted another cow, he could take it upon himself to get one.

A company of militia came in, and there was frantic activity in the stockade compound and the huddled village around it. There had been a pitched battle with Shawnee up on the Ohio, and the militia had won. Men milled about, women gathered to listen, and children ran untended and underfoot.

A tad in shirttails skipped, laughing, into the common and almost went under a wagon's wheels. Eyes wide with horror, Nora ran and caught him. She shook him until his teeth rattled, and she scolded him. Then she dried his tears and took his hand. "Come with me," she said. Marching around the busy compound, she gathered up a

23

dozen or more untended waifs and assembled them in a quiet corner beyond the armory, under the wall. When Ellie came from the washhouse, Nora put her to work tending the children.

By the time their mothers came looking for them, there were twenty children seated in a circle and Nora was singing them a ballad. It was an old song she had learned from Jonathan years before and only vaguely remembered, but she recalled enough to keep them interested. She wondered later how many of them had learned to write their names or been taught to read, how many had ever been taught to recite some lines . . .

The next morning she went timidly to the captain's office and rapped on the door. A militiaman let her in and the captain looked up from his desk.

"There must be a place for the children," she told him. "I want the hay cleared from that building by the gate and the roof patched."

He stared at her.

"Also, if some of your men can build benches, we could have school there."

Weeks passed then without sign or report of Shawnee, and the captain called for volunteers to scout north toward the river. Luther Ferris stepped forward. He was issued powder, lead for shot, and a blanket.

He found his mother at the hay barn that had become a school, directing the work of some of the men. "I'll be gone for a few days," he told her. "Maybe while I'm out I can see our place, see if the house and barn still stand. Maybe we can go home soon."

She looked at him oddly, a confusion in her eyes. "You must be careful, Luther. You don't have to go."

"I'll be all right." He grinned and hugged her. "I want to see the place. If the Indians are gone as they say, there might be time still to put in a crop."

"Just be careful, Luther. Please."

To Ellie, he winked and said, "Any old Shawnee I can't outtalk, I can surely outrun." He wanted to find Kate before he left, but the scouts were assembling at the gate and there was no time. "Ellie, you can do a thing for me. Go to the bakery and find Kate McCarthy. Tell her I've gone but I'll be back. Tell her if she wants to, she can watch from the stockade in the evenings."

His sister cocked her head at him. "Why would she do that?"

He shrugged. "I don't know. But it will please me to think she might."

They watched him as he strode toward the gate, his wide hat straight upon his head, provisions slung at his back, Pennsylvania rifle across his arm, and his ivory-white horn hanging at his side. Nora's eyes were moist and she laid a hand on Ellie's little shoulder. "He does look so like his father, doesn't he?"

Thirty-five young men filed out of the fort. Beyond the village they broke into groups of five, some to the east, some north, and some angling westward. People on the ramparts and in the fields watched them until, one by one, they were gone into the forest.

Kate was in the bake shed mixing dough, her hair tied up and her sleeves rolled high in the heat. She sensed that she was not alone, and she turned. Ellie Ferris sat on the stool just inside the door, watching her. She didn't know how long the child had been there. "You startled me, Ellie," she smiled.

The girl studied her, pixie eyes moving quizzically from the top of her flushed head to the hem of her long skirt, then back to her face. "I guess I don't understand about men," she said.

Kate half turned to resume her mixing, then turned back, her brow creasing. "What do you mean by that?"

"Well, I think you're nice, but I've seen ladies who are prettier. Besides that, you always have flour all over you."

Kate stared at her. "Ellie, I don't know what you're

talking about."

"My brother. He's gone off with the scouts. He said to tell you that you can watch from the stockade in the evenings. Will you do that, do you suppose?"

"Oh." Kate wiped her hands and went to the open door. She looked toward the gate. "How long ago did he leave?"

"A while ago. There were thirty-five scouts. I counted them."

"Oh."

Ellie pursed her lips and raised a brow. "Well, will you?"

Kate gazed across the hot, busy compound. Then, realizing the girl had spoken, she turned. "I'm sorry, Ellie. Will I what?"

As though to make sure she were understood this time, Ellie recited, "Luther said it will please him to think you might watch from the stockade. Will you?"

Julie appeared at the door. Her face was flushed and a young man stood a few yards away, scuffing his feet and twisting his hat. "Kate? Pa says to hurry and get the dough mixed."

Kate stamped her foot in irritation. She rolled her hands in her apron. "Then you come in here and mix it yourself, Julie McCarthy! You tell Tom Jackson he'll just have to wait." She turned to Ellie. "Yes, I expect I might watch from the stockade."

The first scouting party returned after four days, from the northeast. They had gone as far as the fork of the Licking River, then ranged northward. They had found burned ruins at three places and one cabin still standing but deserted. Yet they had seen people returning, anxious to get in one late crop. The next day two more parties came in, one from the northeast and one from the west. The latter reported more extensive burnings, but had seen no Indians.

26

Two days later a party came from the northwest. They had ranged out three days march. They had counted nine burned steads and two still standing, but no recent sign of the Shawnee.

Another two days passed without word, then two more parties came in. They had circled and met, then marched in force all the way to the river's falls. They were grim-faced at what they had seen—and at what they had buried along the way. Some way out they had crossed the trail of another party of scouts moving northward but had not seen them.

Each evening now Kate McCarthy went to the north rampart and gazed into the distance until long after dark. Sometimes there were others there, too, waiting for the five still gone.

The captain sent a patrol of mounted militia to scour the north routes, but they found nothing. In the evening Nora Ferris and Ellie came to stand with Kate. They watched the hills darken until distance blended into starry sky. Off to the east there were lights again in the hills, people returning to rebuild their homes. To the north there was nothing but darkness.

On the fourth day after that last patrol only Kate and Nora stood watch, and the next evening Kate was there alone. The fort was nearly empty now. People had moved back into the village, and many of the refugees were drifting away, frightened but determined to go home.

Then they came from the north, two of them, one helping the other to walk, and women came to peer at them in the distance. Kate and Nora were among the first to turn away. Neither of the distant figures was Luther.

Men brought them in, and women tended the injured one. There had been a fight. They had gone north, all the way to the river, and split up there for a search. Four of them had returned and waited, then had met a party of expeditionaries coming down in boats. They had joined them, crossed the river, and picked up fresh tracks of a war party on the other side. They had followed and attacked. It had been a mistake. Some had made it back to the river, some had not.

But they had learned something. Captain Clark was on the river. He had driven the Shawnee back at two points as he passed. The expeditionaries were an advance party for him. Now the Shawnee had withdrawn entirely across the river, so far as they could tell, and were heading west toward Vincennes.

In the week that followed, Nora Ferris went about her business, occupying herself from dawn to dark with the making of a regular school for the village. Ellie tagged after her, and in the evenings only Kate McCarthy still went to the silent stockade wall.

There had been a summer storm and the night air was washed clear. Kate climbed the rampart and went to her usual place, leaning on crossed arms on the top of the wall. Sadly she watched the day end and darkness descend on the forest to the north. To the east and the west were specks of lantern light. People were rebuilding. There was a light to the north, but it was high and cold. The north star stood where it always had, above a silent land. Kate gazed at it for a time, and when she looked down there was another light, a tiny winking light in the forest beyond the fields. She fixed her eyes on it and saw it move. It disappeared, then appeared again, closer. Holding her breath, she watched it. It was in the far fields, coming nearer. A lantern. Someone with a lantern.

She turned, flew down the ladder, and ran to the fort's main room where there was light in the window. She pounded on the door. "Captain! Captain, please! Come quickly!"

In the glow of approaching lantern light she had seen a reflection, a hint of ivory where it shone. A white powder horn.

When they brought Luther Ferris in he was hurt, sick, and exhausted, and they had to pry his fingers from the rifle he carried. The man who had found him, the one with the lantern, said only, "He come by me out there, talkin' to himself and singin' some kind of ballad. Only there wasn't nobody there to talk to. So I brung him on in."

For several days then it didn't matter whether school kept, and what baking was done was handled by Julie McCarthy and her father. The fevers came and went, and then Luther slept. When he awoke he smiled. "It's still there, Ma. They didn't get it. They tried, but I was there and they didn't burn our place."

Nora Ferris stood before her son and shook her head. "No, Luther, I've decided. I'll not go back there. The land is yours, not mine. I belong here now."

"Then I'll go alone," he said.

She looked long at him, then lowered her eyes. "Yes, I suppose you must."

Riding one mule and leading another, carrying his rifle and looking straight ahead, Luther rode out from the compound at Harrodsburg, his eyes to the north. At the gate he stopped, for Kate McCarthy stood there, a wrapped bag and two boxes resting on the ground at her feet.

"You can't do it alone, Luther," she said.

He got down and lashed her things onto the pack mule, then he took her hand. "You can ride up here with me. We'll swing a little east. They say that there's a preacher at St. Ashban, just past the Tahnessay Trail."

Tenkiller

III

The sun was low above shadowed hills across the valley, its slanting rays just pinking the mist of lowlands where willows grew along a tiny stream. The mists would be frost by morning and the stream would have ice along its edges, but now the only hints of fall were a crispness in the stirring breeze and the falling of bright leaves in the wilderness. On the slope above the willows an old fallen oak lay in a shallow cleft, its bare limbs protruding upward in random pattern, dry bones of a forest giant felled by long-ago storms. About it was a stillness. Nothing stirred there except the sluggish fronds of cedars above, caught by a drifting breeze, and a flock of pigeons still higher, circling in to find shelter for the night.

The breeze touched the cedars again, and a zephyr made tall grasses dance. At the fallen oak it whispered about, turning the gray-brown fur of a barely visible shape that rested there undercover. The fur was raccoon, a pelt with tail in place, a warm cap for the man who wore it. For hours he had crouched there, motionless as death, waiting for the ones he knew would come. The rifle in his hand was charged and ready, and at his belt were a tomahawk and a knife both honed to razor edge.

Eyes as still and pale as the winter sky watched the lazy circling of the pigeons, pairing and grouping as they selected roosts. In the near distance, a little way down the slope, birds veered away in sudden panic and he knew what it meant. They were coming. They had selected the route he thought they would, the one he had planned that they would take. He knew them now. Over a span of four days and nearly a hundred miles of wilderness he had learned all about them. Their patterns, their habits, the way they thought . . . how they would react. He had thought they would circle, and they had. And while they circled he had gone ahead of them, knowing they would turn south again.

They were coming now. Would they be together? He thought not. He had given them cause to spread out and watch their backtrail. He counted on the fact that they would.

There had been eleven of them four days ago, when he first found them. Now there were three. Eight times in four days he had struck them. Four had fallen to his rifle, one to his tomahawk, and two to his knife. The other . . . that one had nearly gotten him. That one had separated and ambushed the ambusher. He carried the cuts and bruises of the encounter, but he was alive and that one was dead like the rest. He had broken his neck.

These were not like the Indians who had raided again and again during the time of the smokes. These were a different tribe—taller, more coppery in coloration, with different craft to their leggings and moccasins, different wearing of their hair.

But they were no less warriors and no less Indian. In that respect, they were like all the others. In at least that way, they were like those that had killed his father and mother, sisters and brother, had burned to the ground the little cabin that had once been home to him.

Would they spread on the path, as he expected? He thought they would. It would be their way. With only three left, they would move silently and apart now. One would come, and then another, and finally the third some way back. They were hunters and warriors, and they knew the country. But he knew them. He waited.

Three years had passed since that bloody summer when Tom Jackson had died in his arms, as did others about him, young men buying peace at a terrible price. He had made it home, stopping off to do a thing that haunted him, to tell Julie Jackson that her husband—her husband of such a short time!—was gone. Then he had gone home and found . . .

For a long time he had done nothing . . . nothing that counted for anything. He had slept in a bunk in the Harrod stockade, doing this or that as needed by those around him. He had just existed. But that became intolerable. Without a word one day, he had gone from there. He had roamed the wilds for a while, then joined a ranger company for a time, then with a horse and provisions had gone hunting.

He had hunted for pelts with those he met sometimes, and then at times he would take the trails alone, still hunting. But not for pelts. He was hunting now.

In the darkening mist below the slope a deer appeared, as though by magic, to pause for a moment beside a thicket, looking back. Then it bounded and was gone. Pale eyes below a coonskin cap narrowed and shifted. Sixty heartbeats passed, and then he saw the first of them angling up the slope on silent moccasins, ghosting through the shrubbery, a tall man-shape more furtive than the deer could ever have been.

The Indian was young, not more than sixteen or seventeen years, he guessed. Younger than himself by a year or two. Dark agate eyes swept the slope, seeing everything there was to see. Not seeing him, though, for he learned from them and others like them. He knew how to hide.

The Indian came nearer and he knew him. He knew them all. This one he thought of as Round Eyes, and he thought that Round Eyes and one of the other two remaining—the one he thought of as Gimp because of a lurch that must come from an old injury—might be brothers. They looked alike in their features. Round Eyes was proving himself now, taking the lead. He was making himself a target, drawing fire so the others—Gimp and Buffalo Tail—might have a chance to find and attack the enemy.

With the still patience of the hunter, he waited, not moving, not looking directly at the approaching Indian. Sometimes people knew when they were being looked at—and from where. He watched from the corner of his eye and waited.

Round Eyes passed within yards of him and went on, and now Buffalo Tail was in sight, coming up the same path, the buffalo tail fastened to his belt twitching behind him. He was an older warrior, maybe thirty or forty years, but it showed only in his face. He was as lithe and muscular as the other two. The hunter waited.

Buffalo Tail passed, and he saw Gimp. Gimp was watching the backtrail, paying less attention to the path than those ahead of him. They had seen what was there. His task was to see what came after.

Now the hunter tensed, and as Gimp came closer, turning to look back, he drew the knife from his sheath. Gimp studied the way back, then continued on, his peculiar gate noticeable on the angling slope. The hunter saw now that he had a deep, ugly scar on the calf of his left leg, along the side. A bear might have done that, or a hog or an enemy. There was no way of knowing. Nor did it matter.

For a moment the Indian was abreast of the hiding place in the fallen oak, then he was past . . . two steps, three . . . maybe he heard something then, or maybe a spirit spoke to him. He jerked his head up and turned—too late. The last thing he saw was the bearded face of a fierce young white man as the hunter's knife drove into his throat and up into his mouth.

As Gimp fell the hunter rolled away from him, scattering the leaves of autumn. Up the path Buffalo Tail turned, brought up his rifle, and fired. But his target was not where his shot went. He was two feet to the right,

33

coming up to a kneel and raising a rifle. The shot shattered Buffalo Tail's breastbone and exploded his heart.

Further up, Round Eyes raised his old musket and its hard thunder echoed across the valley. It was a useless shot. The hunter stood, looked up the rise at him, and poured powder into his long rifle.

Round Eyes shouted, started to run toward him, then turned and disappeared beyond a thicket. The hunter finished reloading, practiced fingers setting and seating the ball while pale eyes scanned the terrain around him.

Rifle loaded, he cleaned his knife on Gimp's leggings and put it away. He strode up the path to where Buffalo Tail lay and rolled him over, then moved on.

Until full dark he hunted, and again at first light. But Round Eyes had vanished. One Indian alone, in a vast wilderness, he could have been anywhere by then. With a sigh, the hunter turned back. He had killed ten. That was enough—this time.

He took no scalps, nor did he notch a stick or tie knots in a line to count them. He needed no trophies, nothing to make him remember. He would always remember.

It was four or five miles to the place he had left his horse, far aside from the line of the hunt. Beyond that, it might be a hundred miles back to where he had started. Up on the Green, maybe he would find those he had hunted pelts with. Some of the packs they cached were his. And with the cold winds coming, they might put in another season before they headed back to the settlements. And when they went back, he would look up Julie. Memory of Tom Jackson had faded with the passing of time. But memory of his widow remained strong in him. He wanted to see her again, now that time had passed.

From a hilltop, dark eyes watched him go. Round Eyes had not gone far. He had only hidden and waited. There was little he could do now, but he wanted to see the white man as much as he could. He wanted to remember every feature of him. He wanted—one day—to have reason to

34

have remembered.

His name was Goga, and in his language the word meant crow. And just as the hunter had given Goga a name—had thought of him as Round Eyes—now Goga gave a name to the white savage who had killed his brother and all the rest of their party. He named him *s'gohidihi*. In the language of Goga's people it meant "tenkiller."

The Springtime Man

IV

Spring 1781

Crispin Blount was a walking man. He came and went with the seasons. When his singing rang down through the hills, it was taken as a sign that spring had come.

"O there is a fair lass at Port Comfort," he sang, "and she carries her coals in a scuttle. Young gentlemen's heads she does turn," his voice rang, "while she winds their poor hearts on her shuttle."

Six inches over six feet tall he stood, storkish and lean as a man made of sticks. He was fluid in motion, big feet pacing the miles, but awkward-seeming when he was at rest. Dappled red hair danced in the breeze and stood in graying tufts before his ears. His proud beak of a nose overshadowed his wide slit of a mouth and separated deep-set brown eyes that laughed at secret things and missed very little of what there was to see.

His clothing was faded, his boots sturdy and scuffed. The mule he led had bells on its pack straps.

"O Rowena, the belle of Port Comfort," he bellowed, "Rowena sweet dream by the sea! If you mus' share the bliss of your apricot kiss, then save all the pits, dear, for me, for me-ee-ee . . ." His voice cracked on the high note, but sheer lung power patched it back together. Startled birds fled the thickets of two hillsides as small creatures peered out in bewilderment. "Oh, aye, save the pits, dear, for me!"

The mule Mystery shook her head, rattling her bells. Crispin Blount looked around, scowling. "Ye've ne'er been in such fine voice yerself," he pointed out.

He topped a ridge and saw cleared fields below. Away in their midst, sprawling out from a low stockade, was a settlement. "Yon is Harrodsburg," he told Mystery. "It's there the smith's name is Cook and the cook's name is Smith. The captain is Clark and his first clark is Butler, an' if any soul of the local gentry has a butler, then times has got better since last we was here. Oh! . . ." he sang out, and Mystery shook her harness bells, "come down to Harrodsburg, down in Kaintuck, seekin' a bed an' a supper. Should a widder wi' cottage be offerin' pottage, a wise man would best take her up-er! . . . Upper? A wise man," he confided to the mule, "takes what's offered." He took her nod for agreement.

He shifted the weight of Old Yellow Dog on his arm. "O . . . a man be a footloose an' quarrelsome thing! A man can ride reckless an' high! But a good woman's kiss-ss-ss an' a measure of bliss-ss-ss . . ." He liked the effect of the drawn-out *ss-ss-ss*. Wind in the pines, it sounded like. "Makes him sweeter than gooseberry pie!" He grinned his satisfaction and ignored Mystery's tinkling protest. The trace pitched downward and he lengthened his long stride. Another mile of the good earth had heard from Crispin Blount.

Down on the flats he cast a practiced eye about him and decided he was within hearing of those in the nearby fields and toward the edge of the town. He raised his voice in finest form.

"O bring out your pots an' your locks an' your buckles! Bring out whate'er needs mendin'! For it's that time o' year an' Crispin Blount's here, so bring on the things as need tendin'!"

"Ho, Crispin!" a man hailed him from a new-furrowed field. "How long's it been? Two seasons?"

37

"Is it George Morley, now?" He shaded his eyes. "I've been far an' afar, George, an' haven't I seen some sights!"

"My woman has a kettle with a sprung seam, Crispin!"

"Bring it around, then." He waved and strode on toward the town. "O hey-diddle-die an' a fresh apple pie an' I'll dance to the tune of a fiddle . . ."

Ahead of him they relayed the message, "Lock up your wives and your daughters, boys. Crispin Blount has come back."

Much had changed about Harrodsburg in that brief time since the bloodletting caused by the red-knife bounties had shifted to other climes. The Shawnee still crossed the river sometimes to raid, but those forays now were far down past the falls in distant backlands. Though no man yet went far unarmed, these upland ranges known to some as Transylvania but to most as Kentuck had known peace now for a time.

The old stockade that had stood through the red fury was now a centerpiece, with a good town spreading around it. Every third cabin he saw was of fresh-peeled timber, and a dozen or more were just coming off the ground amidst the tents and lean-tos of those who would reside there. Even two seasons ago, blackened stumps of some of the first settlement had stood as evidence of the bloody time. Lord Dunsmore had done his worst, and General Hamilton his. Yet here now was a bright and growing place where the burned structures had been cleared away, their sturdy timbers salvaged for better purpose.

To the right, at the edge of the town, he counted two, then three real houses, larger than the cabins that were elsewhere. One of them was a tall and imposing structure with whitewashed framing and glass at its windows.

A flock of shirttails had formed a procession in Mystery's wake, laughing and shouting, darting in and out for glimpse of what her wondrous packs might hold. Over his shoulder, Crispin warned them sternly, "Stand off from the mule there, tads. Her dainty hooves can strike like lightnin'. Not a season past this very mule was sprung on by a painter, and she dispatched that fearsome critter with just one kick."

That backed them off. But one, less credulous than his peers, sidled in again. "Ain't any mule," he declared, "can lick a painter. Must have been some other thing."

Crispin shook his head, never slowing his pace. "It were a painter for a fact," he said. "And the biggest old cat these eyes ever did see. Big as an ox it was, an' its eyes a-flamin' like the pits of perdition. Ol' Mystery here, she just laid back her ears and hind-ended the poor thing right out of its misery."

The boy's eyes were wide with half belief. "If it was that big, I bet you fetched its hide."

"Nope. That mule, she kicked it so hard it flew up in the top of a hickory tree too tall for me to climb. So I had to leave it hangin' there. But I never did see a bigger painter."

The covey kept their distance then, eyeing Mystery with awe and respect.

In a meadow off the road, booted men tended a brush corral where horses were being spring-gentled while others pastured on the lush graze beyond. As Crispin counted the herd his lips compressed in a silent whistle. Something new, indeed. Near a hundred head, he reckoned, and stock that would make a Richmond gentleman's blood run hot. No redland animals these, he noted, but fine-bloods of the best lineage, lean and sturdy regal beasts suited to a racing ground or a king's retinue.

Atop the corral's timber chute two men and a half-grown boy sat, watching intently as handlers worked the horses inside. Nearby, men were building a stable and beyond it stood a new, long barrackslike building.

The three atop the chute were richly dressed, though casually so, as men born to tailored coats and fine linens, as comfortable in finery as other men might be in homespun. One of the men was thickset and stocky, his

39

girth emphasized by the bright lining of his long-tailed coat and the tricorn hat set firmly atop a mane of brown hair. The other man and the boy looked to be father and son, both dark-haired and fine-featured. Both were in shirtsleeves, the new linen snow-white in the sun.

"You, boy," Crispin beckoned, and one of the shirttails hurried forward. "Those fine horses there, whose might those be?"

"Squire Trelawney's, sir," the boy told him. "That's him on the beam yonder, with Captain Post and Christopher. They come up from the river after thaw, bringin' them horses for the squire. Captain Post is a Boston man, sir, but he's seen the Spanish lands, so they say."

Leave it to the children, Crispin thought, to know what's afoot. "And just who might this Squire Trelawney be, tad?"

"He's the Squire, sir," the boy said, as though any fool should know. "He come the past season, with his men an' his baggage, an' they say it taken ten flatboats just to get him here. He come with Virginia warrants that says a good bit of land hereabouts—that folks thought was theirs—is his. That be his house yonder . . . the biggest one."

Absently, Crispin dug into his pouch and came out with an oilcloth bag. From it he withdrew a sweet, then glanced back at the assemblage of youngsters behind him. With a shrug, he replaced the sweet and handed the bag to the boy. "This be horehound, son, an' I charge you share it out wi' the rest of your tribe. Now scat!"

Abreast of the first cabins, he took up his song again. "O bring out your pots an' your locks an' your harness, an' put on a bowl an' a fiddle. For Crispin is here to fix up your gear"—he turned a triumphant grin on Mystery—"an' mayhap to weave you a riddle!"

Captain Post, atop the corral, had turned to see him, and Crispin noted the man's eyes were quick and alert, glittering dark marble in a sun-touched face. The man peered at him, turned away, then turned to look again, scowling aslant as one distracted and puzzled. Crispin waved.

At a stable he found space and good grain for Mystery. He stacked the packs in a corner of the stall, leaned Old Yellow Dog beside them, and spent a time grooming and flanneling the mule. Her contented munching made his stomach rumble. When she was tended, he stepped out into the common, lifted his nose, and breathed deeply. He savored a scent he found there. He returned to the stall, dug through his packs, then went out again and followed his nose. Near the stockade, he asked a man, "Whose house is that yonder?"

"The widow Ferris has it now, and the widow Jackson with her."

"Ah. Wida-women, is it?" He crossed, paused by an open window to test the air again, then rapped on the doorsill. The woman who opened the door was handsome, auburn-haired, and had to tip back her head to look at him as he swept off his hat.

"Ma'am, in your kettle be ham hocks an' beans, cooked wi' clove. There's fresh bread on your table an' a hungry man at your door who'd tell ye a tale, sing ye a song, an' bless your bright eyes were his belly full."

She stared up at him in amazement, then humor tugged at the corners of her lips and she arched an eyebrow. "The hungry man's nose is as keen as it is prominent." She stepped back. "Wipe your feet," she told him. "And duck your head. This house was not built for the likes of you."

He did as he was told. The door-beam, like most, was a scant six feet high and the hewn rafters of the place not much higher. "A cozy house," he admitted, watching her as she closed the door. A fine profile, he thought—eyes that had known sorrow and a chin that had defied it. A handsome woman. She turned quickly and caught his gaze upon her, and Crispin felt his ears going red. There was a recognition in her dark eyes that left him flustered.

41

Crispin had been to Harrodsburg two springs of the past three. It was a wonder to him that he had not set eyes on this woman before. He would have remembered. Still, she looked slightly familiar.

"I do declare!" The voice from across the room brought him around. A young woman was in the pantry door, clutching a pot in apron-wrapped hands. "It's Crispin Blount, it surely is."

Sunlight struck through honey hair to halo a small face that was all dark-shadowed eyes and small, full mouth. Crispin grinned with unabashed delight. "Julie? is it Julie McCarthy I behold? Why, lass, how be you?"

She set the pot on the table, wiped her hands on her apron, and hurried to him. Ignoring the hand he extended, she threw her arms about his midsection and hugged him. Crispin didn't hesitate to return the hug. A wise man takes what's offered.

He well remembered the baker's pretty daughter from past stops at Harrodsburg, but his memory was of a ripe, impetuous child, a quicksilver imp by turns bold and petulant, laughing and somber . . . a lovely powder keg with a burning fuse at its lip. But somewhere through the seasons, there had been a change. The girl with her arms around his waist was no child.

It was a moment only. Then she backed away, laughing. "Oh, I have been impulsive again. But I do declare, Mr. Blount, it's good to see you. Have you brought grand things to trade this year? And stories? I just know you have new stories to tell. Nora, this is Mr. Blount. He travels. And it isn't McCarthy anymore, Mr. Blount. My name is Jackson now. I was married, you see, but he went to siege the forts with Captain Clark and—"

"How do you do, Mr. Blount? I'm Nora Ferris." The older woman's smile was gracious, her interference with Julie's monologue adept. Crispin had the notion she was protecting the girl from her own thoughts. He glanced at her with renewed interest.

"My very great pleasure, Mistress Ferris." His bow,

from a half crouch enforced by the low rafters, was awkward. He grinned at her. "I reckon these old feet for once have not led me astray. Good food and pretty ladies all under one roof. What bliss can a wanderin' man endure?"

"That roof will be your undoing if you don't watch your head, sir. Come, pull a stool to table and sit down before you brain yourself on a rafter."

"You've made enough to feed a brigade," he marveled as Julie ladled food before him. The women were silent for a moment, but he caught the look that passed between them and it puzzled him. Quick anger sparked in Nora Ferris's eyes, and Julie looked afraid.

"Sometimes lately there've been guests," Nora said, biting off the words as though there were more to say but she chose not to.

He waited, inviting clarification. He caught Julie's eye. She was biting her lip.

"Men from the horse camp," she said. "They come sometimes since Captain Clark has been away."

"Clark's away? Then who's in charge at Harrodsburg?"

Nora Ferris looked at him. He was in her house, at her table, but he was a stranger. "That's a bit hard to say at the moment, Mr. Blount. Would you care to speak a grace?"

Puzzled, he waited while the women bowed their heads, then bowed his own. "Lord bless this board and those who tend it, and bless this food and those who'll end it." He glanced up, expecting at least a smile for his words, but the women's faces remained grave. He closed his eyes again. "And let no clouds darken the bright eyes of those who here abide," he added. "Amen."

With no further amenities, Crispin set about demolishing the portions put before him. For a time, the women found themselves hard pressed to keep him supplied.

"It's well we fixed for a brigade," Nora commented, "for it seems that's what we have at our table."

"Good food is like good company," Crispin said. "When a man's been afar, there's no such thing as too much of either." Pausing, he drew a wrapped parcel from his shirt. "From out in the common this old nose savored the vapors of ham hocks and fresh bread a-baking, then these old eyes found beauty in this house and these old ears have thralled at lovely voices. I can contribute a small thing to complete the artistry, if I may."

"I swear we have a strange man here," Nora arched a brow at him. "One minute he drawls like a mountaineer, and the next he proclaims like a scholar. What odd roots you must have, Crispin Blount."

"'Tisn't roots, but the lack of them, that makes for strange admixtures," he winked at her.

Julie took the package from him. "What is it, Crispin?"

"It's coffee, lass. Go and grind a dainty fistful of these beans, then dump them in a boiling pot and we'll finish this fine meal in style."

In these backlands, the packet was a treasure. He shooed Julie off to put it to use, then sat back and patted his belly. "Not in a season," he told Nora, "has this walking appetite been so finely fed. I wonder what service a man might perform to repay for such a meal?"

"None asked," she told him and set about clearing the table.

He leaned back, crossed long legs, and watched her, enjoying the natural grace of her motions. Crispin Blount was a man who cherished beauty where he found it.

Bemused, he crinkled his eyes and chewed his lip, then softly began to sing. "I've seen the ports of Chesapeake, the wonders gathered there . . . the tall ships suited out in sails to venture who knows where . . ." He paused, cocked his head, and continued in a stronger voice. "I've wandered roads that turn an' wind, with riddles ahead an' marvels behind, an' always a-lookin' out to find the sight of a lady fair."

Hands wrapped in her apron, Nora stood by the

44

sideboard, a quizzical smile playing at her lips. Julie had come back from the pantry.

Having hit his stride, Crispin continued in the voice that rang down mountains. "Oh, I've been where sunrise burns the mist, where vapors dance in air . . . where forests whisper and meadows sing, and I've found joy to spare . . ." Dishes rattled on their racks. "But give me a fiddle wi' just one string, or a bell or a drum or any old thing . . . and I'll sing ye a song 'til I've sung ye a sing o' the sight of a lady fair!"

In the ringing silence as he caught a breath, Nora Ferris whispered, "My goodness!" and Julie giggled and clapped her hands. Curious faces peered through the open window.

Swelling his chest, Crispin thumped the tabletop for time and threw back his head. "Oh, hey-nonny-ho for the life o' the road, where a wanderin' man must fare . . . though he muse the bright days and he dream the long nights of a lass with the sun in her hair . . . ." He arched a brow at Nora and it was her turn to blush.

The voice at the window was harsh and demanding, shattering the moment. "Here, now! What's all this caterwaulin'?" A thickset man with bushy brows and flattened nose had pushed through the gathering crowd and was leaning in at the window, beefy hands on the sill.

Crispin's mouth, open for the next resounding rhyme, clamped shut and he turned a somber scowl on the man. "Caterwauling? Is that what you said, sir? Caterwauling?"

"I did," the intruder sneered. "Nora, who is this hollerin' crow and why is he in this house?"

Nora Ferris had gone pale. "Mr. Drummond, you are intruding in my house."

The man glared at her and the glare became a leer. "It isn't me that's sittin' at your table, Nora Ferris, and squallin' like a sow in a mire. I asked you, who is this bumpkin?"

Crispin's jaw dropped open and he sat bolt upright. "Squallin'?" He pointed a long finger at the man. "I have

45

a mule, mister, with a more delicate ear than yours!"

"Then sing to your mule." The man's glare swung back to Crispin and the voice became menacing. "You don't belong in this house."

"I say who belongs in this house!" Nora erupted. "Mr. Blount is my guest here. Withdraw from my window, Mr. Drummond!"

Julie edged back to the pantry doorway, her eyes frightened. At the sudden fury in Nora's voice, Crispin glanced at her. "Mistress Ferris, is this man annoying you?"

It was Drummond's turn to erupt. His heavy shoulders tensed as though he would come through the window. "And if I were, what would you do about it, caterwauler? A man comes callin', expectin' to be fed, and finds some idiot has et his meal and then taken to hollerin' so's the whole town knows he's here. . . ."

"Hollerin'?" Crispin's cheeks went white to the ears. "By damn, sir, I've a mind to . . ." As he came to his feet, his head slammed into a rafter and the world spun. He went to his knees on the plank floor, hands on his head, tears starting from his eyes.

"Haw!" the man at the window roared. "Haw-haw-haw . . ." He pulled back from the window, heading for the door.

"Oh, my heavens," Nora gasped, and ran to drop the bar into place. It fell home and there was a thump, then loud pounding. Nora stood for a moment, wide-eyed, then turned back toward the window. Julie was already there, slamming the heavy shutters.

In the sudden dimness the swelling of interested voices outside was a muted babble. The only light now was from a high midden-window in the far wall. Julie Jackson, her eyes bright with excitement, set about lighting a lamp.

Waves of vertigo swept Crispin, then slowly receded. He caught his breath and blinked watering eyes. The top of his head felt as though a tree had fallen on it. Carefully, keeping one hand there and eyeing the treacherous rafters, he got to his feet. After a moment the room stopped spinning, though his skull hurt terribly. He eyed the barred door. "When I get through with him . . ." he rasped.

"Mr. Blount, for heaven's sake, sit down! You can't go out there. Sam Drummond is a rough man. He'll hurt you."

"Rough man, is it? The man's a dolt, Mistress Ferris, a low clod with no ear for music. By the Lord I intend to . . ."

"Dolt?" The furious voice came from the midden-window. "*Clod?*" Drummond's face almost filled the little window, which normally served only for the passing of slops. Crispin, still keeping one hand on his aching head and ducking low, spun around the table and thrust his face into the window, his nose an inch from Drummond's.

"That's what I said, sir, and I'll say it again. Dolt! Ow!" The last was muffled. Drummond's hand was there and hard fingers abused Crispin's nose. He tried to pull back and howled as the grip tightened. With a muffled curse he squeezed a forearm through the tight window and grasped Drummond's left ear in a hard fist, twisting mercilessly. Drummond twisted his nose in turn and both of them howled.

"Stop it!" Nora Ferris shouted. "Both of you, stop it this instant!" Then she grabbed Blount's shirt at the shoulders, braced a foot against the wall, and pulled. Outside, other hands were pulling Drummond back. In a moment the two were at arm's length through the window, both still gripping, twisting, and yelling. Then they were pulled apart. Crispin stepped back, panting and fuming, one hand on top of his head, the other over his nose. There was a new face at the midden. The dark, intent eyes of Captain Post lingered curiously on Crispin, then fixed on Nora.

"Madam, what is happening here?"

"You might very well ask, sir!" Nora was livid now. "It

47

was your man—or the Squire's—who began it. He came here and insulted Mr. Blount."

"Uninvited," Julie prompted.

"Uninvited," Nora added.

"And the other times," Julie said. "Tell him about those, too."

"Furthermore," Nora agreed, "Mr. Drummond and his friends have been taking liberties for a week now or more."

"Liberties?" The dark eyes glanced aside, then back. "What sort of liberties, mistress?"

"They keep coming to our house for dinner!"

"Uninvited," Julie prompted.

"Uninvited," Nora added.

"They frighten us," Julie said.

"They are rough men," Nora said.

Post looked from one woman to the other. "I can't say I blame them. But very well, it won't happen again. Good day, mistresses." Then he was gone from the window. Outside, his voice continued, "Drummond, I'll see you at the sheds. Bring him along, Mr. Sparrow."

Carefully, Crispin Blount touched his sore nose, pressing first one side and then the other. He decided it was not broken. He turned and his head brushed a rafter. He winced.

"Oh, do sit down, Mr. Blount," Nora ordered him, "before you kill yourself."

"When I see that one again," Crispin fumed, "I intend to . . ."

Julie McCarthy Jackson had gone into the pantry-porch. She returned with a steaming pot. "I believe the coffee is ready," she said.

V

As was his custom when in settlements, Crispin Blount retrieved Mystery from her stable that afternoon and wended through the scant streets and extending ways of the town, singing, banging a copper kettle, and in general making as much noise as he could so there would be no doubt in the minds of the citizenry that he was there.

In place of packs, Mystery now wore a pair of wide racks slung from belts, and into these Crispin placed the wares and possibles he gathered as he went.

His voice this day, as he bellowed a lyric chant along Market Way, had an unusual nasal quality to match the swollen redness of his nose and drew snide comment from some who had heard of the scuffle at the widow's house. "Aye," he retorted more than once, "I've been sore tweaked, but I venture I've given at least one ruffian a better ear for music than he had before." He saw no sign of Sam Drummond or any other "horse camp" men he could recognize. Again he marveled at the growth of the place. It had been a hard winter in the Ohio valley but was developing into a lush spring. Fewer than half the people he saw were those he knew from past seasons. On the north road he saw a baggage train coming in, shuttling people from the river, their belongings stacked in ox carts. He heard there were plans for a foundry, and someone was staking footings for a second mill.

When Mystery's racks were full, he went to the smithy under the stockade wall and arranged with the smith to use his forge and a spare bench. Jason Cook was a busy man, with demands on him for all the chain, harness rings, nails, and tools the settlement needed, and he was pleased to have Blount come along and catch the place up on its "sniggin' tin-smithy" now and again. Cook was a man who best used iron, and he could fit a shoe or temper a share with the best of them. But he had no interest in mending kettles. In past seasons, Crispin had obliged him by crafting cherrywood handles for all his molds.

For a time as Crispin Blount worked, the soreness of his aching nose and the anger of the day's encounter clouded his brow. But not for long. The warm sun and cool breeze of the day, the glow of the breathing forge, the lyric of progress through the town, infected him. He placed a copper pot abaft his anvil to cinch the weld of its seam, and as his hammer rang on it bright lyrics came to mind. "Bring out then a bench for a traveler to rest," he murmured, strengthening the *out* to *oot* and *bench* to *banch* as the old song took hold and the speech of another time prevailed. "Set some honest spring water to hand. Then with me avail an' I'll tell ye a tale o' th' wee folk who came to this land." With each beat, his hammer rang and his voice rose above it. Across the smithy, Jason Cook paused in the bending of a tire and cocked his head.

"Sing it out then, Crispin," he encouraged.

Blount paused, turned the pot, and eyed it judiciously. "Aye," he allowed. Replacing it, he began to hammer again, light taps this time, and his voice came stronger. "'Twas th' eve of St. Michael's," he sang with a will, "a gray bitter day, when the fugitive *Harod* set sail. From Land's End of Wales she set out, so they say, while her passengers prayed at the rail.

"For these were nae gentlefolk sippin' at tea, nor merchantmen bravin' the gale, but the poor folk of Land's End set out to be free, and the quest it were death should it fail. Sixty-one desperate souls and the crew were aboard by head count entered down in th' log. And fourteen more below, of whom none must know, were th' wee folk from Cavendish Bog."

Outside the open shed, people stopped to listen. A sturdy young man near the door peered intently into the shadows, stepping closer for a better look at the singer. Beside him, a pretty young woman held a baby wrapped in a quilt.

Crispin turned the pot again, holding it to the light. Then his hammer and his song resumed. "Old Rube's clan these were, or th' few that was left, for a many had died in th' spring. Yet still proud was each elf, for 'twas old Rube himself who had spat on the foot of a king."

Crispin sang it out, his voice ringing through the town, and people gathered as though drawn by cords to hear him. He was enjoying himself, beating on the anvil, letting the old ballad ring to the distant sky. But now he paused and looked around, surprised. The young man in the doorway had set down his packs and was leaning at the portal, his head cocked, grinning. And he was singing along with Crispin, finding the words to the old song. He had a fine, rich voice, and the words came clear as though he were remembering them from a long time before.

Crispin grinned encouragement, nodded, and took up the song again, and the young man swelled his chest and joined him, in full voice.

"Many days had they fought," they sang together, the young man hesitating over some of the words, then finding them, ". . . fought, there in Cavendish Bog, and many a churl felt the sting o' th' wee deadly darts and th' proud fighting hearts of a folk who would spit on a king. Yet the soldiers were many, the wee folk too few. Scythes and lanches were launched on the land, and each sunset bled for the blood of th' dead tiny warriors, the last faerie clan."

Now the words seemed to have all come back to the

young man. His voice rose clear, matching Crispin's in its power. He was a sturdy, wide-shouldered man, young in years yet sure of himself, with a wide, sober face that broke into quick, honest grins as he found the ballad's words. Dark serious eyes twinkled and dark hair with a touch of red where sunlight hit it curled unkempt around his ears. The young woman with the baby—Crispin was sure he should know her, had seen her before—was pretty in a quiet way, big dark eyes wide now with wonder. She hugged her infant to her breast and stared at her husband in open amazement as he sang.

A fair crowd of people was gathered now around the shed, and many of them tapped their feet and clapped time with their hands, enjoying the entertainment.

The young man hesitated, his eyes slitted as he lost the thread of the song.

"Then the magic and music . . ." Crispin prompted him. "Recall it, lad."

When Blount's hammer faltered, Jason Cook took up the rhythm with his own. "Don't stop now," he urged. "It's been afar too long since Harrodsburg has heard such singin'."

Crispin grinned, turned the pot, and picked up the rhythm with his tapping hammer. He raised his voice, and the young man stayed with him. "Then the magic and music was gone from the bog. The wee folk had spent of their stock"—he slowed, working a sob into the lyric—"to th' last tragic trace. There were tears on his face as Rube counted fourteen in his flock."

The crowd became hushed.

"So to Land's End he led them by darkness of night, 'neath a scarred moon that grieved at th' madness o' kings in their glory who'd end such a story and leave the old world to its sadness."

Crispin's voice faltered. He sniffed, missed the beat, and heard someone in the crowd blowing his nose. One or two wiped away tears. While Crispin cleared his throat the young man went on, his voice rich and true. "Crossbow at his shoulder old Rube led them there where the big folk were sorely oppressed, and they crept aboard *Harod* and hid in her holds to brave the dark seas to the west."

Despite himself, Crispin was impressed. He joined in on the next verse, trying a minor harmony that gave a sad, haunting lilt to the tune. "Not a wee soul was left in th' whole British Isles, only memories of magic they'd shared with th' self-same large race that had done bloody chase until only fourteen boarded *Harod*."

The young man faltered then, forgetting the words, and Crispin sang the verse alone. "Oh, a dark ship was *Harod*. Her crew was but wretches released out of gaol an' stockade, an' th' people she carried were poor souls long-harried, ownin' nought but th' clothes that they'd made."

There was hardly a dry eye among the listening crowd. Crispin bowed slightly to the young man and let him have the next verse. His voice as clear, the tune sure. "Dickie Quist, he was master aboard the sad ship, a man of quick eye and dark mein, and he'd stolen the ship when he'd given the slip to the kin of a noble he'd slain."

Again, Blount joined him. "On that dark howlin' day *Harod* took to the sea. There was ice in the clouds hangin' low over captain and crew and the sixty-one too, and the fourteen wee folk down below. Twenty days the wind held. Dickie Quist held her north, far off of th' known lanes, to drive through the cold northern sea where no frigates would be. Only thus could poor *Harod* survive. West they sailed, ever west, with supplies runnin' low, and gaunt faces peered out to the sea for they knew that out there in the distance somewhere lay a land where poor folk could be free."

At the door corner, Mystery had begun stamping her hoof rhythmically, making her bells chime in time with the tune. Newcomers to the crowd listened and watched, charmed. Someone had found a dulcimer and picked up the tune. A one-eyed man carrying a brace of chickens whistled it as they sang.

"There were children among them and some took the chill." Crispin shifted again to the minor-key harmony and the song became haunting. "There was hunger, and water ran low. Yet still, in the hold, in their dark hidden fold, all the wee folk kept silence below. 'They've done nothing for us,' Old Rube told them there. 'We have seen how the taller folk stand. For it's their kind that killed us and drove us away. Let them perish. I'll not raise a hand.' So they bent to his will and stayed hidden below, content with the course they were plying, but none of them laughed. And it tore at their hearts that, above, human babies were dying."

With a muffled "ahhh," someone in the crowd began to sob. Crispin's singing partner had moisture in his eyes and his rich voice became throaty. Crispin let him carry the verse. "For these were no evil or sorrowless elves, ever given to scurry or crime. No, they were the wee folk, and long friends of man, who had cared for him since before time." Now Crispin raised his voice in a high harmony: "And one was among them, the pixie girl Aella, who knew the old love of her race, and she listened and crept as the human folk wept, and found there were tears on her face. Small and comely she was, barely twelve inches tall, with dark eyes and a humor adept. And there was one who loved her, the stout Belephon, and it most broke his heart when she wept."

Now with the timing of the born entertainer, Crispin stepped forth and raised his hands. The ringing of Jason Cook's hammer stilled. The crowd—seventy strong now and more on the way—hushed itself, waiting. With a wink at his unknown partner, Crispin put a finger to his lips and spoke in an almost-whisper that yet carried to those who listened: "So Belephone went before old Rube himself and he looked his liege-lord in the eye and said,

'Sire, lend an ear, there are no king's men here, only poor folk, and likely to die!'"

Hands on his hips, Crispin let his voice grow. "'I have followed you, Sire, wherever you've led, and I've never been one to ask why. I have fought the king's soldiers. I've stood at your side and I will 'til the day that I die. But now I protest, Sire, for since time began, our way's been to help humans in need. We have lent them our lore and done deeds by the score in the hope that one day they might heed. . . .'"

Now the young man's voice rose to join his own again, and the dulcimer joined in the tune: ". . . that the blindness and foolishness born to their race are the soil from which wisdom might grow. Can we cast them aside after all that have tried through all time, Sire, to help them to know?'"

Suddenly another voice joined the two men. An old woman had pushed forth through the crowd, walking with a cane. Her eyes were rheumy, her frame fragile, but her voice was high and sweet. "As Cook's hammer regained the beat, they sang, 'I would ask for your blessing, but with it or not, I intend to assist them myself. For if I do not come when they need me the most, I can never again be an elf.'"

The blend was so perfect, the harmony so clear, that Crispin Blount laughed aloud and others joined him. Cook's hammer rang, Mystery jingled her harness bells, the dulcimer twanged, and feet stamped the beat as the three who knew the words and others who could only hum or whistle carried the old song forward in a rising swell of sound. Minutes passed and tens of minutes, and the sun crept downward to the west as nearly a hundred people, most of them strangers, gathered in the common at Harrodsburg town to take part in the singing of a fable. Hearts swelled to the words as the wee folk went forth to help the humans on *Harod*. People laughed at the point that Dickie Quist awakened with a tiny man standing on his chest telling him to turn south. Tears of gladness flowed as the magic of the wee folk brought the ailing passengers to good health, and there were cheers and applause when the crew of the old ship guided by elfin craft, outsailed and outfought the best of the king's navy.

Then as one they went silent, and in the evening's stillness only a strumming dulcimer and the sweet voice of a bent old woman sang, "Then leave them behind, all the evils that were. Let the old world inherit its woe. For somewhere out there is a bright summer land, and it's there that we're going to go."

It was a magic moment and silence followed it, then a riot of applause and cheers. At the shed door the young woman with the baby stared wide-eyed at her husband. "Luther, wherever did you learn that song?"

Crispin stepped forth and clapped the younger man on the shoulder. "You're a singer, lad, no doubt of it. Not in a long time have I had such sport."

"My pure pleasure, sir." The man held out a hand. "Luther Ferris is the name. How do you happen to know my father's song?"

"Eh? Your father's song? Why, lad, I've sung that song since I was a boy, when the time of it seemed right. It's an older song than any of us here. I . . ."

He stopped because the young man had turned away. Nora Ferris was coming through the crowd, her eyes sparkling. "Luther!" She threw her arms around him. "And Katie! Oh, my! I didn't know you were coming. But then I heard you singing the wee folks song, and I thought my heart would drop out it sounded so like you and your father when you sang. Mr. Blount, you've met my son? Of course, you sang together. And this is Katie, and little Jonathan. Oh, Katie, do let me hold him . . ."

Crispin Blount looked from mother to son to grandson and felt someone pulling at his sleeve. He looked down. The crone who had joined them in the wee folks song was there, rheumy eyes fixed on his, her brow arched. "Be ye th' man as fixes things?"

"Aye, mother, that I do."

"Then come to my house—it's the one there with the black stoop—and fetch my privet pot. It's bent from being kicked and needs straightenin'. And mind how ye mend it, for it's done better service than th' likes of you."

Behind him, Jason Cook sounded as though he were strangling. Several women nearby turned rosy red while their men collapsed into howls of laughter. Crispin Blount gazed down upon the tottering ancient, so cross and imperious now that the song was done, and blinked in amazement, trying to quell the spasms of mirth that crept upward from his belly.

"Well," she demanded, "will ye fix my pot?"

With a gallant bow and a laugh stifled down to a giggle, Crispin leaned far down to plant a smacking kiss on the old woman's cheek. "Dear soul," he told her, "for the likes of you and your angel voice, I shall not only fix it but tune it so well that it will sing for you in the night."

Taking her hand, he pushed through the thinning crowd and led her slowly across to her house to retrieve the vessel in question. The rest would have to wait. This was a pot that truly merited mending.

In the dim of evening, with the forge coals banked, Crispin took himself off to Cook's well house to wash away the day's sweat and grime. Then, Mystery tended and a pallet spread in the loft above, with a clean shirt on his back and an empty belly within, he presented himself again at Nora Ferris's house where good smells again wafted from the window. But before he could raise a fist to knock a figure came from the shadows there.

"Mr. Blount?"

"Aye." He turned and peered. The man was tall—not so tall as himself, but more than many—rangy and broad in the shoulders, and he carried himself tight-wound.

"My name is Sparrow, sir. Squire Trelawney would speak with you in the morning, he sent me to say."

"Trelawney? And what would he want of the likes of me?"

"He didn't say, sir. Just bid me to fetch you in the morning."

"In the morning I'll be at the smithy, tendin' my trade."

"Most folks come to the Squire, sir. You'll find him at the horse corrals at daybreak. Good evening, sir." And with that he was gone, upstreet in the evening shadows.

VI

It was a family gathering, but Crispin was seldom timid about intrusion. "How do again, Mistress Ferris?" he grinned. "Might there be a place at table for a man as has impressed his head-bone on your rafter?"

"Wipe your feet," she mocked him with a frown, but her eyes said he was welcome if he could behave himself.

He hung his hat on a peg by the door. Then, keeping a protective hand atop his still-sore skull, he accepted a second hug in one fine day from pretty Julie Jackson and pumped the hand of Nora's son Luther. "Need to tell you how I enjoyed our sing today, young feller. It's a fine, strong voice ye have and a pleasure to pair with. And I've met few enough who know the wee folks song . . . Ow!"

"Mr. Blount, if you don't sit down, you are likely to addle yourself!" Nora hurried to set a chair for him, and he nodded gratefully and sat.

"Sight of folks comin' up from the river today," he allowed.

Luther Ferris slumped into a hide-bottom chair by the window, calloused hand reaching out to touch the tresses of his wife, who knelt there tending her baby. It was a casual, gentle gesture, which gave Crispin a pang of loneliness. What riches the young man had. Was he aware of his great fortune? Kate smiled at the touch of her husband's hand.

Crispin had remembered her, after that first glance. Julie's older sister. The quiet one. Both were the daughters of a baker. Sisters, yet so different. Both had the wide-set eyes, the almost buck-toothed thrust of lip, small chins set high . . . . Stubborn chins, he thought. But the similarities ended there. Julie was a striking beauty. Kate was less striking, her beauty deeper, almost hidden by her manner. A serene, thoughtful, quiet person, in contrast to her sister who seemed a tempest held in check.

"The surveyors are working up that way," Luther said quietly. "They've brought warrants from the Squire, setting metes and bounds for his claims."

Nora turned to him, concerned. "Oh, Luther. Your land? . . ."

"I don't know, Ma. They marked a line on our place, with cairns. The surveyors said it's the boundary, that everything west of it is the squire's grant. They said the Transylvania claims have been rescinded. I just don't know. We came in so I could talk to the Squire."

"But the line? Where is it?"

"Through the east field. It wouldn't leave enough to matter."

Crispin held his peace. In the past season he had seen too many claims lost because of Virginia's changing laws. It seemed that Patrick Henry and the Burgesses were far more interested in pandering to their cronies than in protecting the titles of smallholders in the westward provinces. It was nothing new. The Richmonders were easily influenced by land speculators but felt no responsibility to those who purchased the claims the speculators sold. Making war against the king of England was expensive, and the frontier lands were a source of coin to the colonial governments.

"What will you ask of the Squire?" Nora wondered.

"I'll ask him," Luther shrugged, "what would be his price to sell my land back to me. It's all I can do."

"And when he sets a price?"

"I don't know," he said glumly. "I just don't know."

Crispin felt, for the moment, embarrassed to be hearing the concerns of this family—a stranger eavesdropping on private matters—and the thought left him strangely empty. It was not in the nature of Crispin Blount—so he had assured himself for a very long time—to be involved with other people's private affairs. Yet there was a compelling thing about this little family, here in this cozy cabin, sharing the things that families share.

"If Ellie doesn't hurry, she'll miss her supper." Adeptly, Nora changed the subject.

"She took our cow over to Bowman's field," Kate said. "She said she'd be pleased to milk her."

Nora took down a little pewter bell, went to the door, and stepped outside to ring for her daughter. Crispin's eyes followed her as she crossed the room. Taller than some women, she moved with easy grace, and her figure was lean and trim where soft skirts molded her as she walked. A handsome woman, he thought again. A proud woman, tempered by time and the experiences she had collected in this land. A widow, her husband lost to Hamilton's savages. A wife who was no longer a wife because of the doings of kings and generals. A mother whose children had no father. Colonial governments protested tyrannies and the empire reacted and people were pawns on the board. Few families out here had escaped the sorrows of the years of bloody war.

Beyond the open door, the little bell rang again and he heard Nora's voice, calling for Ellie.

In the pantry, Julie bustled about, making things ready for a meal.

Kate knelt beside Luther, her full attention on her baby, fingers checking its swaddling, eyes and ears attuned to its needs.

Crispin Blount lowered his head, tugging at his nose, testing its diminishing soreness. "Aye, Crispin," he muttered to himself. "Ye've been too long alone, when the sight of sweet ladies makes your old heart too big to

61

rest inside your ribs."

"I beg your pardon?" Julie had come in from the pantry, carrying a pot, and she stopped to cock a pretty brow at him.

Nora came in from the stoop and put the bell away. "She's coming along now. Let's get things started."

"Nothin' at all, Julie," Crispin assured. "I was just thinkin' what an honor it would be to speak a blessin' for this family here assembled."

"Then so you shall. And maybe tell us a tale, too."

Luther aroused himself from private thoughts. "That song you sang today, Mr. Blount . . ."

"That *we* sang," Crispin corrected.

"Yes. *We* sang. It was so much like . . . times long ago, when Pa was alive. It filled my heart, Mr. Blount, because when you sing it you sound like Pa."

"No he didn't, either!" There was such outrage in the voice at the door that Crispin came half out of his chair, then thought for a disoriented moment that he had seen a vision. Two Noras stood there, woman and child, and the child-Nora glared at Luther, her chin out-thrust. "How can you say such a thing, Luther Ferris?"

"Ellie!" the woman-Nora scolded. "You mind your manners! We have company!"

Ellie, the child-Nora, carried a pail of milk, little hands firm on the bale, and now she looked across at Crispin and said, "How do you do? Luther was wrong. You didn't sound at all like our father." And with that, she strode across to the pantry, an indignant angel with her chin in the air. From out of sight, her voice continued. "Julie? Do we have a cloth to cover this so it can set for skimming?"

Luther chuckled, and it became a laugh to drive away dark thoughts. "Ah, Ellie, Ellie. Lord, let her never change."

"Pay her no attention, Mr. Blount," Nora shook her fine head. "She's twelve."

Crispin stood, avoiding the treacherous beams with a

respectful crouch, and went around the table to peer into the pantry. The girl was laying wet cloth taut across the milk pail, by the light of a lamp beyond in the cookshed door. She smelled of fresh air and sunshine, and her eyes sparkled with righteous challenge. His expression as serious as hers, Crispin put out a big hand and, when she responded, took her small one in it.

"My name is Crispin Blount, and it's my pleasure to meet you, Ellie. And I make you a pledge. I won't ever sound like anybody you don't want me to. At least not to you."

She thawed somewhat at this, though the carefully practiced elegance of her shrug made it clear that her world was quite sufficient without strangers butting in. "Thank you, Mr. Blount. I'm sure you didn't know that was our father's song. Did Mother invite you for supper or did you just come?"

"Ellie!" Nora scolded from behind Crispin, but he had the doorway blocked.

"Why, lass, I just came, drawn by the promise o' fine food an' fine company."

Ellie wiped her hands on her apron, looked him up and down judiciously, then turned away to retrieve a ladle from its hook. "Well, I suppose there's no harm in that, but you have to realize Mother is far too old to marry anyone."

"Ellie!" Nora shrieked from behind him. Crispin heard Luther roar with laughter, along with the musical giggles of Kate and Julie.

With an effort of will that brought tears to his eyes, Crispin clamped his jaw and set his face sternly. Then he turned, still half crouched in the low doorway, to scrutinize the flushed face of Nora Ferris, a scrutiny that momentarily noticed other interesting features as well.

"Aye," he said slowly, nodding his head. "Most decidedly over the hill. A real pity. An' here I was thinkin' of asking you to the next cotillion."

"Ellie," she rasped, "when I get my hands on you . . ."

"Oh, Mother," the girl scolded. "You said yourself you were too old to even think about . . ."

"Ellie, that's enough!"

Luther was laughing so hard he woke the baby, and its fussing diverted the attention of the women.

Kate arose from the pallet by the chair and crooned to her infant. "I suppose I'd better nurse him before supper," she said.

"You go ahead, Kate. The soup will keep." Nora was still flushed with mortification, but her grandson was a welcome reprieve.

Crispin watched, enchanted, as Kate sat in a chair, exposed one round breast, and positioned the baby to suckle it. The wails cut off abruptly. Then he turned to Luther. "Seems to me I recall seein' a willow tree down by the river road. Want to walk over there with me?"

Luther nodded and picked up his hat. Crispin retrieved his from the peg and glanced out the window. "We'll need a lantern. It's dark."

The night was alive with the tiny songs of spring as they walked across the common. Lights glowed in cabin windows, muffled voices drifted to them. A man passed, leading a brace of oxen.

"Be a fine spring," he nodded in the lantern glow, "though it will be cold yet a time."

"'Tis a crisp evenin'," Crispin waved.

The willow he sought was a big old tree with its freshening tendrils nearly to the ground. While Luther held the lantern he drew his knife and began collecting long branches, choosing those that were finger-wide and had good flex. He kept cutting until he had a good-sized bale of them, singing softly as he worked. "Oh, I be a wee bairn coom a-callin' this night, an' it be a snug home I tae fare, wi' a roof tae keep storms oot, a warm hearth tae sleep by, an' a comfer tae rock me in there . . . aye, a comfer tae comfort me there."

"That sounds Scottish," Luther observed.

"My grandmother was a Scot of Clan McNair. She was

a fine, warm woman. But no, th' song's just somethin' I made up as it came to me, an' it sounded best in th' Scottish manner. It's an old habit of mine. I entertain myself by singin'."

"Where do you know the wee folks song from, Mr. Blount?"

"I've been thinkin' about that all afternoon, since we sang it, and I'm not sure I remember. It seems I've always known that one. I'm not even sure which side of the ocean I got it on."

"You've been on both sides, then?"

"Oh, aye. Both sides." Easing around the base of the tree, peering up, he selected a few more branches, then bound the bale with slim withes, cutting handfuls of these to add to the harvest. "As best I can reckon, Luther, I must be comin' up on forty-seven, forty-eight years old. That's a long time. Man can see a sight of places in that many years . . . if that be all he knows to do is just see places."

When he was satisfied with his bale of branches and bundle of withes, they walked back to Nora's house.

"Sometimes I've thought I'd like to see the world," Luther admitted.

"Oh, you will," Crispin assured. "Every man does that's got eyes to see. But there's two ways of doin' that. A man can be the traveler at the world's door, always on th' move to find a new day somewhere else, an' sure enough, he'll see it. Or a man might just settle in an' put out the welcome mat an' let the world come to him. Had I to do it again, maybe I'd do it this other way. There's precious things a man can miss if he's not home to receive them."

Luther was silent for a time. Bullbats cried above as they wheeled over the silhouette of the old stockade. A quarter moon was rising.

"Like Kate," Luther murmured. "And little Jonathan."

Crispin grinned in the darkness. "Like them. Exactly like them."

"Where have you two been?" Nora asked in a half whisper as they entered the house. But when they started to answer, she put a finger to her lips and pointed. The baby was asleep on its pallet.

Julie looked at the bundle of willow wands. "What are those for?"

"Magical wands for the makin' of magical things," Crispin assured her. "But wizardry comes hard to starvin' men."

"Well, come to table then, before it gets cold."

They gathered around the laden board and Crispin looked around at them: Kate the young mother next to him, the scent of nursing still about her; Luther next, solid and sober in the lamplight; the impish Ellie, so much like her mother, then Nora Ferris, whose eyes met his and there were few secrets between them, because they had both lived too long for pretenses; and pretty Julie, all hopes and sadnesses with eyes too big to hide them. And little Jonathan asleep on his pallet. Crispin bowed his head.

"Lord, maker of wonders, look down upon those here assembled. Bless them and be gentle with them, for of all the wonders of the firmaments there is none half so grand as what this stranger's eyes behold here in this house. Belong among them"—he coughed to cover a choke in his voice—"as they belong to one another. Bless this table and the food it holds, and bless the love that's in its preparation. Amen."

"Amen," they chorused softly. When he looked up, Nora was gazing across at him, her eyes bright as one who has just learned a secret.

Good food and small talk followed, and Crispin luxuriated in the presence of togetherness. It was seldom enough that a traveling man knew such comforts. When finally they were finished, he sat back and patted his belly, and Julie leaned to put a hand on his arm.

"A tale now, Crispin. You must tell us a tale."

"I have a riddle," he said. "Now listen closely, for I'll tell it only once. 'I stand reclining. I am the door to sleep. In every home the future's mine to keep. I serve the large by comforting the small, and sad the house where I'm not seen at all. I am in motion when others are at rest. I walk yet do not move, and that's the test.'"

They were silent for a moment, puzzling over it.

"Is that it?" Ellie stared at him accusingly. "That's not a riddle, that's a rhyme. What's it about?"

"What it's about *is* the riddle," Julie offered. "But what? What walks and does not move?"

"The oxen on a grinding mill," Nora said. "They walk in circles."

"But they are moving, even if it's only around and around."

"Is it a plow?" Luther asked.

"A plow?" Kate turned to him, puzzled. "Wherever do you get the idea of a plow?"

"I don't know. I was just thinking about a plow."

Crispin left them with the riddle and got his bale of willow sticks, setting them on the floor by the table where the lamp cast good light. He sat cross-legged on the floor and began unwrapping withes, then looked up. "Luther, do you want to lend a hand?"

The young man came and sat down in front of him. Loosing one long willow wand, Crispin held it across his chest, measuring it to a full arm span. Then he drew his knife and cut it to length, handing both the cut stick and the knife to Luther. "You cut an' I'll bind. We'll need two like this, and two more a hand shorter, and two more a hand shorter still, and two good thick ones as long as your forearm, and a whole mess of rods an arm's length."

Luther began cutting willow branches.

"'In every home the future's mine to keep,'" Nora pondered. "Maybe it's some sort of a clock."

"That sounds like it might be a book," Kate suggested. "Maybe a Bible?"

Ellie stared at the two men sitting on the floor cutting and manipulating willow lengths. "What are they doing?" she asked of no one in particular.

"'The door to sleep,'" Nora said. "That could be evening, or something that's like evening. And I know something that stands reclining. A bed."

Crispin's left eyebrow raised a fraction of an inch, but he went on working. He bent one of the long rods into the shape of an oxbow and wrapped its legs with double withes to hold it in shape. Then he bent another, shorter one, and nested it inside the first so its ends were even. Then he nested an even shorter one yet and began wrapping the clustered legs with supple withes, strong hands pulling them tight and binding them as he went. He bent hard one of the "forearm-length" pieces, a stout stick, and held firmly until it retained an arc, then set it aside and did the same to the other. Then, starting with a long piece again, he constructed another assembly like the first.

"Those look like big fans," Ellie pointed out. "Except they have no fabric on them."

"They look a whole lot more like chair backs," Luther suggested. "What can 'serve the large by comforting the small,' though? I guess that might be a chicken coop."

"Luther, for heaven's sake," Kate said. "Chicken coop? How do you get to that idea?"

"Well, chickens are small and the folks who eat them—that they're served to—are large."

"Well, I don't think that's the answer," Kate shook her head.

With both "fans" completed, Crispin set them upright, arcs upward, supporting them against his widespread knees. Then he picked up one of the "arm's-length" sticks and attached it with binding to both structures, one at each end. He attached another stick midway on the far side of the two, then began binding in stick after stick, in parallel rows, working downward.

"I'll need two sturdy pieces about a foot long," he told Luther.

These he lashed across the "fans" beneath the lowest of the side board sticks, then laid other sticks side by side on the braces, like flooring. His big hands danced as he placed and set sticks and wrapped their ends tightly with the whipping withes.

"It's a dog!" Julie exclaimed. "A dog guarding a house. Listen: '. . . in motion when others are at rest.' That fits. And 'the future's mine to keep,' and 'it serves the large by comforting the small.' Children play with dogs. I do think it's a dog. Is it a dog, Crispin?"

"I suppose 'stand reclining' might fit a dog," Nora frowned, "but not that 'door to sleep' part. That doesn't fit."

Crispin kept his peace, his hands fairly flying now as he lashed and firmed joint after joint of the structure he was assembling. When it was secure, he tested it for firmness, pressing it one way and then another. Then he picked up one of the bowed sticks and strapped it across the feet of one "fan," bow down, his shoulders rolling with the effort as he lashed it tightly in place.

"Ah?" Ellie's eyes began to widen, her mouth an oval of surprise. Crispin turned the structure around and lashed the other bow into place on the other end, beginning to chuckle. He looked up and winked at Ellie.

"I know what it is!" she chirped. "I know, I know! Oh, charming!"

"What?" her mother asked.

"It's a cradle!"

They all looked then at what Crispin had built. A sturdy cradle of raw willow stood there on the floor, and he brushed its top with a hand so they could see how it rocked.

Kate's dark eyes shone. "Oh, Mr. Blount, it's beautiful!"

He stood, working the stiffness out of his legs and

back. "That bairn there"—he pointed to baby Jonathan—"does deserve better than a pallet on the hard floor."

Luther stared in awe at the cradle he had helped build. "I'll be damned!" he said, then glanced apologetically at his mother. "I didn't know that's what it was."

"Then how about the riddle?" Julie asked.

Ellie stared at her with undisguised impatience. "That's what the riddle is, don't you see? He told us a riddle and showed us a riddle and it was all the same riddle."

"The c—the cradle! Well, of course! Door to sleep, in motion when others are at rest . . . Why, mercy, it does all fit!"

Crispin started to straighten, then winced as his head brushed a rafter. "Criminy, but this house is short!"

Luther carried the cradle across to the hearthside and Nora folded a quilt into it, then Kate lifted her sleeping son and set him down in the nest. Gently she rocked it back and forth, turning a sweet smile on Crispin. "Oh, Mr. Blount, thank you so much."

"My pure pleasure, mistress." He stifled a yawn. "I'd best be gettin' to my own rest, too. I've a bunk over in the common barn."

"But you don't have to go," Ellie said. "There's room here."

"Wouldn't be seemly, child . . ." He paused, then grinned. "And since your mother's too old for marriage, it seems a man must satisfy himself with a fine meal and be on his way."

Nora blushed again, and Crispin admired her fine coloring. "Mistress Ferris," he said, getting his hat, "this has been a fine evenin' for a wanderin' man, an' one I'll not soon forget. A right good night to ye all." With that, he bent low to step through the door into full night, and closing it quietly behind him.

At the stable he looked in on Mystery, inspected his

belongings by the light of a hooded lamp, then filled a pipe and stood a while in the doorway, watching the moon climb in a quiet sky as dark and as deep as the pupils of Nora Ferris's eyes.

The talk when he had gone was of a family nature, muted and cozy by the light from the flickering hearth. Yet each time they looked at the baby in its cradle the talk turned to Crispin Blount. Luther told them of what the tall man had said, about seeing much of the world and about being a traveler at the world's door . . . always on the move to find a new day somewhere else. And about the sadness he thought he had heard when Crispin spoke of the precious things a man might miss if he had no home to receive them.

"He speaks riddles even when he isn't riddling," Luther said. Then he put his arm around Kate's shoulders and glanced again at the cradle. "Yet I felt I understood, even though I don't know whether he was talking about me or about himself." He gazed at the fire and shook his head. "Nor do I know what a man might do should he think he has a home and then discover that he doesn't."

Nora studied her son. There was much of his father in him, a steadiness that had been a mark of Jonathan, a stubborn determination that went hand in hand with his love of the land. The stubbornness and the feel of his land—his place on earth—were one and the same. She knew he was worried now.

"Is it so certain, then?" she asked. "I mean about the claim on the land . . . You said they had marked a boundary, but who is to say that it is a true line?"

"The Squire will hold it true," Luther said. "I can't think why he wouldn't. But I'll speak with him. It's all I can do for now."

"Surveys can be contested," Julie offered. "Mistress

71

Holly claims that the men along Cherry Creek are doing that. They say the survey was in error, and they've petitioned the Burgesses to do another. Your place is not far from there, Luther. And it's at least as far east as those. Maybe it will all come to nothing."

Luther shrugged. "Maybe it will. But it's a poor hope to cling to. The Burgesses favor those who have financed the war and those who have fought in the Continental Army. The new warrants are how they pay them. Unless new surveys change the boundaries, all of the Transylvania patents are at risk."

"It seems just so awfully unfair."

"But when you see the Squire, Luther, what will you offer him to keep your land—providing the survey says it is his?"

"I don't know. Right now I just want to hear what he says."

In her shadowed corner Ellie listened, not understanding all of it but sharing the concern of those older. How the room had changed, she thought. Just a while ago there had been magic and laughter and the cottage had seemed a warm haven. Yet now she heard the dread in her brother's words, the concern in her mother's voice; she saw Kate's eyes dark with worry and Julie's bright with indignation. Ellie wrapped her arms around her knees and huddled there as though a chill had entered.

How the room had changed. It had changed when Crispin Blount left. Even looking at the marvelous willow cradle where baby Jonathan slept was not enough to change it back. She tilted her head, studying her mother's profile in the firelight. She had seen her mother radiant during those hours when the tall man was among them. She didn't remember ever having seen her quite so. It had startled her then, but now she wished she could see it again. There were so many problems. There was so much worry. Somehow, it seemed, Crispin Blount might have found a cure for that.

In her mind she heard again the voice of the stranger and of Luther and the rest as they had sounded in the square. She had stood away from the crowd, just listening, and found that she remembered much of the old song they sang. Dimly, she remembered it being sung in another place and at another time, which seemed so very long ago. And oddly, in a way, it had seemed as though it might have been her father singing it.

How strange, she thought, that she could recall the wee folks song more clearly now than she recalled her father.

The song . . . At first it had offended her, her own brother singing with a stranger the very song their father had given them. But she had listened, and the same fine feelings were there. It was the ballad itself that held them, then, and not those who sang it. And yet . . . Crispin Blount—so ugly he had seemed, so overtall and awkward, with a face like a fishhawk—he had sat to their table and said words to light the very room. His presence was a warmth, and she had decided he was not so ugly after all . . . maybe. Could a person who saw a willow tree and made from it a cradle and a riddle really be ugly?

They were speaking of him again. Julie was reminding Kate of when he had come before, in the time of smokes, and of the stories he had told—bright tales of wonderous places that for a time had pushed back the fear that everyone then had.

But Kate didn't remember it very well. Her mind then had been on other things. Ellie remembered seeing Kate each evening, when the baking was done, up on the rampart of the stockade, looking always to the north. Looking for Luther, even when no one else did.

And Nora only nodded and said, "Yes, I recall him. Though I never met him, really. But I recall when he was here."

"It would be hard not to recall Crispin Blount," Julie giggled, glancing at the shadowed rafters above the table.

73

"He makes an impression."

"Such a fine cradle," Kate said, her voice drowsy now. "And a fine riddle to match."

"I think the man is more a riddle than his riddles are," Luther decided.

Ellie thought about that and decided that Luther was wrong. Crispin Blount was no riddle. She yawned, abruptly overcome by the sudden sleepiness of twelve years old. Luther had put another log on the fire, and its warmth seeped into her. No riddle at all, she thought. Dreamlike, words sang in her mind: . . . *we have lent them our lore and done deeds by the score in the hope that one day they might heed* . . .

Odd, how a person so tall and homely, so—so boisterous, could be so like the wee folk of the song.

VII

In the quiet of morning before first dawn, Crispin Blount opened his eyes and listened for a moment to the darkness—old cautions of a man familiar with the back trails. Then he found his hat, snugged it tight upon his head, and sat up, letting his blankets fall away. Stiff frost crackled where his moist breath had frozen on the blankets in the night. He yawned, shivered, and stretched, then found his boots and stamped his feet into them.

Below in the darkness a horse nickered and hooves stamped a response. Feeling his way cautiously, Crispin found the ladder and climbed down to the stable floor. His long nightshirt flapped around bare legs above the tops of his boots as the night breeze struck him through the open doors.

"Cold," he muttered, and could barely see the puff of steam that was his breath.

He went first to Mystery's stall, edging in with the mule to check her blanket, rub her ears, and tell her how glad he was to see her this morning. Then he went to the corner where his possibles were stacked, found a pot and grinder, ground a handful of coffee beans, and dropped the grindings into the pot.

The rain barrel by the door was empty. He scratched his head, then walked back through the barn with flint, steel, and a wad of guncotton in hand to set a little fire in the cold stable hearth. The fire burning, he strode back to the open front, picked up his pot, and headed out across the common, looking for a cistern.

First light of dawn was on Harrodsburg and there were people about, coming sleepily from their houses to tend the early chores. He tipped his hat to a woman with an egg basket and said, "Morning, mistress." She glanced at his boots, bare legs, and flapping nightshirt, then hurried on her way.

There was a common well beside the old stockade, and he dropped in a rock to break the ice, then drew water to fill his pot and headed back to the barn.

While the coffee was cooking he climbed into the loft again, dressed himself, and folded his blankets. When he came down again the dawn was full and pink, and roosters were crowing.

Patting Mystery's rump as he passed, he walked out front again, breathed deeply of the morning air, then raised his head, flapped his elbows, and crowed at the top of his lungs. The bellowing salute echoed back from walls and fences, and all the roosters went silent. "Give 'em somethin' to strive for," he told himself happily, and went into the barn to get his coffee.

By the time the stablekeep, who wore a wire wig and was named Samuel Calkins, arrived at the barn, Crispin had rubbed down Mystery and turned her out into the enclosed pasture behind, with the suggestion that she "romp a bit to get the juices flowin'."

Calkins carried a musket in his hand and followed his nose to Crispin's coffeepot. "Mornin'," he said, sidling around first one way and then another to demonstrate his interest in the coffeepot. Crispin found a bowl, wiped it out, and poured coffee for the proprietor. "This is coffee," he said.

"Thought it was, from the smell," Calkins nodded. "Ah, that does taste fine. Did you hear a ruckus a bit ago, Mr. Blount?"

76

"Ruckus? Not that I noticed."

"Probably nothin'. My wife said she heard a terrible loud noise an' it woke her up. She made me come out with th' musket to see what it was. She thought maybe it was Injuns. I think maybe she's havin' moon flashes."

Crispin nodded seriously. "Probably comes of wakin' up before breakfast. I don't suppose that fine woman of yours has fixed your breakfast yet?"

"Be ready in a bit," Calkins said. "I brought in a slab of pork from the smokehouse before I came out lookin' for Injuns."

"Did ye fetch a good slab?"

"Fair-sized. And potatoes from the root cellar. I expect some of this coffee would set right well with it, too. Might want to fetch yer rifle along. I expect it would be a comfort to her to set table for two armed men if there's Injuns hollerin' about."

"Be my pleasure," Crispin smiled. "Do ye have a load in that musket, Mr. Calkins?" He picked up Old Yellow Dog.

"No. Is yer rifle loaded, Mr. Blount?"

"No. Powder wastes when it sets up."

"That's all right. I reckon Hanna won't know the difference."

By the time the sun had cleared the hilltop, Crispin's belly was full of breakfast and Hanna Calkins's head was swimming with the praise heaped on her for her cooking.

"I'll fix your rain barrel when I get to it," Crispin promised the stablekeep. With a suppressed belch and a final "Bless your bright eyes" to Hanna, he started back toward the stable. But where the way entered the common, three men blocked his path. The one in front was tall, wide-shouldered, and rangy, and seeing him now in daylight, Crispin noted the hard features, the bleak eyes of a man who took no joy in the morning. The men were spread out so he could not pass. He stopped, smiled uncertainly, and said, "Good day to ye, Mr. Sparrow."

77

"The Squire was to see you at sunup," the man said coldly. "He's been waiting."

"Well, now, sir, I told you where I'd be this morning. I've work at the smithy, and anybody as wants can find me there."

"Let's go," Sparrow inclined his head. The two with him moved in to flank Crispin, and without further word he found himself walking briskly eastward with strong, propelling hands on his arms and shoulders. Sparrow walked ahead, leading the way.

"Here!" Crispin demanded. "You two take your hands off me!"

There was no response. He tried to slow and was shoved forward, off balance, forced to resume his stride to keep from falling. He still carried Old Yellow Dog, and on impulse he thumped the rifle's stock down solidly on the instep of the man on his right, who promptly turned loose of him and veered away, hollering and hopping on one foot.

With that satisfaction accomplished, Crispin gripped the rifle to swing on the other man, but then Sparrow was before him and hands stronger than his own tore the rifle from his grasp.

"There wasn't any need of that," Sparrow said. Then to the howling man, he said, "Abel, hush up. You ain't hurt."

"He broke my foot!" Abel shouted.

Crispin lowered his head to glare around at the other man, who still held him. "I said turn me loose!" When the man didn't respond, he cocked a fist to swing at him. Sparrow shook his head sadly, then caught the tall man's arm and spun him around, twisting the arm behind him. Crispin found himself bent almost double, gasping at the pain in his right shoulder as Sparrow applied pressure there.

"Mr. Blount," Sparrow said, "you are being difficult."

"Turn loose!" Crispin gasped. A moment passed, then the pressure eased. Sparrow released his arm and stepped away. The other one had already backed off. Straightening, Crispin rubbed his arm and growled, "What do ye want, anyway?"

"You're to go see the Squire," Sparrow explained patiently.

"Well, why didn't ye just say so, then?"

"I did."

"All right, but give me back my rifle."

Sparrow handed Old Yellow Dog back to him. "No charge in your pan," he pointed out.

"That's because it isn't loaded!"

The third man came around then, peering at the rifle in genuine interest. "Why do you carry a rifle that isn't loaded?"

Crispin drew himself to his full considerable height and looked down his nose at the man. "For shootin' at things I'd likely miss. It's cheaper that way."

Abel had sat down in the road and pulled off his boot to inspect his foot. Now he pulled the boot back on again and stood up, glaring at Crispin.

"The Squire don't like to wait," Sparrow said, and turned to continue the journey eastward. Crispin followed tamely, his dignity appeased. The other two trailed after them, Abel still cursing under his breath.

Full day was upon the horse corrals, and booted men were beyond in the pasture, tending the herd, gathering the sleek animals toward the corrals for working. Again Crispin was struck by the beauty of that herd. Few such animals had he seen this side of the mountains.

"Here he is, sir," Sparrow said, and Crispin turned around to see Trelawney approaching from a row of sheds. Fresh linen flashed from between the lapels of his buff coat, and his boots glistened. He carried a rust-red tricorn hat in his hand. A wide man, Crispin noted again, wide of body and wide of feature, with a casual arrogance to him that bespoke the use of power and money.

"Where did you find him, Mr. Sparrow?"

"He was dawdlin' in town, sir."

"Dawdlin'?" Blount glared at Sparrow. "My time's my own, an' what I do with it—"

"You are the tinker?" Trelawney interrupted him.

"Upon occasion, when it suits me. What is all this about?"

"Mind your tongue," Sparrow said quietly.

Trelawney looked him up and down. "I don't care for itinerants," he said. "But I suppose you must do. I shall require your services for a week or two. You can work and sleep in that far shed. You will be paid adequately."

Crispin closed his mouth with a snap. Amazement gave way to anger. "Was I lookin' for wages, mister, I might hire me on wi' a thievin' rafter or cad, or even dousin' floor in a low pub. But I'd not do the biddin' of some connivin' backwater warrant-lord that hasn't got the civility to ask me decent whether I—" Before he could finish, Sparrow had him by the arm, whisking him several steps away.

"Mr. Blount," Sparrow said quietly, "that's no way to talk to the Squire. He's a powerful man, and it's best you mind your manners . . ."

Trelawney had stepped up beside them. "That will do, Mr. Sparrow." He looked at Crispin. "Very well, tinker. I was abrupt and I offended your pride. You have my apology. Now will you listen to what I propose?"

Crispin still glared, but he nodded.

"You have seen my horses. Breeding stock for a new venture. Captain Post and I have agreed that this is suitable land for the breeding of fine horses, for which we believe there will be markets both in the east and in the Spanish provinces. We propose to do that—he to provide the stock and perfect the breed, I to develop the markets and arrange distribution."

"That all sounds grand," Crispin growled. "What do you want of me?"

"People of the town say you are a good tinker and take pride in your work. I shall need bins and troughs for my stable, and kettlery for my cribs. I have the materials and the men to build the structures. I need a man to do my tinning and weld seams. I offer the task to you. Do you want it or not?"

Crispin tugged at his chin. "It's a season's work. Staying in one place so long isn't my way, nor is sole employment. I've other things to do. Maybe I'll think on it, but it's doubtful."

"Think, then," Trelawney said. "But don't wait too long. The planks for the troughs are being fined now. If you aren't ready when they are, I shall put someone else to do the work."

"I said I'll think on it."

"Very well." Trelawney turned away. Then he turned back. "Should you not accept my work, tinker, I shall expect you not to remain long at Harrodsburg. You would get no indulgences from me. I care for neither your attitude nor your tongue."

With that, the Squire turned and walked away, again leaving Crispin with his mouth open.

Sparrow looked up at him and shook his head. "Little wonder you travel around, Mr. Blount. A man as can't mind his tongue around the gentry finds his welcomes short."

"The man's a popinjay! Gentry has no business actin' like gentry this side of the mountains."

Sparrow regarded him thoughtfully. "You speak as though that's what mountains are for."

"That might well be . . ." Crispin hestitated, then grinned. Though there was no expression on Sparrow's face, the man had tweaked him well and he knew it. "And how about you, Mr. Sparrow? You're a man wi' meat on his bones an' a head on his shoulders. Why would you choose to do th' biddin' of *Mister* Squire Squatbottom there?"

Sparrow shrugged. "He pays. You may go about your business now, Mr. Blount." He walked away toward the rising stable.

"I'll do as pleases me, bedamme!" Crispin roared.

"What are ye goin' to do for this poor foot of mine, then?"

He whirled to find Abel standing there, staring at him accusingly.

"Ye lamed me, is what ye did," Abel announced. "Ye see this foot here? I can hardly walk on it. What are ye going to do about that?"

Crispin had had enough of the lot of them. He shifted his grip on Old Yellow Dog suggestively. "I reckon I could give ye a second one to match."

Past the corral, where sheds abutted the path, a rider walked his horse directly into Crispin's path and halted there. Crispin squinted up at him, shading his eyes against the bright sky.

The horse was black and unmarked, a superb racer, long of limb and thick of chest. The rider was a boy, a slim youth still outgrowing childhood but garbed in casual finery—tailored breeches, fine linen shirt unsoiled and full in the sleeves, with rolled cuffs. The boots he wore were fitted to him, blacked and waxed.

"Mr. Blount?" The voice, cool and schooled, was that of a youngster but with an edge of easy authority behind it. Crispin squinted into eyes that were like black marble in a sun-dark face, framed by raven hair pulled back into a queue.

"Blount is my name, lad. Can I be of service?"

"I am Christopher Post," the boy said. "Captain Post is my father."

"Aye, young'un. I know who ye be."

The boy remained expressionless. His gaze had force like a man's. "I have heard that you travel, Mr. Blount. Have you been to the west?"

"Well, now, lad, these old eyes have seen a sight of places. I wonder why you'd ask."

"Because I want to know, sir. Have you seen the lands beyond the big river? The Spanish lands? Have you been to the Louisianas?"

Crispin scowled and backed off a step. His neck was

82

becoming cramped. "I ha' been west, lad, but never that far. A man takes his life into his hands who'd venture into the Spanish lands, and to what purpose? None know the trails there, or where the settlements be. No, lad, traders and tinkers may wander a bit, but they find no profit in leaving the known lands."

The boy's face held expression then, a look of disappointment. He looked less aloof then, more of a child.

"Now maybe ye'd tell me why ye wanted to know?" Crispin tilted his head and raised a brow.

"When they said how you had traveled, I thought maybe . . ." he hesitated, "maybe you might have maps—or the means to make them."

"Maps of far country be great treasures, lad, but seldom to youngsters like yourself." He stepped past the horse and continued on toward the town. The boy turned his mount and fell into position beside him.

"Do you know others who may have explored the far lands, Mr. Blount?"

"Nay, lad. I've heard tales o' some that went . . . an' tales of a many that didn't come back. But I know not who'd have maps. What might ye want them for?"

"To study, sir. To study and to learn."

"They told me your father had been there."

"He was, Mr. Blount. He went to the Spanish lands and he came back, though of the twenty who went with him only four returned. And he made maps. But they caught him there, sir. They beat him and they took his maps away, and threw him into a stockade to rot." As he talked the boy's face became harder, his eyes burning with a sullen gleam. "He saved himself and four of his men, Mr. Blount. But later, when he tried to draw maps again from memory, they were poorly done and useless."

"So now he has ye seekin' other maps, does he?"

"They aren't for him, Mr. Blount. My father will never return to the Spanish lands. But I will. I swear one day I will."

Somehow the hard words in such young voice prickled at Crispin's scalp. He thought he had never heard purer resolve.

"Ho, Christopher!"

At the hail from aside, Crispin turned and the boy reined in his horse. The man coming toward them was as handsome and well dressed as his son, his aristocratic face as commanding as when Crispin had seen it through Nora's midden-window. But now he saw something he had not seen before. Captain Edward Post limped on a leg that had been shattered once and poorly set, and the cane he used was not for show but necessary.

As Captain Post approached, Crispin glanced up at the boy and wished at once that he had not. The boy's eyes were on his father, and there was a measure of pride there. But there was another thing, in far greater proportion. It was pity.

Without waiting for the captain to come up to them, Crispin tilted his hat and cradled Old Yellow Dog more easily over his arm. He patted the beautiful black horse once on its glistening shoulder and nodded upward at the elegant boy. "'Tis a strange path ye may be settin' out on, lad. I hope at its end one day ye find a summer land."

When Crispin returned to Jason Cook's smithy it was mid-morning, and Cook pointed to the assemblage of damaged items piled on, around, and under the scudding bench beyond the large bellows. "Folks been by the mornin' long to see if any of those was fixed."

Crispin took up his tools and went to work. "Time be a precious thing, Jason," he said. "I might be of a mind to give it away, but I do balk at havin' it took from me." As he worked he gave the smith a report on his adventures of the morning.

Cook listened, ranking rods of hammered iron over the forge coals then backing away to work his bellows, bringing the coals to a bright hot red corona with hints of cherry. When the rods were heated, he would cut them with a chisel and form links for a chain.

"Not many take to the Squire," he commented. "Especially them whose land patents was issued by the Transylvania Company. Trelawney's land warrants are from the Virginia Burgesses, and they don't recognize the treaty Henderson an' Boone made to get that land. So now everybody with Transylvania land doesn't own it anymore. Trelawney's takin' up what he wants, 'less folks can afford to buy their places back from him."

"How can he do that?"

"Oh, easy. Captain Clark had to go to th' Burgesses to get backin' for his militias, an' if he hadn't there wouldn't be a white family left in all of Kaintuck, for the Shawnee would have wiped us out. But when the Burgesses backed us here, they took it as grounds for sovereignty an' set out to reassign all th' lands they could get hold of, to pay the bill. Henderson an' Boone's treaty with th' Indians never was legal, because th' law says only th' government can treat with Indians . . . not people."

Crispin stopped his tapping and looked up. "But that's Crown law, Jason."

"Well," the blacksmith shrugged, "the war ain't over yet."

Crispin finished crimping a spout on a teapot and set it aside. He picked up a broken axe and selected a stout ash bat to work into a new handle for it. "Many a misery in this ol' world. Could a man rank troubles like steppin' stones, he could walk across floods. Speakin' of which, th' folk that come in yesterday, up from th' river, one of them said that river's like to flood this spring. That's why they come away."

"Is that what they told you?" Cook looked across at him, then went back to turning his link-rods. "Well, that may be so, but that's not why they left the river. Didn't I tell you? Squire Trelawney's warrants cover all that

85

down there. Those folks came in because he owns their land now, an' if they want it back, they have to deal with him."

Crispin stared at him, then set down the axe handle and walked to the open door. He stood there for a time, looking across at the little cabin where Nora Ferris lived.

Behind him, Cook grinned. "Mighty handsome woman," he said.

"What?"

"The widow Ferris. Fine figure of a woman she is. I wonder, now, what it might take to make a fiddlefoot like yourself think of settlin' down?"

Crispin's ears went red. He turned. "Jason, I only met the woman yesterday."

"Aye. And chased Sam Drummond from her house, an' built her a cradle, an' sang with her son as—so it's said—his father once did. Why, Crispin . . ." He stopped. The tall man had turned away thoughtfully.

Crispin went back to the axe handle, shaping it with a rasp. He worked in silence for a while, frowning often as he did. When the axe was done he held it up in large hands and pursed his lips, studying it. It was like most axes he had ever seen. Its broad flaring head with its curved edge and tapered butt weighed about three pounds. The handle he had just fitted to it was a straight shank of rounded ash wood set in a nearly round eye and wedged with seasoned hickory quoins.

In these woodlands, it was the foremost tool of the settlers and the builders. Before the plow must come the axe. Yet it did not please the eye.

"Many a man has worked himself to an early grave wi' those," Cook noted. "The devil's tool itself, they call it. Yet without it, how would a man ever clear his land or build his house or keep his field fenced an' his fire fed?"

"Aye." Crispin squinted at the axe, turning it an arm's length. "So, then, why has it never been improved upon?"

"An axe is an axe," Cook shrugged.

"Were I a man as could turn iron, there's a thing I might try."

"And what might that be?"

He frowned once more at the axe, then set it aside and pointed. "Cast your eye on yonder Brown Bess of yours, standing in the corner there. Wouldn't you say that's as fine an English musket as any there be?"

"I would," Cook agreed.

"Yet, here by th' door stands my Old Yellow Dog. Now would ye say 'a gun is a gun,' Jason Cook? Would ye fire a match with me an' wager a bit of Spanish silver on th' outcome?"

"I would not," Cook said. "A musket—even a fine English musket—be no match for a Pennsylvania long rifle, Crispin, and well do ye know it. But what are ye gettin' at?"

Crispin picked up the axe again. "This axe is what I'm gettin' at, Jason. It's a good axe, like as peas in a pod with every English axe men have carried to these lands. Yet it isn't an axe to fit the land. A heavier head would be better, to my thinkin', and an eye placed so that the head can balance on its haft an' not be forever turnin' in a man's hands when the blade strikes a knot. A longer eye could take a stronger handle, too. Less flare might give a deeper cut, an' a bit of curve to the handle would give a better grip. Then again, why not blunt the backside of it? Seems to me a man has more call to drive stakes in this country than he does to pierce helmets."

Cook had put down his tools and was studying the axe with Crispin. "Could ye draw a picture of it, the way ye describe it? I've a bit of spring stock yonder that might be shaped and would take a good temper."

"Aye, I can draw a picture. And I can hone the edge and shape and set a handle for it. English axes are like English ways, Jason. They stroke too wide an' cut too shallow. They bounce when they should bite an' they break when they're put to the test."

"Aye, an' ye're doin' riddles again, Crispin. Is it axes you're talkin' about now, or is it Squire Trelawney?"

"The subject never came to mind," Crispin said blandly. "I'm just thinkin' there might be a market for a real American axe."

He set the axe aside and picked up the pieces of a broken trivet. Within moments he was hard at work, repairing it. Cook had gone back to his forge and anvil, and Crispin smiled grimly. If nothing else, he had set the man's mind onto more comfortable courses than it had been holding.

He could not help thinking, himself, about the bright eyes and fetching ways of Nora Ferris. But he found talk of the kind Cook had been making uncomfortable. More than that, it was downright unsettling.

"A man be a footloose and quarrelsome thing," the words sounded silently in his mind. *"A man can ride reckless and high. But a good woman's kiss and a measure of bliss makes him sweeter than gooseberry pie."*

The American Axe

VIII

"... for somewhere out there is a bright summer land," Nora sang to herself as she did her long hair into a practiced bun and set a fresh bonnet atop it, peering into the little mirror to see that it was straight. "And it's there that we're going to go."

It was a bright morning, the air outside her windows sparkling with the dance of new sun across the hilltop to the southeast. But most of the shutters remained closed. It had turned cold in the night, a nipping cold that reminded one of how new and vulnerable were the first days of spring.

She had set a fire going in the hearth, moving quietly to avoid disturbing Luther and Kate where they lay close beneath heavy quilts on a floor pallet, or little Jonathan snug in his new cradle. Kate had been up with Jonathan during the night. Nora had heard her. But now they slept and had no need to be up early. Julie and Ellie had both left the house at dawn, Julie to spend the morning at the widow Ferguson's barn, helping with the wash, and Ellie to gather eggs and trade at the morning market, before school.

Then, alone with her kitchen hearth and the house quiet, Nora had heated water, shaved soap, and treated herself to a bath, soaking herself lavishly and sponging herself clean.

Now, dressed fresh for the morning, she sang quietly as she made ready to tend her morning school. She had not heard the strange old song in years, had not thought of it until yesterday when she had heard the singing from the common and had run to greet her son. It had sounded so much like the old times, when Luther and her Jonathan, son and father, had taken turns with the verses on cold winter nights.

So long ago.

She thought of the stranger who had come to her house, who had for a day been so much a part of everything, and a great curiosity grew in her. Crispin Blount. Such an odd man. So tall, so . . . ugly. And yet so utterly charming in his awkward, forthright way. There, she thought, was a man so full of life that he must shout it, so full of song that he must sing it, so full of praise that his words would have been outrageous flattery were they not so obviously sincere.

And full of other things, too, she thought. Deep secrets and old hurts, hidden by the years but still a part of him, lingered like sadness in the turn of his eyes, the sudden glances unaware.

Nora had been a widow for three years and was used to the veiled glances of men, the overtures that ranged from tentative gazes to overt attempts at courtship. She was not displeased that men still found her attractive. She was glad they did. But there was a puzzling quality to Crispin Blount's admiring attentions. Most men saw her, she suspected, as a widow. Crispin saw her as a woman.

Julie knew him from past visits to Harrodsburg, and she doted on him. He was a footloose, magical creature who came and went and seemed to carry a brightness about him for all to share, yet Nora had the feeling he was very lonely.

Certainly he had not been a will-o'-the-wisp all his years. There were hints in him of other times and other situations: the odd speech that was backwoods one moment and educated man the next, the way he had of speaking at length of places and things, but somehow not speaking of himself.

Curious. A most curious man.

With a last glance in her little mirror, Nora pulled her shawl about her, picked up her strap basket, and tiptoed from the house.

Bright morning was upon Harrodsburg, a busy morning full of comings and goings: farmers heading for their fields, women making their way to morning market, draymen hitching their teams, and the air—sharp chill beneath a warming sun.

School was a wide-porched old house within the standing stockade, which Captain Clark had let her use as long as she would tend and teach the children. It was the thing that she had found to do in those dark days when Jonathan was gone and Luther had brought her and Ellie to the stockade's shelter and then had gone with Captain Clark. The stockade days, as she thought of them now, when frightened people, broken families, huddled within the sentried walls and watched the columns of distant smoke that were their homes, watched their young men go off in motley columns, armed with muskets and long rifles, terribly alone in these remote hills, terribly outnumbered yet with their heads high and backs straight. Those had been the Shawnee days. Painted savages from across the river had swept the land, seeking scalps for which British agents would trade red-handled knives.

Until it happened, the Ferris family had not known of the red knives. Jonathan had trusted the Indians, had dealt with them. Jonathan was gone.

Nora opened the schoolhouse, cracked the shutters for light, and set a fire in the hearth. She brought in water from the well, got a broom, and swept around the ranked small tables and benches, then went out and rang the bell. As she waited she looked up at the bright sky, the rising warm sun. It had taken a very long time for the days to turn bright again. The smokes were gone now from the horizons. She wanted never to see them again.

"A fine mornin', Mistress Ferris!" Will Henry waved as he guided his dapple team through the stockade's gateless entrance and into the open court. He halted them before the school and turned. "Off, now, all of ye. Mind yer steps and mind yer manners."

The flock of children that scrambled from the wagon was a dozen in number and ranged in ages from six to fourteen. Four of them were Will's, and the rest belonged to various houses between his place and the town. For his hauling of them he would receive a peck of beans in season, a hot berry pie or a slab of pork, and maybe a chicken now and then. He would have hauled them anyway.

They swarmed from the wagon to cluster bright-eyed before the porch, some looking forward to the day at school, some looking sadly back on the day they would miss by being there.

Will Henry slapped reins on the shining rumps of the dapples and swung the wagon in a tight circle.

"What will you haul today, Will?" she called, and he looked around.

"Winter hay, mistress, from the high fields."

"Luther brought his cow in. We can use hay."

"I'll see to it," he shouted, rolling out of the stockade.

Other children were coming now, some running and some hanging back, and she counted their heads and called them by name. "Good morning, Becky, Tom, Fletcher. Good morning, Samuel. Good morning, Wendy. Good morning, Aloysuis, Mercy, Frederick. Good morning to you, James. And Jared and Julius, good morning. Come in, children. Come in."

They filed past her, those children of Harrodsburg whose parents could spare them for a day in school, and she counted them as they entered. She would keep a roll, but she always counted.

Jared and Julius Bowman, a pair of freckled imps who were more regular in attendance than their attitudes would warrant, shuffled past and avoided her eyes, and she stood in the doorway so she could keep a watch on them inside.

"Good morning, Sarah," she said. "Good morning, Marvin. Theodore. Micah. Good morning, Nathan and Nolan. Good morning, Wilbur . . ."

Seth Michaels hurried through the gate, his hair tousled and his legs too long for his britches, a pair of mongrel dogs trailing behind him. At fourteen, Seth was the oldest of her flock and rarely missed a day in school.

"Set, dogs!" he ordered, and the mongrels obediently moved aside and sat beneath the window, their eyes on him. "Good fellers," he praised them, leaning to rumple the fur of their necks and scratch their ears. Satisfied, the dogs lay down on the porch, prepared to wait the day for him. "Good morning, Mistress Ferris."

"Good morning, Seth. And how is your mother?"

"She's got corns ailin' her, ma'am, but not too bad. Is Ellie here yet?" He peered inside.

"She'll be along, Seth. She went to early market."

Nora smiled to herself as Seth went in. She understood one reason Seth seldom missed school. These three days a week, four months of each year, were almost his only opportunity to gaze starry-eyed at Ellie Ferris. The boy had a hopeless crush on Nora's daughter. If it lasted, he would wind up with a first-rate education.

Most of the flock had arrived, and Nora stepped out in the compound to look through the high gates, then went back to the door. Seth said, "I'll stand by the door if you want, ma'am, 'til everyone's here."

And be the first to spot Ellie. "Very well, Seth. Thank you."

Inside, there was a squeal and a rushing of little girls, and Nora made her way to the far back corner of the room. "What did you bring today, Julius and Jared? Did you bring something?"

The tads looked at the floor, scuffed their shoes, and were silent.

"May I see it?" Nora pressed.

They looked at each other. Julius grinned and Jared looked up at the teacher, then brought his hands suddenly from behind him and thrust them at her. "Boo!"

The skunk the youth held peered at her with beady eyes, upset at the rough handling, and raised its lips in a threatening hiss. Nora cleared her throat, steadied herself, and looked at it carefully. It was just a baby, probably not even weaned. Its little striped tail was curled high over its back in the instinctive defense pose of its kind.

Carefully, Nora held her fingers before its nose, then eased them around to stroke its silky small head. "My," she said. "What a fine skunk. Where did you boys get it?"

"Found it in a fell stump," Jared said, visibly deflated.

"There was three more," Julius said. "I'd have got one too, but Jared said the mother was comin' back."

"May I see it?" she asked, then ran her hand down the creature's quivering back, curling its tail down and under it, and lifted it from Jared's hands. She held it close against her breast and it nestled in her hands, comforted by the warmth and touch of her. "It's probably hungry," she told the children who clustered around now, curious.

"Ick!" Becky Tully squinched her nose and stared at the little dark head peering out from Nora's hands. "If it stinks us, we'll all have to bury our clothes and get scrubbed with yellow soap and turpentine."

"It's too little to spray," she told them. "It's just a baby. It will have to be fed and kept warm and tended to like any baby, or it will get sick and die." She looked at Jared and Julius. "How do you boys plan to feed it?"

Jared stared at her, his eyes large. "I don't know, ma'am. I didn't think about that."

"We just figured we'd raise it up an' make a cap out of it," Julius added.

Nora looked at the animal judiciously. "It's pretty

small for a cap. How far away was that stump where you found it?"

Jared perked up, an answer beginning to dawn, a solution to the awful responsibility for his actions. "It's not far, ma'am. Just down by the creek. We found it on the way here."

"Do you think you'd like to put it back?"

The pair nodded vigorously. "Yes, ma'am!"

Ellie had arrived, trailed into the room by a moon-struck Seth Michaels. She looked at what her mother was holding and stepped back, wide-eyed. "Mother, that's a skunk!"

"Yes, dear, I know. I wonder if you'd go fetch Luther. He's probably awake by now. He could go with these boys to put this baby back where it belongs. Its mother must be frantic."

"I can go along with her if you want, ma'am," Seth offered. "I can knock on the door for her."

"I don't knock on my own door, dummy!" Ellie glared at him and Seth beamed, grateful for her attention. "I'll be right back." Before Nora could comment, Ellie and Seth both were gone on Ellie's errand, Seth's dogs following.

"I have some dried apple," Molly Hays offered. "Could it eat that?"

As they made a snug nest in a basket for the tiny creature, Nora breathed deeply and shook her head. Jared and Julius may have learned a lesson this morning, she thought. But how might Luther take to the idea of returning a baby to a frantic mother skunk? Well, if anyone could handle it, Luther could. Oddly, she found herself wishing Crispin Blount were here.

She got the children unscrambled, counted them again, and seated them in their rows. Another school day had begun.

Luther awakened to fire in the hearth and the quiet

crooning of Kate as she nursed the baby. He folded the quilts and cozies that had been their pallet, stretching the sleep from his shoulders as he did so. Then, with the stacked bedding, he walked across to the pantry, stooping as he passed to kiss his wife's head, just at the spot where the hair parted at the crown, pulled aside in twin braids to reveal a tiny hint of white skin. "Good morning, mistress," he murmured, and winked at the bright smile she turned to him.

In the pantry he stacked the bedding on its shelf and poured tea into a mug.

"Breakfast in a bit," Kate called. "There are eggs."

Carrying his tea, he went back through the main room to the shuttered west window and opened its battens. The morning flowed in bright and chill.

"Cold." He set his mug on the sill and leaned outward, breathing in the icy freshness to bring him fully awake.

"Jonathan slept the night with only one waking." Kate tilted her head toward the willow cradle. "What a strange man, though. Did you know him before?"

Luther shook his head, turning back to the window. "Not that I know. And a person'd not likely forget Crispin Blount."

Beyond in the bright streets, people came and went, shawls pulled up and breaths steaming.

"Been a long time since we lost Pa." He sipped hot tea and hitched himself up to sit on the windowsill. "I guess it's been lonely for her here . . . just Julie and Ellie, and keeping her school, us down by the river and not seeing her but twice a year. Did you see how she looked last night, at supper?"

Kate buttoned her blouse and placed Jonathan snug in his new cradle. Then she came to the window and took a sip of Luther's tea. "Yes. She shone."

"I haven't thought about my mother . . . that way."

"Your mother is still a young woman, Luther."

"And Mr. Blount knew the old song. I never realized others might know it. That seems so strange."

96

Kate gazed out the open window, her hand on her husband's shoulder. "Somewhere out there is a bright summer land," she crooned softly, understanding a new thing about the young man beside her. "Will you teach it to me, Luther?"

"It's just an old song."

"No. It's more than that."

"I wonder who he is," Luther ran a hand over his stubbled chin. "I haven't seen Ma so . . . bright . . . since Pa died."

She took his tea and sipped it again, studying him covertly in the morning light. Sure, he seemed. Square-built and sturdy as his father must have been, strong shoulders that could master plowstaves, square, hard hands that could bend a shoe or touch her cheek as lightly as warm breezes. Blunt, honest face too much given to pensive frowns and hidden thoughts, a face that should laugh more than it did. Dark eyes that had seen violence too young and still carried the images of it. He never spoke of those long days, the savage days, when smokes lined the horizons and she—still Kate McCarthy—had waited and watched from the old stockade, somehow knowing he must return even after others had lost hope.

To her, a part of him would always be a distant lantern in the hostile darkness, a speck of light that bobbed afar, coming slowly closer through the night long after the other young men had returned from the wilderness carrying their sick and wounded. She had kept vigil when they had all lost hope. Then there had been the tiny, distant light and she had watched it, her heart in her throat, as it came, watched it through tears as it shaped itself into a carried lantern, its light glinting on the ivory sheen of a white powder horn.

Suddenly she leaned against him, put her arms around him, and pressed her face against his breast. He smelled of smoke and manhood, and he was hers as Jonathan was theirs.

Sudden pounding at the door sent her hurrying there

with a finger to her lips. She opened it to squabbling voices.

"I told you not to knock, Seth. The baby's probably sleeping."

"I didn't knock so loud."

"You didn't need to knock at all. It's my house."

"Hush," Kate commanded, and they went silent. As one, they peered around the frame toward the cradle, then scowled at each other, fingers to their lips.

"Ma needs Luther," Ellie whispered. "She has a skunk."

Seth looked behind him and waved an open hand. "Set, fellers."

"A skunk?"

"She wants Luther to come and take it home."

"Here?"

Ellie crowded past her, exasperated. "No, its own home. Hi, Luther. Ma needs you at the schoolhouse."

Seth Michaels, timid now, sidled through the door to stand at awkward attention just inside, looking around him at the place where Ellie lived. "It's only a little skunk," he explained. "The twins fetched it."

Luther gulped his tea, then went to find his boots, "A skunk," he muttered.

"A skunk?" he asked Ellie again as they trooped toward the stockade.

"A baby skunk," she repeated with the patience of one who deals always with elders. "Those twins brought it to school and Ma wants you to take it home."

"If it has a home, it has a mother."

"Of course it does."

"Well, if it has a mother, how did the twins get it?"

"Its mother wasn't there."

"Well, I'll bet she is now."

"I can go along if you want," Seth offered. "The fellers probably could help."

They preceded him through the stockade gate—Ellie, Seth, and the fellers—and Luther paused as his glance caught a flurry of activity on down the way. A hundred yards along, a group of men proceeded out toward the east road. Two of them seemed to be pushing a third. As he watched, one of them suddenly broke free and went hopping off on one foot while the center one, a head taller than the others, swung a rifle at the other flanker and a fourth man intervened. In an instant the tall one was bent low, two holding him. Luther's eyes widened. The tall man was Crispin Blount.

"What in blazes? . . ." He turned from the stockade, starting toward them, then the tall man was upright again and they stood clustered there, talking, while the hopper sat down to inspect his foot. Luther paused. One of the men handed Crispin's rifle to him and all four proceeded eastward.

"Luther?" Ellie called from the gate. "Where are you going? School's in here."

He turned back, then turned and looked again. The four were walking together now, seeming amiable, though one in the van had a decided limp.

"Luther!" Ellie scolded. "Come on!"

Luther shrugged away his curiosity and felt the deep gloom returning to take its place. He wanted this to be a good day but saw little hope for it. Somehow it was ominous that he must begin this day by dealing with a skunk, because when that was done—whatever it was— then he must go and deal with Squire Trelawney.

IX

The sun was high when Luther arrived at the big house of Squire Trelawney, and he found others waiting there. At least thirty men stood or sat around the railed dooryard. One or two of them he recognized as distant neighbors of his, landholders to the north. Most of the remainder, he assumed, were from nearby. One large group stood aside, scowling toward the house. There were two men on the porch, both holding muskets.

Luther hesitated, looking around at the men there, then went to the rail fence and pushed open the gate. One of the men on the porch raised his musket and barked, "You there! What's your business?"

"I've come to see the Squire," Luther told him.

"Aye, and hasn't everybody? Why do you want to see him?"

"Because he has claimed my land . . . or most of it. I've come to speak to him about that."

The man grinned. "So has everybody else out there. You'll wait your turn like the rest. Outside of that gate."

Luther sighed, closed the gate, and started to turn away.

"Where is the land you claim was yours?" the man called.

"North. On Rolling Fork."

"So you're one of those," the man said. "You've come

a long way, young feller."

"Four days on the road."

"Well, you wasted the journey. The Squire is only considerin' lands here in the valley now. The rest ain't surveyed yet."

"They came and ran a line . . . right through my fields. They said it was a warrant boundary."

"'Twas only a try-line, son. Surveyors will be along later. After that maybe the Squire will talk to you, if he sees fit."

"If he sees fit?" Luther's big hands rolled into fists. "The man has taken my land and won't even have the decency to talk to me about it?"

"Nothin' to talk about," the guard shrugged. "Until it's surveyed, don't neither you nor him know what kind of boundaries there might be."

"I know my boundaries. They're from the Henderson survey."

"Not anymore. Henderson never had legal land to survey, and anybody livin' on that land is just squatters." The man grinned again, then squinted at Luther, suddenly seeing the expression on the sturdy young man's face. He twitched the musket. "Here now, you just back off like I said. You got no business here anyway."

Luther turned away, red-faced and defeated. He tried not to look at the men gathered there, but one came forward and put a gentle hand on his shoulder. "Easy, son," he said. "We've all got the same problems."

Luther willed the hard anger away. The man was trying to be friendly. "Then what are you doing about them? What can *I* do?"

"Not much," the man admitted. "You bein' out yonder like that, you might get another crop or two in afore they run you off. Those of us closer in, some of us maybe can buy back what was took from us. Or maybe a few of us will recover somethin' if we can get a new survey." He looked around sadly. "Some of us will be movin' on, I reckon."

"To where?"

"West someplace. Anywhere past the bedammed Burgess warrants. There's land out there, somewhere." As though musing to himself, he added, "Somewhere a summer land." Then he looked at Luther again, more closely. "You're the one as sang that song. I know you now. Ah, 'twas a rare good sing, lad. For a time at least, the sun shone on a few bedarkened souls."

Luther shook his head and looked again at the house with its porch guards. "Did it?" he wondered. "A song doesn't change things. No more than does a rainbow."

For hours then, Luther wandered about the little town and the countryside around, deep in thought. He had talked with others. He knew what they knew. Some of them had petitioned for a resurvey of their lands. A waste of time, others said. The Burgesses had already commissioned official surveys, at the demands of Trelawney and other warrant buyers. Some of these had bought their patents on faith. Others, though, were withholding payment until exact surveys were at hand—though like Trelawney, they were already consolidating their claims.

Among the dispossessed, many were proclaiming for a land act—a new law for the Virginia territories, something to prevent what had happened from ever happening again. There was confidence that such a law would come into being. But it would not help those whose Transylvania titles had been voided. Throughout much of the land beyond the Cumberland, men whose sweat had cleared fields and whose blood had fallen on them now stood by in bleak silence as those same fields were divided among others. No man knew for sure, outside of a few square miles of surveyed townsite—single-acre in-lots and ten-acre out-lots and the wider lands immediately beyond—exactly who owned what. But the Burgesses had decreed the old titles void and were paying their debts by selling off the land, and what they said would be the law.

And through it all there came new smallholders, veterans of the Continental Army, each with a legal claim to some dimly specified piece of land and each came to claim it. What they claimed would be theirs, survey or not. The honor of Virginia was at stake. They came trickling into the Kaintuck territory, only a few at first but always a few more.

The investors would have their realms and the soldiers their acres. But for those who had settled the bloody land and held it through the long days of the red knife massacres, there would be nothing. In the turmoil of war, Crown law had uprooted them and Colonial law had taken away their lands.

Captain Clark himself had intervened, they said, and his prestige was such that a few parcels had been salvaged. But not many.

Luther had been among them and had listened.

A few spoke of taking up arms. Some, in their anger, threatened burning and pillage. But most of those would change their minds. Nothing would be gained by lawlessness.

Many more spoke of moving on. Some were thoughtful on this, considering where legal claims might be made. Others would just go and put down where they could and hope next time to be more lucky.

Luther thought of the little farmstead up toward the river, the place where he had buried his father, the place he had defended single-handed against marauders, the place to which he had taken his Kate when the smokes were gone. Hot moisture welled in his eyes as he remembered. They had journeyed there from the fort at Harrodsburg and found the old cabin still stood firm. He had entered first, then turned to hold the door wide.

"This is home, Kate," he had said. "This place is ours."

Baby Jonathan had been born there, just a season past.

He felt lost and betrayed now, wondering where to turn. The land had not betrayed him, but the laws of the land had. And somehow the land itself no longer was a comfort to him.

"We have little money," he had told Kate after the boundsmarkers came. "But if I can just talk to the man Trelawney, maybe it will work out. If a price is set, I can offer him my indenture. I will if I have to. A few years service to him . . . I can manage that, Kate."

Yet now even that seemed a false dream. Trelawney would have no use for servitude in return for parcels of land. The land itself was what he wanted. He had plans for it.

Move on, some said. But where? Out there was only wilderness, and if it was beyond the reach of the Burgesses, then it was beyond their protection as well. Could a man take his wife and child into wilderness? Pa had, but there had been no war then, no British generals offering red-handled knives for settler scalps. Then, the Indians had been generally friendly. Some might be friendly again, but most would not. They would not forget.

The sun was low when Luther found himself again on the main east-west street of the town. Ahead was the old fort, across from it was the smithy and the stables, and just beyond, his mother's house. Kate would be waiting, wondering about him. What could he tell her?

The voice from the smithy startled him as he passed. "Ho, there, Luther! You wear the very face of trouble."

Crispin Blount was at the rain barrel, washing grime from his hands. As Luther turned, he gazed at him from behind bushy brows. "Ah, it *is* trouble, is it? Lad, I swear we'll have a dry season, for no storm cloud would dare to show its face about ye, for fear it would die of shame."

Luther tried to put on a smile and failed. "Will you come to supper again this evening, Mr. Blount?"

Crispin shook his head. "My empty belly has talked of little else this day, but I've imposed too much already on the folk of that fair house. A stranger at the same door too often soon wears out his welcome."

Luther nodded, understanding the civility. He started on, then turned back. "Mr. Blount, it would be a favor to me if you would come. So I ask again, if you please."

Crispin dried his arms on a strip of blanket hanging at the door. "Do ye suppose another riddle might soften the mood of your eyes, then, Luther? It might be that I could . . ."

"No, it isn't that. Thought maybe you would sit with me a while when we've eaten."

"Sit? It's a thing I do well when I put my mind to it."

"I'll explain to my mother that I begged you to come."

"In which case, I'd be honored. But only if you will tell me what troubles you so."

Luther looked at his feet, finding the words. Then he looked up, and his gaze was level and earnest. "There was a time, a long time ago, when if a thing bothered me, I would tell my father about it. Sometimes he could find an answer, other times he could only listen. It was a long time ago, and I was just a boy. Now he's gone . . . and I'm a man. But . . . well, sometimes I still need to tell him about things . . . when I can find no answer. . . ." He ran out of words then and faltered. He was embarrassed.

Crispin stood in silence for a moment, then a slow grin spread across his face. "I've had kind words come my way now and again, Luther, but never any that have touched deeper fiber than those. Lad, if I can listen to you as your father did and if it be a help to you, then there's naught could ever please me more."

"Then come." Luther scuffed his feet, abashed at the things he had said. Blount was a stranger here. But then, Luther reminded himself, so was he.

Jason Cook, the smith, came from the shed and handed an object to Crispin, then turned to offer his hand to Luther. "Fine evenin' to you, young Ferris. Will you come again soon to sing wi' this big rooster here? It did sound rarely fine, the music yesterday."

Crispin was turning the object over in his hands, eyeing it critically. It appeared to be a splitting wedge, though narrower than most that Luther had seen and with a graceful curve along each side. Then he saw that there was a hole through it, an oval hole set back in the wide part. It was a new-forged axe-head, but of a design Luther had not seen before.

Crispin handed it to him. "Try th' heft of this, lad. When it's done, you've the shoulders to test it for us if you'd like."

"Looks more like a 'Hican tomahawk than an axe," Cook noted. "But it's an axe, right enough. Mayhap the first of its breed."

"An American axe," Crispin added. "A new blade for a new breed."

Luther turned it over, trying to be impressed with it then beginning to understand. It was a straightforward instrument, simple and businesslike, with none of the flare and sweep of the axes he had used—that same flare and sweep that had made men curse the tool since before any could remember. "It looks American," he allowed. "Shaped to do what it is meant to do."

Crispin grinned at him. "Well-chosen words, those. Had the popinjay British ever understood that, they'd have pursued a harder war . . . or mayhap not bothered at all."

Luther added the words to his store of riddles and handed back the axe-head. "What do you mean to do with it?"

"Fashion it," Crispin shrugged. "And others like it, if there's a market for such." He in turn handed it back to Cook. "If ye'll grind this tomorrow, I'll use a bit of that bent ash to put a handle to it. Then we'll see what we have."

In the clear evening air a hand-bell sounded from the door of Nora Ferris's house.

Crispin cocked a brow and grinned. "The very music of good food and fine company. Hurry along, then, Luther, and I'll not be far behind you. I'll see to Mystery and then I'll be along."

As Luther walked away he heard Crispin's voice behind him, talking to Jason Cook. "It's a vagrant world, Jason, that can mold a tad to the comforts of hearth and home, then pull it all away. Many's the man that's had to come of age too young an' in too harsh a world."

And neither of them heard Jason Cook's words to Samuel Calkins: "A wager for you, Sam'l. I say that this time yon tall singin' crow will stay on at Harrodsburg for more than just a season."

Calkins adjusted his wire wig and peered toward his stables, where Crispin Blount was emerging to cross the street toward Nora Ferris's house. "The man's been footloose all his life, Jason. Why would he change his ways now?"

Cook shrugged. "Maybe because the Squire has got his dander up, or maybe because the widda Ferris can cook. Or maybe it's that Crispin's own years are talkin' to him. At any rate, it's the first time I've known him to propose a venture that might last more than a season." He handed the axe-head to Calkins. "There's still forest an' plenty to be cleared in this land, Sam'l. Yonder to the west. But mayhap Crispin knows it's younger men than him who'll do th' clearin'."

Will Henry did not haul winter hay that day. When he reached his high fields after depositing his wagonload of children at Nora Ferris's school, he found men there setting cairns. "This be claimed land," they told him. "The Squire has need for it for summer graze, so Mr. Sparrow sent us to plot the roads an' fences."

"But this is where I take hay for the town," he insisted. "Everybody knows that. I've harvested here since . . . well, since most any of us came."

"It isn't your land." The overseer spread his hands in a gesture that said he had no say in the matter but recognized the facts as they stood. "It's needed now by him that owns it. Mayhap there's winter hay some

107

other place."

For a time Will stood beside his wagon, watching them work. Some hauled slabs of stone, some placed them, and the overseer made marks on a chart when each landmark was completed. Outside of the marked grounds, little remained of the hayfields Will Henry had harvested for these past seasons. And with each cairn raised, Will Henry saw a bit of his world dissolve.

He did not, in fact, own any of the land the fields encompassed. Question of ownership had not arisen before. Since the time of the smokes, although new folk had moved into the region, no one had contested his right to the hayfields. It had always been the practice that each man who owned an out-lot of the town of Harrodsburg could farm his acres and add a little income by whatever he could fetch from the open lands beyond. Seldom had any man encroached upon another. Just as Sam Michaels harvested firewood from the forests beyond his out-lot south of the town, and Cull Barnett quarried building stone from the ledges beyond his plots, so had Will Henry been accustomed to harvest winter hay in the high fields beyond his. It was claim by right of enterprise, and none had contested it until now.

The hay from these fields had supplemented his produce from his own ten acres. It was what had made it possible for him to feed his family, with an occasional sweet at the supper table.

Without it . . . A dread grew in Will Henry as he watched the laying of the cairns.

Still, he had made promises. So after a time, he climbed aboard his wagon again and headed further out, into the hills. Here and there in the unsettled lands were deadfall clearings and old burnovers where ample grass cured through the winter. Several of these he found, then busied himself with scythe and rake, felling, baling, and binding until he had a wagonload. One load to show for a day's work. In the hayfields it would have been four or five. A man who counted on the produce of the hills for

108

barter to supplant the meager harvest of his crops could not subsist for long on such short pickings.

Winding homeward, he found a good stand of post cedar and was calculating the trade value of fencewood when he saw stone cairns. Here, too, someone was claiming ground.

Circling around to come in on the high road, Will passed Sam Michaels's woodlot and reined in. Men were working there, felling trees, but they were not Sam or his helpers. Nor were these men selecting for cordwood. Their axes and saws sang in the brisk air, and where they had been no tree stood. They were not harvesting, they were clearing. Again Will spotted the familiar stone cairns, marking new-claimed boundaries.

So much has changed, so fast, he thought. Just since the thaw, nothing has been the same.

Will had heard the talk, the wonder at the arrival of the Squire with his great assemblage of carts and draft animals, servants and hired crews. He had watched the work on the new horse pens, stables, and pastures, had seen how almost overnight—so it seemed—Trelawney's great house had risen from its stone foundations to overshadow all the rest of the town. He had watched with awe the caravans of goods and materials coming up from raft docks on the river after the thaw. And like, he supposed, everyone else, he had not inquired into what was taking place. Everyone knew that Trelawney held land warrants from the Burgesses, even that the warrants covered some claimed lands in some areas. But it had been a bright and busy spring, and none had taken the time to ponder over what might come next.

He remembered the Virginia delegation that had arrived last fall, the magistrate and his clerks who had posted notices on the town boards and had called meetings to publicize that all land claims must be recorded and approved or be subject to—what had the magistrate called it?—*readjustment*.

People claiming Transylvania land had been notified—

those close in who could be reached—that they should bring their claims to St. Albans for hearing if they wanted their claims verified.

But St. Albans was a journey of weeks, across wilderness. Will did not recall hearing of any who had gone. Probably those located in the territories beyond the trade roads had never been notified at all.

Swinging past the woodlot onto the road, Will saw young Seth Michaels walking toward him in the distance, his ever-present pair of dogs at his heels. He glanced at the sun and saw that the day was late. The widow Ferris would be waiting for him to pick up children at the school, to deliver to their homes.

At a trot then, he guided his wagon along the high road past the first out-lots of Harrodsburg, and pulled rein at the old stables where he kept his hay. It was only a few minutes' work to unload the wagon. He climbed aboard again and headed for the old fort, waving at Seth Michaels and a few others as he passed.

The magnitude of what he had seen this day was only beginning to dawn on him as he made the turn and pulled into the stockade grounds. His hayfields . . . Sam Michaels's woodlot . . . stands of fencewood . . . What else would be closed to the people of Harrodsburg? And beyond, in the territories, what of those out there, who had not even town lots to bind their homestead rights?

Will Henry had come to Harrodsburg—Harrod's town it was called then—in the first season of its life. He had helped to build the stockade there, and then had helped to defend it in the time of distant smokes. Will Henry knew the taste of fear.

But the fear he felt now was different. The threat was not the erratic, deadly violence of savages driven into a white men's war. The fear now was of law, law born in distant places, law bred by the need for wealth to pursue a continuing war, law that had come to Harrodsburg and even now was rearranging everything to suit its own purposes.

Law that would have no place in it for many of those who were his neighbors here, and did not care.

With a wagonload of children collected from Mistress Ferris at the stockade school, Will Henry turned again toward the high road and flipped his reins. His route of delivery would be a half circle beyond the out-lots, dropping children at their dooryards. Then with his own brood, he would head home. He wondered what he should say to Sarah, how to broach the subject. She would have to know, of course. When there was no hay to sell, it was Sarah who would suffer more than he. She scrimped now to make ends meet, to keep a larder stocked and meals at table for all of them. What would she do without the few pennies from the hay?

At the foot of the high road, where foot-trails angled up to the street, a horseman appeared. He paused, looking around, a long rifle across his saddle. As he turned his head, the striped tail of his coonskin cap fell over a buckskinned shoulder. He tapped heels to his mount and came on then, leading a pair of pack horses laden with bundled hides. Will squinted at him as he neared, then raised a hand to wave. It was nearly two years since he had seen Leander Haynes. The young man had changed with the seasons. The shoulders that bulged his buckskin jacket were hard muscle, and the whiskers of his cheeks had become a beard, a thick bronze mane clipped in the manner of a woodsman and lighter in color than the hair that fell from his cap. As he neared, Will saw other changes as well. Leander's eyes were not the lost-orphan eyes of the frightened lad who had left Harrodsburg after the death of his family, the boy who had paced silently about the fort for a time, then had taken up his rifle and disappeared. Those eyes now were eyes that had seen much and said little. They were strange eyes.

It was Leander, he recalled, who had brought word of the death of the Jackson lad, the one Julie McCarthy had married before they went off with Colonel Clark, making for Kaskaskia. Leander had gone to young Julie, they

111

said, and had talked with her for a time, then had gone home . . . and had found there was no home there to go to. The marauders had come while he was away.

They neared and Will drew his reins. Leander stopped alongside him, his head tipped as one who is trying to remember.

"Will Henry," Will said. "I helped your pa roof his house . . . back then. You toted bales for us."

The distant blue eyes brightened. "I remember you now, Mr. Henry. How do?"

"Passable," Will shrugged. "It's been a time, Leander. Some said you must be dead. Others said maybe you'd gone with the rangers."

"I did that for a time," Leander nodded. "A ninety-day tour to get coin for supplies. Since then, I've had a look at some country, Mr. Henry."

Will gazed at the bundles of hides on the two horses. A winter's worth of long-haired plew. The lad had been to the north, probably. Or to the west. No, he decided, to the north. Maybe up toward the lakes. Men spoke of the trapping up there, in the woods between the Shawnee and the Sauk lands. Those who came back alive spoke of it. But had he been west, far enough that no word would have come back, he would have encountered worse. Fort Massac stood out there, on the Ohio beyond the mouth of the Wabash, but beyond the reaches of its little patrols was wilderness.

And in the wilderness was Nicolet. A chill went up Will's spine even at the name. Nicolet, chief of the sixth tribe. Of all the great chiefs of the Cherokee, not one— not even the formidable Dragging Canoe—could have mustered a force of renegade Senecas, Chicamaugans, Creeks, and the armed refugees from the Iroquois battles. But Nicolet had done it, so they said, and no man went to hunt the forests of west Kentucky save at his own peril.

All Will said, gazing at the bundled furs, was, "Prime plew, Leander." But the young man caught his thoughts and a slow grin parted his bronze whiskers.

"From west," he said quietly.

Will stared at the young man, openmouthed.

"I'm needing a meal and a bed," Leander said. "And to know where I might sell these furs, if there be a buyer hereabouts."

Will shook his head and closed his mouth. "Becket's house yonder is an inn now," he pointed. "You might put up there. As to the plew, I'd ask Jason Cook about that. He'll be at his smithy, now or in the mornin'."

"Pleased to see you again, Mr. Henry," Leander touched his cap in salute. He eased his reins, then drew them tight again. "Ah, Mr. Henry? . . ."

"Aye?"

"Tom Jackson's widow—Julie McCarthy she was before—ah, is she still about?"

"Aye, she's here, Leander. She keeps house with the widow Ferris now."

"Then she isn't . . . ah, she hasn't? . . ."

It was Will's turn to smile. "No, Leander, she's not married again. Though many's the young buck that would court her, she's still alone to this day."

X

"Unsettled times breed unsettled times," Crispin Blount told Luther Ferris. "Just as riddles breed more riddles." Wrapped snug in linsey-woolsey blankets, they sat in frosty starlight on the stoop of Nora's house, smoking their pipes. Inside, three women, a child, and a baby were snug abed. Luther had told Crispin of his fears, of the seemingly inevitable loss of his beloved plot of land up by the river and of his uncertainty of what he must do. For a long time Crispin had simply listened, letting his mind rove through and through the young man's dilemma and wishing he had the wisdom to resolve it with a word. Finally, Luther sighed and sat in silence.

"Precious little have I done with the days I've had," Crispin admitted, "except to walk afar and see a sight or two . . . that and think on riddles. But it seems to me the answer to any riddle is in its parts, an' the trick is to see all the parts as one." He tamped his pipe, letting his thoughts roam as they would. He spoke as though to himself. Luther could listen or not, respond or not, as he chose. And if Crispin could offer no more than the sound of another man's voice to be a brace against the loneliness, then that was enough.

"See yonder star, Luther. The bright one, low down to the west. Evening star, some call it, and some say 'tis the same orb as the morning star, though in a different place.

114

But seen at evening it holds in the west, so that some have called it the western star, an' I've stood atop a mountain ridge with men who pointed at it of evening and called on it for luck. An' I've wondered if maybe it's in our blood—those of us who've left the tidelands an' the shores—to face the west when we look for good fortune."

Luther muttered something and Crispin tipped his head toward him. "It's like what I heard my pa say," Luther repeated. "He said those who face east are looking at the past. I've thought it a thing a wise man might say."

"Or a man of riddles," Crispin shrugged. "But then, who's to say they aren't the same?" In the starlight, each word was a tiny thread of mist. "But there's a thing about that star out there. It comes and goes with the seasons, yet it has a pattern to its travels the way the sun does makin' days for us or the moon as it marks the months. Have ye watched the swallows, Luther?"

"Birds?"

"Aye, the swallows at morning, when first they find the new day's sky. How they do wheel and dance on the rise, each circling all the others like the strands in a lassie's braid or gentlefolk performing a minuet by shine of chandelier. They climb from shadow into sun, and had they threads to pull with them, they'd weave a brightness there. A sight to see, Luther. Truly a sight to see."

"I see the falcons up there waiting for them," Luther muttered, gloomy in the darkness.

"Aye, there are hawks." Crispin shrugged. "Every critter that's there is part of the weave, though, and that's what makes for riddles. The swallows and the hawks, they spiral in the sky. The sun and the moon and the western star, they do, too, in their way. Yet down here on the earth, don't we weave a spiral, too? Henry Hamilton sends his redcoats out from Detroit and his redskins out from Vincennes. Then Colonel Clark takes his militia and takes the river and Vincennes, and that's an end to that. But it's no end, lad. It's just a pause. The Delaware at Gnadenhutten and the Shawnee at Chillicothe, they spiral like swallows between the Georgies and the Boones. The Cherokee hold the high places south of Cumberland, and some are our friends and others not. And yonder on the tidewaters, they build ships to fight the British at sea and assemble armies to fight them on land . . . and the Spanish king deals with the French king and the coin is the land where we stand."

"The French are on our side . . . aren't they?"

"Kings are on their own sides, lad. Never forget that. It's not a favor to these colonies that brings the likes of Lafayette to these shores, but a disfavor to the British. Yet out here, all that is far away for now. Except for the paying of the bill."

"With my land," Luther breathed.

"Aye, it looks that way. Yours and many others. The swallows and the hawks they fly, and everyone must dance."

"Pa thought the land was ours."

"A place for roots, aye, Like the oak in summer. But even oaks fall sometimes."

"Yes."

"Then the acorn puts down other roots somewhere else and begins over again. Your pa was not born to that bit of land where he died, Luther. He came to it from some other place. And there's no more shortage of other places now than there was then. Only the times are different."

"When Pa moved to a new place, he knew where to look for it."

"I expect he did, right enough. Nor am I sayin' that you should move on, Luther. Each day's mornin' brings new things to think on. But should it come to that, I've a notion you'd know where to look, too."

After Luther had gone inside to join his family, Crispin sat for a time in the night shadows, thinking his own thoughts. The stolid sadness of the young man troubled him, and the depth of it surprised him. It had not been his way to become deeply involved with people . . . not for many a year. With the tenacity of one who is too easily hurt by the hurts of those around him, Crispin Blount had removed himself from such harm by resolving never to stay in one place any longer than the season demanded and never to accept friendship that went beyond a pleasant how-do. And yet here, in the span of days, he had become involved with a family that was not his family, and he felt the complexities of its loves and fears to the very soul of him.

Does it come of age, he wondered, this business of the heart? Have I spent so long alone that I've forgotten how to stay that way?

Or was it the bright eyes of Nora Ferris that had done him?

Women's eyes . . . Eyes that saw to the core of a man and accepted what they saw there. Eyes that had seen how it was to be wife, mother, and grandmother; to be companion, teacher, and nurse . . . When those eyes were upon him, he felt there was nothing he could hide and nothing that he would want to. And, he thought, my heart tells me that she sees in my eyes just what I see in hers.

All that and a promise—just a suggestion, but to be claimed as promise if either of them wished it—of a friend and companion to share the remaining years. Have you been alone long enough? The eyes asked it. If so, they said, then maybe I have, too.

He thought of Mystery in her stall, of Old Yellow Dog standing in its corner, and of long roads to be walked and new songs yet to be sung to the lonely hillsides. But Mystery could be mule to two as well as one, and Old Yellow Dog could put meat on a table as well as a lonely campfire. And the songs . . . The songs were better by far when there were other ears than his to listen to them.

On the morrow, he would trim and taper a handle for his axe. He pictured it in the night sky, a graceful, sweeping handle of stout wood, tapered and slightly curved from the head, then recurved near the butt where

117

a man's hands gripped, completing a stroke.

A true American axe. He should name it, he thought. Then he chuckled. Name it for himself? A man named Blount giving his name to an axe? The idea made him laugh aloud. It would be like a man named Square giving his name to some new kind of wheel. How many fine things had faded into obscurity? How many noble inventions died a-borning for lack of a decent name? No man in his right mind would pay coin for a Square wheel, nor for a Blount axe.

Still chuckling, he stood and started across the night-quiet street, seeking his bed in the loft. American axe he had called it, and American axe it would be. What prouder name than that for a blade to tame the American land?

Better to dwell on such things—on the feel of fine tools to skilled hands, on the turn of a phrase that could evoke laughter or tears, on the sound of a song in the forest—than to risk looking back at the years that have slipped away.

What had he to show for two score and seven or more years? Fond memories, fleeting and unconnected, but fond. He thought of Luther, young and stubborn, worried and determined. A young man sorely troubled but with a pretty wife by his side and a healthy babe to carry his name, the first acorn to his oak. So far as he knew, Crispin Blount had no children. Had never had, and that knowledge was a coldness within him.

Luther Ferris would know his share of trouble in this life, but where he went he would sink his plowshare deep into God's earth and leave his mark upon it. Crispin glanced back. In the starlight he could not even see his own footprints where he had passed.

The door of the inn, further along the street, opened for a moment, lamplight washing the pebbled roadway in front of it. The brief light reminded Crispin that if he were to stay here long enough to get Cook started in an axeworks, he would need to find a bed. The stable loft was adequate for a night or two, certainly no worse than a blanket roll on a cold trail camp, but he had begun to admit to himself these recent years that there were times he longed for a soft bed, times when his bones of morning creaked and various aches punished him. It was a thing a man could ignore in the wilds. Out there, there was no better to be had. But in town the aches each morning were worse, magnified by feeling sorry for himself, he supposed.

He started to enter the stable, then paused. A man had come from the door of the inn and now stood on the stoop there, leaning against a rail. Starlight told him only that the man was tall, bearded, and young. But what gave him pause was the man's gaze. He was looking toward Nora's house, as though to fix its every detail in his mind.

Ellie had dozed for a time, troubled images tumbling through her mind, bits of the talk she had heard, the uncertainty in all their voices, especially Luther's. Her brother was fretting, and she was aware of his mood as she had always been. The opening and closing of the door awakened her and she listened, then relaxed. It was Luther, coming in. He lit no lamp but walked carefully to the pallet where Kate slept and sat down there. In the darkness, Ellie could distinguish each move as though she could see him.

She heard him pull off his boots, then drop his galluses and remove his shirt—he always sighed faintly as he did that, stretching his arms and rolling his shoulders as though removing a weight from them. Even when she was very small, back in that other cabin that she remembered so well, Luther had always done that. And so had Pa. She tried to bring Pa's face to mind and found its features dim in recollection, really more like Luther's features now, and trying to recall how Luther had looked then was even more difficult.

Things changed so much. People changed and sur-

119

roundings changed. Everything seemed always to be changing. People of the town were there for a time, then they were gone and others came. And lately, even she had been changing—the little swellings on her chest, the soreness there sometimes, fits of temper that she sometimes wondered about later . . . She found herself cross sometimes for no reason, and at other times joyous for no reason. The breast tenderness, she knew about that. She would start to grow there soon, as women did, and her hips would widen and she would bleed sometimes just the way that Ma and Julie and, she supposed, Kate did. She had talked about such things with Mary McCoy, who had been her friend until the McCoys moved on, heading up the Tahnessay with Judge Henderson.

"Just like the lowest beast," Mary had said, "we prepare ourselves to calve, and some man will come along and plant his seed in us just as he plants his fields." Mary had said it with a giggle and a sneer, but Ellie kept her counsel. Life didn't have to be so base, she felt. Not simple like that—bleed, breed, and carry the seed. Were that all that life was about, she felt, then Mary would be right that they were just like the lowest beast.

She didn't believe it. If God had meant people to be as beasts, then why did people see beauty? Why were there songs? Why did folks glow when they were pleasured and pine when they were lonely? There was far more to it than anything Mary had said. There must be.

The tall man who had come . . . Crispin Blount. Such an ugly man and yet . . . She found no words in her mind, only that, ugly as he was, when he made riddles and told tales and when his rasping voice intoned on improbable rhymes and his big hands bent withes to form a baby's cradle, in those moments he was not ugly at all.

Luther's problems were not his problems, yet he had listened to them and thought about them with Luther . . . just the way she thought Pa would have done had he been here.

The man wanted to please Ma. Ellie saw it in his

manner, the need of it in his eyes. And he *did* please Ma, she knew. He wasn't Pa, would never be, but Pa was gone a long time now, and if Ma could glow at the company of the tall man, was that so bad? She tried to imagine Ma having another baby, being with an infant as Kate was with little Jonathan, and could not imagine it. And yet, she supposed, Ma *could* do that. If you bleed, you can breed, Mary McCoy said. In that respect, Ma was no different from Kate or Julie. Ellie helped with the wash. She knew.

So much to think about. And everything always changing, nothing staying the same.

What stayed the same was the songs. Words in tune wandered drowsy through her mind. *And there was one among them, the pixie Aella, who felt the old love of her race, and she listened adept as the human folk wept, and found there were tears on her face.*

Such an old song. She couldn't remember when she had first heard it. It had just always been there. *And there was one who loved her, the stout Belephon. Oh, it near broke his heart when she cried.*

The stout Belephon . . . Somehow it made her think about Christopher Post, handsome and dashing, alive with dark intent, tall and booted atop his big black racing horse. She saw him sometimes, about the town. He was like a song himself, a troubling song, full of hidden drives and dark ambitions. A boy—certainly not much older than herself, maybe fourteen or so—but fiercely impatient to be a man because, she felt it somehow, to do whatever it was he meant to do, one must be a man grown.

Often his image came to Ellie's mind, and sometimes it made her heart beat more rapidly to think of him. It was an excitement, thrilling and frightening . . .

Much easier, if she must think of boys, to think about Seth Michaels. Seth was comfortable. Seth was devoted to Ellie just the way Seth's two dogs were devoted to him. She knew that and found no fault with it. Sometimes he was pleasant to be around. Christopher Post would not be pleasant to be around. She didn't even know him, only who he was. But she saw him sometimes and thought of him afterward.

. . . but Aella went to him and she took his hand and she turned his face back to the sun . . . Could anyone turn Christopher Post's face anywhere but where he had set it? Seth Michaels would face any direction Ellie wanted him to. They were nothing alike.

The thoughts came slow and sleepy, and she snugged her covers about her and closed her eyes. *Aella . . .* Why is her part of the old song the part I remember best? Vaguely, she wondered about it.

Why does Ellie sound like the name Aella?

Why is it so simple for the people in the songs? They have but one tale. Why do real folk have so many, and they all keep right on changing?

XI

"Dan'l Boone may have been the first to come here," Jarod Cole spoke as though to the fire, rather than to the men around it. "He claims he was, an' I've heard none dispute it. But the thing is, it wasn't so long ago, any of it. It just seems so because of all that has come since. But say Boone was first. When was that? Maybe twelve, fifteen years ago? An' there sure warn't folks here then. Injuns, an' plenty, o'course, but even they didn't live here. Nobody did. Injuns just come to hunt the land, Cherokee down from the mountains, the Shawnee, Delaware, Seneca, an' them comin' along time to time from up across the Ohio. Nobody lived in Kaintuck. Nobody at all. But look at it now. Land, there's folks everyplace a body looks. Somebody said there's better'n three hundred right here at Harrodsburg."

"Not for long," Piney Sullivan snorted. "Ol' Squire gets done, there won't be a dozen left."

There were nine men in all around the fire. Dancing flames guttered to the dripping grease from cuts of venison on a spit and gave half light to the faces of them as they talked. Jarod Cole, Davey Ross, and Colin McLeod wore the furs and slicked buckskins of men long away from civilization, and their whiskers were untrimmed and matted. They had come as far as the Salt River with Leander Haynes but had stopped short of the town, preferring to camp under the stars rather than to seek the shelters of roof and hearth. The rest were men who had come out to meet them, curious at sight of a fire out beyond the cabins and sheds. Piney Sullivan and Sam Michaels had seen the glow from the out-lots at full dark and walked out, carrying their rifles. George Morley had seen the long hunters pass, their pack animals laden with pelts, and had come to seek news from the backlands. Sam Drummond, Arthur Wills, and Abel McCall had been railing fence alongside the horse camp, not a hundred yards away, when the four hunters parted by the trader rocks, three to make camp there, the fourth going on into town.

For two seasons the hunters had roamed the Green River country, all the way down to the lower Cumberland, and there was much to tell.

"Thing about it is," Jarod Cole gestured with his pipe stem, "out past Green River a man might swear there'd never been nobody in Kaintuck all along, wasn't for the stubs of burn-out cabins here an' yonder. Th' war's took its toll out there, right enough. From th' Green down to th' Cumberland, it's like it was before ever Dan'l crossed the gap. Not a white man in sight."

"Injuns, though," Colin McLeod put in, his one eye a fierce gleam in the fire's light. "We seen a passel of huntin' parties, time to time. An' there was one bunch, back afore first snow, that seen us, too. Had to fight that time, we did."

"How many?" It was Sam Michaels who asked it.

"Seven. We got good count because we taken out three right off, then Davey and me, we was out four days trackin' down the other four. Didn't want any of them goin' back where they come from to tell about us. They was Cherokees, all but one that Davey made to be a Wyandot. Bein' mixed thataway, they might of been Nicolet's bunch."

"We heard Nicolet was over there someplace," Morley said. "Ranger dispatcher was through a while back. Said

Nicolet's got twelve hundred warriors over past th' Cumberland. Cherokees with Shawnee an' Delaware an' whatnot mixed in. I never heard they'd mix that way."

"Tribes generally don't." McLeod shook his bearded head, his leather eye patch a darkness on his scarred face. "Some of th' Ohio tribes'll run together, but Cherokee won't have anything to do with 'em. Too much bad blood, it's said. Goes a long way back. But Nicolet's a renegade, an' so are those with him. I don't know about any twelve hundred. Might be four, five hundred, though, if they've banded thataway."

"But you said they weren't out there."

"No, not where we were. We camped with traders over nigh the big river th' first summer out. They said they'd heard of a Cherokee leader drawin' renegades to him down yonder, in the Carolina back lands. But we figured that must be Dragging Canoe. Him an' his Chicamaugans, they been hostile ever since Henderson's bunch pushed up the Nolichucky. But we seen a Frenchman later as said Dragging Canoe's settled farther south. So maybe the traders was talkin' about Nicolet."

Will Henry had sat quietly, listening to the talk, chewing on a sassafras twig. Now he squinted at Jarod Cole. "You said you seen British out yonder, Jarod. Tell us about that."

"That was year afore last, when we went nigh to the Mississip. We was all four up a a ridge, havin' a look at th' trade roads comin' up th' river on th' Spanish side, an' first thing we knowed ol' Leander let out a hiss an' there was a redcoat foot patrol danged near right under out noses, comin' along big as ye please from th' north. We let 'em go by, then we follered along, an' when one of 'em split off to wet th' bushes, we captured him an' had us a talk. Name of Billy Doyle, he was. A private soldier, an' friendly as ye please after we taken his Brown Bess away an' give him grace to get his britches buttoned. We kept him a day or so. He said the Georgies has a big base at Mobile, an' fair got their hands full tryin' to keep Galvez an' his Spaniards from shippin' guns an' powder upriver. Said there'd already been better'n two thousand kegs of it got through. Likely all the powder in Kaintuck this minute be Spanish powder, less 'n you fellers back here is makin' some."

"Homer Willis was," Sam Michaels admitted. "But it wasn't very good powder. He gave it up after he blown up his milk shed."

"Jason Cook taken some in trade that come down the Ohio from Fort Pitt," Will reminded him. "I got some of that."

"Then you got Spanish powder, too," Jared nodded. "That's where a mess of the Spaniards' goods have been goin' to."

"What did you do with Billy Doyle?" someone wanted to know.

"The redcoat? Nothin'. We thought some about knockin' him in the head or trading him off to th' Spanish, but Leander couldn't see fit to do that. So we give him back his musket an' set him loose. Just as well. 'Cept for bein' th' enemy, he seemed like a decent sort of young'un. Told us if we's ever in Culney, we should look him up."

"Where's Culney?"

"It's in England someplace."

Sam Drummond raised a hand, tentatively. As a horse camp man, newly arrived from the undermountain country, he felt shy and slightly outnumbered in this situation. But since the day when Crispin Blount had stretched his ear, he had heard little news because Captain Post had sent him out on fence duty to keep him out of trouble. Still, his curiosity was stirred. "You said all that land yonder past the Green is empty now? No settlers?"

"Nary a one," Jarod repeated.

"But all that's still proclamation land, ain't it?"

Cole just shrugged. Sam Michaels said, "Might be. Unless there's Burgess warrants bein' give on it, like around here." He couldn't resist a glare at Drummond and his partners. Being in the employ of Squire Trelawney, they must suffer the ire of those who rightly belonged here.

Drummond looked away, feeling uncomfortable. He knew little of what his employer was doing out here in the back lands. His job was to tote and fetch, and now and then to raise rail fence. But still he was curious. He had heard the talk in past years, back in the undermountain country, about Kentucky land for the taking. And he had thought about a place of his own from time to time, just like any other man.

"There was four of you fellers rode in," he noted. "But there's only three of ye here now. How come is that?"

Again it was a local who answered him. Will Henry said, 'That was Leander Haynes. He's from these parts."

"He's a strange one," Cole said. "Hunted with us a time, then he just taken off on his lonesome for five, six months, then he found us again, comin' back. Said he wanted to visit a woman here."

"Julie Jackson," Will agreed. "I believe that's who he's lookin' for."

Sam Drummond glowered and muttered to himself, knowing defeat. For a time there, he and his mates had counted on the hospitality of the widows Ferris and Jackson, and the meals they served up. Now he felt that such comforts were long behind him. If people kept showing up at the rate they were, calling on the widows, there would never again be room at their table for honest beggars.

Far to the southwest, across three ranges of serrated mountain ridge, the sullen Clinch River growled across shoals beneath cold starlight, then widened and became momentarily placid at a cut-bank bend where gravel bottom formed dark ripples at a natural ford. Here at this hour no night birds sang and no woodland creatures prowled. They would return, but only after a time. The rotten-egg smell of burning powder had been whisked away on the evening breeze, its scent gone. But even in the chill there was the sweet smell of fresh blood mingling with the vapors of night.

Where waters whispered through a stand of browned cane, a body floated facedown, turning sluggishly to nudge the stalks. Beyond and above were others, one caught among the rocks in the shoals, another sprawled at the edge of the riverbank, three scattered among the stepped floodbanks above, and two in the fringe of willows just beyond. Except for those in the water, each carried the mark of final defeat of the Kentucky frontier—facial skin sagging beneath a gaping crown where a hand span of scalp had been ringed by blade and pulled free.

James Chandler's party, seven undermountain men out to scout new lands beyond the grasp of the Virginia Burgesses, had gone southward, across the Cumberland and into the narrow valleys of the Tennessee uplands. As a result, they had done a thing the smaller party led by Jarod Cole had not. Chandler and his men had found Nicolet. The encounter had been fierce, abrupt, and final. Though Dragging Canoe's Chicamaugans had been defeated only days earlier in pitched battle far from the quiet hills of Tennessee, Nicolet and his band were no longer among the Cherokee marauders facing the settlers of Kentucky. Quietly, the new leader of outcasts had taken his followers south.

It was a party of these followers—sixteen Bird Clan warriors accompanied by three Delaware and five Wyandots—that found James Chandler's long hunters. The Indians were thorough. None of them wanted white survivors returning to the dark lands to report where Nicolet had gone. They wanted a season or two of isolation to build their strength, hunt and feast, and gather supplies from the unwary while silent runners went out seeking others to join them. Then, Nicolet said,

128

they could consider what to do about the invaders among them.

Two of the Wyandots took the scalps of those who had not fallen in the water and hung them from a tree limb on the far bank of the Clinch. That way, any who happened by and read the sign might believe the ambush was done by Shawnee or Iroquois hunters heading north, or possibly by a roving band of Piankesha bound upstream in search of woods buffalo, leaving their trophies for others who would follow behind.

They were careful to leave no sign that might say otherwise. "Until the leaves fall again," Nicolet had told them, "we must be as the night owl in the thicket. It is a time to plant corn, to weave shields, to do those things that are done by the light of the moon. The shamen say when winter comes again it will be a hard winter. But we will be strong then and the winter will be our friend. When snow falls we will drink the black drink and know what we must do."

It was the talk of a leader, carefully chosen words in the *Tsalagi* style to imply that no decision would be made until the time of decision was at hand, and then the decision would be made by all. But privately, Nicolet knew what must be done. Dragging Canoe had held that the *Aniyunwiya*, the true people, should regain their ancestral lands that the white man now called Kentucky. But Nicolet held no such dreams. Those lands had been lost so long ago that they were only legend. They had been lost to people coming from the west, red people like themselves but of lesser stature and greater numbers. Maybe the Shawnee and Iroquois. Legend had it that they had come from the west in times long gone. Then they in turn had lost the lands that the Cherokee now called the "dark and bloody ground" to white-skinned savages coming from beyond the morning mountains. No, those lands could not be regained. But neither would the whites stop there, he knew. They would spread like smoke on the wind.

Nicolet's dream was of a summer land where no such savages would threaten his children and his people. His dream was of the morning sun glistening on the backs of his enemies. His plan was more practical. With strength, they would decide between two courses: either to remove themselves from this English land of war and chaos, to places west where the Spanish were only a handful in the wilderness ill-equipped to govern settlement or incursion, or as an alternate, to seek the valleys of Tennessee and scourge them of white men, then deal from force with the settlers of the Charles Town colony to the east. Nicolet had a spy system the equal of anything General Washington or the British ranks could field. In his opinion, though the fighting was heavy around Charles Town now, the season's end would see withdrawal of the British. That would be the time to make treaty with Charles Town and Carolina. They would be weak then from their war. They would be ready to concede lands to those who could hold them.

On a sun-struck morning when spears of sunlight drew splendor from the hilltops and stood in the crimson sky like spikes from a golden crown, Crispin Blount came down from the stable loft and made himself a breakfast of parched corn and jerky, adding oats from the stabler's bins and a steaming pan of coffee.

Then he cleaned Old Yellow Dog carefully, poured powder and placed a patched ball in her breech, dusted fine powder into her flare pan, and strode out into the square. There were people about, here and there, and he waved at some of them and whistled a sprightly tune as he turned full circle, holding the long rifle above his head. Up the street he saw a group of horse camp men walking toward the wellspring and he grinned. Mr. Sparrow was in the lead, trailed closely by Sam Drummond and Abel McCall. Crispin could have asked for nothing more.

Still a hundred yards away, the horse camp men, intent

on some quest, veered leftward to pass the corner of the old stockade, close beneath its standing blockhouse. A gourd on a strap hung there, high above them, left by repairmen notching shingles against the spring rains. The blockhouses now were used for the storage of grain, and those who used them saw to their maintenance.

Partly by plan, partly by inspiration, Crispin brought Old Yellow Dog to his shoulder and sighted on the gourd. As the horse camp men passed beneath it, he set his trigger and fired. The gourd exploded and a shower of cold droplets rained on the men below. Crispin raised his hands, again holding Old Yellow Dog over his head, and grinned at them, his teeth flashing in the new light. Then he turned full circle again, sweeping off his hat to bow for those who stood about, flabbergasted at the sudden performance.

The smoke cleared hesitantly in still air, tops of the puff drifting into new sunlight. Crispin bowed again, this time a courtly sweep toward the three men charging across the compound at him. Sparrow was in the lead, heavy brows lowered like a gathering of thunders.

Sparrow came to a skidding halt in front of Crispin, his nose thrust to within inches of the tinker's chin. Abel McCall and Sam Drummond were close behind, bristling like hound dogs to the kill.

Crispin smiled his most disarming smile at them. "Fine mornin' to th' lot of ye, lads. Now that I've . . ."

"What did you do that for?" Sparrow glared at him, the words an angry hiss.

"If it's yonder gourd that frets ye, I do intend to pay its owner full value on it. And well worth the price, for a fair test of a fine rifle, I'd say. It's well to blow out her bore now an' again, just to keep her sprightly." He turned Old Yellow Dog in his hand, gazing at her with affection.

"You know what I mean," Sparrow growled. "What did you do that for?"

"Mainly, ye see, I wanted to get your attention. Seems

131

to me as how I've done that, right enough."

"That water's cold," Abel fumed.

"Take your mind off your sore foot," Crispin suggested.

Sam Drummond's flat face twisted into a leer. "I've a good mind to—"

"There could be some debate about that. It—"

Sparrow could stand it no longer. He raised a big fist and shook it under Crispin's nose. "Are you goin' to explain yourself?"

"I already did. I wanted to get your attention. I've a mind to have words with his righteousness the Squire, ye see. I allow th' three of ye could manage to tell him that."

Drummond's mouth dropped open in disbelief. Sparrow just stared for a moment, then shook his head as though he hadn't heard it right. "If you want to see the Squire," he explained slowly, "then it's you that goes to him. You don't send messages, just get along up there an' tell 'em at the door who ye are. If he wants to see you, he will."

Crispin smiled and shook his head. "No, that be'nt how it goes, for I've my business to tend and no time to wait on the pleasure of Squire Tidewater nor anybody else. So, since th' three of ye are in his employ, it's fitten that you take my message for me. Just tell his rampancy that Crispin Blount desires to speak wi' him regarding a matter previously discussed. Tell him I'll see him yonder at th' blacksmith's shed ere yon sun lights th' base of that flagpole there. Mind him be prompt about it, as well, for I don't intend to wait."

Drummond's eyes were wide at the audacity of it. Sparrow gritted his teeth. "See here, Blount . . ."

"*Mr.* Blount, if ye please, Mr. Sparrow. Don't fret yerself now, just take my message."

"If you think Squire Trelawney is going to . . ."

"If he wants his troughs seamed, he'll come," Crispin shrugged. "It's that I want to discuss wi' him."

"You're going to get yourself in a lot of trouble," Sparrow whispered, glancing around at the sizeable crowd that had gathered there.

Crispin cupped a hand to his ear. "Speak up, man. There's nothin' to be said that these folks shouldn't hear."

"I said," Sparrow stated, "you are behaving in an unwise manner, *Mr.* Blount."

"I am behavin' in th' manner most appropriate for dealin' wi' squatbottom gentry this side o' yonder mountains, *Mr.* Sparrow. If the Squire doesn't like bein' dealt so, then ye might suggest he stop bein' such a rare nuisance in how he deals wi' others." Having had his say, he turned away and looked around at the crowd in the street. "If the man as belongs to yonder holed gourd will see me at th' smith's, I'll pay him his damages. Good mornin' to the lot of ye." He grinned, winked broadly, and sauntered off, Old Yellow Dog resting across his shoulder.

At the door to Nora Ferris's house he knocked, removed his hat, and executed a sweeping bow to a startled Ellie. "No fairer sight is any man's eyes shown," he said, "than a lass who'll be a menace when she's grown."

She scowled up at him and he grinned, enchanted at how she resembled her mother. "An' that be no riddle, lass," he added. "But only a simple statement of fact."

"Folks usually don't fire their guns in town," she scolded. "You woke the baby."

From the shadows beyond came Nora's voice, "Ellie, for heaven's sake, either close the door or invite him in."

Ellie closed the door.

When it was reopened a moment later, this time by Nora, Crispin still stood outside, hat and rifle in hand and nearly convulsed with laughter. Nora shook her head. "That child!" she muttered. "I meant for her to invite you in, Mr. Blount." Her expression wavered as she saw tears of mirth in his eyes, and she giggled. "She's twelve, you know."

"Yes, missus, I know. An' nothin' would delight me

133

more than to spend a pleasant hour with such rich company. But, in truth, it's Luther I'm lookin' for this mornin'. Is he about?"

"Why, no. Luther has gone to Boone's Town with Leander Haynes. They went to sell furs."

"Haynes?"

"A young man of Julie's acquaintance. He was a friend of her husband. He's been to the west and just recently returned."

"Ah, West, is it? Does he bring news of those parts?"

"He says the country is unsettled. Really, I've hardly spoken to him. He comes to see Julie and they go off walking, but Luther has visited with him at length. Possibly—"

"Aye. I'll discuss it wi' him. Did he say when to expect him, then?"

"Two or three days. They just left this morning, before light."

Kate had appeared in the door light, beyond Nora. She held her baby at her breast, and Crispin nodded to her, started to bow his departure, then had a thought. "Mistress Kate, tell me, is your man a hand at felling trees and shaping boles?"

"He is," she nodded. "Just the past season he cleared a grove of cedar and made fence around eight acres."

"Aye," he tugged at his lip. "By the shoulders on him, I'd thought he might be. Fine mornin' to ye, ladies. Oh, an' please tell Miss Ellie that I've a riddle for her. 'Fair breeze and stormy gale, I am the wind; I change yet am as changeless as the sea; I will not break, yet ever bend, and man has all the world if he has me.' Ah, I see she heard me. 'Tis a good riddle, lass, so think on it well."

With a wide smile for all of them, he turned and headed up the street.

Jason Cook was waiting for him at the smithy. "Charley Finney brought in yonder cook pot, Crispin. Said if ye'll mend the bale on it, he'll call it even for the gourd ye shot. What was that all about, anyway? Half the folk in town are sayin' ye've challenged the Squire."

"Small enough challenge, Jason. I just sent word to him to come an' talk wi' me." He glanced at the flagstaff across the street. "He should be here directly."

"Ye've called the Squire to come at your bidding? What for?"

"Why, Jason, I've a mind to offer the gentleman a wager."

It was a dour and angry Joseph Trelawney who rode down from his great house to rein his fine mount before the open wall of the smithy and lean from the saddle to glare at Crispin Blount.

"You have made your point, tinker," he said. "I'd suggest you press it no further. Have you decided to accept my contract for the troughs?"

"I've given it a mite o' thought." Crispin stepped to the open frame and leaned his lanky height there. "As I said before, long-term work has not been to my likin', yet I *ha'* considered stayin' on here for a time, an' such bein' the case, I reckon I could do the work for ye . . . for a fair price."

"I'll not be swindled," Trelawney warned him. "I know what such work is worth."

"Aye, yonder where there's others fit to do it. But here there's not so many. Still, I said fair price an' meant it. However, betimes I'm a wagerin' man, Squire, so I've in mind to offer ye a chance to get the work done for free, an' by the best craftsman at hand, which is me."

Trelawney frowned more deeply. "What is it you propose, tinker?"

"A contest," Crispin shrugged. "A simple contest to provide a bit o' sport."

Trelawney glanced back at the blockhouse where the exploded gourd still hung. "I'm told you consider yourself a fair shot," he said. "But I vow that Mr. Sparrow is better. Would you contest with him?"

135

"I'm a fair shot as needs be," Crispin admitted. "But unless you yourself will honor me, then it'll need to be your man against mine. You choose yours, I choose mine."

Trelawney pursed his lips. He had the feeling he was being maneuvered along blind ways. Sparrow was a crack shot with a long rifle, he knew. But then, so were many of these woodsmen in Kentucky. He wondered who the tinker intended to have do his shooting, if not himself. "State the wager you propose," he said.

"You against me or your man against mine, a straightforward contest. I choose the manner of it and you choose the place. My wager is free seaming of your troughs and bins, an' my word they'll be done in fine fashion."

"And my wager?"

"A fair exchange, considerin'. There's decent folk hereabouts that stand to lose their holdin's through no fault of their own, and it's you that stands to gain. Should I win—or my man—then to each man dispossessed by your warrants in Kentucky County you make reimbursement."

"I have paid for the lands I own. I'll not pay twice!"

Crispin shook his head. "Not for the lands, Squire. Th' Burgesses may be liable for what they've done, but I reckon you've bought fair an' square. No, I've in mind that you pay for the improvements that each man has made. A quit-claim settlement. 'Twould do wonders for the feelin's these folk have about you, you know."

Trelawney squinted at him. A quit-claim settlement? The idea had not occurred to him. Such might go far toward achieving better cooperation from these back landers. In the long run, it might even save him money.

"I'd consider that," he said finally. "Some modest amount, at least. But is that your wager? What would you demand for yourself?"

"Strap iron from the best Pennsylvania foundry an' smith's wages for a month."

136

"*What?*"

"Jason yonder an' me are thinkin' of goin' into business," Crispin said. "If you lose, you can finance our venture for the first month."

A smith for a month and enough strap iron to keep him busy. Trelawney calculated it, twenty pounds sterling at the outside. He nodded. "Done. When will the contest take place?"

"When my man gets hisself back from Boone's Town. A few days at most."

"Who is this shooter of yours, then?"

"Squire, I said nothin' whatever about a shootin' contest. The manner of contest I choose is choppin'. Each man to fell an' clear a like log, with his two hands an' a simple axe. You choose who you like. I choose Luther Ferris."

At least thirty people witnessed the making of the wager.

When it was done and the Squire had gone, Jason Cook shook his head at Crispin. "I swear, your mind is as twisty as a dung beetle's path. What kind of wager was that?"

"A fair one, Jason. An' a good test for our new venture, as well. What better way to make a market for the American axe?"

XII

Through a long morning, Crispin Blount worked with
rasp and drawblade, turning down a bat of cured hickory
wood for a handle for his axe. Wide-egg oval he made it at
the head, ready for fine-fitting into the tempered socket
of its cutting head. Three feet and two inches in length he
cut it, subtly curved along the shank and reversing more
sharply forward in the last ten inches of its grip. A
pleasing shape, he thought, holding it up in the sunlight.
A graceful shape, almost delicate in its arcs yet sturdy
and purposeful.

"I haven't seen the like," Jason Cook admitted,
turning it in grimy hands. "It's a pretty thing, right
enough. But should an axe handle be pretty? You've
curved it like a dulcimer's spine."

"So where does it say that a tool must be a graceless
thing?" Crispin grinned. "When a man uses a tool, it
isn't just the muscle an' sinew of him that's usin' it. It's
all of him. I've watched ye swing that mallet yonder,
when yer eyes was fixed on the cherry red of a heated bit
an' yer ears was hearin' the music o' your beat. There's
a music in any man that masters a trade, Jason, or he'd
never ha' mastered it. That music comes when he's usin'
his tools. Curved like a dulcimer, is it? Aye an' why not,
when its task is to ring clear through the dark forests an'
sing out th' song o' th' good earth bein' put to the use o'

them that claims it?"

"Be that as may," Jason frowned, "'tis still only a tool. Wood and metal, nothin' more."

"Is a dulcimer anything more? Or a fiddle? Wood an' metal, that's all they be. Yet no more stirrin' sounds be known than those they sing . . . 'less it be the voices o' angels."

Cook squinted, studying the tall tinker. "Ye still speak in riddles, Crispin Blount. But yer riddles have took on a different rhyme than ere before. Ye've not been th' same man since th' day ye came here an' followed yer nose to th' widda Ferris's table. Are ye riddlin' to yourself as well, Crispin, or do ye know what you're about?"

Easy answers came to Crispin then, the answers of evasion. But Cook's question was an honest one, and Cook was a friend. 'Then ye know I've changed my mind about movin' on."

"Of course I know. I knew it th' minute ye started talkin' about this axe. Maybe I knew it before that, as well. Maybe from the time ye sang wi' Luther Ferris to th' wee folks song. Home an' family, Crispin. Ye've felt it an' it's clung to you. An' is aught wrong with that, then?"

"It could come hard to change, Jason. I've been a wanderin' man nigh longer than I'd want to think on."

'Aye. Like a bird on th' wing. But now I mind ye've seen a nest that'll comfort ye."

"Would such be comfort, Jason, or a mess of troubles? I've always found it best to know just a little about folks and stay on just a bit, then go afore I'm caught up in their troubles. A man can save his peace of mind that way."

"Aye, I reckon. But him as fights shy of other folks' troubles misses th' good times, too. Th' bird that will not land to nest must be a lonely old bird, Crispin."

"Aye." The talk made him gloomy and he returned to his shaping of the axe handle, letting the rhythm of the rasp strokes draw tunes to his mind.

"Not my business, o' course," Jason added a final point. "But do ye intend to court the widda Ferris, I'd counsel ye get to it. That be a warm woman yonder. Once her fire's been stoked, *somebody* will receive its heat."

"I've stoked no fires," Crispin pointed out.

Cook looked at him pityingly. "For a man your age, Crispin, there's a passel ye don't know. Why, man, ye've stoked since the day ye walked into Harrodsburg. I know that for a fact."

Crispin stared at him. "How would you know such a thing?"

"Same way everybody else does. I heard it from my Becky, that heard it from Mistress Oakes, that got it from her son Harold, an' he heard it from his good wife Martha, that heard it from her sister, that heard it straight as you please from Ellie Ferris."

"Heard what?"

"Why, that Nora Ferris's cheeks has been bright as fresh apples mornin', noon, an' night since th' first time ye visited that house. That's what. What could be straighter than that?"

By the time the sun was quartering to the west, Crispin had a fine handle finished and fitted to a shining new axe head with the edge of a razor and the temper of Jason Cook's best skills. Both of them looked at the implement for a time, admiring it. No such axe had ever been seen before, there or anywhere else. It held little resemblance to the British axes common to every household of the time, nor did it look like a Spanish axe or even, as Cook had once suggested, a large tomahawk. It looked like no other thing except itself, and as they turned it over in their hands and felt its heft, each man knew that they had made a new thing . . . and a better thing than all that had come before it.

Its cutting edge was a scant five inches from top to bottom and only slightly curved—just enough to take kindly to the whetstone. Its rear face, only an inch from the tapered handle in its socket, was a flat rectangle of tough iron. Each tried a swing of it against a stump, and its curved grip slid neatly to extend the reach and bring power to bear on the cut.

They put it away then, and Crispin washed up at the trough and put on his coat. At the stable he fondled the alert ears of Mystery, then slipped her headstall on her and took up the lead. With Old Yellow Dog over his shoulder and Mystery tagging behind, making music with her harness bells, Crispin walked to the high road and turned toward the hills.

Past the out-lots and the fields he strode, and some turned from their labors to look at him as he passed. George Morley even waved his hat, though he stood as one stunned and let his plow tip in its furrow. Was the tinker leaving again? he wondered. He had heard the talk, too, and allowed that this time Crispin Blount had met his match. This time, he had thought, the singing man would stay.

But Crispin walked on, big feet scuffing the trace as long legs found the measure of the road and Mystery's harness bells fell into a tinkling rhythm at his back to match his pace.

"O, I come down to Harrodsburg, down in Kaintuck," he muttered. "For ought but to see how it lay . . . an' to sing a few songs an' to sit to a table . . . an' then just to be on my way."

A simple tune fit itself to the words and he sang it, feeling the echoes of the fields and woodlands about him, hearing the traces of it coming back from the lonely hills. Mystery shook her head and the bells were a shifting counterpoint. A short way off, on a side trail, children were leading cows in to milk and they turned to watch him.

"O, there's trouble at Harrodsburg, down in Kaintuck," he sang, "For they've sold out the lands for a tuppence. Yet the Squire be a man who will do as he can, an' he swallows a rightful comeuppance."

He heard the irritated jingle of the mule behind him as his voice grew in strength, and he grinned. The bright air of evening was sweet in his lungs and his feet had the feel

141

of the road.

"But there's aught can be done beyond lendin' a hand, afore a man packs up his packs!" He had the stride of it now and the hills rang to his singing. "An' th' law o' the land be a sturdy young man who can swing an American axe!"

In the echoes, faint among them, he heard quick distant footfalls, but the song had him now and he sang it out with a will.

"So a hey-heighdy-ho for th' life o' th' road, for a man needs a time to be free . . . when all that needs doin' an' can be is done, an' there's yet th' far places to see . . . an' a man be a footloose an' quarrelsome thing . . ."

The footfalls were close now, and he heard quick breathing, panting. Crispin turned. Ellie Ferris was running to catch him. White-knuckled small fists clutched at her skirts and little feet were a blur of motion, clipping at the gravel of the trail. A moment, then she was beside him, her shoulders heaving as she fell into step, two or three of her steps to each one of his.

"I've—I've an answer to your riddle," she said, trying to catch her breath. "I thought you'd want to know it."

Riddle? He remembered then. He had forgotten.

"You said, 'Fair breeze and stormy gale, I am the wind,'" she reminded him. "'I change yet am as changeless as the sea; I will not break, yet ever bend, and man has all the world if he has me.' Well, I thought about it. I know what it is."

"You do, do you?" he glanced back. The children with the milk cows were far behind now, going toward the town. Ellie should be with them. Yet she strode beside him, her small chin high and proud, as though wherever he went she would go, too, no matter that it might be far away.

"It's my mother," she said. "It all fits, and it's so like her that for a time I couldn't think of it. I am right, aren't I?"

For once in his life, Crispin Blount was speechless. He

142

tumbled the riddle-words in his mind and they were indeed Nora Ferris. Fair breeze and stormy gale . . . the wind . . . will not break, yet ever bend . . . and man has . . .

In his own words the child had found what he didn't know was there. The riddle was a rhyme and a song and a celebration of a woman . . . of Nora Ferris.

"You have the right of it, lass," he said softly. "It could never be any other than your mother."

"I knew I was right," she said. She looked up at him with eyes as wide and wise as only innocence can be. "Mr. Blount, I might have been wrong . . . before. Maybe my mother isn't too old to marry . . . if that's what would make her happy."

'He wouldn't tell her that the riddle—so he had thought—had been about herself. She would be a woman one day, and maybe then she would know that it had been.

A half mile more he walked then, the girl child striding along at his side. In the evening breeze were hints of echoes, memories of songs thrown back at him by the lonely hills along a thousand lonely trails. Mystery's bells jingled softly and he wondered for a moment if mules knew aught of times of change—of taking one last look at how things had been, then putting them away to make room for how things would be.

"An' how might a man go about th' courting of your mother?" he asked.

Ellie thought about it for a time. "I suppose you should tell her you'd like to marry her," she said finally.

"Plain words may be too simple for a grand occasion," he suggested. "Maybe a riddle . . ." He grinned, threw back his head, and sang, "A riddle an' a rhyme an' a song for th' time covers words that a man be afraid of. A trick an' a riddle to th' tune of a fiddle . . . for that's what *occasions* are made of."

He glanced down at her, expecting approval. She frowned in thought, pursing small lips. Then she shook

143

her head. "It might pleasure her for you to do tricks. I believe it does. But if you want to marry my mother, I think she'll make you ask her straight out."

Crispin sighed. Mystery's bells jingled and the hills rang tiny echoes. "I reckon a man's never too old to learn new ways," he admitted, "long as he guards against th' old ones."

Atop a rise he stopped and took a long look around. The wide land lay before him, brilliant in evening's last sunlight, shadowed hills rising in the distance. Errant breezes whispered in a stand of cedar, and the greening tops of willows thrust pale from misted streambanks.

"Hey-heighdy-ho for th' life o' th' road," he breathed, "where a wanderin' man can roam free . . . 'till the time comes to rest an' to find him a nest . . . then other folks' roads yon will be."

He pulled his hat firm on his head, laid Old Yellow Dog across the nubs of Mystery's packstraps, tugged the lead, and turned the mule around. To Ellie he said, pointing, "See how far we've come, young'un. I'd not intended so long a walk, but I'm pleasured by yer company."

Partway down the slope toward the village of Harrodsburg Ellie walked close beside him and reached out to take his hand.

"Do ye suppose your mother might invite a walkin' man in to supper again?" he asked.

"Maybe, if you wipe your feet."

Hand in hand they walked together then, heading home.

XIII

On a day when great V's of geese winged northward over the hills and buds of apple-green befurred the boughs of sluggish chestnut trees, men came from the town and from the horse camp to witness the contest between Luther Ferris and Matthew Sparrow. Word had spread throughout the area about the wager between Squire Trelawney and Crispin Blount, and the story grew with the telling. By the time Luther returned from Boone's Town with Leander Haynes it was an accomplished fact that he and Mr. Sparrow were scheduled to either clear an acre of forest apiece or to do battle with axes, following which Squire Trelawney was to either cede claims back to their original owners or to pay quitclaims for the properties he took . . . although some had it that either Crispin Blount was going into the horse business with the squire, or maybe it was that Luther and Mr. Sparrow were going to chop a tree together.

Luther finally got the straight of it from Crispin himself, who met him at Cook's smithy and handed him a bright new axe, then led him out of town and down into the forest across the creek. Crispin selected a straight ash tree ten inches across at the base and pointed to it. "Cut that down," he said.

Luther rolled up his sleeves, spat on his hands, and went to work. Square-built and solid on legs attuned to the heaving of a plow, Luther yet had the rolling shoulders, thick arms, and hard belly of a woodsman. He was no stranger to the swinging of the axe.

Still, almost from the first slice of blade into timber, Luther knew he was wielding a new thing here. The subtle curve of the slim handle rode in his hand sleekly, and the stubby, tineless blade hummed true and cut deep. In half the strokes it might have taken with an ordinary tool, the tall tree toppled cleanly and with a satisfying crash.

"Now top an' trim it," Crispin said. "Pace it out to thirty feet. No sense in wastin' yer effort. We'll sell it to th' Squire for roof timber."

Luther paced the required length and again the sleek axe sang its song. Five strokes each side, wedges of white wood flying clean from the cuts, and the tree was topped. Most of the branches took only a single cut to trim away. None took more than four. He stooped to roll the trimmed log one more time, to show that it was clean.

Crispin whistled a merry tune and looked around, not caring to have them spied upon, and saw that they were not alone. Ellie had seen her brother ride into town, then had seen him go with Crispin into the woods. Half hidden by budding vinery she had watched the entire performance. Now she stepped out wide-eyed and clapped her hands. "I just knew you'd have a trick in mind," she said to Crispin.

"No trick, lass," he shrugged. "Your brother is a cutter an' I've shown him a better axe."

Luther held the axe before him, studying its lines. "It's a marvel," he said. "Never have I held such an axe."

"But I think it must be our secret for the time," Crispin urged them. Then he told Luther the straight of his deal with Trelawney, and the young man's eyes went grave. "It will be Mr. Sparrow," he said. "I've seen him. He is a strong man, maybe stronger than me."

"That's as may be, son. But the test is in the bite o' the blade. Your blade will be th' one there in your hand."

146

"I'll do it," Luther decided. "I've naught to lose. But you do, Mr. Blount."

"Not overmuch." Crispin grinned and winked at Ellie. "It may be that I'll be stayin' on here after all, an' I'd not mind doin' th' Squire's troughs for him if it came to that. 'Twould explain my presence now an' again at yer mother's door."

Ellie giggled, then went to Luther to look at his axe. Abruptly she laughed again, at words in her mind, and she sang them, her clear young voice rich and true in the hush of the forest, "Now gather around me, Rube said to his tribe, we can help if we all lend a hand. There are skills we must share with the big folk up there if we all are to reach a new land."

Luther frowned at her, wondering what had prompted that. Then the meaning came to him, and he chuckled and continued the song, taking it up further along. "For this old ship is blind, just the way I have been, but all that she needs is craft's hand, then we'll show her sting to the ships of the king and we'll sail to a bright summer land."

"It is craft," Ellie nodded at the axe.

"I be no elf, young'un," Crispin noted.

"Maybe you are. How would you know?"

Nora had heard at the school that Luther was back from Boone's, and when she reached her house Leander Haynes was there, sitting on the stoop with Julie. She had the impression as she stepped past them that neither realized she was there, and it pleased her. Julie had been alone too long. It was time she paid notice to young men again, although she wondered if one as wanderish as the quiet Leander would be a proper choice. Still, that was not her affair. She entered her house and knelt beside little Jonathan in his willow cradle, nuzzling his sleeping face and checking his wrapped britches at the same time. Kate looked in from the pantry. "Luther's back," she said. "He got a price for his root harvest at Boone's and said Leander did well with his pelts."

Luther's bedroll, rifle, and white powder horn were in

147

the corner by the fireplace. Nora glanced at them and Kate spread her hands and shrugged. "He went to find Crispin. He said he'd heard all sorts of strange things about the contest."

"I'm certain he has."

They heard the voices then and Kate went to the window. She pulled back the shutter and leaned out, then leaned further. "Nora, come look."

They were coming up the road from the creek, Luther on the left with something long and slim wrapped in his coat, Crispin on the right, tall and gawkish lean, and Ellie between them, holding each by the hand and skipping to the time of the song they sang together. Their separate voices blended and twined to carry the lyric to all and sundry within earshot, "Then up from the hold came Old Rube and his tribe to the decks where the fugitives huddled, and they spread stern to tip through the groaning old ship 'midst a deck crew amazed and befuddled . . ."

Nora laughed and Kate giggled at the sheer exuberance of it, as other shutters opened along the way and folk peered out to see what was amiss.

"Belephon found the helmsman and made him kneel down," the three sang, "to learn to read rudder and fife, and the deck crew all stared at the wee men who dared set all sail. And the ship came to life . . ."

The three spotted them at the window. Luther grinned and Crispin tipped his hat, and they picked up the tempo and the volume. "Now she sang and she hummed and she clove through the waves and she took the cold spray on her bow. Belephon and the helmsman they hauled hard a'lee. They would make for the shipping lanes now. Dickie Quist was asleep but he woke with a start, for a tiny man stood on his chest. There was frost on his whiskers and fire in his eyes and he carried a crossbow at rest . . ."

Fed by the power of Crispin Blount's lungs, enriched by Luther's strong lyric, and bewitched by the girl-angel voice of Ellie, the old song bounded along the street and drew a chorus of echoes from the walls of cabin, barn, and shed. In his cradle, Jonathan awoke with a howl of outrage and added a new voice to the skirl.

"We go south! sang old Rube. We make for the lanes where this *Harod* can run with the sea, and if frigates await they shall find out too late that oppressed folk can fight to be free."

A door banged open across the way and a man ran out, carrying a stringed lute. He fell in abreast of the three and picked up their melody with dancing notes. "The blockade was there," they sang, "men-of-war three abreast when old *Harod* drove out of the north. The king wanted her dead. 'Sink the *Harod*,' they said, and they loaded their guns and sailed forth. Lightly armed was the old ship, and heavy with age, yet she danced and she dodged and she blasted 'til two were aground on the shoals of a sound and the third man-of-war was dismasted."

Applause and laughter came from those now thronging the street. "Wi' Crispin Blount's voice, ye know not whether it's a song or a ruckus," someone shouted.

"Aye," another answered. "Yet th' rest of it's right fetchin'."

Blount stared sadly at the hecklers, then swept off his hat and bowed to Luther and Ellie, giving them the song. Luther hesitated a moment, but Ellie tugged at his sleeve and the lutist caught up the tune strongly, urging.

Luther grinned and raised his head, the evening sun strong on his ruddy face. "Dickie Quist and Old Rube plotted course by the wind," he sang as Ellie linked elbows with a woodsman and launched him into a whirling jig. "Belephon and his helmsmen trimmed keen, and the courage of men and the craft of their kin brought to *Harrod* a magic not seen since the long-ago time in the age before kings when the large and the small folk were one . . ."

Towering a head above most of the crowd, Crispin

149

looked toward the window again and held Nora's eyes as he joined in, not following the tune but adding a Gaelic harmony to it: ". . . and Aella's eyes shone, for she saw reborn what a king's whim had nearly undone."

The song went on and others joined in. The dusty little road rang with it, burly woodsmen and far-eyed long hunters, planters and townsmen pounding the earth with booted feet in whirling jigs while women laughed with delight at the spectacle and children peeped from behind their skirts. Matthew Sparrow, lean and hard-shouldered, came from somewhere and leaned on a lashed hitch rail, narrowed eyes missing nothing, his weathered features telling nothing. Yet he noted with interest the coat-wrapped parcel in Luther's hands, scrutinizing the wide shoulders and bulging arms of the young planter. He had not met the man with whom he would compete for the squire's pleasure, but he knew him.

Crispin Blount had lifted Ellie Ferris to his shoulder and she perched there, a sprite with blowing hair the color of the evening sun, to sing the final verse alone, her child-voice lifted above the stamping and strumming of the crowd: "Then leave them behind, all the evils that were. Let the old world inherit its woe. For somewhere out there is a bright summer land, and it's there that we're going to go."

At the window, Nora Ferris glanced aside at Kate, then looked again. The younger woman's eyes were fixed on Luther as though there were no one else about, just she and her husband and the cooing baby in her arms. And there were tears in her dark eyes. "He's beautiful," she whispered. "Oh, isn't he beautiful?"

Nora put an arm around Kate's shoulders. Yes. He was beautiful. All three of them were. And Ellie as well, and the tall, ugly man on whose shoulder she perched . . . He, she realized, was as beautiful as those who were hers.

She glanced aside again and Kate was looking at her, her lips twitching with a secret smile.

"They sing for their suppers," Kate said. "We had

better set out the plates."

Again in the evening Crispin Blount was among them, tall and stooped in the little cabin, awkward and enthusiastic and, Nora decided, altogether improbable. And when they were done and he left to find his loft, a secret smile formed itself on Nora's lips. She had decided a thing, she realized. Should the man one day come to supper and then not want to leave, she would not hesitate to let him stay.

And so on a bright day the town turned out and the horse camp, too. Squire Trelawney came down in his polished coach, with Captain Post and Joel Simms riding with him, and Matthew Sparrow with a glisten-edged broadaxe of fine British make. Christopher Post cantered alongside on his tall black racer, and many a young girl of the town turned eyes toward him as he passed. Behind came a dozen of the squire's men, some riding his fine stock and some afoot, as suited them. The people of the town came out to meet them, and some from the hills around.

Where the creek curved through a meadow with a spring the squire stepped down and selected two fat cedars as alike as could be found. He turned to Crispin Blount and his dark eyes glinted beneath the butternut tricorn on his head. "Do these suit you?" he asked.

Crispin nodded. "As fair a choice as I myself might make, though I'd have thought of hardwood an' not cedar."

The squire walked up the rise to where young oaks formed a grove. He marked one, and then another. "And these?" he asked.

"They be as fair as t'other pair," Crispin admitted. "Which then shall they be?"

"Those there for the wager, tinker, and I'll stand by it, though I've heard of your marvelous axe. Let your man win and I'll pay quit-claims to all who've improved on the lands that are mine. Belike he *will* win, for Mr. Sparrow has told me of the cleared rooftree in the forest there

151

and the strokes he counted on it. You've tweaked me, but you've done it fair and I'll stand by what we said . . . about the quit-claim payments."

"Then what trees are these?" Crispin waved at the oaks.

"These are for the rest of it, tinker. But the manner of it will be different. You yourself will chop one down, and I myself the other. For the strap iron and smith's wages you so want. Now I know what you've in mind, I've thoughts of my own about it."

"And what might those be?"

"Whether it's better that you and your friend Cook make a hundred of those strange axes in a breezy smithy and put a few coins in your purses, or whether it's better that the three of us consign a patent to some proper ironworks in the East where they can build a thousand or five thousand or ten, and mayhap we'll all become wealthy."

"Ye say if I win ye would finance such a venture?"

The smile on Trelawney's face was a surprise. Few in these lands had ever seen him so. "I say rather that if *I* win, you and the smith *allow* me to finance it, for shares. I pride myself that I know a venture when I see one, tinker."

Crispin laughed aloud and slapped the great man on the back, a thing that brought gasps from many about them. "Then to make it interestin', Squire," he said, "we'll take turns and both use Luther's American axe. Ye might as well get the feel of where your money is goin'."

So those who gathered on the meadow that day saw two contests, not one. And they were as unlike as any two could be.

At the cedars, Sparrow wiped down his axe and Luther unwrapped his, and people gawked at the difference between them. The British axe with its broad, curved blade and counterspike, its clublike long handle and pole socket, seemed twice the size of the American axe, though they were of nearly equal weight. Yet when the two men rolled up their sleeves and took their first swings, the British axe did as all men were accustomed to. It bounded and thrashed and chewed at the cedar trunk, while Luther's blade clove clean and deep, down and up, down and up, thick chips of red-white wood flying aside as alike as peas in a pod. The contest was over when Luther's tree fell, for Sparrow's was not yet half through.

Sparrow wiped his brow and gazed at Luther. "How might it have been had we traded axes?" he asked.

Luther shrugged. "It would have been the other way around."

Trelawney climbed up onto the boot of his carriage and raised his arms. His tailed coat flared out like batwings and his tricorn was tipped sharply forward on his head. Barrel-chested and slightly bowlegged in white breeches and stockings, waistcoat drawn tight across a midriff as wide and solid as an oak stump, he looked every inch the aristocrat in a land that no longer had room for the breed. "Hear ye all," he boomed. "Let each man as has claims on land that is mine come before my good clerk, Mr. Simms, and state to him what improvements have been made there. Each claim will be validated, and each of you will be paid what's due, in proper course. The young man there has fairly won this day."

One among them more direct than most peered up at the squire to ask, "An' will what we're paid buy back the land we've held?"

"There are some holdings that I need," Trelawney said. "But mayhap there are some that I do not. We will consider what is offered."

He climbed down then and sent Simms and the rest of them away, townspeople and claimants following in their wake. When only a few were left on the meadow he went to Luther and took the axe from him. He turned it over in his hands, admiring it. "So simple," he muttered. "So very simple."

"Like the folk who'll use it," Crispin Blount said. "They have no need of flaring blades or counterspikes,

153

no more than they need th' trappin's of old places. They'll not pay court to th' forests yonder, nor ever bend th' knee to 'em. Like kings an' nobles, lords an' gentry . . . be they in the way they'll cut 'em down.''

"Come along, then, tinker," Trelawney said, and stalked away up the rise. Crispin bid the rest to stay, then followed him.

At the pair of oaks Trelawney removed his coat and hat and rolled up his sleeves. He chose a tree, braced his feet, and swung the axe. Its bite was deep and solid. He swung again and a wedge of white wood fell. "Squire Squat-bottom, is it?" he asked Crispin, frowning. "Tidewater gentry, is it?"

"Ye heard about that, then."

"Every word of it, tinker. Every word." He swung the axe twice more and the tree was notched for fair. "Nuisance, is it? That's what you called me, tinker. Nuisance, am I then?"

He handed the axe to Crispin and stood back. Crispin squared off on the second tree and swung a ringing slice. "As ever was," he grunted. "Nuisance an' worse, when ye bring old worn-out custom to a place that's got no use for it." He swung again and a wedge flew. "We've had war in this land, good man against good man, an' all for th' riddance o' European custom. Yet even now th' tidewater gentry clings to that they've fought as though it were th' best there ever was." He swung again, and yet again, then stooped to look at his notch. It was a good notch, but less deep than the squire's. He frowned and handed back the axe. "An' I'll thank ye to quit callin' me tinker, sir. 'Tis old country custom t' reduce a man to what he does in trade. Here's new country where a man's a man of all his parts an' none born higher than th' next."

Trelawney spat on his hands and swung the axe. It bit half blade-length into the tree, driven by powerful arms. "Nor any born less, either," he grunted. "Is it proper custom then for some chirping minstrel to wander about in vagrant sloth and do slander to the good names of

154

those who at least accept responsibility when they find it?"

The color drained from Crispin's face. He stared at the squire. "Chirpin' minstrel, is it? *Vagrant sloth?*" His outrage was drowned by the squire's next ringing cut and the two that followed. The oak was notched clean to its core. "What manner o' man," he shouted, "cries slander in th' same breath as he commits it?" His ears had gone from white to red. "I've a good mind to—"

Trelawney handed him the axe. "Your turn," he said.

Crispin put his back and his rage into it, and missed his mark. The axe bit above his first notch, wasting a cut. He swore and swung again, then twice more. He felt sweat running down his cheek and noticed that the squire's shirt was soaked. The man mopped his face with a kerchief, squinting at him. "Generally, I hire younger men to do this sort of thing."

"An' do ye apologize in person, or do ye hire men to do that, as well?"

Trelawney licked his lips, catching his breath. "That," he said, "I like to do myself. But only if it's mutual."

Crispin peered at the other's tree. "I have to admit, yon's not th' notch o' a squatbottom tidewater gentry-man. Mayhap I was presumptious about that."

Trelawney shrugged. "And perhaps I misjudged a . . . well, a passable voice for chirping minstrelsy."

"'Tis possible," Crispin conceded, "that a man could get over bein' a bloody nuisance if he set his mind to it."

"And I suppose a man might outgrow vagrancy if he had a reason to," Trelawney nodded. "It will take a time, I suppose, to secure a patent on a new axe. Those thimbleheads in Williamsburg have things in a sorry state right now. I wonder if you'd consider seaming a few troughs while we are waiting."

"For a fair price, I'd consider it," Crispin agreed.

Trelawney squared his shoulders and retrieved his hat. "I'll not be swindled, Mr. Blount."

"Nor will I, Squire," Crispin assured him. "Nor will I."

At the foot of the rise a puzzled and worried group awaited them. Crispin went straight to Nora Ferris and grasped her shoulders in his big hands. "What man be wiser than he knows, an' never knows the reason, save has no fear o' winter's snows no matter what th' season?"

She gazed up at him with eyes as wise as his own. "A husband," she said. "But you'll have to do better than that if we are to discuss such matters."

Beside her Ellie's rippling laughter rose like starlings on the wind. "I told you," she squealed in delight. "I told you it wouldn't be easy."

Trelawney had turned to look back at the two notched trees standing side by side on the rise. "Let them stand," he said. "I've no need of them."

A puzzled Luther took back his axe, wondering about all that had occurred there. "They're strong oaks," he assured the squire. "In a season they'll heal over, but they'll bear their scars as they grow."

"Aye." Trelawney buttoned his greatcoat and beckoned Sparrow to bring him a horse to ride. "Aye, they will. But then, don't we all?"

A Gathering of Storms

XIV

They came down from the Cumberland with the coming of new spring. Where trails divided in the greening hills they made camp to counsel and to study their maps. Sixteen were in the party since the undermountain lands, where three groups had met two days hence, and traveled together from there as men do in wild country.

For Thomas Dodd, who came with two men and mules to carry their packs, the goal was the settlements beyond, where charts could be perfected and landmarks noted. His packs carried his tools: folding rods and lengths of light chain, compasses and calibrated protractors, brass telescope and sextant, dividers and pens, a pair of tripods and a theodolite. In the summer ahead it would be his task to survey the valleys of the Kentucky, the Salt, and the Rolling Fork.

For too long, controversies had raged over the lands variously known as Kaintuck, Vandalia, Transylvania, Kentucky County of Virginia, the Old Indian Lands, and The Overmountain. Now with the British troops withdrawn, with Continental soldiers being mustered out and jobs shut down, thousands would be turning toward the west to find homes. There must be a measuring now of lands. Thomas Dodd was one of many who would rectify the old boundary disputes. Each commonwealth with wilderness claims sought now to know exactly what it held and who owned what. Dodd did not know how many other surveyors would be working the Virginia back lands, but their task was the same—to work from land offices, to adjust the chaotic mess of boundaries, try-lines, stepped-off claims, and landmark lines to a consistent, somehow workable pattern. Their lines would become law.

From the slopes beyond the gap, Stephen Moliere had looked further. His was the largest party, nine men in all, and the bladed devices in his packs were for the working of timber and the construction of broad-horn boats. One of his animals carried a pair of fine pit saws strapped stem to stern, one on each side of its pack frame. Another carried a bale of ten axes—the new design that some called the Kentucky axe but most knew as the American axe. Not until two seasons hence had Moliere seen one of these tools, yet now they were common among those going into the wilderness. Originated by a smith and a tinker somewhere in the Kentucky wilderness, they said. Now they were the product of a half-dozen foundries and shops on the New England coast, and no man who ever felled a tree with one was satisfied to again use a clumsy British axe. Even in England, they said, the new axes were sold and brought a fair price.

Axes and saws, planes and studding mallets—tools of the forester and the shipwright were the treasures Stephen Moliere brought into the wilderness. Somewhere north was the Ohio River, and along its banks were great woodlands that could be reduced for timber. Moliere was a young man with an idea, and the idea had brought him here along the Wilderness Road.

The remaining four in the party were young men adrift by circumstance. David Hastings, Ben Rusk, and William McDowell had served at Yorktown with the Continental Army. They came now with a few coins among them and warrants for land to be found.

Leander Haynes owned nothing save the rifle he carried

and the horse he rode . . . those, and a knowledge of the lands west of the mountains. He was a Kentuckian.

Where the Wilderness Road branched the sixteen found good spring water and paused there to roast venison over an oakwood fire.

The right fork was an ancient road, wide and dim. Centuries of dark warriors whose moccasins had left faint impressions of their passage had come this way, so many for so long that even now the land retained evidence of their route. To the left, northwest, the Wilderness Road went on, down through the hills.

"I'm for the settlements," Dodd told them. "Harrod's marks will be my starting point, the bench marks that he set. I'll fix a base, then work toward the river. Six miles to the march would have me finished in two seasons, I think."

"We may part here, then," Stephen Moliere said. "The old Indian path goes straightest toward the Ohio and I'm anxious to get started. We'll spend a month at least, just cutting timber and digging pits, before we can begin to build a boat, and I want four boats ready when the corn comes ripe."

"You're gambling there will be cargo," Dodd noted.

Moliere grinned, dark eyes quick in a serene face that could be by turns pensive and laughing, thoughtful and grim, exuberant and sad. Despite his name, Stephen Moliere spoke little French. Born on the coast of Normandy, he was most comfortable in English. Training as a shipwright had earned his passage to America with the fleet of General Lafayette. He had never intended to go back. Yet, though he spoke the language of the recent colonies, his features retained the mobility of Gallic ancestry. "Not so much of a gamble," he said now. "Where men put seed in the soil there are those with goods to sell. They say wheat is grown now in Kentucky, and flax and hemp as well. Where there is wheat there will be mills, and there are markets in New Orleans for flour. Also for tobacco and spirits . . . and always for salt

159

meat. We will build our broadhorns. When they float I think there will be cargo to fill them."

"William's father was a millwright," David Hastings said, pointing a thumb toward the stocky McDowell.

McDowell nodded. "Aye. And he taught me as well. But it takes money to build a mill, and I've little enough of that."

"Money goes where profit is," Moliere shrugged. "Me, I never had two shillings at the same time before. But then one day I brushed my coat and went to see a man in Baltimore, and I said, 'There's money to be made in the produce of the western lands if they can be transported to New Orleans. I can do that.'"

"And he gave you money?"

"Of course he did. I showed him how to make a profit. He risks his money and I risk my life, and if I don't get killed, then we may both be rich. Those pit saws there"— he nodded toward his packs—"they cost twenty pounds apiece at the mill in Connecticut. And there's another eighty pounds worth of timbering tools there, as well as a set of shipwright's tools that I couldn't set a price upon. All that, and supplies for a year and wages for my men—it cost him a lord's plenty to outfit this venture. But I can repay his capital with a single good haul to New Orleans. And the boats I can sell there to outfit us for another season. After that, we will make plenty of money."

"Can a flour mill grind grist?" Ben Rusk asked.

McDowell nodded. "A mill is a mill. It's in how the stone is set."

"I know a way to make whiskey from barleycorn grist that's faster and purer than the soak-grain method. But who in Kentucky would have the means to provide for stills?"

"There are always means," Moliere grinned. "You consign to me a hundred kegs of good whiskey, my friend, and I'll bring you enough money to produce a thousand more."

Through the conversation, Leander had sat in

thoughtful silence, puffing on a pipe. Now he turned narrowed eyes on Moliere. "How do you get back?"

"Ah," Moliere breathed. "The heart of the problem. Flatboats—broadhorn or any kind—they only go one way. My plan is to return overland. I hope to find scouts who can show me the way."

"That be all Indian country down there now. Since th' British pulled out along the Mississippi, the river itself's the only safe road . . . for most folks, anyways."

"Oh, there are always roads. It's just a matter of finding someone who can find them."

"New Orleans is Spanish, isn't it?" Hastings asked. "I heard that was part of the treaty."

"It is Spanish," Moliere agreed. "They set a line through the Choctaw country, straight east from the Mississippi to the Atlantic. South of it is Spanish. North of it's ours."

"Whose?"

"The colonies . . . the Confederacy . . . who knows, except it isn't British or French or Spanish. It's ours."

"This is all Virginia land," Thomas Dodd said. "From the other side of the Cumberland bend yonder all the way up to the Ohio and out to the Mississippi. South is the Carolina territory, past that are others. Nobody knows rightly just what belongs to who. The Congress is debating that right now."

"There's just a whole lot of it that the Indians say is theirs," Leander said. "You'll be lucky if you don't get your hair lifted. Th' redskins know what surveyin' means."

"I thought Kentucky was quiet."

"Kentucky's never been quiet, Mr. Dodd. Never. Shawnees and Delawares still raid across the Ohio, time to time, an' there's Cherokee off yonder that don't stop at bashin' a white skull if they feel like it. An' somewhere out there"—he waved his arm, spanning an arc from west to south—"is Nicolet's bunch. They've hit Nashborough a time or two, an' them that's gone lookin' for 'em just don't come back. Some say th' Spanish shelters 'em across th' river sometimes. Nobody knows for sure."

"You know much of this land?" Moliere studied the woodsman.

"A mite. I been down th' Holston a piece, scoutin' for settlin' lands for Judge Treece. He's a New Yorker. Afore that I spent two seasons west with hunters. Good bunch. Jarod Cole, Colin McLeod, an' a couple of others. We saw far places. Come to searchin' out Indian sign an' back land trails, Mr. Moliere, you might think about them. They know their way around."

"Jarod Cole? I met a man by that name a week ago, over on the Yadkin."

"Likely was him. He hires out to ride trail sometimes. Carries mail an' the like. What was he doin' yonder?"

"You might say carrying mail," Moliere grinned. "He had a proclamation from some people up past the falls, to relay on to Williamsburg. He was showing it around. Basically, it said the people up there don't consider themselves to be Virginians, and the House of Burgesses can damned well bugger itself if they expect to regulate where and how they settle."

"Yeah. That'd be the Scioto bunch. The more hell they raise over there, the more Wyandots an' Delawares an' Shawnees we get pushin' raids over here. Surprised Jarod's totin' for them."

"He's just carrying the mail, far as I know. I recall part of that proclamation, though. It said, 'All mankind have an undoubted right to pass into any vacant country and there form their constitution, and the Confederation of the whole United States Congress is not empowered to forbid them."

Leander shrugged. The wages of that kind of talk didn't come from Congresses, but from Indians. He knew about Indians.

Moliere made a decision. In the two days trip down through the gap, he had made note of the Kentuckian. A quiet man, that one, reserved and contemplative. Yet his pale blue eyes seemed never to miss anything, and he carried his rifle as though it were an extension of his arm. Moliere knew too little of the Kentucky lands. But Leander knew them.

"Where do you go from here?" he asked him.

Leander put away his pipe. "Harrod's town. Most call it Fort Harrod now. I generally head back there time to time . . . no special reason."

"A woman," Moliere nodded. "No special reason usually means a woman. Is she your woman, Leander?"

"I've thought on it. Even spoken of such wi' her, but I come up short each time. A man as can't set in one spot's a bad bargain for a woman, seems to me."

"Well, that's your business, not mine. But since you know this land, I'd pay you to take me and mine on up to the Ohio. I have a map, but I'd like a scout better."

"Maps don't show where the Shawnee cross," Leander agreed. "I guess I could lead you yonder an' show you how the land lays, but not up the Warriors Road like you said. If you follow me, it'll be over to Harod's, then cut back down th' Kaintuck."

"Because of your woman?" Moliere's eyes sparkled.

"Partly. I do like to look on Julie now an' again, even if I ain't decided what to do about her yet. But mainly it's that I don't need wages bad enough to follow th' Indian road in springtime. That be an old trail, Mr. Moliere, but it's still in use. Cherokees call Kaintuck th' dark an' bloody ground. There's still reasons why they do."

Moliere considered it. He was impatient to reach the Ohio and put his men and his tools to work, but he relished the thought of Indian troubles no more than any other man. "How much further will it be, through Fort Harrod?"

"Few days. Maybe add a week. If ye want to do that, then I'll take ye on from there."

"Then we won't separate here after all," the trader told Thomas Dodd. "If you see fit, we'll travel together a few days more."

Dodd agreed readily. The larger the party in these parts, the safer the travel. As they tightened packs and prepared to travel again, he asked Leander, "Do you know Daniel Boone and Judge Henderson?"

"Met Boone a time or two. Seen Henderson. Why?"

"I could use their help. They were the first to lay claim in Kentucky. Even before Harrod. To some extent, every boundary that's been recorded since is based on their original claims. The Commonwealth has told me to try to preserve the original claims as far as possible. They don't want to dispossess people. They only want an orderly system of properties."

Leander's pale blue eyes were cold as he gazed at the surveyor—eyes too old for the young face they were in. "Yer too late for that, mister. Last I heard, Henderson's down around Nashborough some'ere, tryin' to scrape together a claim. Boone's gone. He left last year."

"Gone? Where?"

"West. First white man ever to lay claim in Kentucky, they say. Lot of good it done him. Burgess warrants took part of what he had, Continental Army warrants took some more, speculators done him out of the rest. Amongst 'em they taken every acre of land old Dan'l owned, an' not a thing he could do about it. He picked up an' left. Maybe out on th' Green some'ers. You talk good, Mr. Dodd. Could have used you out here a few years back. Boone an' a lot just like him could have used your help."

Dodd shook his head. "I'm sorry he's gone. That's hardly just."

"Not much is, in Kaintuck. Joel Simms—he's Squire Trelawney's clerk—he reckons that for every ten men as ever laid claim to land out here, nine of 'em lost all they had an' moved on."

"It was the war, I suppose."

"The war? Who was we fightin' against, Mr. Dodd? Some say it was the British, but I wonder. 'Pears to me like most folks' fightin' is amongst their ownselves."

David Hastings, Ben Rusk, and William McDowell had drawn apart from the rest. Now they stepped up into their saddles, touched their hat brims to the rest, and headed west into the wooded hills.

Leander looked after them. "I reckon for every man as loses somethin', there's another as gains. Them three, it ain't their fault they was paid off in land that somebody else might have thought was theirs. But I can surely see how it might bother 'em to hear it spoke of."

"You're right," Moliere allowed. "It isn't their fault."

"Nope. Not any more than it'll be the fault of them as comes later, after Mr. Dodd an' th' others do their new surveys an' takes the land that them three are fixin' to claim."

Miles away to the south a young man slipped through high forest, climbing a path that was known to few now, though in its time it had been known to many. His name was Edahi, and he wore his hair cropped and plumed in the Iroquois fashion, although the three feathers fixed atop his head and the high moccasins on his feet were Cherokee.

Edahi was of the Bird Clan of his tribe, and thus a kinsman of Goga the Crow. Taller than many, and with the knotted legs of a mountaineer and runner of high places, Edahi had set himself a task that he hoped would one day lead to legends in which his name would be honored. Since the first thaw, he and one other had scouted the dark land far north of the mountain sanctuaries of his people, high in the folded mountains above the headwaters of the Cumberland.

Edahi had been watching. Day after day through the change of a moon he had lain in hiding on the steep slopes above the river gap that the white men used as a road. He had seen the man Goga described twice now. He had seen him cross through the gap to the valley lands beyond, going toward the settlements there. Now he had seen him

165

return, in company with many other men who led pack animals. He had marked the direction of his journey, then turned south, leaving Chula to follow and watch.

Edahi's swift legs, they said, were like the wings of an eagle in the mountains. He used them now, carrying word to Goga, as well as a plan.

The one called Tenkiller had returned to the dark land. Edahi felt in his heart that this would be the season when they would go and find him. Chula would have marked the way.

XV

Next to George Rogers Clark, Joseph Trelawney maintained the most effective communication system west of the mountains. It was essential to his investments that he keep abreast of myriad happenings to the east, and he in turn kept Crispin Blount advised when they met periodically on business. And when Crispin knew something of general interest, it was not long before everyone in the region knew it as well. Thus, when it was learned in Williamsburg that Thomas Grenville and Benjamin Franklin were in Paris negotiating for peace, and that the last of the British troops had sailed from Charleston and Savannah, and that someone had constructed an engine powered by steam, and that a new bank had been established in Philadelphia, it was only a matter of weeks before these things became general knowledge in central Kentucky.

In like manner, Trelawney knew when the Burgesses approved yet another new land act for the western territories, and when the plan was approved to send out public surveyors to perfect existing claims—or change them.

Blount was typically blunt in his reaction to that. "Serves ye right, ye greedy brush-lord," he said amiably. "I mind how high ye rode scant seasons back when th' law took folks' property away from them an' gave ye th' opportunity to buy it. So now it comes around again an' them as took gets taken."

"Everything I own I bought legally and fairly," Trelawney blustered, slapping his noggin of toddy down on the plank table between them. "I did more than that, if you'll recall. I paid quit-claim money to every man who'd left his sweat on the land."

"Ye did that because I hornswoggled ye, *Squire*." Crispin grinned and sipped his own toddy, a concoction Nora had introduced soon after she and Crispin moved into their new house, when the squire and Captain Post had come to call and Trelawney and Crispin nearly came to blows over philosophy—or, as she insisted, over far too much naked run in their bellies. As a widower with no woman in his household, Trelawney had become accustomed to excess whenever he felt the whim. Nora had taken it upon herself to civilize both her husband and his friend.

"I concede that," Trelawney nodded. "Though I probably would have done it anyway. It saved me from quite a lot of mischief in the long run."

"Not to mention the money ye saved. I've told ye since, some of those claimers was that far from organizin' regulator gangs th' way they've done in Tennessee. It would have cost ye dearly to defend yerself had they done it."

"I concede that as well," Trelawney sighed. "It's only that this new thing is grossly unjust. No good can come of it."

"Them as takes by th' law gets taken by th' law," Crispin chuckled. "It's only in that way that th' laws o' man has ever promoted justice."

Trelawney picked up his toddy and sipped it, as aware as Crispin that Nora Blount was just beyond the door, ready to intervene at the first sign that the two of them were becoming violent. "It's my own fault," he said. "I should never have trusted Jefferson."

"So this is Jefferson's doin', then?" Crispin was surprised. In his opinion, Thomas Jefferson was a fair and thoughtful man—for tidewater gentry.

"Partly. He pushes for expansion, more than Washington does. But now he talks of prime meridians and ranges and township lines . . . the whole 'rectangular geography' notion. And you know how those nitwits running the commonwealth respond to his ideas."

"It seems to me the only difference between range and township an' th' old way—boundin' by landmarks an' such—is everything will wind up bein' in straight lines. I have to admit, though, such a thing offends th' soul. Had the good Lord wanted straight lines on his blessed earth, he'd have put them there."

"I'll have to sell a great deal of what I own," Trelawney muttered, the toddy making him glum in proportion to how cheerful it made Blount.

"Either that or pay taxes on it, 's my prediction."

"I *pay* taxes, bedamme! More than my fair share!"

The sitting room door creaked and both of them glanced around. "No problem here, lady love," Crispin assured the door. "Th' squire's just levelin' lovely dire slanders at Thomas Jefferson."

Beyond the door Ellie giggled and Nora shushed her. A sweet odor wafted through the sitting room. The two of them were in the kitchen beyond, rolling sugar-rind from berries they had preserved in the fall.

Trelawney's nose twiched. "You are a fortunate man, Crispin Blount."

Crispin leaned his elbows on the table. "Far more than I'll probably ever understand, Joseph, for a fact."

"Well, it's that I've come to see you about this day. It has been my observation that a man who is richly blessed with the joys of domesticity . . ."

"An' what would the likes of you know about such things?"

"Very little. Let me finish. . . . But first, it seems my noggin has run dry. Do you suppose your good wife might permit . . . ?"

169

Crispin finished his own with a gulp. "Problem wi' blendin' good spirits down like this, a man's got to near founder his self to enjoy 'em." He eyed the kitchen door, then threw back his head and spread his arms. "Lady o' th' house," he sang at the top of his lungs. "'Tis fact, my sugarplum, that sober conversation ends when men run out of rum!" He grinned apologetically at the Squire, whose eyes had gone suddenly round. "There was a time I was better at such."

There was bustling in the next room, accompanied by Ellie's renewed giggling, and Nora pushed open the door and entered, carrying a lidded pitcher. "Honestly!" she said.

She filled their noggins and stared sternly at each in turn. "When this is gone, there'll be no more. You've both had too much already."

When she was gone, Crispin leaned back contentedly. "What bliss can come to a wanderin' man when he stops his feet from itchin'."

The changes in Nora Ferris, now Nora Blount, had been subtle, but in the three years since Crispin had come to Harrod's Post and decided to stay, they had accumulated. Always a handsome woman, tall and graceful, she was more handsome now than ever. Old hurts had fallen away with time, and the wisdoms in her eyes now were contented wisdoms. Little joys and humors twinkled there, and at times she seemed radiant. The seasons had been good to her and she cherished them.

Ellie came through carrying a pan of sugar-rinds to set out on the porch, and she paused to curtsy to them. "Mother always acts that way when Crispin sings in the house," she confided to Trelawney. "She swears the house is not built to stand it."

If the changes in Nora had been subtle, those in Ellie had not. At fifteen she was a thorned rose, as pleasing to the eye as morning sunlight and as quicksilver change-able as the moon on a stormy night. As Crispin put it,

170

"Her mother all over again, she is, as though th' Lord saw he'd done one thing right so He repeated th' performance."

"You were sayin'? . . ."

Trelawney stifled a belch and drank more toddy. "Yes. I was. I should never have placed my trust in Jefferson. The man is a visionary surrounded by idiots, and—"

"That wasn't it," Crispin pointed out. "You said ye came here for a reason."

"Oh yes. That." He glanced at the hearth where Old Yellow Dog hung above a stone mantel. "Crispin, a man a'flounder in wedded bliss has—"

"I think ye said that, too."

"Confound it, man!" Trelawney slapped his noggin down on the table. "Will you let me finish?"

"If ye think ye're up to it," Crispin shrugged.

"Don't for one minute think I'm not! It is my custom to say what I've a mind to say, and I do not care for interruption!"

"Well, ye're in my house now an' I'll thank ye to be civil about it!" Crispin glared at him. "I can take those seams out o' yer bedammed troughs just as slick as I put 'em in there!"

"I paid for those! Twice what they're worth an' more! . . ."

"*Twice what they're worth?* Now ye're sayin' ye been cheated, is it? My God, I only charged half price, an' that because I felt sorry for ye! . . ."

"Gentlemen!" Nora stood in the doorway, her hands on her hips. Ellie hurried in from the porch and crossed the room to tug at her mother's arm. "Leave them alone, Mother," she whispered. "They're only having a good time."

"Well, they might be a little quieter about it! Mercy!"

The squire bowed toward her. "Madam, my profound apologies. It is only that this lout of a husband of yours—"

"*Lout?*" Crispin hissed. "Lout, is it? I've a mind to—"

171

"Crispin!"

"Ah? Oh. Yes, dear. I apologize, too. But this crude—" He caught himself and sagged back in his chair. "The squire was just about to tell me why he came here today. I think."

"Well, behave yourselves."

The door closed behind the two females.

"Fine woman, that," Trelawney said.

"Wonderful wife," Crispin added.

"Such comforts could addle a man," Trelawney expanded.

"Truly," Crispin agreed.

"It's why you should give yourself a reprieve."

"It's why I should . . . what?"

"I think you need to get away from all this for a time."

"I do?"

"Well, what I mean is, I've been thinking of a hunt. How long has it been since you've taken a hunt? I had thought about possibly a party to go north for a few days. We could hunt, you know . . . and possibly stop off to look at some boundaries that I've been concerned—"

"Are we back to that now?"

"To what?"

"Are we goin' to get back to boundaries an' range-line surveyin'? I thought we covered all that."

"Well, there's no justice to it. But no, I thought you might like to go along. We could go to the river, possibly. We might even stop by Luther's place if you—"

"Did I ever tell ye that was a right noble thing ye done? Sellin' that ground back to th' lad?"

"Several times."

"I still think ye overcharged him unmercifully, considerin'—"

"Overcharged? By God, all I charged him was what I offered him for a quit-claim! The fact is, I *gave* it to him!"

"Not th' way I saw it, ye didn't. Had ye paid a fair quit-claim, then charged a modest price, th' lad would've had a nice balance to put in his purse."

172

"That's ridiculous!"

"How would we travel . . . if we went huntin' up that way?"

"Well, not by foot and leading your mule! The thing is, I've a fine span of six matched horses on pasture, newly trained and needing some saddle time. I thought—"

"Ye thought I'd help ye weather yer horses."

"Well, it's better than walking! Though on second thought, no more of a rider than you are—"

"I can ride anything you can breed!"

"You are as stubborn as a goat!"

"Goat, is it? Better a goat than a snag-toothed old—"

"Can you even shoot that rifle there? Or is it only decoration?"

"I can outshoot an' outhunt ye any day o' th'—!"

"I was thinking we'd leave tomorrow!"

"I'll have to speak to my wife about it!"

Nora's voice came from the doorway, sharp with irritation. "Crispin!"

"Yes, dear?"

"Go hunting with the squire!"

"Yes, dear."

"And take your time coming back!"

"I am certain they will be quite safe and comfortable while we are away," Trelawney said.

"Aye, they'll be all right," Crispin nodded. "Between Seth Michaels spendin' his every free hour here pesterin' Ellie, an' half th' young bucks in Kentucky wanderin' by hoping for a smile from Julie, there was never a house more securely observed or enthusiastically guarded."

When first Nora Ferris and Crispin Blount were wed, and moved into the new house that Crispin and Luther built for them—a fine big house with five rooms and high ceilings (Crispin had been emphatic about high ceilings) —Julie Jackson stayed on in the old house for a time. She tended the school for Nora while they were finishing

173

their house, and the cozy cabin near the stockade was convenient for her. Then when the sisters Becky Chandler and Lib Gates showed up at the town with a flock of small children and no place to rest, she took them in and for a time the little cabin rang with bustling life.

But it was a hollow time, as well. The sisters had come down from the gap, escorted by a group of long hunters from the undermountain land, expecting to find their husbands at Harrodsburg. But they were not there. They had been there, some said, but had found no land that they could claim in the vicinity. So they had organized a party of men like themselves and had gone to the Green River to look for land on its headwaters or above. Some thought the James Chandler party may have been going farther on from there, possibly over into Tennessee.

No one had heard from them again. Like so many before them, they had simply disappeared. A small enough thing, just seven more young men who had gone into the wilderness and had never come back. It happened all the time.

But it didn't happen all the time to Becky Chandler and Lib Gates, nor to their children. Like all other young mothers and babies, the loss of husbands and fathers in the wilderness was a terrible and unique thing.

Finally, they had found travelers to take them back— to whatever was left where they had come from.

And the little house was lonely then. Oh, she had callers—young men, mostly. They stopped by, some achingly shy and some forthright, some tentative and one or two so determined that she had barred the door until they went away. Mostly they were lonely, far from home and looking for company. Some among them were gentlemen. Yet she found none that seemed to fit her needs. Maybe even Tom Jackson wouldn't have, in time. She would never know now. She had been smitten with Tom . . . or with being smitten. At times since, she had wondered which. But that had been so brief. They had been married such a scant few days and nights, and then

174

he was away and then he was gone—dead somewhere in the wilderness.

There had come a day when she went to the tackle lofts in the back of the old fort and found there her father's pans and ovens, put away when the baker died. She had wept then, remembering. Her father's death had stunned her, but coming so soon upon Tom's death it had somehow been just one more blow. There had been too little room left for grief. Later, though, seeing the pans and ovens, the grief came. Her father's few things, mute evidence of a life gone and over. For most of a day she sat in the dim recesses of the tackle loft, turning this and that thing over in her hands . . . mourning. In its time, the mourning had come.

And among the legacy-things of Calvin McCarthy was one that she hugged to her breast as she wept, because she had seen it so often as a child and had thought so little about it then. It was a small brass-bound telescope, a long-ago gift to her father from some friend whose name she should remember and never would.

On the following day she had gone to Nora Blount with a proposal. And Nora had talked with Crispin about it, and Crispin with the squire. Agreements had been made, and the little cabin near the fort had become a bakery. Julie spent her days up to her elbows in flour and her nights at the Blounts' house, where she was provided a room. It was a far better arrangement.

All through that time, now and again, Leander Haynes had shown up—grim and distant usually, smelling of woodsmoke and far places, always anxious to sit with her and talk, but always having little really to say. Yet he came and came again, and always she could see in his eyes the longing that he could not seem to speak. Once he had almost spoken of marriage. She had been sure he was leading up to that, and she had trembled because she did not know what her answer to him would be. He frightened her in some way. Something in the remote, secret parts of him even repelled her. Something that was

175

cold and angry and always ravenous. Something she could not draw out of him to see in the light of day.

Almost he had spoken of the two of them, then had shied away, and she felt that a war raged within him. He wanted her. But there was something else he wanted as much, something dark and secret and frightening.

He would come sometimes to call and be about the town for a day or a week, and then he would be gone again and she never really knew where he went.

But she thought of him, more than of any of the others, and she both prayed and feared that one day he would speak his mind to her. She feared, because then she would have to know how she felt about him. Yet she didn't really know him at all.

She should marry again, she knew. A woman should be married. Still, she hesitated. She could take her pick of the young men in Kentucky, Nora said, and she supposed that she could. But since Tom . . . well, she had to admit that only one had appealed to her since, and that was the problem. That one was Leander Haynes. In a way, he frightened her just a little. She thought that he frightened others, too. Luther had traveled with him a time or two, over to Boone's or St. Ashban, but Luther's comments about Leander were always guarded. "Luther says he doesn't really know Leander," Kate had told her. "He says there is something about him that troubles him. He doesn't know what."

Crispin Blount had spoken of him to her, but then Crispin was always Crispin, and if one didn't understand his riddles, then one didn't understand what he had to say. The tall man never ceased to delight Julie. He could make her laugh when there seemed no laughter in the world. Yet commenting about Leander one evening he had gone pensive . . . thoughtful. "Some rivers run too deep for me," he'd said. "What lies beneath's not plain. Like storm clouds on a summer's day had filled them with cold rain."

She knew what it meant, and yet she didn't. Something

176

very dark and very secret lurked just behind Leander's pale eyes, and she wondered if anyone at all knew what it was.

One bright morning Julie went to the stockade well to clean oven racks, and she climbed to the old rampart to stand for a moment, letting the fresh breeze play around her. It was just below this platform, she thought, that her father and Kate had baked the bread and corncakes for those who came crowding in in those terrible seasons of the red knives. Just down there, not twelve feet from where she stood now, Calvin McCarthy had worked with his ovens while Kate mixed in the sheds just over there. Julie herself had helped, but not enough, she thought now. There had been so much excitement, so much fear, yet such vital bustling about, so many people doing so many things. And the boys . . . young men they had been, yet still boys. And all of them had looked at her—couldn't help looking when she passed—and that was part of the excitement, too. Even then, Tom Jackson had been coming to call whenever he could.

And through it all, Kate had worked alongside their father . . . just there, so few feet away . . . there where the shadow of the old flagstaff fell each day at noon. And there across the compound, on the rampart of the far wall, there was where Kate had gone each evening after the patrols went out. Julie remembered how the crowds there had dwindled with the passing of time, how for many long evenings there had been no one there except Kate and Nora, and sometimes little Ellie. Then, after that, only Kate. Kate had never given up hope.

And, finally, Luther had returned. As Kate had known he would.

I want that, she thought. I want a strong young man to come for me and make me feel that way. I want to know devotion, to give my soul to him and receive his in return . . . and no secrets ever between us. No secrets. Ever.

She turned to look out over the south wall. In the back

177

street below, Samuel Calkins was passing, pushing a wheelbarrow laden with stones. His wire wig glistened in the early morning light. Mr. Calkins and some of the other townsmen had been hauling stone since first thaw, bringing it up from the old Harrod cairn that had become a stone heap when first these lands were cleared. They intended to use it for the foundation of the new church over by the high road.

In the near out-lots, men were in their fields, planting. Just beyond, Seth Michaels walked along the road, his gun over his shoulder, his two old mongrel dogs pacing along at either side of him. Seth was eighteen now, tall and gawkish in britches long outgrown. And he was as hopelessly smitten with Ellie as anyone could be. She watched him, saw him glance back over his shoulder, and knew where he was looking. Even now, off on a day's hunt for turkey or pigeons or whatever he could find, he took a moment to glance back, to glance at the house where Ellie Ferris lived.

And again it tugged at her, the seeing of devotion. So many people came and went, appeared and disappeared. Things changed so all the time. Yet there was steadfast purpose, and it showed itself in people like Kate and Luther, like Nora and Squire Trelawney . . . like young Seth Michaels. Some people knew exactly what they wanted and never changed.

Seth walked on, along the high road past the out-lots, then turned where a pathway led off through the woodlots, off toward the distant forest. The two old dogs tagged after him as always. Brought in by someone from a burned homestead, it was said the two could smell an Indian a mile away. Sunlight gleamed on snowy muzzles. Just a pair of mismatched old dogs, but they loved Seth Michaels.

And there it was again. Devotion. I want that, she admitted to herself. I want to feel about someone the way those old dogs feel about Seth. And I want that someone to feel that way about me.

178

Did Leander feel devotion toward her? He was constant, in his way. He always came to see her when he was about. His pale eyes never left her when they sat and talked, and though there was much there that she could not read, there was no doubting his desire to be with her. Maybe that was devotion, too. She sighed and turned toward the ladder. A day was begun and there was work to do. She found that she enjoyed the work most times.

It was later in the day that she heard the bell in the old Bowman loft. A few minutes later the twins, Jared and Julius Bowman, came racing into town to spread the word that a large party was coming up the trail. "Better'n a dozen an' two strings o' pack critters," Jared puffed.

"Leander Haynes is leadin' 'em," Julius added. "We didn't know th' rest."

XVI

Seth Michaels had intended to be out earlier on this day. The geese were moving now, and he had thought to waylay a brace of fat ones fresh from their wintering swamps. But when he went to the barn in the dark hour before dawn, Ma's old cow was down and lowing and it had taken time to get the tottering critter up on its feet and moving. So he had gotten a late start. Still, he strapped on his powder horn, dropped his little bag of precious shot into his pouch, shouldered his musket, and set out, hoping. Sometimes geese would stay around a pond for a day or two, even in this season, if there was a stand of wild rice nearby or an abandoned cornfield that still had grain on the ground.

The dogs saw his preparations and went to stand by the door, wagging and grinning big dog-grins. Seth put on his hat and stepped out, noticing that the sun's edge was already over the hills. He shook his head and shrugged.

"Come on, fellers," he said. Still wagging their enthusiasm, the dogs fell in on either side as he headed for the high road. Partway out the high road, he paused and glanced back toward the Blount house, wondering whether he had told Ellie that he would be gone today. He was sure he had—or at least he had meant to. Things got so busy sometimes. Well, if he hadn't already missed the geese rising, maybe he could knock down an extra one and take it to Mrs. Blount. Maybe Ellie would be around to help him clean and pluck the goose.

Pa had cautioned him not to go past the creek pond, for there had been some talk of Indians of late, but Seth thought little about it. There was always talk of Indians. The Shawnee and the Delaware and some of the Iroquois still crossed the Ohio now and again, usually just small scouting parties, though there were skirmishes sometimes. And there was always talk of the renegade Nicolet and his mixed band, but they were away off somewhere, it was thought, over in the Tennessee hills. What had set it off just lately was a hunter down from the upper Cumberland who said he thought he had seen mountain Cherokee over by the pass, though what they would be doing there no one knew. But it wasn't a raiding party, so far as he knew. He had seen just a glimpse of one, or maybe two.

It was little to worry about.

Past the outer fields he turned right, at the trail up through the woodlots. Beyond was forest and beyond that the goose pond.

Chula stayed far off the trail, only approaching cautiously where there was good cover, and then only close enough to know that the white men were still moving northward along it and that Tenkiller was still with them.

Like the fox that was his namesake, Chula ghosted through the empty lands on silent feet, every sense alert, every skill of the hunter serving him. From the moment Edahi had turned southward into the mountains to tell Goga and the other clansmen of the Bird that Tenkiller had returned to the dark land, Chula had stalked the white men on the trail and left his mark here and there in ways that Bird Clan warriors would know. He felt as Edahi did—the winds spoke of it and he listened—that this was the season for vengeance against Tenkiller.

181

Edahi would take the word and Goga would come. Three winters had passed since the day Goga had seen Tenkiller, in the hills far to the west, but Goga the Crow never forgot. He had seen the face of Tenkiller and described the white man so that all of them would know him on sight.

And through the seasons they had watched for him. Watched and scouted and talked with those of other tribes whom they sometimes met. From the Delaware runner Hattentay, who carried the red stone pipe, they learned that others besides the *Aniyunwiya* had been hunted and killed by the man Tenkiller. A *Sawani* brave had tracked him once, then watched from a hilltop as Tenkiller stalked and murdered every member of a Wyandot hunting party in the forests beyond the little spirit river. But the *Sawani* had not seen him so closely as had Goga the Crow. Goga knew the color of his pale eyes, the whiskers of his beard, the slant of his brows, the measure of his moccasin track.

Three winters they had searched and waited. Now they had found him. Chula ghosted through the forest at a distance, staying far back from the white men's road but never losing track of Tenkiller. Edahi would bring Goga and others, and they would find Chula and Chula would lead them to Tenkiller.

The white men were going toward a settlement, and from a rise Chula saw the smokes of it in the early light of dawn. They would reach that place at midday. Probably they would stop there. It would be difficult then for Chula to keep track of Tenkiller. He would have to stay well away from the white men's town and their fields and roads. He could not have any of them know he was here. Maybe he would have to spend days patrolling a great circle around the settlement to be sure that Tenkiller did not leave—or, if he left, that Chula did not lose him.

If that was what he must do, then that was what he would do. He climbed a tall tree to see the trail camp where the white men had stopped for the night. Tenkiller was still with them. On the ground again Chula found a spring and washed himself with the cold water. Then he ate a handful of pemmican from his travel pouch and moved on, looking for another vantage somewhere ahead, a place to look at the white men another time as they approached the settlement.

There had been geese on the pond. Seth found fresh droppings along its verges. But they had flown with the sun and the chances of another flock seeking the water before late afternoon were slim. There were plenty of ducks about, but he hated to waste a load of shot on a duck. There wasn't enough meat to justify the expense. To load his musket with shot required almost two ounces of dropped lead—melted atop a tower, dropped from there into a shallow pond, then raked out and sieved for proper size pellets. Good shot was hard to come by and Seth hated to waste a large load on a small bird.

Beyond the pond the forest began again, climbing away over the rolling hills. A few miles beyond, he had heard, were natural meadows where turkeys could be found.

"What do y'think, fellers?" he asked. "Shame to go home empty when we've come this far."

The dogs wagged their tails and grinned up at him. Something scurried through the brush a few yards away, and both of them yodeled and went after it.

"Come back here, fellers!" he shouted, and they turned, watching him. "It's just a rabbit. Come on, now. Let's find somethin' better."

They glanced back at the brush where the rabbit had gone and returned to him, and he set out around the pond, splashing through icy water at its lower end where a little creak ran away into the brush. "We shouldn't walk too far," he told the dogs. "Wet moccasins fetch up scald feet if a body isn't careful."

Beyond the stream he angled around the up side of the pond and found a deer trail—only a suggestion of a path, but visible—leading into the forest beyond. "Well," he told them, "we can go on for a bit. Brace of fat turkey hens'd be worth takin' home." He entered the woods and the dogs pranced along beside him, excited at exploring new terrain.

It was farther than he had expected. For nearly two miles, fingers of forest and stands of cedar cloaked the rising ridges like a quilt, with scarcely a break anywhere. Game generally liked the open places, meadows surrounded by forest where they could come out to feed or skitter away to hide in the shadows. In that respect, turkeys were like deer. They favored the same sort of places, and where you found one you might find the other.

Atop the second crest, Seth sat down on a deadfall log and pulled off his wet moccasins. His feet were beginning to cook, sealed within the moist buckskin without circulation to cool them. Nothing Seth had ever put on his feet beat good moccasins for general comfort, but scald feet could be a problem if a man wasn't careful. Pa said that George Morley had once been laid up a'bed for nearly a week from it.

He turned the moccasins inside out and hung them on branches to air while he flexed his feet on the cool moss and new grasses of the forest floor. The dogs circled around, noses to the ground, then came back to him and he scratched their ears. He could scarcely recall the time he had not had them with him. Both mongrels and mismatched at that, they were still the best friends he had ever had . . . except for Ellie Ferris.

He enjoyed thinking about Ellie. Pretty as a picture she was, and in the past two years she had grown in just the right ways. He wasn't sure when it had happened, all that filling out and subtle changing. It just had, and he was glad of it. Sometimes it near took his breath away, just being around her. She looked like her mother now, they said, and he supposed it was so in some superficial respects. But he couldn't see anybody else being like

Ellie. Ellie was just . . . Ellie. There wasn't anybody else to match her.

When his feet had cooled he rubbed the moccasins briskly together, fluffing the buckskin, then put them on his feet again. He stood, picked up his gun, and headed on. "Come on, fellers."

The dogs were beside him even as he said it.

Chula had one more glimpse of the white men on the road to assure himself that Tenkiller was still among them and that they were going to the settlement ahead. Then he headed deeper into the forest. The cleared fields ahead, ringing the white men's town, extended farther to the east than they did to the west, so he went west. He needed to move fast now. He must scout the village without anyone knowing he was there. That meant long distances to cover, a great circle beyond the outer fields. Also it meant great care. If he were seen, they would come and hunt him down—or try to. Chula was not afraid of the white men. If they came for him, he would not die easily. But then Tenkiller might get away. He thought for a moment of ways to enter the white settlement and find Tenkiller and kill him himself. But that was not the way. Goga wanted Tenkiller. He should wait for Edahi to bring Goga and others. Then they would stalk Tenkiller and rid the land of him.

The Indian would not have thought so of a man—even a white man—who had killed in open combat. Even if it were his kin who died, he would respect that. But Tenkiller did not war. Tenkiller hunted, and the game he hunted were people. He must be treated then as one would treat a puma that had tasted human blood and stalked the people's villages seeking more.

Even the Wyandot would not tolerate such behavior.

Chula held a hunter's pace, angling to pass a comfortable distance to the west of the town. Hills and forests knew his fleeting shadow, then the land opened

185

out and was dotted with natural meadows. These he avoided, choosing a snaking route that held to the cover of the trees—a path that a fleeing deer might choose. He saw many deer along the way, browsing in the fringes of the forest or just beyond in the open places. And turkey, here and there. Some of the turkeys saw him pass and darted for cover. None of the deer saw him.

Then at a gap between cedar stands, where a brushy meadow spread beyond, he froze. Like a cat in reeds he sank down until only his eyes were above the level of the low brush. For a minute he watched, his dark eyes fixed on a point across the meadow, then for part of another. Then there was movement there, and a man stepped out into the open, a young white man with a gun over his shoulder. A pair of dogs bounded past him, then stopped to scent the air.

The problem with thinking about Ellie Ferris was that it always wound up with him thinking about Christopher Post, and Seth didn't care for those thoughts at all.

Since Mistress Ferris and Mr. Blount had married, and Mr. Blount had gone into business with Squire Trelawney —patenting axes and who knew what else—things had changed for Ellie. Seth was no part of that change, but Christopher was. Even gone off to Massachusetts to school, it was as though he were still around. And when he *was* around . . . He had seen her eyes when Christopher rode by the house, high and handsome on that big black racer that he always rode. Like a person out of another world, he was striking—dark hair and fierce dark eyes, dark hat and coat and fresh-blacked riding boots for all the world like a Prussian grenadier's, and always fine, clean linen to his throat that gleamed as white as his teeth.

Christopher was Captain Post's son, and the captain also did business with Squire Trelawney, and sometimes

186

Seth felt as though his whole world had run off and left him.

He didn't hate Christopher Post. It wouldn't have taken much to make him hate him. Seth was willing to hate him. But Christopher had never given him reason to hate him. He wasn't even certain that Christopher Post was aware he existed, except maybe as someone to walk around to go up the steps of Ellie's house. And something bothered him more: He wasn't sure that Christopher even had any interest in Ellie. He wasn't sure what it was that drove Christopher, that made that intense fire burn in his dark eyes the way it did. But someone had said the captain's crippled leg had come about over in the Spanish lands and that Christopher intended to do something about that somehow.

Seth was thinking such thoughts when he approached the second meadow, and he willed them from his mind. He wasn't out here to worry about Christopher Post. He was out here to put some birds on some tables. So he slowed, working from tree to tree and keeping the dogs behind him with a wave of his hand. From the shadows he saw the telltale bobbing of turkeys, off toward the other side of the clearing. There were several of them. He was thinking of how to approach them near enough to shoot, when abruptly they ducked out of sight, every one of them. Turkeys could do that, when they were nervous about something. Yet he was sure he had done nothing to alert them, and what breeze there was came across from them to him, so they had not caught a scent.

For an instant he thought he had seen movement over there, beyond the fringe of trees on the other side, but he saw nothing now and was not sure he ever had.

"We'll step out an' have a look," he whispered to the dogs. "Maybe them birds are comin' this way."

Cautiously, he stepped out, scanning the brushy clearing. "Down an' quiet, fellers," he muttered. "Stay down an' quiet now."

The mid morning breeze gusted and he felt it cool on his face. First one dog and then the other jerked their heads up, nostrils quivering. Seth had never known them to catch the scent of turkeys in the open.

One gave a startled yip, then set to baying, and the other barked in chorus. Without even glancing back, they went streaking out across the meadow, scattering turkeys ahead of them. Heavy wings drummed the air as at least ten big birds took flight, going in all directions. One homed toward Seth and he raised his musket, held just above its outthrust head, and fired. It tumbled and bounced almost to his feet. The dogs were still going and he yelled at them. What in God's name were they after? He ran after them, then realized he was carrying an unloaded gun. He stopped, poured powder and began loading, and saw the fellers disappear into the woods beyond. Their clamor was throaty and threatening, and Seth felt a deep fear for them. If they had scented a bear or puma and tackled it, they could be hurt. His fingers flew as he set wads, poured shot, set cap-wad, and rammed his load home. He tipped the musket down, charged the frizzen pan, and ran, trying to follow the baying of the fellers. And suddenly there was nothing to hear. One voice went silent, then—abruptly—the other.

When Chula saw the dogs he went flat to the ground, perfectly hidden in the undergrowth among the trees. But when the stalks above rustled to a change in the breeze and he heard the dogs' chorus, he knew they had his scent. They would come and so would the man with them. His hand tightened on his bow. Then he heard the flurry of rising turkeys and heard the musket's thump, and he relaxed. At least for a moment the man would not come. He was hunting.

Braced low to the ground, Chula scurried backward,

still hidden, then edged aside and darted for heavier cover, deeper into the forest. The dogs were close, and for a moment he was tempted to outrun them. They were not racing dogs, just dogs. But it would take too much time. He darted again, to his left, changing the direction of his retreat. The dogs were into the trees now and he knew the white man could not see where they went. When he was satisfied, he turned and waited.

The taller of the two dogs crashed out of the brush, saw him, snarled, and leapt at him, waist-high. When its feet had cleared the ground, he sidestepped, ducked, and lashed out with his knife. The dog rolled lifeless beyond him, open from heart to entrails. The other was coming for his knees, and its teeth nipped the skin of his leg before his war club took it between the ears, shattering its skull.

The dogs lay still. Chula stood in silence, letting his ears tell him where the hunter was. He heard him coming through the meadow, running, heading for where the dogs had entered the forest. He took the time, then, to reload his weapon. Again Chula gripped his bow, and again he caught himself. He did not know how long it would be before Goga and Edahi and the rest arrived where he was. In the meantime, it was best that no one suspect his presence. It was best to leave no trace, no sign that anyone might try to find.

Chula wrapped the disemboweled dog in his cloak so that its blood would leave no trail. He scuffed old leaf-fall over the pooled blood and picked up the bundle. Carrying both dogs, one in a bundle and the other by its scruff, he headed deeper into the forest, again moving at a right angle to the track the man was on. When he had gone far enough, he found a ravine where old runoffs had cut through soft rock. He dumped the carcasses of the dogs there and covered them over with stone and brush.

Somewhere in the distance he could still hear the man's voice, a young voice with the traces of childhood still in it. Over and over he heard him call, "Fellers? Where are you, fellers? Here, fellers!"

Through most of a day, Seth Michaels searched the forests and meadows, looking for his fellers. It was only when dusk deepened the shadows on the land and nightfall threatened to catch him out, far from home, that he turned wearily and headed for Harrod's.

The walk home was the longest, loneliest walk of his life.

XVII

From the village where Ganasini was chief, the young men went out with their bows and stout arrows, their knives and their clubs, their heads wrapped for war, and provisions on their backs for a long march. They went with bellies purified by the black drink, the words of shamen to guide them, and the intention never to return. Goga the Crow led them, and Goga was in agreement with the old chief and all of the others who had counselled in the longhouse upon Edahi's return. No man could tell them they must not go, nor tell them what they might or might not do. But the people of the five tribes who held Ganasini—called Gone Seen by the white men—as their principal chief were at present in a state of peace with the Carolina leaders. Treaties were being made and it was best that nothing interfere.

Goga agreed, and those who chose to follow him agreed as well. Going into the dark land to seek out the one called Tenkiller meant that they could not return to the five tribes of the *Aniyunwiya*. To do so would be to invite the vengeance of the Kentuckians and their mountain neighbors to the south.

Among themselves, the young warriors agreed. They would go into the dark land to avenge Goga's brother. Then they would go west and try to find the sixth tribe. Nicolet had no peace with the white people. They would be welcome where Nicolet was.

They went out and Ganasini watched them go, and in the heart of the chief was a great longing. Had he not been principal chief, he would have gone with them.

Kentucky, the white men called the land beyond the mountains. But to Ganasini and all the rest of the *Aniyunwiya,* whom others called Tsalagi or Cherokee, it was the dark and bloody ground. In times so ancient that only the legends remained, it had been home to their ancestors.

They had come from an island, they said, in a time when the earth trembled. They had crossed a sea in boats and come to a new land, and had followed the seashore northward until the land was as wide as the path of the sun in its heaven. Then they had turned east. They had settled many times in many places, building their cities and their mounds, and each time had come the generation that moved on, ever eastward, until they reached a land so fair that it was home to them for a long time. It was a land where no one had ever lived before, and it was their land.

But then came others. They came from the west in great numbers, and for many seasons they fought the people on their land until a time came when they shared the land, the people—the real people—on the south of it, and the others who had many names on the north.

The people learned new ways from some of them and mingled with them when they were at peace, and a time came when the *Aniyunwiya* thought of those to the north as neighbors while they in turn thought of the *Aniyunwiya* as "the other Iroquois" or as the Southern Iroquois.

But then still others came from the west in great number, the *Sawani* whom some called "Popos," along with their cousins. And in a time of great turmoil the Iroquois and the *Sawani,* or Shawnee, made war upon the *Aniyunwiya.* So long and fierce was the war that all the land was stained with the blood of the dead, and so it had its name—the Dark and Bloody Ground. They fought until the "true people" were driven south into the mountains and their enemies were driven north across the river Oha'i-yo. And those became the forest tribes, with some allied ones as well. Then the dark lands between became only a shared hunting ground and no people lived there, and the ages passed that way.

Yet still the *Aniyunwiya* remembered. It had once been their home.

Ganasini wondered how that land had been so many times ago—before the white savages came to it, before the long wars, before the coming of the short people from the west. How had it been for his grandfathers' grandfathers, when the dark land had been the bright land and only true people had roamed its hills?

The New World, the white man called this land. Ganasini had been to their old world. When he was very young he had gone with the chiefs of the seven tribes to cross the ocean on a white man's ship. They had spent two seasons in the city of London. He recalled some of the party enjoying the visit so much that they became ill, but he had not enjoyed it at all. Never had he seen such filth.

The old world of the white men was poor and ugly and scarred beyond belief, but Ganasini knew it was not old . . . not like the Dark and Bloody Ground was old. The white men only *thought* that the land across the ocean was old and this one here was new . . . because they were ignorant.

Ganasini saw the young men go out, proud warriors seeking honor, and his heart went with them. He would have gone, too, if he could.

And beside him old Kitsicum the Hatasi leaned on his walking stick and looked beyond, where the mists of distance obscured the horizons, and he too was thinking of old times, though not so long ago. Once, out there, he had befriended a white man. And though so much had happened since that time, though the white men's wars

193

had driven him from his own people to live out his life as shaman among the tall Tsalagi, still he did not regret that day. He had learned from Hasana Ferris that the white man, however strange his ways or violent his disposition, was yet as human as anyone else.

Ellie Ferris went with her mother to watch the hunters leave, six men mounted on splendid fresh horses with a line of other mounts behind them bearing pack saddles. Matched horses for mismatched men, she thought. An odd assortment they were, with two blustery old men as different as any pair could be, the squire square and sturdy and dour, Crispin Blount long and awkward and boisterous. Then came Jason Cook just behind them, sitting his horse the way a monkey might cling to a swinging barrel, Captain Matthew Post elegant in his saddle, favoring his outthrust crippled leg, and Mr. Sparrow, powerful shoulders stretching his buckskin coat, leading the way. Such a company to venture forth into the wild lands to the north. The words pleased her and she sang them in a hushed voice, putting a little tune to them as Crispin often did when a turn of phrase pleased him. "Such a company ventures forth," she repeated, "into the wild lands to the north." She thought about it for a moment and added, "And let the birds and beasts beware if any such be waiting there."

Nora pursed her lips in mock horror. "Sometimes you sound just like Crispin," she said.

"Will they stop to visit Luther and Kate?"

"They intend to, before they return. But they'll be in no hurry about it. The squire says he wants to look at some stone markers first, and of course they'll be hunting along the way. Though I expect all of that is just an excuse to go. What they really want to do is go charging about through the forest on those horses, and sit around campfires and argue and swear, and sleep on the hard ground and become so filthy that their whiskers will stand out like pennants in a wind."

"Why would they want to do that?"

"Because they are men."

"I can't imagine Captain Post becoming filthy. I can't even imagine him with a soiled collar."

"Well," Nora admitted, "maybe not Captain Post. But the rest of them will."

"I wonder if Christopher will be back this season. The captain said he has finished the forms at his school."

Nora shrugged. "That young man does as he pleases. There is no accounting for him." Nonetheless, she glanced again at her daughter, suddenly concerned. "Are you . . . interested in Christopher, Ellie?"

The girl hesitated, and Nora noticed again how her daughter had flowered . . . so suddenly, it seemed. She had been a little girl. Just so recently, she had still been a child. But she was no child now. Abruptly, Nora recalled that she had been only sixteen when she was married to Jonathan Ferris. Ellie was fifteen now.

Ellie shook her head. "I don't know, mother. Sometimes I think about when he came to call last summer. It's just that I don't know anything about him. He's . . . well, he's so different from anyone else I know. Sometimes I think he is given to moods, and then I think he just isn't like the rest of us. He wants . . . I don't know what he wants, really, except that he spoke of the Spanish lands and was like a huntsman talking about a bear. He frightens me . . . sometimes."

"You know Seth Michaels simply adores you, Ellie."

"Seth is a good friend, mother. That's all. We're just friends."

Nora put a hand to her chin thoughtfully. "I wonder if he knows that."

They walked back to the house. The Negro girl, Hattie, was already there, busy with broom and bucket. Hattie was the property of Squire Trelawney, but the squire

195

permitted her to tend house for Nora two days each week, for wages. The money, as Ellie understood it, was hers to keep.

Ellie was in the sitting room, carding dark buffalo wool by the window, when she saw Seth pass on the high road, his gun on his shoulder and his fellers pacing him aflank. He had said he planned to look for spring geese this day, but he was off to a late start for it. The sun was already in the sky. He went by, then paused to look back, as though he could see her there at the window. But she knew he couldn't, unless he saw motion in the shadows. She started to wave at him, then changed her mind and sat still until he turned away. What her mother had said puzzled her. Did he feel more than friendship? She wasn't at all sure that would be pleasant if he did. She could hardly recall a time when Seth hadn't been her best friend. If that were to change . . . She put the thought away for another time and hummed a tune to the rhythm of her fingers working the wool. Such a company ventures forth . . . the words mingled with the tune and made her smile. Such a company ventures forth into the wild lands to the north . . . so let the birds and beasts beware if any such be waiting there.

When she glanced out again, Seth and his dogs were small figures in the distance, passing the far out-lots. Had she ever seen Seth without his fellers? She couldn't remember. They were always together. The dogs were as much a part of him as were his arms, it seemed.

Seth and his fellers, she thought. Seth and his fellers venture there . . . and geese for the pot await somewhere . . . such common sights does God arrange . . . Ellie's fingers went still on the wool and she blinked. Suddenly there was a tightness in her throat, as though a sadness had lodged there, a sadness that was in the words that presented themselves to her to complete the rhyme. Such common sights does God arrange . . . why is it, then, that things must change?

196

She wished such thoughts had waited until another time, when Crispin Blount was back from his adventure. She lacked the tall man's skill at coating hard words with merriment.

She turned her thoughts away to Luther and Kate instead. Not since the thaw had they been back to visit, and she missed them. Somehow, it seemed, there had always been a special closeness between her brother and herself. Though they were seldom together nowadays, still when they were it was as though Luther had never been away. She teased him fondly and he smiled when she did, and between them they could always make Kate laugh.

The thought of it brightened her spirit. She studied them one by one in her mind, Luther so strong and solid, so sure in many ways yet uncertain in others . . . Kate beside him, as she always was, the bond between them so strong that it seemed sometimes a person could see it there. And little Jonathan, strong and stocky, looking at his world with eyes that would puzzle things out and deal with them as they came along. A sturdy little boy, full of inquisitive mischief. And the baby, Michael, a slighter child than Jonathan had been and sometimes colicky, but so special in his own way—bright and alert in his cradle, and with eyes that were the image of Kate's.

She wished she had sent a letter with Crispin. She had thought about it but hadn't made the time to write. But Crispin would convey their good wishes, of course. And anyway, Luther had said they would be coming back to town after he had his fields planted. He was planning a new shed for his cows and would need ironwork to make it as he wanted.

It was noon when she heard the bell out at the Bowman loft, then saw the Bowman twins running up the road. Someone was coming in, from the pass. She put down her work and went out to the porch. In the distance were riders and pack animals, just rounding the creek bend. A

197

large party this time, a dozen or more. And one of them was Julie's friend, the pale-eyed woodsman Leander Haynes.

It was Jarod Cole's misfortune to have left the undermountain country the day he did—even the hour he did—on his return to Kentucky. He had tarried for a while at Callan's Crossing, persuading Caleb Becker's servant girl to permit him favors, and so had missed the chance to travel with a party. Stephen Moliere had invited anyone who wished company through the gap to join him. But Jarod had stayed around for a few more days. He had thought that Colin McLeod would join him and they could ride back together. But McLeod didn't arrive, and Piney Sullivan had decided to go on to Williamsburg with the post rider. So after a few days on the Yadkin, Jarod set off alone.

He was a trail-wise and wary man, one who had put in a good bit of time in the wild country, and from the time Callan's Crossing was behind him he rode alert and cautious, taking no chances.

At the head of the gap, where the trail wound alongside the Cumberland River between rising shoulders of bright clay, he met travelers coming the other way, a party of traders from Boonesborough taking hides to market. The trail was "clear as ever was," they assured him. No Indian sign at all, not even on the Warriors Path.

"A mite early, I allow," one said, and Jarod agreed. Generally, there would be a few redskins creeping through Kaintuck in the spring—Cherokees or an occasional Creek hunting party going north, or sometimes a handful of Delaware southbound, but nowadays a large band anywhere along the eastern ridges was unlikely.

"They done learned their lessons," some said. "Don't 'spect th' tribes are fixin' to fool with Kentuckians anymore." And there was reason behind the assumption.

There had been no real Indian trouble this side of the Green for a long time. Three or four years, as anybody could recall. Oh, a skirmish now and then, two or three sneaking redskins flushed from cover by a hunting party, and sometimes they fought. But more often they ran away.

Kentucky, some felt, was becoming almost peaceful.

Jarod Cole knew better. It paid to be cautious, and he would stay that way. If a man knew the back lands and kept his eyes open, he could get by. If not, then that was just bad luck.

Jarod Cole's luck went bad two days later, a day west of the gap and within sight of the Warriors Road fork. He hadn't seen the warriors there, but they had seen him coming and when he did see them it was too late. Before he could even raise his rifle, an arrow pierced his throat and another went into his chest. As he pitched from his saddle two more struck him, cutting off the scream that was bubbling in his ruined throat. He lit on his back on the hard ground, and the arrow in his back was driven through his heart.

A dozen young warriors gathered around him there, and Goga the Crow peered closely at his face. "This is not Tenkiller," he said.

"Tenkiller is out there." Edahi pointed northward. "Chula is following him so that we can find him. Chula will mark the way."

"Put this one on his horse and tie him there," Goga said. "Then set the horse free."

"When he is found the white men will know we are here," Edahi pointed out.

"It will not matter," Goga said. "The ones who seek us will be behind us. We will move faster than they can spread the word. If Chula has found Tenkiller, then we will avenge our people. If we do not find Tenkiller, we will go away. Either way it does not matter. From this place, we are at war. Let us proceed as warriors."

The Adventurer

XVIII

On his eighteenth birthday Christopher Post stood for examination in general sciences at Sibley Academy on the outskirts of Boston. Headmaster John Wesley Nesbitt and a hearing board of four senior facultymen tested him on mathematics, elocution, logic, and the literary arts, and pronounced him learned. Then, as was his custom, Headmaster Nesbitt invited the young man to deliver a brief discourse on modern philosophy. "Please be brief, young sir," he instructed him. "We require only a measure of your perceptions, not a dissertation."

Christopher nodded and stood, facing them. "I shall be very brief, sir. It has become customary, I understand, to expostulate on the proper courses for the regulating and governing of a newly independent nation. I have little interest in those affairs. The Continental Congress will draft and the commonwealths will ratify a document that will be the basis of government of this confederacy, and whether the confederacy succeeds or fails then is a matter beyond my control. My concern, for my own reasons, is in how the commonwealths determine to deal with their western territories. At present, the northern colonies are willing to cede their territories to the control of a national government of some sort, while the southern colonies have no such intention . . ."

"We know all that," Nesbitt interrupted. "What we question—since such is your chosen subject—are your own feelings on the matter."

"Yes, sir. My feeling is that regulation of the western territories by a central government would virtually assure an orderly, systematic development of those lands, with the expansion of settlement there limited by the designs of treaties and land acts."

"You favor such, then."

"No, sir, I do not. Orderly expansion will breed a tame and manageable populace in those lands, and almost certainly will preclude our ever expanding beyond the Mississippi River."

The teachers glanced at one another in dismay. Nesbitt frowned his disapproval. "Young sir, I am disappointed. You should know that our nation has no ambitions in that direction. Only a handful of firebrands have ever even suggested such."

"Our nation may not have such plans," Christopher said, "but I do. Are we discussing our nation's philosophies . . . or mine?"

Nesbitt eased back into his chair. "Yours, of course. I stand corrected. Whatever this academy can do toward properly molding you, young sir, it has already done. The purpose of this discourse is for us to understand what the result has been."

"Yes, sir. Then understand this. I came here to learn, not to be molded. I have achieved what I came for."

"And obviously not a whit more," Dr. Thaddeus Reed grunted.

Nesbitt hushed him and sighed. "Nor a whit less, Doctor," he said. "Refer to the gentleman's marks." To Christopher he said, "I have a question then, regarding relativity. On the one hand you espouse some sort of personal . . . ah . . . incursion into lands not governed by your government. Yet on the other hand you espouse the permitting of unfettered and chaotic population in our western territories. Can you make us see a con-

201

nection there?"

"I think so, sir. I feel that westward expansion, whether or not the people we send to Philadelphia will it, is inevitable. It will occur, and it will not be the result of some grand plan played out on a treaty table. It will be spontaneous and chaotic, and the role of government will be to ratify it after the fact and clean up the mess as best it can."

"Barbarian thinking," Reed grumbled.

"But why," Nesbitt persisted, "do you favor the festering of howling mobs in the territories?"

"Because it will not be the landed gentry of the seaboard who bring about expansion, sir. It will be those howling mobs, as you put it." He paused, lowered his head in thought, then raised it again, his dark eyes flashing like black agate. "Consider it thusly, sir: Had Attila had an army of shipping clerks at his back, we would still be subjects of Rome."

When the examination was ended and he had gone, Dr. Reed turned to Nesbitt and shook his head. "If Christopher Post is what this land will breed, then by the Lord I would wish that we had lost our revolution."

The headmaster sat in deep thought, his eyes focused on distances beyond the shadowed chamber. "I don't know," he admitted. "What we have won here will not go untested. I think the British will be back, when they have the leisure to retake what they have momentarily lost. Possibly we will have need of the like of Christopher Post one day."

"I do not care for the young man," Reed said. "His ambitions are beyond my comprehension."

A cold smile played across Nesbitt's lips, then was gone. "I wonder," he sighed, "whether in fact we have just interviewed Attila."

From Sibley Academy, Christopher Post went to his family's solicitors on Beacon Hill and had the bequests held in trust for him audited and presented. The trust had been until he turned eighteen. He was now eighteen. He had the proper documents drawn and signed, then registered them, and in that act took control of his own fortunes. Almost as an afterthought, he had a letter drafted in his presence, citing the agreements of principle between the commonwealths of Massachusetts and Virginia and naming himself as executor for certain Massachusetts investors interested in mineral exploration in the "territories to the west of Virginia." The "investors" were his own trusts, though that was not clarified.

Spring breezes were on the hills above the bay. As the packet glided southward on waters brushed flat by the same offshore winds that filled its sails, Christopher stood at the stern rail and watched the shoreline creep past. Ahead, over the midships benches of the launch, a canopy had been rigged and two ladies sat beneath it, one of near his own age, the other older. Now and then he felt the young woman's eyes on him, and once he turned abruptly to catch her startled gaze. Large, lustrous eyes nearly as dark as his own held his for a moment, eyes wide-set in a heart-shaped face framed by dark curls and partly hidden by a heavy veil falling from one side of her bonnet. Christopher smiled to himself. He had purchased passenger lists and other information in Boston. He had planned carefully to be on *this* particular boat.

The harbors and coves along the rough shore showed the effects of the war. Here and there abandoned hulks of battered warships stood at their hawsers, some afloat, some partially submerged. Yet among them were the lofts and towers of industry—foundries, shipyards, casting plants, and ironworks shouldered among stores and warehouses, sheds and mills. Yet it had changed in the past year, since he had last seen it. There was not the bustle of activity everywhere now. Many of the stacks were cold, and everywhere there were buildings boarded up. Gangs of men stood along quays, or walked the waterfronts or fished at the docks.

Spoils of war, he thought. The ravages of revolution side by side with the ventures of feverish investment—and now both stilled by the onslaught of numbing peace.

The men there had been employed by war and by the making of weapons. Now there was little employment. The Admiralty's white fleet was withdrawn to more pressing engagements in other wars, and the privateers had returned to the hauling of goods or to the slave-and-sugar lanes. The little American fleet, though still commissioned, was consigned to coastal patrol. And nobody was buying ships or guns now. The new nation's fresh-hatched war economy was floundering.

Those men there—he studied a distant group gathered outside a tavern—without employment would move on. They, and untold thousands of others like them. But where could they go? See how they face the sea, he thought. This is their nation now, and they know not what to do with it. They stand and look out to the sea . . . toward England. Like dogs who have broken their leashes and rid themselves of their masters, and now stand bewildered by the lack of them. And just beyond them is the nation they have won, a tattered thread of civilization thrown up on a hostile shore and simply clinging there, waiting for another wave to come and carry it away again.

Turn around, he wanted to say to them. Turn and look the other way. When the fledgling leaves the nest it must fly or fall. Turn around. There is what you've won, there behind you. A huge land is there for the taking. Have you been so long bound by foreign chains that you don't know what to do with your freedom?

They would learn. Necessity would require it. Without employment, they would go the only direction that was left to them to go. They looked eastward, out to sea, yet westward was where the future lay.

A hand tugged at his sleeve and he whirled around. It was the packet's choreboy, a grimy-faced urchin with a saber scar across his freckled cheek. "Beg par'n, sir. Th' lady yon asks, be ye ill?"

"My health is excellent, thank you," he said loudly enough for the women beyond to hear. Both of them were turned now, looking toward him. The younger might have been a beauty but for a strawberry stigma emblazoned on her cheek. "Pray thank the ladies," he told the boy. "But I am in good health. I was only distracted."

The boy glanced back, then leaned toward him. "Th' young lady, sor . . . she said ye may ha' a fever, ye looked that grim. She e'en ast Cap'n f' yer name."

"And did he tell her?" Christopher answered the whisper with a whisper.

"Aye, sor. He did. Christ'er Pos', 'e said. O' Virginia."

"Then I believe the ladies have the advantage of me." He found a halfpenny and handed it to the boy, then strode past him and bowed soberly toward the open canopy. "Ladies, your concern is appreciated. Christopher Post, in fine health and at your service." The blush on the younger one's face was satisfying. Her veil covered the birthmark on her cheek.

"We . . . ah . . . I was afraid you might have a sickness," the matron said. "These small craft, they do rock so at times."

"Not more than a spirited horse, mistress"—he turned his gaze to the young one—"or the laughing eyes of a lovely lady."

Again her color heightened, and she put a small fist to her lips to cover a smile. "I believe it's true then," she said. "You must be from the South."

"Virginia, miss, though from Boston originally. And you?"

The older one intervened. "I am Mary Chase. My husband is Clayton Chase, a member of the Virginia assembly. This is my daughter, Elizabeth. If you'd care to join us here, there is room."

He hesitated. "Chase? Colonel Chase is your husband?"

"Yes. We are on our way home from Boston. Please, Mr. Post, do be seated."

He joined them beneath the canopy, stifling a smile. Destiny was what one made it be, he thought. More than anyone except Patrick Henry and Thomas Jefferson, Clayton Chase controlled the destiny of the Virginia territories. Any man who had the authority to designate civil militias was the hand of destiny itself.

"It would please me greatly," he told the ladies, "if you would accept my services as escort until we reach Williamsburg."

"Do you have family in Williamsburg, Mr. Post? I don't recall the name there."

"Only a few acquaintances, mistress. My father is an associate of Squire Joseph Trelawney, in Kentucky. I've been away to school."

"Squire Trelawney. Yes, of course. Why, I believe an escort would be a comfort, don't you, Elizabeth?"

"I would be very pleased," the girl said.

As the packet put out for New Bedford, where passengers would board a larger vessel for the voyage to the Chesapeake ports, Mary Chase studied the young man at leisure and plied him with deft questions. Though she had not heard the name Post among her Virginia circles, she was well acquainted with it from her friends in Boston. Matthew Post was the second son of a family that had done well for itself. An adventurer, they said of Matthew Post. He had gone to Pennsylvania, then down the Ohio with a band of adventurers that had come to a violent end somewhere in the Spanish wilderness to the west. He had survived to return to Boston, had made a good marriage and fathered a son. Then his wife had died of fever and he had gone off again, this time to Virginia.

A man of high dreams and misfortunes, breeding first-rate horses now, somewhere in the overmountain lands.

In Christopher Post, the son, Mary Chase found qualities that she recognized and understood. Bred to the use of wealth and power, Christopher Post carried in him

206

the quality his father most lacked. That quality was ambition. Mary Chase approved of ambition.

It surprised her to learn that the young man was just eighteen. She had taken him to be older. Still, age was what one made of it.

For his part, Christopher was fully aware of the scrutiny of Mistress Chase and guessed at its source. The daughter, Elizabeth, was nearly twenty years old and still unmarried. Something to do with a young officer lost at sea, they indicated. And perhaps more to do with the unfortunate stigma on her face, he thought. The mother was scouting and probably viewed every young man of means as a candidate.

At mid morning they bore east from Plymouth to skirt Cape Cod with the wind astern. The little ship rose on long swells and sheeted water from its bows to glisten in the sunlight. Little rainbows appeared each time a swell was crested and Christopher pointed out how they danced there, as if by magic.

"I've need to stretch my legs a bit," he said, standing. "Miss Chase, have you ever seen the waters curl beneath the keel of a vessel? Sometimes the sheets at the prow look like bolts of woven silk."

"I am sure I've never seen such a thing," she admitted.

"Then perhaps you would like to stroll forward with me now and test my description of it." He offered his arm. She smiled, stood, and took it.

Mary Chase watched them go. They might be well matched, she thought. And somehow Elizabeth did not seem so shy, so nervous and withdrawn, in the presence of Christopher Post as she did with most young men. Has she overcome her embarrassment, she wondered, or is it this particular young man?

Well, there would be time to observe him more. They would be several days in the passage from New Bedford to Chesapeake. She would know more about him by then. And once in Williamsburg, should there seem to be reason for it, she could learn a great deal in a short time

207

about Christopher Post. She was fairly sure that the young gentleman was not exactly what he seemed to be. The question was, then, was he less or was he more?

No matter how ambitious, very young men were inexperienced in matters of the heart and therefore slow in their progress. She would have plenty of time to decide at leisure whether Master Christopher Post might be a suitable match for Elizabeth.

At New Bedford, after laying over for a day, they boarded the three-master *Sotheby* along with nearly sixty other passengers, most of them displaced men seeking employment or adventure in the southerly commonwealths—Virginia or the Carolinas. With a crew of thirty-three, *Sotheby* was limited to four passenger cabins. The rest must seek space on the deck or in the crowded holds. The Chase ladies had one cabin, by advance registration. Christopher Post paid coin to a Baltimore trader for the one next to it. That same afternoon, as *Sotheby* rounded off Montauk for its run down the coast, Christopher put on a spotless linen shirt with folded cravat, his gray weskit and black coat, white breeches, polished boots, and black tricorn hat. He dropped a bag of coin into one tail pocket and a primed pistol into the other, and buckled on the gold-hilted saber he had won at Sibley. Then he rapped at the sill of the next cubicle. When Elizabeth opened the portal, he doffed his hat and bowed. "These quarters are stuffy and close," he said. "Come walk with me upon the deck and we'll breathe sea air that does not stink of bilges." Before the mother could object, he added, "And you as well, Mistress Chase. I would be honored."

Accompanied by both ladies, he emerged on the windswept afterdeck and took a deep breath. "Much better," he said. He turned to the deck officer. "My compliments to Captain Rigg, and I wonder if I might have a word with him here on deck."

The junior officer hesitated, then sent a man below. A few minutes later the captain came up and Christopher met him at the ladder. They spoke quietly for a few seconds, then Christopher led the captain back and introduced him. "That seems a comfortable bench, there by the after rail," he added. "It would honor Captain Rigg to sit there for a time with you, Mistress Chase, while Elizabeth and I stroll the deck."

Mary Chase was startled. "There are so many men there," she faltered. "They seem . . . rough men for the most part."

"Sturdy lads." Christopher smiled. "I might find I have business with a few among them. We shall be back directly." With Elizabeth's arm firmly fixed in his, he circled forward, leaving the captain to attend to Mary Chase.

Elizabeth giggled. "My mother is not accustomed to being so adroitly manipulated," she said.

"I doubt it happens often." He shrugged. "I expect it is usually the other way around."

She looked up at him, puzzled. "Almost always," she admitted.

The deck was crowded with men, both passengers and crew. One group, apart and wary, he identified by various items of clothing among them. They had all been British marines. Were they paroled, he wondered, with their pay in their purses, or had they deserted and stolen the fare to make their way south? With Elizabeth at his side, he turned to them and spoke to the strongest-looking among them. "Are you men seeking employment?"

"What be that to you?" the man sneered, then turned to leer at Elizabeth.

"Address me, if you will," Christopher said mildly. "It was I who asked the question, and the lady is not here for your pleasure."

The man's shoulders tightened and his eyes narrowed. Some of the others, behind him, grinned.

"I asked a civil question," Christopher said coldly. "Answer it now."

"I don't answer popinjays, sonny, an' that sword at yer

209

belt makes no difference to me." He raised a big fist and grinned.

"I don't need a sword." Christopher loosed Elizabeth's arm and eased her back away from him. Around them, crew and passengers watched, hoping for a bit of entertainment. "Either use those hands, deck-monkey, or answer my question."

With a hiss, the man swung at him. Hardly seeming to move, Christopher slid aside, then stepped in close to beat hard knuckles into the fellow's breadbasket. As the man doubled over, he brought both fists down hard on the back of his neck. The man sagged and sprawled on the deck. It had lasted only a second. Christopher put a foot on the fallen man's back and looked at the rest. "My question was, are you men seeking employment?"

"That we be," one of them nodded, wide-eyed.

Christopher pulled out a few coins and handed them to him. "This will buy you food and a bed at Williamsburg," he said. "Bide one week's time as you will, then look for me at the wellhouse square. If I need men as I expect, then I shall sign you on."

The man looked at the coins, at his companions, then at Christopher again. "We'll think on it. Who do we ask for at th' square . . . should we decide to?"

"Christopher Post," he told them. "*Captain* Christopher Post."

Without a further glance he turned away, took Elizabeth's arm, and resumed his stroll. Her eyes were huge as she glanced back, where the burly ex-marine was just being helped to his feet. "You did that intentionally," she said.

"Of course. Such men wouldn't think of following a person as young as I am unless they are shown that age has no significance."

"But—but you said *Captain*. Do you have such a title, Christopher?"

"Not at the moment. But I will. And a wife as well, if she'll accept me."

210

"A—a wife?"

They arrived at the midships cable shrouds and he cleared space for them with a look. Every man on deck had seen the burly marine fall. When they were alone at the shrouds he took her shoulders in his hands. "I'll not court you slowly, Elizabeth, nor build for you a castle of little lies to entrap and win you. Such is not my way, and I've no time for it. If you will marry me, Elizabeth, I shall make of you an empress or a widow. And either way, I promise you, you will never have cause to regret."

She stared up at him, openmouthed, her scarf falling away.

"A season past," he said, "we were all subjects of the British Empire. A season hence we may again be subjects, whether of the Crown or of something of our own device. But this season now is mine, Elizabeth. And yours if you will share it with me. Never has there been such an opportunity to reshape a land and make of it what we will. I do not intend to let such opportunity pass."

She licked her lips, unable to move, hardly able to speak. "But, Christopher, I . . . how can I know . . . I have not thought of . . ."

"How can anyone know, Elizabeth? When does one know? Ever? I know only one thing. On this day I live and the world is mine to take—as much of it as I can manage. Tomorrow? . . . I don't know what tomorrow is, Elizabeth. Nor do you. So why waste today wondering about it?"

"Christopher, I have to think about it. I must . . . oh, mercy! I have to have time to think! Please? . . ."

He smiled and nodded. "Of course. Think about it, do. But don't think too long, Elizabeth. I have no use for tomorrows."

Many of the men on deck were within earshot, but he ignored them. Elizabeth turned away, looking out to sea. Fifty feet away on the afterdeck Mary Chase was trying to listen to the captain's conversation and keep an eye on her daughter at the same time.

211

After a few minutes Elizabeth turned to him again. The startlement and confusion were gone from her eyes. Now there were only questions. "Christopher, why did the captain of the ship do your bidding?"

"I paid him," he said. "Before we sailed, I bought a favor from him. I needed this time with you. He provided it."

"That was deliberate, too, then."

"Yes."

"I see. When did you decide that you wanted me, then?"

He had no hesitation. "When I learned who you are."

"When you learned who my father is?"

"Yes. I find you attractive, Elizabeth. But many women are attractive. Your father has power in Virginia. Virginia controls the West and the West is the gateway to New Spain."

"The land you seek . . . is that where it is?"

"Yes. There are empires to be had, Elizabeth. My father saw them, but he lacked the ambition to pursue them. I have that ambition."

"That's what you meant . . . that I'd be an empress or a widow."

"Yes."

"Do you expect me to love you, Christopher?"

"Only if you choose to."

"Then it would be a marriage of convenience?"

"Of course. You need a husband, Elizabeth. My name will be your freedom and my fortune your security. And I'll make no demand that you be a wife."

"Where would I live . . . as your wife?"

"In Williamsburg or in Kentucky, as you choose. With a house and servants. With whatever you need."

"And no demands."

"One only . . . that you support me in what I ask of your father."

"And what will that be?"

"I have a request for commission. He can grant that.

212

And he can grant me discretion in how I use it."

"How will you use it?"

He glanced around then. "There are too many ears here, Elizabeth. Including yours . . . until you are my wife."

They returned to the afterdeck and Christopher stood before Mary Chase. "I have asked Elizabeth to marry me," he said. "I would like your blessing, Mistress Chase. But Elizabeth's answer will suffice."

Later, in the privacy of a tiny cabin below deck, they talked at length. Christopher told them what he would and Mary Chase guessed at the rest. "You intend to enter New Spain before any treaties can be arranged between Spain and the united colonies," she said. "And you want a commission at discretion so that there is no question of treason against the Virginia colony."

He grinned and his dark eyes studied the older woman with respect. "I offer your daughter . . . and her family . . . a share in the venture. But time is critical."

"It is a business arrangement."

"It is."

"And my husband's influence . . ."

". . . will diminish when the Continental Congress reaches a decision on union of the commonwealths. I offer him the chance to rise rather than fall."

She shook her head, trying to remind herself that this man was hardly more than a boy, that he was the same age Clayton Chase had been when he followed George Washington to Fort Duquesne and won his field captaincy. "You are audacious," she said. "What do you hope to gain?"

"Wealth and power, mistress. What else does anyone seek?"

"By personal invasion of the dominions of a foreign power?"

"It will not be an uncommon thing. New Spain is there and ripe for the taking, and everyone knows it who considers such things. I will not be the only one to try it.

There will be many. I do, though, intend to be the first."

Christopher Post and Elizabeth Chase were married at sea, one day out from Chesapeake, by Captain Hosiah Rigg. It was Mary Chase's suggestion. Things would go more smoothly if her husband were presented with an established fact when they arrived at Williamsburg.

The Dark and Bloody Ground

XIX

Leander Haynes put away his horse and trappings, then went straight to Julie's. She was elbow-deep in flour, smelled of sunshine and fresh bread, and was in all ways about the prettiest sight he had ever seen. He pulled off his coonskin cap and gazed at her as she wiped the flour from her hands. But as usual he held his tongue, except to say, "How do, Julie? I'm back from the Yadkin."

"I can surely see that you are, Leander. Well, don't just stand there gawking. Come in and sit, and I'll put water on the fire to boil. Squire had some fresh tea sent over and I got a bit of it."

He came in and sat, quiet and inscrutable as always but never taking his eyes from her. And as always, she wondered what sort of thoughts were in his mind that haunted him so. As she got the kettle hung and a flame scraped up under it, he said, "I won't be but a day or so this trip. I'm goin' on up to the river, scoutin' for hire."

"Oh?" She got out tea leaves and crushed them into the strainer. "The people you came in with?"

"Part of 'em. Feller named Moliere got a notion about buildin' broad-horn boats an' floatin' cargo down to New Orleans to sell. I said I'd see him settled in up yonder."

"I hope you will be very careful, Leander. They say there has been Indian trouble up there again. I've been worried about Kate and Luther. They are so isolated

215

where they are."

"No need to worry about Luther defendin' his place," he said. "He's done it afore."

Even as he said it, though, Julie noticed that odd distraction that took him sometimes, a sort of distance that grew in him, a coldness in his pale eyes. Talk of Indians almost always caused it. Of course, he had lost his family to the redman, but that was years ago, and the same had happened to a lot of people back then. Why was it so different for Leander? She had wondered about it often.

"Tell ye what, though," he offered, seeming to shrug off the mood. "Where I'm takin' that bunch mayn't be so far from their place. Happen I can, I'll swing over there an' look in. Meantime, though, there's another man in with th' same bunch. Surveyor name of Dodd, he's lookin' for a place to stow his maps. I said I'd ask around. Anybody hereabouts got spare room these days?"

"Squire Trelawney, I suppose. But he's away. He and Crispin and Jason Cook and some others, they went off to hunt. What does he need?"

"Said he needs a table an' a chair to work at, an' a corner for a map bin."

She glanced around. "Well, how about right here? Mercy, I don't use half the space here for mixing. Mostly I'm out with the ovens. How long does he need it for?"

"A spell, I reckon. He says where he puts his map is a land office. Can a bakery be a land office, too?"

"I don't see why not. Tell him to come by."

"I will. How much do you want him to pay?"

She blinked, surprised at the thought of receiving rents. "He can pay?"

"Reckon he can. He's got a contract from th' commonwealth. Ye'll prob'ly get shinplasters instead o' coin, but no sense not takin' what's offered."

"No sense at all." Her mind was turning over the idea of another source of income. It would be well to have a little something to put aside. Leander had hinted a time

216

or two that his income from furs, scouting, and whatnot was being stowed away . . . toward the purchase of a claim, she thought. She'd had the notion that it was such a goal that kept him always distant when their talk veered toward the two of them. She felt close to Leander, drawn to him even, but there were those strange parts of him that she didn't understand. Possibly this was one of them, some sort of a pride that wouldn't allow him to talk man-talk to a woman until he had a place to offer her. Men could be peculiar that way.

When the water boiled she poured tea and they sat at her mixing table. That distant, odd mood had come over Leander again, and he seemed preoccupied with his own thoughts.

"Tell me what ye heard about Indian trouble," he said.

"Not very much, just the talk at market. They said some people are settling over across the Ohio and the Indians don't like it, and sometimes they cross the river and bother people on this side."

"Well, I'd heard that much." He shrugged. "I wonder who might know where they cross over when they come."

"I don't know. Jason Cook said he heard about it from Colin McLeod. Maybe he knows."

He looked up from his tea. His eyes reminded her of ice on a still pond. "Colin been around lately?"

"Now and again. Why are you so interested in the Indians, Leander?"

He was silent for a moment, as someone whose thoughts are far away. Again she felt the dark strangeness of him, like a fearsome presence just behind his eyes, an awful, brooding violence barely held in check.

"No reason," he said finally. "'Cept if I'm to scout a mess o' frontlanders up thereabouts, I'd like to know where to watch out for."

She took a deep breath, squared her shoulders, and looked straight into his eyes. "Do you care for me, Leander?"

217

The question caught him off guard. He blinked and fumbled for words. "Why do you ask me that?"

"Because I want to know. Often I think you do, but you never really speak of it and I hardly ever know what you're thinking."

"Julie . . ." He paused and started again. "Julie, it's hard for me to say, an' maybe there's reasons why I should never say it, but I care for you more than I've ever cared for any living soul. Didn't I come back here because of you? Don't I always come here? There's only one reason I'd ever come to this place, Julie. It's because you're here. Maybe I thought you knew that."

"I thought so, but . . . oh, Leander, there are so many things you never say. Things it seems you want to say but just never do, and other things as well. I wait for you to come, and I'm pleasured when you do. But then when we're together your secrets rise up like a fence between us. What is it that torments you, Leander? What is it that you never talk about?"

"Nothin'!" he snapped. "Some things are nobody's business but my own!" The change in him was so abrupt, so violent, that her eyes widened. A chill went through her as though, just for a moment, she had found herself face to face with a stalking beast. Trembling, she stood and turned away.

A moment passed in silence. Then he said, softly, "I'm sorry, Julie. I truly am. I had no call to speak that way to you."

Still facing away, she bit her lip. The sudden violence of him had stunned her. It was not like anything she had ever seen before.

She heard him get to his feet, heard the sorrow in his voice. "I'd best leave, Julie. And if you want me to never come back, I'd understand . . . though without you to come to, there'd be little left in this world for me."

"You frightened me, Leander. Somehow you always frighten me."

He came to her then and turned her with strong, gentle

218

hands. "I'd not frighten you for all the riches on earth, Julie Jackson. There's no one I care for as I care for you, and you'd best know that. Maybe I should have spoken of it long since, but—"

"Maybe you should have," she agreed.

"—but, Julie, don't be frightened. Don't ever be frightened, not of me. I'd never do anything to bring harm to you or to anybody as matters to you. Y'have to know that, Julie."

Before she could respond he drew her to him and kissed her, lingeringly, full on her lips. Then he stepped back and turned his head away, unwilling to meet her eyes. "If that kiss offends ye, Julie, then I apologize for that as well. But for me, I'll cherish that kiss as long as I live, even if I never have another."

He plopped his coonskin cap onto his head, picked up his rifle, and left the cabin without another word. The door swung shut behind him and bounced open again, its drop-bolt uncaught. Julie stood where she was for a moment, her mind a turmoil of surprise, anger, pleasure, and a hundred kinds of doubts, all swirling in confusion. She shook her head and touched her fingers to her lips wonderingly.

From outside then, through the open door, she heard his voice again. He was asking someone where he might find Colin McLeod.

Puzzled and confused, Julie went to close the door.

In mid afternoon she was outside, kneeling before her ovens, when a shadow fell across her. She looked around. The man who stood there was tall and well-groomed, with the robust features of a woodsman though his clothing was of fine cut and fit. She stood, turning, and he doffed his hat. His smile was unabashed, a grin of surprise and appreciation. "Ah . . . Mistress Jackson? Julie Jackson?"

"I am," she said.

"Beg pardon, but I had not expected such a pleasant vision. My name is Dodd, Miss . . . ah, ma'am. Thomas Dodd. I'm a commonwealth surveyor and I've come to

219

see about space for my land office."

Again she made tea, and again she sat across her mixing table from an attractive young man, but there the similarity ended. Thomas Dodd was as cheerful and outgoing as Leander Haynes was moody and secret. His enthusiasm for his work bubbled into his speech, and there was an excitement in his knowledge of land measure, his mastery of rods and chains, of yards and feet and furlongs, of acres and sections and townships . . . a way of looking at the world that seemed to Julie strange and wondrous.

"Forty-three thousand five hundred and sixty square feet make every acre, no matter how it's shaped," he explained when she questioned what it was that he would do. "Sixteen and a half feet are in a rod, so a mile being five thousand two hundred and eighty feet, then a long acre is a rod wide and a half mile long. Public domain should be standard, long acres north and south within square mile sections, six hundred and forty to the section . . . Ah, listen to me prattle on, as though a lovely lady cared for such things! Have a care what you ask of me, mistress. Bright eyes and polite questions set my tongue to running every time."

She blushed. It was almost like talking to Crispin Blount, except that Crispin had never been so handsome. "I only wondered what it would do, such a dividing of the land into little squares. It won't change where the streams flow or where the hills are, or how lie the fields that folks can plant."

"No, it won't change the land," he agreed. "But it will bring order and stability to the ownership of it. But then, it might not ever occur, though it's argued. Range and township isn't the law . . . not yet, anyway. And there are many who oppose it. But that's not my worry. The politicians will decide that. I'll just place some bench marks and squat at my theodolite and put pretty marks on foolscap sheets . . . and be paid for the doing of it just as though it made good sense."

"Squire Trelawney is one who opposes such measure," she said. "Crispin—that's Mr. Blount; I live in their house—Crispin says the squire thinks range and township will ruin him."

"I don't see how." Dodd shrugged. "It won't change what he owns. Though maybe it will change how he is taxed."

Julie noticed abruptly that her tea had become cold and that the room had grown murky. They must have been talking for hours, she realized. With a rueful smile, she got up and lit candles.

Dodd chuckled. "It's how things go, I reckon. By light of day I sit and splendor in a lady's company, then at dusk when the candles glow we must do business. That half of this room would do nicely for my use, if you could let it to me."

"Well, I have no use for it," she said. "All my mixing is done here, by the pantry and the midden. But I have to use this table."

"I can get a table, and anything else I need." He eyed the far end of the room, unfurnished except for a bed that had been left there. It was a good rope bed, but Crispin had built new ones when they moved to the new house.

"I'll only be here from time to time," he said. "But I'll need to stow equipment and charts, and work on them when I am in town. Would that trouble you?"

"Not in the slightest, that I can see."

"And you'll be paid, of course. The commonwealth may skimp on its post routes and the wages for its clerks, but it pays adequately for land offices."

Outside, dusk of evening lay on the town. The faint crackling of ovens cooling came from the midden window, and the room smelled of candles and fresh bread.

"It's done, then?" he asked. "Do we have an agreement?"

"Of course we do. It should work out very well."

He stood, flinching slightly as his head rose to within

221

an inch of the beams. He grinned. "I'll have to remember not to enter with a hat on my head. It isn't a tall house."

He looked down at her and held out his hand. "To amicable arrangements," he said. She took his hand, then abruptly he leaned down and kissed her, a quick peck on the lips. "Pardon, lady," he said, "but somehow I just couldn't resist. It's a rare beauty that you have."

"I . . . it's all right," she said.

"Good. No offense intended, none taken. Now I have let the afternoon pass and have yet to find a place to sleep, so I must go and attend to that. Though at this hour I may wind up in the stable loft."

On impulse, she gestured toward the rope bed in the far corner. "Nonsense," she said. "You've rented the space, you might as well use it. Sleep there."

"You wouldn't mind?"

"I wouldn't mind at all. Consider it your home—that half of it, at any rate."

So this time it was Julie who left and another who stayed at the little house as evening fell upon Harrodsburg. And as she walked along the street, toward the Blount house where Nora and Ellie would have supper waiting, she put her fingers again to her lips and thought of what a strange day it had been. It had been too long a time since she had been kissed, she thought. Yet now she had been kissed twice in one day.

She found the surveyor charming and would be glad for his company on those days when he worked in his "land office." But now her thoughts turned again to the brooding eyes of Leander, and a strange dread hung over her, a dread that had no reason to be there but was there all the same.

XX

Because the weather was fine, Luther took little Jonathan with him to seed the high field. Through the morning Kate could see them out there on the plowed ground, the little boy trudging along with his sack of seed, dropping a few at each step, while Luther came along behind with his hoe, covering the corn.

In autumn they would have a fine crop, she thought. Luther had expanded the field so that it now ran to more than twelve acres. He had two other fields as well, but they were farther away and not visible from the cabin. She had not seen them since Michael's birth, although Luther told her of his progress there. One he had put into wheat, planting in hard ground before the thaw. The other he intended to plant with flax and oats. And of course he would plant other things as well—pumpkins and sweet-roots, turnips and cabbages along the low end where there was the best moisture, peas and onions and other things in the door garden. . . . She smiled a contented smile when she saw Jonathan stop and point back down the row, and Luther shrug, set down his hoe, and go back to get his gun where he had left it leaning against a stump. Jonathan had heard them talk, had heard Luther expound upon the importance of a man keeping his weapon close at hand. Leave it to a four-year-old, Kate thought, to see to it that grown-ups behaved as they should. Luther wore his shot-pouch and powder horn, so they were always at hand. But to use the hoe he had to set down his rifle. And sometimes he neglected to stay close to it.

Michael had been fussy again in the night, but now he cooed and chirped in his cradle, content to fondle the wooden horse Crispin had carved for him. Kate worked on the porch, with the door open so she could keep an eye on him. Michael had discovered that he had hands to pull up with and legs that could push, so there were pelt rugs piled around the cradle. He might throw himself from the cradle as he had done several times, but the fall would do no more than make him angry.

Michael was as different from Jonathan, she thought, as night was from day. Almost since birth he had been given to moods and tantrums, and they had wondered sometimes whether his infant rancor was caused by colic or whether it was the other way around. Sometimes the milk of her breasts had disagreed with him. But at other times not. She still nursed him but he was weaning now, and the porridge and cow's milk were making him grow. And his tempers were more rare now, though still unpredictable.

Pausing at her labors—the churn sometimes made her back ache—she looked toward the high field again. Luther's big dog had come in from the woods and joined them out there, following along behind Jonathan, nosing each seed that he dropped. The dog was a huge beast, shaggy and fierce-looking, its head as high as Jonathan's when they walked together. Luther had bought it from a river family, two years before. But from the day the dog and Jonathan discovered each other there had been no doubt whose dog it really was. It answered to Luther. It adored Jonathan. And Luther's expressed disgust at the situation was a thin mask to hide the pride he felt when he watched them together.

With no more stumps nearby, Luther had fixed a rope sling to his rifle and it hung at his back now, swinging awkwardly as he worked his hoe. In the distance they made a strange parade. Jonathan and the dog could almost have been a sturdy, strapping man and a shaggy horse. If so, then Luther behind them was a burdened giant doing their bidding.

She went back to the churn's plunger, and inside the door Michael howled abruptly. She turned to look. His wooden horse had escaped him. It lay on the pelts outside the cradle and he was up on precarious legs, striving to reach it. His howls were pure outrage.

"Oh, Michael," she muttered. "Have mercy." She went and retrieved his toy and he threw it halfway across the room, still howling.

"You little savage," she told him. "What am I going to do with you?"

She had dried apples on a shelf, and she dipped a slice in honey and held it for him to taste. Abruptly the howls ended as he gnawed at it with new-emerging teeth. Those teeth were one of the reasons he was weaning. Kate had felt the sharpness of them on her nipples more than once. She held the apple slice for him until its honeyed end was a pulp, then she dropped the wooden horse back into his cradle. His temper was gone as quickly as it had come. He dropped to his bottom and started playing with his toy.

Kate stepped out on the porch again and had her hand on the churn when movement caught her eye. She turned, peering westward where the trail led away beyond the barn, into the near woods. Birds were erupting from the trees out there, spiraling upward as something below startled them. It might be the Joneses, she thought, coming from their claim downriver, but then she remembered that the Joneses had boarded up and gone inland two weeks ago.

But someone was out there. More birds rose from the gray mist of the forest tops. Someone was coming this way. She turned toward the field. Luther and Jonathan and the dog were near the top of the rise, going the other way. Setting the churn plunger, she went inside and got down the musket, checking its prime the way Luther had taught her to do. With the gun in hand, she went back out to the porch. There was movement among the trees out there now, but she couldn't identify it. She thought of the talk she had heard, talk of Indians crossing from the treaty lands to prowl the Kentucky side. Farther down, they said, near the mouth of the Green, though the trouble seemed to be because of people settling over on the Scioto, which Luther said was almost straight north.

Again she caught vague movement in the forest. Luther still had not looked back. With a sigh she hauled on the bell rope, calling him in.

In the field Luther dropped his hoe and came at a run, his rifle in one hand and Jonathan in the other. She could tell that he had seen the birds.

He was nearly to the house when riders broke from the trees beyond the barn, a string of them on matched horses. Kate's eyes went wide. Mr. Sparrow led, followed by Crispin Blount, Jason Cook, and others behind.

Luther hurried up to her, still carrying rifle and son. "Well, look who's here!" he puffed. "Look there. I believe that's Squire Trelawney yonder."

"I couldn't see who it was," she said, "so I rang you in."

The dog had run beside him, its dog-eyes not seeing the movement beyond the barn. But now it caught the scent of them and bristled, dancing around on stiff legs, showing its fangs. "Tick!" Luther barked. "Down, boy!"

He set Jonathan on his feet and pointed. "Look'ee yonder, Jonathan. Company's here." The boy looked, then scrambled behind Kate to peer from there. Except for Mr. Sparrow, the party did take some recognizing. Grimy and besplattered, with fur robes over their hunting shirts and pelt caps on their heads, they were a wild-looking bunch of riders. As they neared the barn, Crispin raised Old Yellow Dog in a wave and Mr. Sparrow halloed the house. "We're friendly," he called. "Can we come in?"

226

"Come an' welcome," Luther called back. "The door is open." He handed his rifle to Kate and hurried off to help them with the mounts and their packs. Kate shooed Jonathan into the cabin and followed him. By the time she heard their footsteps approaching, she had a good fire going and pot and kettle hung to heat. Crispin was the first to the door and she met him there, throwing her arms around him. "Mercy, but it's good to see . . ." She backed off abruptly, wrinkling her nose. "Ooo . . . what have you been doing?"

"Huntin', lass." He grinned. "An' I reckon forgettin' to bathe." He turned to the squire. "We been enjoyin' our own company too long."

"Speak for yourself, tinker." Trelawney frowned. "Morning, mistress, and if you'll point us to a trough, we'll get ourselves a bit more presentable before we enter your house."

Of them all, only Captain Matthew Post looked halfway civilized, though Mr. Sparrow seemed clean enough in the way of the practiced woodsman whose home is the outdoors. But one and all, they shooed themselves off to the trough to become presentable. When Luther led them into the cabin an hour later, Kate didn't even order them to wipe their feet.

They had brought haunches of venison to hang in the shed and a field-dressed black bear to render for tallow—though a bear in this season would be a scrawny thing, they admitted. They had packs of smoke-cured turkey and a hundred pounds of jerked buffalo strip, as well as fresh sassafras root and a huge bale of what Mr. Sparrow called "thurleigh shoots."

"Boil these down with honey an' a bit of clove," the woodsman told Kate. "They'll do for peas until the peas come ripe."

"Crispin has been fretting about all the hungry mouths to be fed here"—Trelawney looked at Jonathan and the baby—"until we sort of had the notion that there was an army of you up here. Possibly we were a bit enthusiastic in collecting provisions."

"An' was it me that shot at everything as moved, all the way up here?" Crispin asked him.

"I did no such thing! I took only fair shots!"

"At least *I* hit everything I shot at," Crispin concluded.

At the hearth Kate turned away to hide her grin, and she wondered how Nora was getting along.

Never since coming here with Luther, as his bride, had Kate realized how small the cabin really was. But now it seemed packed to the rafters with men, and she set about serving them refreshments.

They made a meal from her pot and their packs, then most of them went outside with Luther to see to the tending of their game, Jonathan and the dog trailing after them. But Crispin hung back, and when they were alone he sat at the table and filled his pipe, his eyes on the baby in its cradle. "Yon bairn's th' image of ye, Kate. Truly a beautiful boy."

"He can be a problem." She brought tea to the table and sat across from him. "Tell me all the news. We hear so little up here."

His deep eyes twinkled. "News, is it? Well, they say Ben Franklin is havin' himself a lovely time in Paris, though he has taken time from the ladies there to strike an accord wi' th' British envoy. England's prepared to grant independence to th' American commonwealths. Some say we'll go to war amongst ourselves now for th' lack of anything better to do. Th' Continental Congress is back in Philadelphia, squabblin' like so many old maids all tryin' to weave at th' same loom. Tom Jefferson is tryin' to get them to agree on principles o' unity, an' some say there's scarce a one among 'em as knows what either word means. . . ."

"Crispin!"

"Aye?"

"You know what I mean. What is the news?"

He chuckled. "Leave it to women to concern themselves wi' what matters. Well, let's see. . . . Julie's well. Her bakery's flourished so that she'll have to put on servants to tend to it before long. She sees a mite of Leander Haynes when he's about, though I ha' some misgivin's about th' young man myself. Yet she's a woman grown an' must make her own choices."

She shook her head. "Poor Julie. Life's uncertainties seek her out."

"As would every young buck for miles around were they not all a-feared o' Leander Haynes. That sister o' yours is ripe for matchin', Kate. A body wi' eyes can see it."

"And Nora and Ellie? They're well?"

"Well as can be. Do ye recollect th' old song, Kate? Th' wee folks one?"

"Of course I do. I've tried to get Luther to teach it to me."

"Is that so? Well, Ellie's been at me to learn it, an' I believe she knows every word. I believe she adds some to it now and again, as suits her."

"I wonder where she learned such things." She grinned.

"Nora worries herself about th' lot of ye . . . out here in th' wilds an' all. She hears talk of Indian trouble an' it frets her."

"We are all right," Kate said. "Luther has talked with the trader Fosse. . . . Do you know him?"

"Know of him." He nodded. "A good man, they say, for all of bein' a heathen."

"Well, he lives among them. Luther says he has a wife and children at Gnadenhutten."

"Aye. Fosse married a woman of th' *Leni-Lanape*. A rare beauty, they say."

"She has given him six children, Luther says. Fosse has told Luther that we should be safe here. He says the Indians—the Delawares and Wyandots—have put secret signs around our place to protect us. He says even the Shawnee will respect the signs. And all the time we've been here, there's been no trouble. We never even see Indians."

" 'Tis a comfort," he said. "It's th' way o' most redmen to keep their contracts . . . at least until somebody else breaks them first. O' course, there's other Indians besides th' Delaware an' Shawnee and whatnot, an' they might not honor any such covenant. But they're all far to th' south, th' Cherokee an' such. They'd seldom come here now. I'll tell Nora about that. It will comfort her."

His eyes fell on the gnawed slice of dried apple beside the cradle and he smiled. "Teethin', be he?"

"He has teeth like a tiny badger," she winced.

He reached into his pouch and drew out a little packet wrapped in doeskin. "We thought he might be. Nora mixed this poultice for ye. She says a woman's life be hard enough wi'out bein' blessed wi' toothmarks." He dug further into the pouch and drew forth a small bag. "An' this be horehound, that I brought for young Jonathan. I had to hide it well or th' squire'd have been into it all th' way up here. Th' man's a natural thief where sweets be concerned."

She tucked the treasures away on her shelf. "You haven't yet said how you come to be 'way off up here, Crispin."

"No more reason than I gave." He shrugged. " 'Twas th' squire's notion, that we should go a-huntin' an' try out th' new breed of horses Captain Post has bred up. O' course, what th' squire had in mind was to swing westerly an' look at claim markers, but I said what kind o' man would go out lookin' at claim markers when there's starvin' folk at Luther's place . . . though I see now that none of ye be starvin'."

"Nor likely to, with the game you've brought."

"We'll stay th' night, I reckon, then go out an' see th' cairns. . . . Squire's said a hundred times if he's said it once, 'Just whose trip is this, tinker? Yours or mine?' "

His imitation of Trelawney's gruff voice made her laugh aloud.

"I expect, though, that we could stop back this way afore we head for home. Just to look in one more time."

The hunters made beds for themselves in the barn and stayed for the night. And that evening after supper, as they sat on the porch and in the dooryard, Jason Cook laid his rifle across his knees and began tapping on it with his knifeblade, a steady ringing beat. For a time they talked on, then Crispin glanced around at him. "Ye've been a blacksmith far too long, Jason, if ye can't hold metal in your hand without beatin' on it."

"'Tisn't beatin'," Cook said. "This is music . . . or at least th' beginnin's of it."

"No stranger pairin's ere been tried, an' oft I've heard it said, than to match what man holds in his hand to that what's in his head."

Kate giggled and Jonathan laughed at the rhyme, but Trelawney glared at Crispin. "Only a lout would say such things in front of a lady."

"Lout, is it?" Crispin bristled. "Who's the lout, then, Squire Squatbottom, th' one as voices high-minded thoughts or th' one as thinks low-minded ones an' takes exception?"

Captain Post glanced from one to the other of them, mystified. "Do you two never stop?"

Still Jason Cook continued tapping his knife against his gun barrel, his expression set and stubborn. Mr. Sparrow leaned toward Crispin. "Why is he doing that?"

"He says it's music."

"I said 'tis th' beginnin's of it!" Cook grunted. "I'm doin' my part, an' waitin' for others to do theirs."

Crispin's brows went up. "Oh, then it's a sing ye want?"

"Why else would I be doin' this?" Cook paused. "It's been long years since first I heard you an' Luther sing about th' wee folk, Crispin. Let's hear it again now." He started tapping again and Crispin glanced at Luther, then waved a hand at him, inviting.

Luther took his wife's hand in his, cleared his throat,

231

and began it. "Now bring out a bench for this traveler's rest, with some honest spring water to hand. Then with me avail, for I'll tell you a tale of the wee folk who came to this land. . . ."

Kate noticed again how the words changed from time to time, just small changes to suit the mood of the singer, and she wondered how old the song might be and whether it had ever been sung quite the same twice. Yet it was the same, clear and sweet with a tune that held true yet changed itself from moment to moment to match the mood of the story.

Crispin joined in, his strong voice ringing off through the darkening forest, and Jason Cook's knife blade rang a steady beat. And sometimes, in those parts that she knew, Kate sang with them, her soft voice blending with theirs like velvet smoothing iron. The others there did not know the song, so they only listened, nodding and tapping their toes as people do in backcountry lands when there's a bit of music to be heard.

They sang as the wilderness darkened about them. The old song went on and on, and sometimes there were parts of it that Crispin sang alone and Kate wondered whether she had ever heard those parts. Maybe they were new, added into it along the way.

Then toward the end she found herself singing alone, an entire section of it, while the shadow-faces of the men around her held to her, listening. "For the world is far greater than any king's realm," she sang, glad that Luther had taught her at least some of it, "and with new lands abundantly blessed. And many a king's found that among those he's bound there are brave ones who'll look to the west . . . past the enemies lurking, the deserts and bogs, past the cold night and wintering sea . . . and they may not know where but they know that out there is a place where one day they'll be free."

And as she sang it she thought of her blessings, of Luther who loved her and of little Jonathan a-romp in bright meadows, of the dark eyes of baby Michael that sometimes were like looking into a mirror at herself. . . . She thought these things and a great fullness grew within her that touched high in her throat and made her voice rich with its joy. Then the others were singing again, and Luther let Crispin carry it while he leaned close and whispered in her ear, "I love you, Kate. I always will."

She thought then that never—not since the dusk when she had stood alone upon a stockade wall and seen lantern light against a white powder horn and known that he was yet alive—could she recall knowing so well how blessed she was and how rich life could be. Not until this moment, when the music of people rang out across the wilderness and its echoes sang in the breeze.

From Fort Harrod, Leander Haynes took the trail northward with Stephen Moliere and his crew. He would guide them to a place he knew, where thick forests spanned the miles along the south bank of the Ohio River and then went inland for a distance. He had learned from Colin McLeod of the likely crossings of Shawnee and Delaware, places below the falls of the Ohio where hunters had found traces of their passage. He would point these out to Moliere and show him how to guard against the savages. Then, because it was not many miles upriver, he had in mind to visit with Luther Ferris and his Kate. They would enjoy the company, and they might have further news of Indians.

At times, Leander thought of crossing over into the treaty lands. There were settlers there now, on the Scioto River. And there were Indians. It was almost a year since he had hunted Indians, and the craving was strong upon him. Across the Ohio, past the Scioto settlements, were Indians in plenty. But he hesitated. He did not know the land over there as he did on this side. He would be in strange country. The knob hills up there and the forests beyond were the redmen's territory, a wild and brooding land where few white men knew the paths. But the word of Indians crossing to Kentucky excited him and the old dark hunger built within him. Soon, he would have to go hunting.

One report puzzled him, a vague enough thing, that a small-planter near Harrod's thought he had seen an Indian in his woodlot. Just a glimpse, but he had reported it. And he swore the Indian was no Shawnee. He said it was a Cherokee.

Chula saw the white men leave the town, a large party of them with many packs. They went northward, and Chula marked their path and left a sign for Edahi and Goga the Crow to follow.

One of the white men was Tenkiller.

XXI

It was the first time Luther had taken Jonathan out to the far fields, and it was an adventure for the boy. Sitting up on the mule's pack frame between sacks of grain, holding his father's rifle across his lap while Luther walked ahead carrying his rake, his eyes widened at every movement and sound in the forest and he rattled questions as they went.

"What makes the leaves so green?" he wondered.

Without looking around, Luther said, "Those aren't leaves yet. They're just buds. They'll be leaves soon enough, though, and they're green because God made them that way."

"Buds are baby leaves," Jonathan clarified for himself. "Those yonder aren't green. They're white. Why are they white?"

"Those aren't leaves or buds, Jonathan. Those are flowers. That's a dogwood plant. Don't you remember the dogwood branches mama had on the shelf last spring?"

"I didn't know what those were. Why do we have two different kinds of seeds for one field?"

"The big sack is wheat. That's what we want to grow in the field. The other one is oats to sow around the edges. I want to see if the critters will eat the oats and leave the wheat alone."

"If we killed all the critters, we could have wheat and oats both."

Luther glanced around. "If we killed all the critters, then there wouldn't be any critters left. Then what would we hunt when we need meat?"

"We don't need meat," the boy pointed out. "The shed's plumb full."

"Well, with appetites like yours and mine, it won't stay that way."

Jonathan shifted his position on the pack frame and pulled the rifle closer to him. The long gun weighed more than ten pounds. Its weight on his lap made his legs hurt, but he was mightily proud to be carrying it for his father.

"Besides," Luther told him, looking back again, "we don't kill critters unless they threaten us or we need the meat. You know that."

"Yep. I just forgot. Is Michael a bud?"

"Michael is a baby. Little leaves are buds."

"Mama says Michael is a mixed blessing."

The forest gave way to stands of cedar as they topped a rise, then to thinning brush where the path plunged downward toward the new field. Luther had found the rich meadow three years earlier, identifying it by its flatness among the hills around it and by the abundant stands of wild peach and cherry laurel that grew there. Such were the things a man looked for when he sought good farming land. It had taken him the spare days of two seasons to clear it for plowing, then a third season to break out the virgin loam, clear away stumps and rocks, and turn the soil for planting. It was the farthest from the cabin of any field he had—almost a mile.

"And below were the wee folk from Cave and Dish Bog," Jonathan crooned to himself, keeping time to the rocking of the pack frame as the mule plodded along behind Luther. The dog came back from scouting ahead, satisfied itself that they were still moving, then headed off on another scout.

Jonathan shifted the rifle again. "If we see an Indian,

236

can I shoot him?"

"If there's shooting to be done, son, I'll do it," Luther said. "You aren't big enough yet."

"When will I be big enough?"

"Maybe when you're seven or eight. We'll see."

"How long will that be?"

Luther glanced back again. "How old are you now, Jonathan?"

"I'm almost five."

"You're four. And how many is eight less four?"

He puzzled over it, then brightened. "Eight less four makes four."

"That's right. So you'll be eight years old in four years."

"Maybe I'll be big enough to shoot when I'm seven. Seven less four is only three." He thought about it some more. "And seven less five is two. In two years, I'll be big enough to shoot. We better get me a rifle, I guess."

They came down to the cleared field and Jonathan looked in awe at the expanse of ground turned by his father's plow. "Are we going to sow all of that?"

"Every bit of it, son. It's what we've come to do."

Where heavy stands of timber lined the high banks of the Ohio, Stephen Moliere and his team made their camp, and Leander Haynes scouted a wide circle around the area while they raised their lean-tos and threw up a pole corral for their stock. Twice in three days he rode out, looking for sign, and the feeling was strong upon him that there were eyes in the forest, watching where he went. But he found no sign anywhere. If any man, white or red, had set foot upon these parts it had been a long time ago. Not even the faint old trails of warriors in the time of the massacres passed through these woods. Still, from time to time as he scouted out, he might have sworn that someone was there—someone who watched and waited and was not friendly.

The sound of axes rang through the forest, echoing for most of a mile, when he returned to the broad-horn camp the second time. They had dug their saw pits and now were felling the choicest trees to saw for planking.

Moliere stepped from his planning shed and waved as Leander rode in. He swept an arm toward the great forest behind him, its greening spires stepping down toward the river. "It's said a squirrel can go from branch to branch in this land, from the Atlantic shore to the Mississippi, and never need to touch the ground. I've been too much in the settled places, Leander. I didn't believe it. You've located us well, my friend. Did you find anything on your expedition?"

"Not a sign." Leander stepped down from his saddle and began loosing its cinches. "I've had a feelin', though, that there be redskins about. Just a notion, I reckon, but I'd urge ye put out a guard an' don't have anybody runnin' around alone out there." He slipped the saddle from his tired mount and signaled one of the hands to lead it away and bring him another. "I might be gone a few days, Mr. Moliere, but I reckon you'll not need me for a bit."

"Your friends upriver?"

"Aye, it's time I go an' look in on them. Shall I tell Luther ye'll buy his wheat come fall?"

"Tell him and have him spread the word to all he sees. Tell him I'll have docks here and a wagon road cleared by the time he harvests. I'll have boats waiting and I'll buy all they can hold." He held out a hand. "Have a nice visit, Leander. How far is this Luther's place?"

Leander squinted at the morning sun just breaking through the boughs to the east. "Not over-far," he said. "An' your man brings me a fast horse, I'll be there afore the sun goes down."

Within sound of the axes, Edahi and Goga the Crow crept down the dawning hills and found Chula waiting for

238

them where the last marker had said.

"Tenkiller is there," Chula pointed. "Many men are there, but Tenkiller rides out alone. I have seen him twice, once so near that I could have reached him with my war club. But it is Goga's mark he bears upon him, so I have waited to let Goga see him die."

They spread silently, slipping into forest shadows as though they had never been there. Such were the arts of the *Aniyunwiya*, whom even the Huron feared when they were at war—and whom even the sharp-eyed *Leni-Lanape* sometimes could not track. It was a thing few but the *Tsalagi* would have attempted—a dozen warriors crossing the breadth of Kentucky, through the settled areas, in search of a white man—yet on their entire march only two white men had seen them. And both of those now were dead, one bound to a loosed horse where trails crossed at the mountain pass, the other left facedown in his field within sight of a white man's town.

They spread and circled about the place of the ringing axes, then they returned to Goga and Chula said, "Tenkiller has changed horses and gone out again, but this time he went up the river."

"It is well," Goga decided. "There are many men in this camp. It is better if we find Tenkiller alone."

They were less than an hour behind Leander Haynes when they took to the forest trail, and they moved swiftly on silent moccasins. In the lead now went Edahi the mountain-runner, swift and sure, following the tracks of a single horse.

It was no more than a hunch that made Leander decide to check his back trail late in the afternoon. He was within a few miles of Luther Ferris's place, far from the heavy forest and into rolling lands shared by forest, cedar hillside, spotty brush, and sudden little meadows, but the uneasy feeling he had had before came over him again, making his scalp crawl beneath his coonskin cap. At a place where the woodland trail crested a low ridge capped with cedar he heeled the horse, drumming its ribs, and ran the hundred yards to the next good cover, then swung to his right and circled back to where he had altered his pace. He had not pressed his mount through the day, but had just held a steady pace, pausing only twice at streams to give it water and a bit of grain. Whatever he had sensed back there at the broad-horn camp, though, should be long since far behind him. But something—some woodsman's sense that was not sight, sound, or smell but only a feeling of something not right—kept talking to him.

Near the crest among the cedars he halted the horse, stepped down, and tied its reins in good cover. Then he crept back to the trail and found a place from which to watch. With the patience of the hunter, he prepared himself for a wait, but it was only a minute or two before he saw the Indian—a tall copper figure ghosting up the rise on long, tireless legs that covered ground at a pace that would have tired a horse. Where the trail curved, the Indian pulled a few pebbles from a belt-pouch and dropped them, hardly breaking his stride. There were others behind him, then. It was a signal left on the path.

When cedars intervened for a moment, hiding the approaching warrior, Leander leapt to a brush-shrouded old tree right at the edge of the path and burrowed into cover, blending with the vegetation there. The Indian was in sight again, fifty yards away and seeming almost to fly over the trail as he ran. Leander took a deep breath, let it out slowly, and looked slightly away from the warrior, watching him only from the corner of his eye. He gauged his steps and judged distance, then leapt.

Edahi never knew what killed him. He saw only an explosion of underbrush at his right, a hurtling dark figure, and the gleaming edge of a tomahawk as it bit into his forehead.

Leander knelt over him for just a moment, prying loose his tomahawk, then he stood and looked back down the trail with pale, cold eyes, a slight smile forming at his lips. He didn't know how many others there might be back there, but they wouldn't be far away. This one had been the fleetest among them and had taken the lead, but he wouldn't have gone too far ahead.

There would be more than one. Had there been only two of them, they would have stayed together. The runner in the lead might mean a large party, but this was not one of the tribes from across the river. This one was taller, more copper-red than brown in his skin. The kind Leander had found to the south, where the mountains rose beyond the Cumberland. The kind he had killed ten of on one hunt a few seasons back—and maybe that many again on other hunts. So it would not be a large band. They were too far from home. Likely there were four of them in all. Likely there were three more coming behind this one.

He left the dead Indian there and raced back to his horse, a fierce excitement driving him. In the saddle again he retraced his back circle and emerged on the next rise, in a narrow gap where he could see the back trail. The dead Indian lay half across it, and there was movement beyond.

He raised his rifle, held on the narrow path back there, and eased his breathing. An Indian appeared among the cedars, then another, steps faltering as they saw the body before them. Leander set his sight-blade on the naked chest of the first one and fired. The Indian fell across the body lying there. He saw two more disappear into cover and smiled as he swung the horse around and drummed it with his heels, raising his powder horn to reload.

He was pouring powder when the horse snorted and faltered, and something burned his leg. An arrow stood in the animal's side, driven so deep that only its fletching and a foot of shaft remained. It had scored his leg and gone into the horse's lungs. Suddenly there were Indians on both sides of him, scrambling from the brush. He

241

ducked and an arrow whisked past his ear. A warrior came up almost under him and he swung his empty rifle, feeling bone break beneath the weight of it. The horse pitched and stumbled, but it was still moving and he kicked it with his heels, trying to gain space. It bunched powerful haunches and, somehow, it ran. Fifty yards, a hundred yards, and it was still moving. The trail curved and he was out of sight. He pulled free of his strirrups, got his feet on the saddle, and jumped, sailing over the fringe of brush to roll beyond, and he kept moving, scurrying into a low, shadowy cover beneath matted vines. He stopped then and lay very still, just listening. His ear pressed the thorned ground and he searched with his eyes until he picked out a sliver of opening with space beyond it, a narrow peephole from which he could see the trail. Dimly he heard the drumming hooves of his horse, going away, faltering now but still moving.

Then he saw them, and he counted them as they passed—those that he could see. He had been wrong. This was a large party—and not a hunting party. This was a war party hot on the scent. Then for just an instant he saw a face he had seen before and his blood went cold. An instant and he was gone. But Leander remembered him. It was the young Indian from that hunt—the one that got away. The one he had called Round Eyes.

He lay still until they had passed, counting his breaths and the beats of his heart. Then in the distance, not far away, he heard the clanging of a bell.

The hunters from Harrodsburg had taken more than a week to find and inspect all of the boundary claims the squire wanted to see, and they were fairly tired of being in the wilderness. Had it not been for Crispin's insistence, they would have turned toward home. But Crispin had promised to stop by and look in on Luther and Kate once more, so they made their way up toward the river on a winding, angling game trail that only Mr. Sparrow among them could have followed. A fresh wolf trail, he said. Probably it would lead to some new-cleared field where rodents had been plentiful during the winter. It was going in the proper direction, so they followed it.

In late afternoon they found the field, and Crispin pointed. "Yon be Luther an' his bairn . . . a better sight than any cairn."

"I really wish you would quit doing that," Trelawney grumbled.

Luther had finished with his day's planting and was just loading a very tired little boy onto the back of his mule when his dog told him people were coming. He turned and saw them coming around the field, and his grin told them how happy he was that they were back.

He finished his loading and put a tie around the drowsy Jonathan so that he wouldn't go to sleep and fall off. Then they headed for his house, Luther walking, leading the mule, and the hunters riding alongside with their pack animals coming behind. They hadn't brought meat this time, and he was glad. He wouldn't have known what to do with it.

They had gone a half mile when they heard a rifle shot somewhere to the north. "Somebody up that way?" Crispin asked.

Luther shook his head, his brow lowering with worry. "Not that I know of." It was only minutes later that they heard the bell.

Kate had just taken wash off her strung line when she heard hoofbeats beyond the barn. She set the basket on the porch and turned to see a riderless horse galloping into the clearing. It ran on crazy legs, seeming half to dance and half to stumble, and it screamed and tossed its head as it came. She started to go to it, to head it off, then saw the blood on its side and the feathers there. She backed away, onto the porch, and it circled in the dooryard, then went down as its back legs collapsed. The arrow snapped beneath it as it rolled, and it screamed again, trying to get to its feet.

Inside the house Michael awakened with a howl and Kate turned to look through the door, then turned back. The horse lay just a few steps away, writhing and crying in agony. And beyond, just clearing the trees past the barn, were Indians.

For an instant Kate just stared at them, shock mounting upon shock, seeing their faces as they came around the barn, the weapons in their hands, how their legs moved as they ran. Then Michael howled again and she whirled around, grabbed the bell cord, and pulled it with all her might. They were almost to the dooryard when she sprang through the door and bolted it behind her, then ran to get the musket.

With shock-clouded eyes she looked around, hearing Indian voices outside. Her eyes went wide. The window was full open, its shutters left wide to let in the balmy breeze of spring's first warm day. Again Michael howled, and she spun toward him, wanting to hush him. A shadow moved and she whirled again. There was an Indian at the window, drawing a bow. She started to raise the musket, but another squeal from Michael caught the savage's attention and he turned, the drawn bow aligning on the willow cradle. Kate screamed and the musket rattled to the floor. She threw herself into the path of the arrow.

Pain flooded through her, so intense that for a moment there was nothing else in all the world except a growing, glowing pain. Then there was Michael, and she lay sprawled across his cradle, holding him to her breast, shielding him. Beyond were chaotic sounds—shouts and running horses, guns going off, wild yips and yells. . . . She couldn't understand it, nor really see how it mattered. The baby was crying. She ran a gentle hand along his cheek, pressing him close, feeling with numb fingers the little features that were so much like her own. "Oh, Michael, be still," her mind said, though she couldn't hear her voice saying it. "Be still, baby Michael.

244

Everything is all right. . . ." Then, oddly, "I see a white horn. It's all right now."

She couldn't find Michael's face . . . couldn't even find her hand in search for it again, but out of the searing pain that still was there somewhere grew soft rose light . . . light that lay gentle on waving green meadows where a little brook meandered and shadows walked . . . shadows that held out their hands to her and called her and sang to her. . . .

Somewhere, they said—and it was a song—somewhere out there is a bright summer land . . . and it's there that we're going to go. . . .

XXII

Up on the rise there was a stone, a shaped thing that Luther had worked a winter on to replace the weathered old wooden marker that had been there. The chiseled letters on the stone said what the letters on the cross had said: *Jonathan Ferris, 1733–1775.*

Beside the stone they dug fresh graves and buried their dead, and Squire Trelawney thumbed through his old Anglican Bible and muttered to himself as each body was placed in the ground. Captain Matthew Post would see no more new strains of racing horse come from his stables. Of them all, he had been the first to charge among the savages, through the smoke of his own rifle. Of them all, it had been this quiet, distant man who struck first. And when he was pulled from his horse and three of them fell upon him with war clubs, only two had gotten up again.

Mr. Sparrow knelt by that grave and tossed in a handful of earth, gently. The first earth should be applied gently, he felt. Then the thumping spadefuls that followed would not matter because they could do no more than had already been done.

It took a time to pry Luther's arms from the body of his wife. He simply knelt there by the cradle, holding her and sobbing, and did not know that they were trying to pull him loose. Finally he relaxed a little, and they brought him away and wrapped her in a blanket and two hides. The blood on her back had begun to dry, but Luther's tears on her breast were warm and wet.

He could barely see to walk when Crispin Blount led him from the cabin and up the hill to where the graves were, but then Jason Cook brought Jonathan and Michael to him. The blacksmith placed the baby in his arms and he held onto him as he had held onto Kate. Then Jonathan reached up to touch his fingers, and Luther took the child's hand in his own and raised his streaked face to gaze with unseeing eyes at the field beyond the graves, the forests beyond the fields, the hills beyond the forests.

The third grave was a bit aside from the others, and not so deep. It was for one of the squire's horse-handlers, a man whose only name had been Buto.

Through it all, Leander Haynes held to himself, distant from the rest, keeping his own counsel. He walked about the clearing, counting the fallen Indians. Five in all, plus two others that he knew about, back on the forest trail. How many had there been? He wasn't sure. A dozen or more, he thought. They had driven them off, but he knew they were not far away. He knew because nowhere among the dead was the one he had recognized—the one he had seen before. Round Eyes.

By first light of morning they packed what they could, took what stock they could manage and turned the rest loose, and set out for Harrodsburg. Crispin Blount took Jonathan up to ride with him, and Jason handed the bundled baby up to Luther. With a throat so tight it threatened to burst, Crispin watched the young man arrange blankets around his baby . . . and felt the boy Jonathan watching, too. There were no tears on Luther's face now. There was nothing there at all. Only a face. Yet in the big, hard hands that cradled the infant there was such an exquisite gentleness that Crispin's own eyes went moist.

"Th' very image of its mother," he whispered, to no one but himself. Yet beside him he heard Trelawney sniffle and knew that he had heard.

Leander Haynes had ridden up the trail, looking for sign. Now he returned, grim and bleak, pale eyes as cold as winter snow. "No sign of 'em," he said. "Maybe they're gone. We can go now, if ye're ready."

For the second time then Luther Ferris turned his back on his fields, his cabin and barns, on all that had been home, and rode away, and there was fresh-mounded sod up on the rise.

This time he didn't turn to look back.

When the white men were gone and he was sure they would not return, Goga the Crow led his clansmen back to the clearing and walked here and there, looking at the faces of the dead. Ugidatli lay sprawled on his back near the barn, his head twisted oddly to the side, the blood of an enemy crusting on his hands. Tsatsi had fallen across the waist-high rail of the dooryard fence and hung there, holed through by a rifle ball. U'sdi-tsani, whom the white men at the Carolina trading posts had called Little John, lay behind the house, just under the open window, hacked to death with a tomahawk. His broken bow had been flung across his body. Ganahida had taken three balls through his chest and had crumpled like a straw doll beside the dead horse. Chiya the Otter they found beneath a bitterbrush a hundred yards away. He had crawled that far with a sliced throat before he died.

Goga walked among the dead and squatted on his heels beside each one, saying their names in turn. He stood then and looked back the way they had come and said the names of Edahi and Chula, whom Tenkiller had ambushed on the trail. Then when they brought Yona-adisi in from the forest, staggering and holding his belly closed with his hands, Goga said his name, too, because Yona-adisi would not see the sun rise again.

It had been a trap. Tenkiller had taunted them and led them to the slaughter, and now of the twelve of them only

248

four remained.

As the white men had buried their dead now the red men buried theirs, only forty yards from the first graves. Through the dusk hours and into the moonlit night they dug holes in the dark earth, and as each was laid to rest the four took turns depositing handfuls of earth— gently—atop them. It was the final service one man could perform for another. Atop each grave they placed a stone, to say that an honored person slept there.

Then with Goga the Crow leading, they went south and west into the deep woods. Had they been Shawnee, they would go home now. Had they been Wyandot, there would be none left. But they were Cherokee. They could wait for the white man *S'gohidihi*, the Tenkiller. Goga would not forget. A great sadness walked with Goga now, and in the night he heard the songs of the little people in their secret glades—the ancient wee folk whose legend was so much a part of the heritage of the *Aniyunwiya*. They danced and sang in their hidden places and only a few ever heard them, but those who did sometimes received gifts from them. Goga's gift was a vision that was dark and ominous.

Tenkiller was only a man. One man. But the wee ones sang and Goga the Crow knew that Tenkiller also was a kind, and soon his kind would burst forth upon the dark and bloody ground and go out in great number. And as the one man had a name in Goga's mind—*S'gohidihi*, the Tenkiller—so did the kind have a name, and soon all of the red people would know it. The name was Tsotsi Danawa. The name was Enemy.

Peter and Carter Framington were brothers, green-grocers from New York whose business had become miniscule with the collapse of the fleet trade in New York Harbor. Clive Serrey was a kiln-owner from Connecticut, though not since Yorktown had there been trade to keep his chimneys smoking. Separately and in keeping with

249

many others like them, they turned their eyes to the West and set out to make new lives. Where their two parties came together in Pennsylvania they combined their lot for the safety of numbers, and the number of souls boarding their three flatboats was twenty-seven— six men, four women, twelve children, and five Negro servants. Their destination was the Scioto settlement in the Ohio wilderness.

White Bird was sixteen years old when he joined his first forage, a young buck like many others, seeking glory and a proud name. The party that made its way eastward along the Ohio was eighteen in number—fourteen young braves like White Bird and four seasoned warriors. Along wilderness trails they ran, aiming for the Scioto settlement and the chance to strike back at hunters from there who had raided their village in the time of snow melting. The hunters had killed four people and stolen young women and winter stores of meat and grain. White Bird and the rest followed the warrior Lone Elk and shared his outrage at the behavior of the white trespassers.

The river had been high for a month, flowing swift with the thaws of spring, and was curtained by rain when the three flatboats passed the mouth of the Scioto and pushed on downstream, never knowing that they had missed their destination. Four days and ninety miles later they put in at the mouth of the Miami River and made camp. Five of the six men set out on foot, hoping to learn where they were, while Clive Serrey stayed with the camp to guard the women and children.

On the second morning, Long Elk's party found them and attacked. Peter Framington's wife and a black manservant were killed on the bank of the Miami. The rest, under fire and without most of their provisions, made it to two of the flatboats and pushed off into the river, while Long Elk and his warriors pressed them from the shore. At the river's mouth, heavy currents swung them close ashore and the Indians attacked again. With arrows whisking over and around them the emigrants managed to lash the two boats together and pole them out into the Ohio's current. Long Elk divided his forces then, sending some across the river while he and others remained on the trails along the north side. White Bird was one who crossed, swimming driftwood through cold waters for more than a mile to reach the south bank. Where the river curved, a half-day downstream, the warriors scrambled down the banks on both sides to rain arrows at the emigrants as they passed. Clive Serrey had one dry load in his rifle, and he leveled it and fired. White Bird's search for glory ended that day.

Four days later, the wreckage of the two flatboats grounded in a backwater below the falls of the Ohio and a scout from Stephen Moliere's lumber camp helped the survivors to shore. Clive Serrey had a broken leg, the only one of the survivors with any injury . . . though the survivors numbered only five—Clive Serrey, Carter Framington's sister Beth, two children, and a Negro named Josephus.

In the meantime, far to the northeast, the Framingtons and their cousins reached the Scioto settlement and returned to the Miami camp with a group of ten, to find the body of Peter Framington's wife. She was identifiable only from a few scraps of clothing and a gold ring. There were trackers among the Scioto men, and they set out along the Ohio shore. They never found Long Elk and his band, but they did find three Wyandots digging roots. They took their scalps back to the Scioto settlement and displayed them on a post.

And the word spread. From settlement to cabin clearing, from timber camp to the crossing of trails, where men met in the wilderness land they exchanged news. They talked of the finding of Jarod Cole, arrow-killed and left tied in his saddle. They talked of Will Henry, found facedown in his hayfield a mile from Fort Harrod. They talked of the pitiful survivors of the flatboat massacre and of the death of Matthew Post and

251

of Luther Ferris's wife Kate. They talked, and many remembered times past, when the old hunting ground they called Kentucky had become killing ground and when Chief Dragging Canoe had said, "This land is known as the dark and bloody ground. I will make it so again." And when the British general, Henry Hamilton, had offered red-handled knives for patriot scalps and the land had swarmed with Shawnee raiders—the time of the smokes. They met and talked and spread the word.

"Must we go into the forts again?" the women asked. And the men primed their rifles and gathered their neighbors and said, "There be a Lord's plenty of us here to rid Kaintuck o' heathens. So we best get started at it."

Relays of riders went out from Boonesboro and Bryant's Station, from Limestone and Fort Harrod, from Point of Rocks and Kanawha, bearing messages to Virginia, seeking "a force of rangers to move against the general uprising of the Indians." The recent movement of the capital from Williamsburg to Richmond brought the seat of government closer by that much to the undermountain and overmountain lands, and the posts moved with great speed. And even as the messengers neared Cumberland Gap, they met others coming westward with news to alert the settlements. America's French and Spanish allies, without whom the colonists might never have evicted the British from their lands, now had decided to divide the spoils of war.

"Lafayette an' Rochambeau an' all th' rest of 'em," a dour long rider paused to say, "they never was here for th' likes of us. They was here for their own reasons, jus' like Patrick Henry said. ''Twasn't our war they come to fight, it was their own.'"

"So what is it they've a mind to split?" Colin McLeod squinted his good eye, anxious to be on his way.

"Kentucky, among other things. Seems like France promised to take Gibraltar from th' Georgies an' give it to Spain, but th' redcoats held it. So now France has offered th' west half of Kentucky to Spain instead."

252

"Kentucky?" McLeod gawked at the man, stunned at the treachery of it.

"An' Tennessee an' th' whole Chickasaw an' Choctaw country, right down to Mobile Bay. Th' way they've got it cut out, everything from Vincennes south will be Spanish land afore th' year's out. Way I hear it, they'll put Spanish forts at Massac, Nashborough, an' Muscle Shoals, an' lay a Spanish line right down th' foothills."

"So what are they fixin' to do about it, then?"

"Who?"

"Th' commonwealths! Th' Continental Congress! George Washington! Anybody?"

"Oh. Well, that part don't make much sense. They say th' French an' Spanish has offered all th' fur country past th' Ohio back to th' British. Washington an' Jefferson are both sayin' we got to take that country an' run th' Canadians out, so we won't lose Kentucky an' all to th' Spanish. They're sayin' we need a new alliance."

"With who?"

"With England."

"But you just said . . ."

"Yeah, I know. On one hand we're fixin' to whale th' redcoats out of th' Northwest Territory, an' at th' same time we're goin' to say, 'Please, King George, ol' bean, see what ye can do about keepin' th' Frogs an' th' Spaniards out o' Kaintuck an' whatnot.'" The man shook his head. "Some says it's all Benjamin Franklin's idea . . . an' you know how *his* ideas gets."

It was beyond the both of them. "That what's in th' tote sack?" McLeod asked. "Ye got anything else?"

The man shrugged. "Bits and pieces. You know Captain Post?"

"Used to. Injuns got him."

The man removed his hat for a moment, then put it on his head again. "Shame. Got a post here for him. His son Christopher has got hisself appointed head of Rangers for everything west o' the Kaintuck River."

"Christopher? He's just a tad."

"Well, not no more, he ain't. His daddy-in-law is Colonel Clayton Chase." The man grinned crookedly. "One more thing, too. Word's in from Philadelphia not a week hence. Th' king's ministers in Paris signed th' treaty. Th' colonies is now thirteen free an' independent states. Peace is here. Th' 'times that try men's souls' is over."

McLeod stared at him with his good eye. Somehow the news that the war with England had ended had little meaning to him, and he wondered why. He turned to look back toward the dark and bloody ground. "Peace . . ." he muttered. "Where?"

Leander Haynes hung around Harrod's for a time after they brought Luther and the babies to Crispin Blount's house. He saw Julie there, but he hung back and didn't speak to her . . . or to any of them. Kate's death hung like a pall over the house, and he was saddened and ashamed. He wanted to go to Julie, to tell her how it had been and why it had happened . . . to tell her about Round Eyes. He wanted to get down on his knees and ask her forgiveness. Had it not been for him, he wanted to say, Kate would not have died. The Indians had been after him, and he had led them straight to Luther's family.

Of course, he realized, if he told about it, then everyone would know. And he had kept it secret all alone . . . the hunts and the kills, the insatiable longing that crept upon him now and again, that drove him to the forests and the wilderness trails, looking for redmen . . . looking for Indians to kill. Why was it a secret? He didn't know. Other men had killed Indians . . . and would again. It was a common enough thing to do. And yet, his hunts . . . the pleasure they gave him was more than just a satisfaction at revenge. He hunted, and he killed, and each time a redman died there was a starburst glory in him that was almost physical. A release, as though for that moment all the world was at rights. The

254

pleasure . . . somehow he knew . . . was not a normal thing, and so he was silent about it.

And now it had come to this. If Luther ever learned that he had led savages down upon his wife, he would kill Leander. There were some hurts that no man could stand, and somehow the notion of Luther—solid, rock-steady Luther, whose temper was as level as water in a deep well—in a killing mood was terrifying.

He stayed away from the house, his guilt tormenting him. No one must ever know. Still, he had a need to tell Julie, to somehow make her understand that it was his fault, though he had never intended such a thing. If she knew, then maybe she might choose to forgive him one day. And if Julie could forgive him, then maybe he could forgive himself.

He even approached the little cabin where she mixed her dough, hoping to talk to her there, but she was not alone. Through the window he saw the surveyor, Thomas Dodd, working at charts on a table. Leander remembered that he had directed the man there, to inquire about space. He turned and walked away.

On a rainy evening word came that a band of Shawnee had been seen—a hunting party most likely—over on Green River. Men gathered at the inn and talked of it, and some raised their cups in agreement. With first light they would go out in force to find the Indians. Too much had happened. Kentucky must be ridded of savages.

Leander didn't wait for first light. He went to the stable and got his horse, loaded his gear, and left Fort Harrod, silent and alone. Indians on the Green River. The hunger for killing came over him and fed upon his guilt, and there was no saying nay to it. Indians had done it. They had done it all. The Indians were the source of all evils.

It was time to go hunting.

XXIII

By the time the messages from Kentucky had reached Richmond, there were other messages coming up behind them. A gang of armed settlers out of Killdevil Cross had ambushed a migrating village of Wyandots on the old Warriors Trail. Thirty-four Indians were dead—men, women, and children. A hundred or so more had escaped. An immigrant party from Pennsylvania had stumbled across an Indian camp on the Monongahela flats and killed fourteen of the redmen in a running battle, though some of them had circled back and retaliated against the immigrant women and children. There were six casualties, they said.

There were conflicting reports of Shawnee amassing on the far bank of the Ohio, most of them armed with Brown Bess muskets. The reports differed as to just where the Indians were. A patrol from the little fort at Blue Crest had gone to scout the Ohio in their vicinity and had never reached the river. Indians had ambushed them almost within sight of their fort. Nine of the fifteen men had made it back, three of them wounded. That night the mutilated body of Captain William Walden had been cast over the wall, into the fort. He had died slowly and cruelly.

In the hills above the Warriors Trail an entire family—four adults and seven children—had been wiped out by Indians. A hunter had seen a large band of Wyandots near the place. By hiding, he had escaped them. There were dozens of other episodes as well—isolated, random, casual killings of Indians by whites and whites by Indians. In the first weeks of spring in the year 1783, all-out war had erupted in Kentucky. Some said it had started the very day word was received in Philadelphia that the war with England was over. Some—a few in central Kentucky—said it had begun the day Kate Ferris and Captain Matthew Post died. Both might have been right, for those things had happened on the same day, March 24. Others, though, said the war in Kentucky was just another flurry in a strife that had never ended since the day in 1773 when Daniel Boone's son had died in a battle with Indians . . . or that maybe it had been going on since the Seven Years War broke out in 1755. The war then had been between France and England, but it was settlers and redmen who died. Later the war had been between England and the colonies, but in Kentucky it was settlers and redmen who died. And after that it had been between Canadian Rangers and the Virginia militias, but it was settlers and redmen who died.

Now the war seemed to be between settlers and redmen—at least they were the ones dying—and the men who read the reports in Richmond and Philadelphia looked at one another with hard cynicism and didn't believe it. There had to be reasons beyond what were obvious.

In Richmond, Colonel Clayton Chase paced the length of what would be the Territorial Ministry when the transfer of archives from Williamsburg was completed. Veteran of both Trenton and Charlottesville, Chase had served as aide to John Jay in the interim and had gone with him to Spain to seek Madrid's help in the cause against England. Like Jay, he had returned to the colonies with a thorough distaste for the Spanish. In his new—and not yet thoroughly accepted—son-in-law, he had found an unexpected ally at least in this respect. It

257

was this grudging alliance between the father and the young husband of Elizabeth Chase Post, as well as Christopher's knowledge of the frontier, that led to his calling on the "upstart young adventurer" when conflict erupted in Kentucky. And that had led to his giving Christopher an interim appointment as captain of militias for the west districts—at least that seemed to have led to it, though Chase suspected that his son-in-law had planned the entire discussion in advance.

And now he had called on him again. When the door was closed and they were alone, he stopped his pacing and faced the young captain. "Tell me again what you said about the governor general at New Madrid."

Christopher nodded. "I said that he will waste no time in consolidating his claim to western Kentucky, now that France has offered the territory to Spain."

"Yes. Now tell me, Captain . . . ah . . . Christopher . . . oh, blast! Do sit down, and I will, too. I—I may have need of your advice."

"Yes, sir." They sat.

"Tell me, Christopher, how did you even know that France would so betray the colonies? At the time of your arrival from Boston, we didn't know that any such offer had been made."

"It was known in Boston, sir. I heard of it when I was there."

"The colonies whose territory is jeopardized are Virginia, the Carolinas, and Georgia. So why was it first known in Massachusetts?"

"That isn't unusual." Christopher shrugged. "It is a popular activity in Massachusetts to keep abreast of other people's business. Mr. Paine commented on that some time ago, in a published paper. He said something to the effect that Boston merchants are so insatiably curious about the affairs of others, it would lead one to think they have no affairs of their own."

"So they knew it. Why didn't they tell us?"

"Why should they? It isn't their territories being

given away."

"A reasoning that only a Massachusetts man might understand." Chase glared at the young man suspiciously. "Very well. Then, recognizing that the frost-bitten gentlemen knew that, what else do they know that is our business and not theirs?"

"It isn't what they know, sir. It's what they expect will happen next that concerns me. Spain is not our friend, sir . . . as you well know. The Spanish never wanted the American colonies to be independent from England. They are afraid of us, and everyone knows it."

"With good reason."

"Sir?"

"I've heard your own thoughts regarding New Spain, Christopher. The Spanish have good reason to fear us."

"Yes, sir. And now that we are independent states, they will not trust France's offer of territories. They will move to establish their claim."

Chase dropped his chin against his chest. "As you said before. Yes. Christopher, what is your opinion of the fighting in Kentucky now? Is there more to it than what Mr. Brook believes?"

"Mr. Brook, sir?"

"The North Carolina assemblyman. He believes the slaughter west of Cumberland is spontaneous, possibly started by the Kentuckians themselves . . . or some of them."

"I hadn't heard of that, sir."

"He cites a conversation some of his constitutents have had with an old Indian, a Delaware living among the Cherokee in Tennessee. A shaman of some sort . . . Kitsicum is his name. Brook says Kitsicum spoke of a quest by some of the young Cherokee warriors to find and eliminate a white man they call Tenkiller. The man has been murdering Indians for years, they say."

"I know nothing of that, sir. But the Indian I encourage you to think about also is a Cherokee, though not of the tribes. He is a renegade and has a strong tribe of his own."

"Do you mean Nicolet? We know of him. But there hasn't been a sign of him in at least two years. My people believe he has crossed the Mississippi to seek a haven in the Spanish lands."

Christopher said nothing. But the dark eyes that gazed at his father-in-law glittered with the knowledge of Chase's intuition.

Chase cleared his throat. Damn, but the upstart was disconcerting. Did he know everything? What had Elizabeth brought upon them? "Is that what you think will happen, Christopher? You believe the Spanish governor-general will turn Nicolet on us?"

The slight smile on the younger man's face was cold and certain. "If I were him, I would."

"And if I were to assign you—assign the captain of militias of the west territory—to proceed to Kentucky and protect the interests of the commonwealth of Virginia there, what would you do?"

"I would go, sir."

"Go . . . and do what?"

"Whatever is necessary."

"I cannot mount a campaign on the basis of a rumor from Massachusetts. You know that."

"Of course not, sir."

"Nor can I put troops in the field—even if I had them—on the sheer supposition that some Spaniard may take hostile action against our western territories."

"I know that, too, sir."

"Then understand also that I can do no more than encourage defense of home and property against the depredations of savages. Nothing more."

"What are you saying, sir?"

"Damme, young sir! What I am saying is *defense!* Nothing more. We are *not* at war with Spain."

"*We,* sir? Who do you mean?"

"*We!* The Commonwealth of Virginia. The united colonies, the independent states, the . . . whoever in

260

God's name the Continental Congress decides we are—if it ever manages to decide. There is to be no incursion beyond the Mississippi River by subjects of Virginia, is that clear?"

"Very clear, sir."

"Then are there any questions?"

"Only one, sir. Is the Concordance of 1774 still in effect?"

"The Continental Association? Of course it is. Why?"

"I may assume, then, that compliance with its directives is compliance with orders?"

"Of course."

"Thank you, sir. I wanted to be clear regarding conduct in the field." Christopher stood and picked up his hat. "By your leave, sir, I must arrange a coach to Williamsburg, so that I can be ready to depart when your orders are written."

"Yes, by all means. Give my love to the ladies, please. Tell Mary that I shall be home within the week, when the press of this"—he looked around him at the half-finished office—"this *progress* has been dealt with."

"Yes, sir."

"Oh, and Christopher? . . ."

"Sir?"

"About your father . . . my deepest sympathy."

"Thank you, sir."

The following day Chase met with the Territorial Committee and received approval for a modest assembly of militia in the west territory, in view of the fighting reported there and the possibility of Indian incursion from Tennesee and the Northwest Territories. With that authorization, he issued the necessary orders to Christopher Post, to be delivered immediately at Williamsburg.

It was two days later when he received his archives and ministry records, and had the opportunity to again read the articles of the Concordance of 1774 and the Continental Association. After a time he put the papers aside, crossed his arms on his table, and rested his chin

261

on them. "The devil," he muttered. "The very devil. What has Elizabeth brought upon us?"

The article was an appendage to the colonial boundaries agreements, an afterthought probably, but it was very clear. It agreed that the militias of each colony could, at their initiative, cross any continental boundary if in "immediate pursuit" of hostiles.

On April 9, Christopher Post, age eighteen and a provisional captain of Virginia militia, crossed through Cumberland Gap and into Kentucky with the beginnings of a company at his back. The party included a clerk, a pair of dispatch riders, and five mounted ex-marines fresh from the British fleet and the New Bedford stockade. Colin McLeod met them at the Holston settlement and rode with them from there.

Christopher had been offered additional men and horses but had declined. There were better horses to be had at Fort Harrod—his father's own breed of racers—than any that Virginia could supply. And as for men, he would find them in Kentucky. Men to match the wilderness of Kentucky might come from the tidewater lands or the undermountains, but he preferred a more tested breed—men who had tasted the bitter winds of the dark and bloody ground, who were tempered by its moods and knew its secret places. Men of the sort that Headmaster John Wesley Nesbitt called "the howling mobs of the territories." He and his reformed marines could mold an army from such men, if such were needed. Even Attila could have asked for no fiercer stock from which to draw his fighters.

Oban Calloway was fifty-nine years old and had emigrated twice—or "times it was needed," as he saw it. Born to a shepherd's wife near Shipbourne Fairlawn in Kent, he had apprenticed to a stonecutter as a boy, then run away to sea aboard a merchantman and eventually wound up on the shores of the new world, penniless and alone. But a good set of shoulders had earned him employment with a furring company, and two seasons wages had paid for his equipment and provisions to join a brigade into the Huron lands. The expedition had earned him a modest profit and a great hunger to see more of the wild back lands beyond the colonies. At the age of twenty-three he went with Celeron de Blainville as a scout when the Frenchman visited his country's claimed lands along the Ohio. He helped with the burying of leaden plates at the mouths of four tributaries as evidence of French claim, then was tried and fined by the commander at Fort Stanwix, on a charge of liaison. Penniless again, Oban wandered southward from the Alleghenies to the Appalachians, doing various jobs for wages. He was with Thomas Walker in 1750 when Walker discovered the Cumberland Gap.

Then with the outset of the French and Indian War, Oban found use for his apprentice skills. He worked as a stonecutter at New York, then as a stonemason at Philadelphia, where he met and married Comfort Shanding. Children were born to them, and then more children, and Oban worked each day except the Sabbath, when he sometimes looked to the west and dreamed of the places he had seen.

Thus had time and events gone by, until a day came when there was no work to be had for a man of his age. Nor was there work even for his sons and his daughters' husbands. It was then that Oban Calloway decided to follow his dream.

Three generations of Calloways and kin made their way overland to the Susquehanna Valley, then on to Fort Pitt and the staging docks, where hundreds of emigrants were trading goods for boats to seek the golden frontier.

With the purchase of four boats, the remaining assets of the Calloway tribe included seven rifles with powder and lead, six of the new American axes, three augers, various personal implements, four pigs, a crosscut saw, a loom and two spinning wheels, a bag of salt, and five bags

263

of seed corn.

"We ask the blessing of the good Lord upon us," Oban said as they bowed their heads before stepping aboard the boats, "for we are but poor folk as Thou can plainly see, but grant us safe pasage and a bit of good land at the end of it, and we'll be rich enough soon enough. All we ask is that Thou see to it that we get there, and we'll thank ye kindly when it's done. Amen."

Then Oban led Comfort aboard the first boat and the rest set about boarding—sons and daughters, grand-children, pigs and in-laws. There was ice on the river, but it was breaking up and the flow was good. They averaged three miles to the hour and sometimes as much as seven. On a bright March day, two days beyond a long bend where the river had swung westerly, Oban studied his charts and then put them away and pointed toward the left bank. "Yonder is Kentucky," he said. "God has kept his end of our bargain." Near the mouth of the Scioto, two men in a canoe, going the other way, confirmed his estimate. They had indeed reached Kentucky.

Where there was a path and a cleared bank, they put ashore and scouted inland, then came across new-planted fields with a deserted cabin and barn beyond, where they stopped a bit to rest. There was meat in the shed and grain in the barn and a message over the hearth of the cabin. "Gone to Fort Harrod," it said. "Travelers use what you need and repair what needs fixing." It was signed "C. Blount."

They lingered there for a bit because two of the children had developed a fever. Then Comfort came to Oban and said, "It's time we found a settlement, Mr. Calloway. The babies are ill and they need attention. And three others have a fever."

His sons had found a path and they took it, finding two other new-planted fields as they set out. "It is a prime land," Oban said. "And the man who tamed it here used a firm and gentle hand."

Four miles along, an old horse came from the wood to

follow along after them. They slung the babies to its back and let them ride.

Though there were other places closer by, they did not know of them, and they followed the trail that Luther Ferris had made, coming finally to Fort Harrod, which people were again starting to call Harrodsburg as it continued to grow. At the edge of the town they met a young man, and Oban asked him who in the place might be skilled at medicine.

"Dr. Ford's away," he said. "Maybe Dr. Christian is about, though." He stepped close to the horse to look at the babies in their slung cradles. "They look spotty," he said. "Is it a pox?"

"It might be the cowpox," Comfort said. "There was complaint of it at a place we stopped, up the river."

The young man's name was Seth Michaels, and he led them into the town, toward the old stockade that stood at its center.

They saw children coming from the stockade. A good many children, of various ages. "Mistress Blount keeps school there," Seth told them. "Dr. Christian's house isn't far beyond."

As they passed, two women came from the old fort, so alike that anyone could tell they were mother and daughter. Seth smiled at the daughter, then turned to the mother. "Some of these folks are sick. Is Dr. Christian about, do you know?"

The woman came and looked at the babies, and her eyes widened. She turned to the young woman. "Ellie . . . no, stay back . . . go find Dr. Christian and tell him to come to the school. Then run home and tell Crispin to have the squire send men down here, with blankets and soap and turpentine. Hurry, please."

They hurried away and the woman turned to Oban. "I'm Nora Blount," she said. "Please, bring the babies and come with me. All of you. We can make room for you in the school." Other people were approaching along the street and she waved them back. "Stand away," she told

265

them. "Stand away! These children have a pox!"

At the stockade gate Seth started to turn away and she waved him on. "You, too, Seth. We must both stay here with them until we learn what it is. And no one else is to come near until Dr. Christian says it is all right."

When they were all inside, Oban Calloway had two of his sons repair the wagon gate and close it. Meantime, Nora and the emigrant women began bathing the children with water from the rain barrels. When one of the young men took a bucket and started toward the enclosed well, she called him back. No one was to use the well or even to go near it.

"You've seen pox before, then?" Oban asked her.

"In Philadelphia." She nodded. "I was very young, but I remember. When you came here—since you left the place where they spoke of illness—did you see anyone else?"

"Few folks . . ."

"Oban," Comfort interrupted. "The lady means did any of us *touch* anyone. No, Mistress. We didn't. There wasn't anybody that close for us to touch."

"That is a blessing," Nora said.

"We did stop, though, at a cabin. No one was there, but we rested there. 'Twas where little Evan first had the fever."

"There was a message," Oban added. "A welcome. Signed by C. Blount. That is your name, isn't it? Blount?"

"Yes. That would be Luther's cabin. But there should be no one there to be infected."

"We saw fresh graves there," Oban said.

"Yes. Yes, there are graves. But unless someone else happens by . . . did you leave anything there? Blankets or clothing, anything like that?"

"No, mistress. I'm sure we left nothing."

But Comfort had gone pale. "The boats, Oban. You remember. We left things with the boats." She turned to Nora. "We thought we would go right back to the boats,

266

but then the babies were fevered, so we came looking for a doctor."

Even then, though, the boats were no longer where they had left them. A group of Delaware, fleeing from the white raiders out of the Scioto settlement, had found them. They had taken what they wanted, then had cut them loose to drift on down the river toward the falls.

XXIV

Two doctors practiced at Harrodsburg. Just a few years earlier they would have been sworn enemies—a New York Tory and a Charles Town Whig. But when it became certain that those within the stockade carried variola—the smallpox, it was called, to distinguish it from the great pox or syphilis—they worked as a team, James Ford outside the stockade and Robert Christian inside. Where most ailments were concerned, medicine was an inexact art and those who practiced it could rarely be certain how to proceed. But both of the doctors knew the nature of variola. Both had seen epidemics and knew the measures to take against the disease.

In the closed stockade Christian worked—and those not infected assisted him—to keep the ill ones clean and comfortable, with elixirs of camphor, turpentine and oil of bay to thin their blood, saleratas and extracts of snakeroot and cinnamon to keep their fevers down, and herbal liniments to dress the pustules as they formed, to limit disfigurement. They kept a fire going and water boiling, and every article of clothing that was taken off was washed with yellow soap.

Outside, Ford organized a search for anyone who might have come into contact with the infected people, and he supervised the supplying of the needs of those inside in such manner that none of them could come into contact with other people until the disease had run its course. He reread his books and the journals he had made during his study in New York, and he answered the worried questions of those outside as best he could . . . and asked a few questions of his own. Of those inside, how many had ever been exposed to cowpox or the chicken pox or festula? It had been noted that those agrarian ailments seemed to impart a degree of immunity against variola, at least in some cases.

"I don't think you need worry overmuch about your son," he told Sam Michaels. "Seth is a healthy lad, and the mild pox he had as a child may protect him . . . at least against the pox. I'm not sure anything will protect him against Bob Christian's elixirs."

When Crispin Blount heard of this, he took it upon himself to seek the same hope. Striding up to the stockade gate, he called, "Nora? Nora, lass! Come to th' wall! I've a delicate question to ask!"

She waved and started for the rampart ladder, and he backed away to stand in the middle of the street, ignoring the curious people passing by. When she appeared above, at the top of the north wall, he called, "Nora, lass, there's a thing I've never asked because it seemed not fitten, but now I need to know!"

"Well, what is it?" she called back. "We're busy in here."

"Nora, those lovely wee dimples here an' there on yer backside, that no one knows about but us, be they perchance old pox marks?"

Her face went as red as ever her hair had been, and people on the street paused to gawk. "Crispin!" she scolded. "For mercy's sake!"

"Well, if ye'll answer my question, then mayhap I won't fret so much!"

"Oh, mercy!"

Jason Cook stepped out of his smithy and called, "Why don't ye sing it to her, Crispin? Ye'd draw a better crowd!"

At the little cabin beyond, both Julie Jackson and Thomas Dodd peered out the door. "What is he yelling about?" the surveyor asked.

"Crispin? Crispin yells whatever is on his mind. It's how he is."

Crispin ignored them all. "Please, my love! 'Tis most important that I know! What was it so bedappled yer lovely behind?"

Nora sighed visibly. "Well, if you have to know, it was the cowpox! I had it when I was a little girl!"

"Th' cowpox, was it? Why did ye get it there an' not on yer face like most do?"

"I don't know, Crispin! Honestly! Now will you go away? I'm busy!"

"Oh, aye!" He grinned at her. "But, lovely lady, ye'll never know what peace of mind I find in th' topography of yer tender posterior!"

Still rose-red, Nora returned to her washtubs in the enclave.

Comfort Calloway was ladling up linens for Oban to hang. "That was your husband, then?" she asked. "He seems a lovely man."

"Plainly, he says what's on his mind," Oban agreed. "Does he sing as well?"

"At the top of his lungs," Nora admitted.

As he approached his house, Crispin saw Luther sitting on the porch, arms over his knees and head hung like a man deep in thought. He frowned, concerned at how the young man clung to his brooding. Certainly, it had been only short weeks since he lost his Kate, but it seemed to Crispin that somewhere in that gloom, sometime soon, there should be at least a trace of sunshine. For the first few days, Luther had wandered about blindly, as one in shock. But that had worn itself away, and a bit of the old Luther had emerged. But only a bit. There seemed no spark in him now, no interest in anything . . . nothing but a hurt so deep that nothing else mattered. The children were comfort of a sort. Crispin had seen how he clung to them, how his eyes seldom left them when they were together. But even the habitual howls of Michael, even the now-and-again abrupt sobbing of Jonathan—the child was of an age to realize that his mother was gone, but not yet old enough to understand why—seemed not to reach beyond his gloom.

He stepped onto the porch and placed a hand on Luther's shoulder, and the bereft young man looked up.

"I've passin' good news," Crispin told him. "Yer mother has had th' cowpox, so it's likely she'll not get th' smallpox."

"I know," Luther said. "Dr. Ford came by and told us. He said to tell you not to worry too much, if she did catch the disease it likely would be the minor strain."

"An' how would he know she'd ever had a cowpox?" Crispin turned to look back at the town suspiciously.

"He heard her tell you. He said everybody heard. He just wasn't sure you'd know what it meant, so he told us." As though forgetting he was there, then, Luther gazed off into the distance, his face expressionless.

"Well, it's good news."

"Yes," the younger man said distantly. "Yes, it is."

Inside the house Michael yowled abruptly and they could hear Ellie hurrying to attend to him. Crispin stepped toward the door, then paused when the bell from the Bowman place sounded. He turned, walked out to the gate, and waited. Minutes passed, then Jared and Julius Bowman came running up the road. "Riders comin'," they shouted. "Christopher Post is home!"

As they passed, the door opened and Ellie came out to stand beside Crispin, looking down the road. Riders came into view, and Crispin squinted. The tads were right. There was no mistaking Christopher Post, even at the distance. Elegant and severe on a tall, dark horse, white linen shining between the lapels of a black riding coat, black boots high-polished, it was Christopher as ever was. But there was something else about him now, a sureness of purpose that Crispin had not seen before. The boy had gone away and come home a man. Several men rode with him, and Crispin recognized only one—Colin McLeod. But there was a thing about them all that echoed and reflected the subtle change in Christopher Post. They rode with him, but not casually as men who travel together. These men were Christopher's men. He was their leader.

Crispin glanced down at Ellie Ferris, then looked again.

Ellie was Ellie, little girl grown woman-size but Ellie as ever was. And yet there was a look to her now that Crispin had not seen before. It was not an expression—she wore no expression—just something in her eyes as she watched the riders coming up the road.

In that moment, Ellie had the look of woman in her eyes. They were Nora's eyes as they must have been at fifteen—eyes that saw what they saw, that could sparkle or storm at will, that could say everything a man wanted to know . . . or that could say nothing at all if she chose.

In that moment, Crispin Blount—tamed old wanderer, singer to the hills, riddler and occasional roisterer—was the first to learn a thing that he would not have guessed such as he could know. Ellie had grown up.

"The world is full of many kinds of people," Awigadoga said. "There are dark people and pale people, and the *aniyunwiya*—the real people—are not the only people. Sometimes it comes about that there are too many people for the land to hold, then they must fight and some must move away. Some people believe that the world can be portioned into little squares of land and each person can own one of those little squares. But the deer and the buffalo, they do not know where the little squares are. The land is the land, and they go where they must. So if everyplace is little squares of land, then where can the people hunt?

272

"Now the white chiefs in Richmond and Charles Town send men to Echota to tell us that the *aniyunwiya* have held forty thousand square miles of land, and since it is that much, it is too much for us to have. They say we must farm the land as they do, so that we will not need so much of it. The white people have short memories. They do not remember that it was the *aniyunwiya* who taught them to farm the land, and it was they who taught us to hunt. They say that they will teach us what we taught them, so there will be more room for them. Ganasini knows this. But Ganasini is chief, so Ganasini must agree, or there will be war and the people will suffer. The white people are like the Shawnee. They are only friendly when people give them what they want.

"Dragging Canoe could not agree to give the white people what they asked at Sycamore Shoals, so he fought with them. The spirit of Dragging Canoe will live forever on the land, but he could not win his fight. Nicolet could not agree, so Nicolet is gone to the west. Nicolet would rather deal with the Spanish than with these whom the English have left behind.

"And Awi-gadoga cannot agree. So Awi-gadoga also will leave Echota. There are places to the north where the laws of the English king may still protect the true people. I will go to live among the Huron."

So Awi-gadoga went out from the people, and his people went with him—his sons and daughters and grandchildren, along with others who did not agree with the council. They traveled north from Echota, through the mountains and across the Cumberland River, then down into the rolling forests of Kentucky, staying far to the west of the known settlements of the white people. They hunted as they went, and where they rested they made deer hides into buckskin and other hides into soft pelts. If they were fortunate, they would winter in northern lands beyond the realms of the deep-forest Shawnee. They would need warm clothing.

273

Even this far west they found signs of the white men—traces of their long hunters, and here and there a clearing where corn was planted and a cabin stood. They moved slowly, giving these a wide berth. On a spring night in dark forests, they heard the little people singing. "The wee folk," some of the women told the children. "They gather in the secret places, and they sing and dance, and they are our friends but it is best not to look for them."

When the children asked Awi-gadoga, who was *edudu*—grandfather—to many of them, he said, "The wee people have always gone where the *aniyunwiya* go. Since the beginning they have been there, and sometimes they have helped us and given us comfort. It is what they most enjoy, the comforting of people. But sometimes the comfort they offer is not what we seek. One time there was an old man who went to the *Yunhwi-Tsuns'di* and they sang and danced for him and invited him to their cave, and when he was there they invited him to stay and sleep. But the next morning when he woke up, ten years had passed."

Their eyes were huge in the firelight, and he nodded wisely. "Listen to your mothers. If your mothers say, 'Do not go to find the *Yunhwi-Tsuns'di*,' then do not go."

A very small one, a little girl, came close to him and tugged at his arm. "Edudu, sing to us about the wee people."

Awi-gadoga cast back into distant memory. It was a very long time since his Edudu had so sung to him, and he remembered only parts of it. Yet one of the young warriors had begun to beat softly on a stretched hide, and others came forward and began to chant, their voices no more than whispers in the night.

"From a place beyond the sea," he husked, "the people once were driven. In canoes they paddled west, with nothing left among them. But small canoes followed behind, though the people did not see them, and in the small canoes were those the people called the wee ones.

274

For while the people's land had shook, and fires had smoked the heavens, the wee folks also were cast out, for they had fought the raven."

In the forest around, shadows crept and dark branches whispered to the night breeze. Awi-gadoga raised his eyes, remembering, and the old words sang in his husky old-man's voice. "When the people lost all hope and could no longer paddle, and slept beneath the sea's dark sky and thought they'd never waken, the wee folk came upon them there and saw that they were sleeping. 'These people are as lost as we,' they said to he who led them. 'They are cast out, the same as us, the ones who fought the raven.' So they tied thongs to their canoes, and through the time of darkness they paddled westward, pulling them, the ones who did not know them. Then Man-Above looked down at them and saw where they were going, and made the nighttime last until a new land lay before them. Then the people woke and went ashore where new lands lay about them, and saw a pathway leading north to where the lands were wider."

As night winds whispered in the forest and a pale moon rose above the trees, Awi-gadoga sang softly to the children . . . of how the people journeyed north and encountered others there, and stayed among them for many years until there was war, and how they migrated north again, then turned toward the east, and always the wee people were with them, seldom seen but sometimes heard in the forests at night. Generations of migration he sang, sometimes staying in one place long enough to raise the mounds that recorded their travels, sometimes only long enough to leave the little mounds where those who died were buried, yet with each sunrise seeing a hope renewed, that they would find a land so fair that they would stay forever and not have to wander again. And always there were the faint songs of the *Yunhwi-Tsuns'di* to guide them and give them comfort. . . .

He paused and looked around. The tiny one had fallen

asleep upon the robes of his lap, and most of the other children slept too. Awi-gadoga put a finger to his lips and the quiet chanting ceased. "We will sing again another night," Awi-gadoga said. "It is a long story."

West of Linden Valley, Leander Haynes killed two Indians, then went on, searching. He knew he should go back to Harrodsburg. He should talk to Julie and tell her . . . but tell her what? That it was his fault Kate was dead? But was it really? It had just happened, the way things sometimes do. Maybe Round Eyes hadn't been after him at all. Mabye he had just happened along. But he knew better than that and didn't try to deceive himself. The Indians had come to find him because he had killed brothers of theirs. It wasn't a thing Indians would often do, he thought, but those had. Round Eyes had seen him once and had gotten away. Then Round Eyes had come back with a party and had come hunting for him . . . and had found him!

It was that, among other things, that bothered Leander. He was not vain about his woodsmanship, but he knew for a fact that he was as at home out here as most Indians. More than most. Indians generally didn't *live* out in the wilderness, any more than white men did. They had their villages, their settlements, the same as white people did. He had seen them. They planted corn and raised children and . . . The images blurred, pushed into the background by other, darker images: a burned cabin, the too-long-dead remains of a father and a mother, a sister and two tiny corpses barely more than babies. Those he remembered the most cruelly. The two least ones had been cut apart.

No, the Indians were not like white people. They were butchers and murderers, and if others did not go out and hunt them down as he did, it was because others had not seen what he had seen.

He pushed the thoughts away. Indians didn't *live* in

these lands. They only travelled through them and hunted on them from time to time. But *he* could live here. In the past few years he had come to know the wild lands as he knew the palms of his hands. As long as his powder held out and the black urge was upon him, he could live here and hunt redmen. And there was no hurry about going back. With time, the hurts back there would fade. Then he could think about what to do. He would think of something. Julie was his. He had told her that, the best way he knew how. And when he returned he would know what to do. He would think of something.

At the edge of a bluegrass meadow he found Indian sign aplenty. A large party had passed this way, maybe an entire small village migrating. He held his powder horns to the sun to see the levels in them. The smaller hunting horn was less than half full, but the big supply horn held plenty to fill it a few more times, and his pouch was weighty against his hip, a good supply of cast rifle balls waiting there. He tested the edges of tomahawk and knife, then pulled his coonskin cap around so that its tail dangled behind his right ear and he could feel the direction of the slightest wind in its fur. Pale eyes bright with blood lust, he set out on the trail of those who had passed.

XXV

Christopher Post wasted no time in the organization of the Kentucky Militia. From his headquarters at his father's horse camp just outside Harrodsburg's town lots, he sent his five sergeants to Cay Cross, Lexington, St. Ashban, Bryant's Station, and Boonesboro to recruit volunteers. These and Harrodsburg were the gathering points of those hardest hit by the Indian wars—the very places to recruit those "howling mobs" he sought. Within eight days he had three hundred men either encamped in the old hay meadow or on their way. "Once and for all time," he told them, "it shall be our purpose to rid the County of Kentucky of the red menace."

All of them provided their own arms. Those who survived in the back land depended upon their long rifles, and no man among them would willingly have exchanged his rifle for any issue weapon.

Some had horses of their own, and some of the rest were issued fine racers from Post stock. He sent his sergeants out again, through the near settlements. "Bring me two hundred more," he told them. "The fields are planted now, and I've summer employment for them. Let them know that the plan is to make one full sweep in strength up to the Ohio, then as far to the west as necessary to clear every redman out of the settled areas. Tell them they will be home in time for harvest, with pay in their purses."

Five hundred men. He would divide them into five companies, two mounted and three foot. It would not be the largest company of Kentuckians to set out against the Indians. Clark had led a thousand in his Scioto raid, Crawford nearly seven hundred up the Miami. But these were not Kentuckians raiding into the Northwest Territories. These would be Kentuckians defending their home ground as they saw it, marching to eliminate a threat to their homes and their families. Five hundred would be adequate.

He concluded a letter to his father-in-law: "Sir, I am wagering that our estimate regarding a treaty of land with the king's envoys is correct. By summer's end I shall be at the Mississippi River, holding the western tip of Kentucky by presence and force of arms. Further, I expect similar expeditions to be mounted westward in Tennessee and the Carolina territories. If a treaty can be perfected by that time, it will stand unopposed, as the Spanish will be confined to the west of their river. I assure you that, before the fields ripen, no force of Spain or their Indian allies shall hold so much as a foot of Kentucky."

Michael had been a screaming little tyrant all afternoon, but by sundown Ellie had him fed, cleaned, wrapped, and asleep in his little bed, and she went out to sit on the porch and watch the twilight play in storm clouds over the distant dark hills beyond the out-lots. Down the road she saw Luther approaching, head down and listless, while Jonathan tagged close beside him. Something in a far field caught the boy's attention and he tugged at his father's britches, pointing. But Luther didn't look around. Ellie sighed, shaking her head. "Oh, Luther," she whispered, "can't you comfort your son? He's just as lonely as you are."

As we all are, she thought. In recent days they had

279

hardly seen Crispin. He came home only to sleep. Through the daylight hours he haunted the area around the old fort, worrying about Nora, missing her terribly despite his bluster and denial. There were so many sick people quarantined in there. Twenty-two people, they said, and more than half of them abed with fevers and pox. Some might die of it, they said. It was the smallpox, and it could kill. Yet Dr. Christian was there with them and Dr. Ford outside working with him, and though some were very ill, none had died yet. Those who had escaped infection were attending those who had not, doing everything that was known to keep their fevers down and the poisons in them abated.

But still, the closing of the old wagon gate had spread a pall over the area. People in the town kept to themselves, not sure that some among them might not carry the infection and afraid to risk contact until they were sure. Hattie was there all the time now—the squire had sent her to help with Kate's children, and Nora had made a cot for her in the pantry—but rarely did anyone else come.

And with so many of the men camped out in the old hay meadow, getting ready to march with Christopher Post against the Indians, the town seemed a ghost of itself these past days.

Thoughts of Christopher brought back old feelings that had never gone away, but she thought of him now as a thing from her childhood, a focal point for the dreams and the feelings that had been part of growing up. Christopher had never been a part of her life, not really. He was an illusion that she had enjoyed, someone to dream about when it was so urgently important that she dream. But he had never been close, never interested in her . . . or in anyone, so far as she could recall. He had a wife now, they said. A beautiful young woman with a shawl always over one side of her face because of an ugly stigma there. He had married her aboard a ship bound from New England to Virginia. Her father, they said, was

280

a powerful man in Virginia. Obviously, Christopher had made good use of that. Captain of Militia for the West . . . at eighteen! It was a provisional commission only, the squire had told Crispin. But provisional or not, Christopher was making use of it. Some said he would have five hundred men in his militia soon.

Eighteen. Brilliant, wealthy, ambitious . . . driven Christopher Post. Eighteen. What would he be at twenty, or at thirty, or at forty?

Such contrast . . . Seth Michaels was also eighteen. Eighteen and lonely. He missed his dogs. The fellers. How odd that they had both disappeared that way, both at once. He talked about them, was lonely for them, kept saying to everyone that they would come back, though it was only himself he was saying it to. Ellie didn't remember Seth ever being without his fellers. They had been part of him. And she found that she missed them, too. Just as she missed Seth now. He was in the fort, too, one of those exposed. Nora was safe from the smallpox, the doctor said. Cowpox was a protection. He said Seth was safe, too, but there was a hesitancy there. Wasn't he sure? Didn't chicken pox carry immunity as well? They thought so, he said. No one was really certain.

Had Christopher Post ever been uncertain about anything? In a way, she doubted it. She pictured him clearly in her mind, as he always appeared there—tall, slim, elegant in a casual way . . . but not casual. Christopher was never casual. Handsome of feature, striking of pose—a person for a young girl to dream about. But she knew he had never noticed her, not in any way that mattered. She wondered how it might be for his wife. Did he notice *her* in ways that mattered? Or did people matter to Christopher? It was an odd thought. If people didn't matter to a person, then what would? People mattered to her. Luther mattered, and her mother, and Crispin, and Julie, though Julie could be so strange at times—like a person lost in a fog and running in all directions looking for a way out. But Julie mattered, and—and those two little boys who would never know their mother because Kate had died.

Luther and Jonathan were near now. The boy tagged along slightly behind his father, his pace and posture a miniature of Luther's—head down, his whole self slumped a bit as he walked. He wasn't mimicking his father, Ellie knew. He was only learning—from the only person who could teach him—how one behaves in grief.

Her throat tightened at the knowledge, and there was moisture in her eyes. Don't teach the child the ways of grief, Luther, she thought. Kate wouldn't want that. Teach him to laugh. Sing for your son, Luther, the way our father sang for us. The way Crispin Blount brought back for us . . .

And there was one among them, the pixie Aella,
who felt the old love of her race,
and she listened adept as the human folk wept,
and found there were tears on her face. . . .

The door opened and closed quietly behind her, and after a moment she felt a hesitant hand on her shoulder. She turned. Hattie stood there, deep concern on her dark features.

"What troublin' you, Miss Ellie?" She knelt beside her. "Why, look at you. You cryin'."

Thomas Dodd had been out with his scouts and his crew. From the stone cairn that marked Harrod's original claim, he had worked due north to where his line-of-sight measure intersected the Kentucky River, then had done compass readings along its meandering course until he reached the forks of the Elkhorn. With these readings and his charts he had established a meridian that he labeled "Principal Meridian for the Kentucky River surveys."

He returned to Harrodsburg full of excitement and urgency, unpacked his duffel, and went straight to work at his table in Julie Jackson's mixing cabin . . . now officially designated the "land office."

"If you were to walk a hundred paces down that street out there," he told Julie, "to where that pile of stones is, you would be standing at exactly eighty-four degrees, forty-eight minutes, and eleven seconds west longitude."

"I would?" She cocked her head at him, intrigued by the excitement in his manner and wondering what he was talking about.

"That means how far you are west of Greenwich . . . in terms of degrees of longitude."

"It certainly is good to know that," she assured him. "Where is . . . Grenidge?"

"It's a place in England. It's where the Meridian of Greenwich is established. The Prime Meridian for the entire world. It's where navigators and geographers count from. And Harrod's bench mark is exactly eighty-four, forty-eight, eleven west of it. A truly marvelous conicdence!"

"Well, I'm awfully glad," she said. "What does it mean?"

"Ah, Julie," he chuckled. "Dear lady, if you keep looking at me that way, I shall surely embarrass the both of us by kissing you again." His eyes narrowed and his chuckle faded. "I've had a devil of a time trying not to think overmuch about the first time, you know." He tore his eyes away and prodded at his charts with a stiff finger. "What it means is Harrod's claim heap is on the same meridian as the mouth of the Greater Miami River, which comes down to the Ohio through the Northwest Territories. What it means is that *if* the Continental Congress passes a land act for those territories, based on rectangular measure as it is proposed, and *if* a Geographer's Line is extended from Pennsylvania, as proposed, and *if* that line is measured westward by ranges, as proposed, and *if* I survey a meridian line from here to the mouth of the Greater Miami on the Ohio, which I believe is due north, then I will have established the First Principal Meridian."

Still she gazed at him, hopelessly lost. He chuckled again, then laughed outright. "Julie . . . ah, Julie. Were you to chirp at me about the proper mixing of bread dough, I might look just as perplexed."

"Mixing bread dough is simple," she said.

"Well, geography has never been simple. All it amounts to is that a proper surveyor has two goals in mind: first, to get his numbers right and be paid promptly for them; second, to leave behind a significant point or line from which others will survey later."

"Is that all a proper surveyor ever wants, Thomas?" If she hadn't comprehended the business about meridians and geographic lines, she had clearly caught the subtle urgency of his joke about a kiss, and that was a thing she well understood. She hadn't been kissed since the evening they met, and the last person to have kissed her was him. She had thought about it since. Thomas Dodd was not a person she minded being kissed by. Not, she realized, at all.

"Well, I suppose there are some other things that are important." He shrugged, and that look was in his eyes again.

"Short of embarrassing us both, of course."

"Oh, of course."

"But still, you have been gone for a time. A seemly welcome home might not be that embarrassing."

"Possibly not if it were . . . well, seemly," he agreed, pushing back his chair.

It was a kiss unlike any kiss Julie had ever had before. It left them both flushed and breathless. "Welcome home, Thomas," she breathed after a moment.

"I'm wondering, Julie . . . if I were to go outside, then come in again, do you suppose I might be welcomed home again?"

He helped her finish her loaves and clean her ovens, then they sat at his work table and made a meal of fresh bread, dried venison, and tea. After a time, he said, "I heard there is a company of militia forming, to march north to the Ohio and then sweep westward. Is that their camp I saw, east of town?"

"Yes. Christopher Post will lead them. They plan to leave in two or three days, I heard."

"The country should be quite safe for travel where they have passed, shouldn't it?"

"It surely should be. They intend to push all the Indians out of Kentucky."

"I see." He tapped his fingers against the tabletop, thinking, then looked at her. "Julie, when was the last time you got out to take a look at the countryside? I mean, beyond just these fields and woodlots here. A journey . . . an adventure."

"I've never been away from Harrodsburg, Thomas. Not since I was just a little girl, when we came here from the Holston. It seems I've lived my life since then either in or in sight of that stockade fort over there."

"Stifling," he said. "There are beautiful places out there, Julie. Places where the forests grow so thick that full sun never hits the ground beneath their branches. Meadows of blue grass where a dozen kinds of flowers spring from every rock and ledge, and the air is so sweet you can taste it. Springs where the water comes cold from the stone to make little laughing streams with ferns along their banks. Would you like to see some of those places, Julie? With me?"

She gazed at him with large eyes, and a dimple danced on her cheek. "I don't know, Thomas. Would it be seemly?"

"Absolutely seemly." He grinned. "A survey crew in the field has little time for interludes. It works from dawn to dark."

"What about after dark? How much seemliness could there be then?"

"As much as you want, Julie. I would promise you that."

"It sounds . . . exciting. Thrilling. But I don't know. . . ."

"You have hired help for the bakery, Julie. . . ."

"Only temporarily, while the militia is encamped."

"Extend their service, then. A week or two of wages won't hurt that much, surely. They could run the bakery while we are away. I'm offering you a holiday, Julie Jackson. I hope you take me up on my offer."

"Why?"

"Because I would much rather have you with me than to spend that many lonely hours thinking about you from far away."

In the old fort, Seth Michaels finished folding clean blankets from the day's wash and went to a barrel for water. He leaned there, sipping, letting the coolness slide down his parched throat, realizing that he was extremely tired. His joints ached and his throat hurt, and it was far too warm for comfort. Slowly he climbed to the rampart and leaned his elbows there, looking off to the east. The Blount house was clearly visible in the evening light, and there were people on the porch. Was Ellie there? He squinted, and the view seemed to blur. His eyes ached. He was very tired.

He slumped against the old logs of the wall and looked away to the south. The fellers could be out there somewhere. They could be right out there, just there . . . or there . . . maybe on their way home . . . maybe trying to come home. He squinted again. They wouldn't have gone far away; they should be showing up any time. . . . No! He shook his head. They were gone. If they were alive, he would have found them. Or they would have found him. No, something had happened to them.

And yet . . . the world seemed to tilt a bit, and things shifted this way and that, and yes, those shadows away off there, those could be them. He pictured them, trotting along side by side, one at each flank as he walked with them. Where were they?

Where was Ellie? He hadn't seen Ellie in a long time. Had something happened to Ellie? He drew deep breaths into sore lungs, trying to cool off. It was hot. So awfully hot. Fellers? He thought he heard them, somewhere. But it wasn't the fellers. Only voices . . . Ellie's mother's voice, saying something to him. Calling his name.

But where was she? The light had grown so dim, just a sullen, swirling murk of dull red and black . . . and it was hot.

XXVI

Joseph Trelawney had his carriage out, exercising a team, and at sunrise he pulled up in front of Crispin's gate. When Hattie opened the door, he called, "Tell the tinker the militia is moving out. If he wants to come with me and watch, he'd best not dawdle."

Crispin peered out, then turned to those inside. "Who wants to go along to see the militia march?"

"I do!" Jonathan ran to him.

"Then take yerself out there an' climb up in th' squire's contraption," he told the boy. "An' mind ye don't let him sell ye anything." As the boy scrambled past him, Crispin put on his hat. "Luther, come along for the ride, son. 'Twill be a sight worth seein'. Ellie, would ye like to go see Christopher off?"

Luther went to find his hat, but Ellie shook her head. "I've seen him enough, Crispin. I'll stay with the baby."

"Any more word about Seth yet this mornin'?"

"Nothing, except that he is very ill."

Crispin went to the girl and put a hand on her shoulder. "Seth'll be all right, Ellie. It's yer own mother who's takin' care of him, isn't it?"

The dog had come from under the porch to join Jonathan in the squire's bright carriage, and Trelawney turned a frown on Crispin as he opened the gate.

288

"Creatures of my acquaintance generally don't ride, tinker."

Crispin shrugged and climbed aboard, Luther following. "One o' the tragedies o' squatbottom gentry," he said. "They miss association wi' th' proper class o' creatures."

At the hay meadow Jonathan's eyes went huge. Five hundred militiamen were assembled there, nearly two hundred of them mounted and all armed with rifles, knives, and hand axes, laden with powder horns and shot pouches, possible packs, bedding, and tack. The boy had never before seen so many men together in one place. Handlers were tightening pack frame straps on a string of mules, and among them all rode five large, grim-faced men wearing the dun-collared red coats and tricorns of Royal Marines, shouting orders and assembling groups. Over his British coat, each wore the strapping of frontier militia and the shoulder patches of Virginia regulars. The effect was odd—almost comical at first glance, but then something else . . . something altogether fierce and warlike.

"His sergeants." Trelawney indicated the redcoats. "He recruited them directly from their paroles."

"I can see why," Crispin said. "'Twould be a rare irregular as would tempt th' temper o' th' likes of them."

Armed men waved the carriage into the encampment and directed them to a knoll where noted personages awaited. Giles Bowman was there, and Samuel Calkins in his wire wig, along with the magistrate Ethan Shane and Captains Haymon Roberts and Charles McKinnon from Lexington and Boonesboro, and a bearded man from Bryant's Station who wore a green sash over his buckskins.

"Kentucky's finest," Crispin allowed. "Yon Christopher is makin' all this nice an' official, it seems."

"It *is* official." Trelawney nodded. "It's no mob that goes out from here this day, but the muscle and might of

289

Kentucky with the blessing of Virginia to back it up."

"An' a lad o' eighteen in charge," Crispin muttered.

"A lad of eighteen, indeed. Tell me, Blount, how old were you when you took charge of your own life?"

"Maybe sixteen . . . seventeen. A many's done it younger, I reckon. But not in such high manner as this."

"Not many are Christopher Post, either."

At the far end of the camp a calling horn sounded and handlers led out a magnificent black horse—Christopher's favorite hunter. Then Christopher himself appeared from a tent and mounted. He rode straight across to the knoll and tipped his hat to those assembled there. "Gentlemen," he said, "by your leave, I present to you the Militia of Kentucky." He swung the horse around, and more horns sounded. Sergeants shouted and men scrambled to form companies, facing those on the knoll. There had been little drill for these men—and they would have tolerated very little of it—but they ranked in presentable fashion, rifle barrels aglint in the morning sun.

Christopher raised his hand for silence, then rode forward to inspect each company, one by one. When he was satisfied he walked his mount away twenty yards, then turned and addressed the militia.

"Too much Christian blood has fallen on the soil of Kentucky," he said. "For too long the red menace has been a pall over these lands. Many have fought the red men, and many have died. Many have tried to live in peace with the red men and have died. If any man among you has not lost a loved one to the attacks of savages, let him look to his neighbor and know how it has been for him.

"On this day, the tide must turn. No longer are we Englishmen, suppliants of a foreign king awaiting his troops to protect us. Nor have we allies in any foreign power . . . indeed, we have been betrayed by those who offered their help to us. The ministries of Europe, intent upon their own dreams of empire, have played their games upon our soil and have made to divide the spoils among them. Each king attempts to placate another king by granting him a share in what we have won here. France has offered all of western Kentucky to Spain as a prize of war. But Kentucky is not France's to give, nor Spain's to claim. Kentucky belongs to us! The people of the Commonwealth of Virginia, the people of our allies— the other Confederated Commonwealths who choose to come here to dwell among us in peace—but mostly to the people of Kentucky itself, whose blood has darkened this ground and whose sweat has cleared fields in the wilderness.

"Those fields are planted now, and they shall not bear for the benefit of red raiders or Canadian rangers or French adventurers . . . and most certainly not for the benefit of the Governor-General of New Spain! We go forth now to put an end to such pretentions, and when we return you yourselves shall harvest what you have sown. We shall sweep Kentucky clean of all who would take it from us, right down to the Mississippi River. And should any across that river seek to impede us, then we shall drive directly across that river and assure ourselves that they will not trouble us again!"

Without further ceremony he turned his mount, put on his hat, and trotted to the foot of the knoll. "By your leave, gentlemen, good day."

The sergeants had the militia moving smartly even as he finished his words, and he wheeled away to ride out at the head of his companies. For a time there was silence among those who had come to watch, then voices erupted all around. Startled questions flew. Crispin turned to Trelawney, whose broad face was hard as hill rock. "I take it he's thinkin' on crossin' into New Spain."

"He is," Trelawney said. "Oh, they'll make a sweep for Indians first, but to Christopher that is only an incidental task. He intends to ride right up the funnel at Horseshoe Bend and look the Governor General in the eye across his river. And I fear that if the Spaniards give him an ounce of provocation, then New Madrid is going to go up in flames and that Governor General is going to feel the blade of Christopher's sword."

Crispin looked after the departing Kentuckians. "I've known since first I set eyes on him—he was no more than a tad then—that he intended ill against th' Spanish an' New Spain. But I've never known why."

"I know why."

Crispin jerked his head around. Mr. Sparrow had come up to the carriage on silent moccasins. "When Captain Post died out yonder," he said quietly, "it grieved me to lose him and it grieved me that there were times I didn't understand him. But I placed soil in his grave and made my peace with him that way. Christopher never had a chance to make peace with his father, never when he was alive and never in death."

"Peace? Make peace for what, Mr. Sparrow?"

"For his shame, Mr. Blount."

"Shame? For havin' a bad leg?"

"Shame for how he got it, maybe. The captain got that wound from the Spaniards yonder, and Christopher could never bring himself to forgive him."

"For being wounded?"

"For failing, Mr. Blount. For failing."

On the drive back, Jonathan clung to the seat rest at Crispin's shoulder, his eyes still large and excited. "Pa says when I'm big enough he'll give me his white horn," he chattered. "And I'll have a rifle, too, and the white horn. . . . Pa said he made it for his pa, and his name was the same as mine. Jonathan Ferris."

"Takes a big man to shoulder a rifle, tad," Crispin told him, "and a big man to know when not to, as well."

"I'll be a big man," the boy assured him. "When I get my rifle I'll shoot a turkey for everybody to eat, and a deer and—and then I'll shoot some Indians." He looked back to where the militia had gone. "And I'll go with those men and—and go to New Spain and shoot

Spaniards, too."

In the seat behind, Luther chuckled. It was the first time anyone had heard him laugh since that bleak day up by the river, and both Crispin and Trelawney turned to look at him. Luther chuckled again, but it was not the laughter of humor. His eyes were bleak. "He sounds as fierce as Christopher Post, doesn't he? Had the boy been me, he'd be out there now, with that militia, tearing off to wreak wrath in the wilderness. But not me. I had the chance to go, but I didn't."

Crispin arched a brow, studying him. "Did ye want to go, then?"

"I don't know. It seems right that I should, I suppose. I've as much reason to as any. The Indians . . . they . . ." His voice broke. Crispin turned away, not wanting to have the young man shamed. But then Luther breathed deep to calm himself. "No, I don't wish that I had gone. I don't know what I want to do, but that's not it. Kate— Kate wouldn't have wanted me to. Such things are not my way, and I think she knew me better than I know myself."

"Generally women do." Crispin nodded, turning to him again. "Don't mind what the boy says, Luther. He's a wee tad an' playin' with thoughts. 'Tis a natural thing. But there's those as goes off to play at war an' there's those that don't, an' well that be, for if all the men went off to war, then who'd mind th' stores an' tend th' fields an' chop th' firewood? Boys dream o' war an' adventures. Men must think o' other things as well."

"And listen at who is talking about mature responsibility," Squire Trelawney muttered.

Crispin ignored him. "It's th' price of growin' up," he told Luther.

Luther shrugged and looked away, disinterested eyes watching the out-lots pace by. "Sometimes I think I was born grown up," he said.

At Crispin's bidding, the squire turned right off the

high road, past sheds and houses beyond which they could see the new stone church going up. Scaffolds were slung upon its face, ready for placement of a roof-tree. The work had been delayed while Samuel Calkins assisted in the building of wooden coffins, resin-sealed and treated with camphor. Three of those in the stockade now had died of the smallpox, and there might be more. The special coffins were the only way Dr. Ford and Dr. Christian would allow the bodies to be taken out to the community graveyard, sealed inside the fort and then set by the gate to be picked up by men using poles and slings. There was complaint, both inside and out, at such treatment of the dead. But so far no one outside had been exposed to the disease.

Among those at the gate were several of the Michaels family and Ellie. Nora was above, at the rampart, and Crispin waved at her as the carriage pulled up. Ellie hurried over to them. "Mother says Seth should be all right," she said. "Dr. Christian brought his fever down. He probably will have scars, but he will recover, they say." She looked up at the rampart, then back at Crispin, and her eyes were liquid. "He kept calling for me, mother said. All through the fever he called for me. Why would he do that, Crispin?"

He stepped down from the carriage, walked around, and took the girl's hand. "Step up there, Ellie, lass. Sit beside yer brother an' ask him that. It seems to me it's high time both of you think hard about how he'll answer that question." To the glowering squire, he said, "Ye won't mind takin' these young'uns to my house, will ye, Squire?"

"This is no jitney, tinker."

"Well, 'tisn't like ye had anything better to do, is it? An' while yer about it, why not raid yer precious warehouse again for candles an' lamp oil? Seemed to me last night there was precious little light in yonder."

Trelawney muttered and grunted, but he went off on

294

the errands. Crispin stood for a moment, looking up at his wife atop the rampart. She looked tired and disheveled, and he noticed for the first time that there were bits of silver lacing her auburn hair. But the smile she sent down for him was that same smile, unchanged by the toil or the years, and his heart swelled within him. There was a thing he had told Luther once—in another time, it seemed—that he had thought was meant for the younger man but in fact was for himself. Every man sees the world . . . that's got eyes to see. He can be a traveler at the world's door, finding each new day in another place, and sure enough he'll see the world. Or he can settle in and put out the welcome mat and let the world come to him. There's precious things a man might miss if he's not home to receive them.

Looking at the tired face of his wife now, twelve feet above him and separated from him by a log wall, the words came back and with them a rush of gladness that no part of his old traveling ways could ever have produced.

On impulse he pulled off his hat, held it against his chest, and gazed into the eyes above him. "I've seen the ports of Chesapeake," he sang in a voice that was just for her, "the wonders gathered there . . . the tall ships suited out in sails to venture who knows where . . . I've wandered roads that turn an' wind, wi' riddles ahead an' marvels behind, an' always just lookin' out to find . . . the sight of a lady fair."

She blushed and glanced about quickly at others passing on the street, many of them stopping to listen. Then her eyes returned to him and she shrugged. "I didn't marry a private man, did I, Crispin Blount?"

"A private man's old heart would burst for sure, Nora, had he th' pleasure th' sight of you gives me this minute . . . an' no way to release it from within him." He threw back his head, grinned, and sang in the voice that rang down mountains, "An' it's that brings an end to th' life o' th' road where a wanderin' man must fare, while he dreams th' dark days an' th' long, lonely nights o' a lass with th' sun in her hair! Aye, but some have th' fortune to find what they lack, an' a few have th' sense then to never look back . . . an' I pledge thee, my lady, this one's found th' track . . ." He paused and shook with laughter. "Ah, dear heart, could only life be like a song, so simple that every line can rhyme!" Then he straightened his face and gazed directly into her eyes. "I pledge thee, beloved, there's no turnin' back . . . when a man's found his lady fair."

"Seth Michaels loves you, Ellie." Luther turned from the door, puzzled. She had asked him the same question she had asked Crispin Blount, just after the squire let them off at the house. "Don't you know that? If you don't, you're the only one who doesn't."

"Oh, I know," she said. "At least I suppose he does. We have been friends a very long time. Of course we are fond of each other. But, Luther, when he was so ill and out of his head with the fever, mother said he didn't ask about his family, or call for his fellers as he did at first, or anything like that. She said he just kept saying my name. Why did he? If I were so ill, I don't know if I would say his. I don't know what I should do, Luther."

"What did mother think you should do?"

"I don't know. How can people talk about anything when there is a stockade wall between them?"

He hung his hat on a door peg and went to sit by the window. From another room they could hear Hattie's voice, singing softly to the baby. "I don't know, Ellie. All I know of anything like that is how it was . . . for me. But that's over now."

"How can it be over when you are so sad, Luther? A thing that's over is done."

He gazed out the window, trying not to remember, trying not to think about Kate. But Ellie pulled a bench from the hearthside and joined him there, her eyes intent on his face. "Please, Luther. Crispin said you could tell me. What is it when a person loves someone that way?"

He rubbed his face, then looked at his hands—big, hard hands that had touched angel skin. . . . Why did they still look the same? Nothing could ever be the same. "I'd as soon not talk about it, Ellie. I don't know what I can say."

Yet still she gazed at him, and memory was a nudge. Even when she was so little, tagging after him when they gathered nuts in the forest, even then there had been that about his sister. She persisted. Ellie was Ellie. Always.

What did it mean to Seth to love her? The same as it had meant to him, he supposed . . . his love for Kate. But how to answer Ellie's question?

"It's comfort," he said, stumbling on the word. "A comfort in all things, I suppose. He loves you, so no matter what things may be wrong, all's right despite them. As long as you are there. And—and what's important to him is important because you're a part of it. I expect it pleasures him to be with you, and to think about you when he's not. I guess he'd give his life for you if he had to . . . and gladly give it to you if you wanted it. Still, if all he could ever be to you is your best friend, then I guess he'd be grateful for that as well. . . . Ellie, I don't know what more to say. It's so hard to talk about such things, when . . . ah, look at me, for heaven's sake! What way is this for a man to behave?"

He turned away abruptly, lacking the words to tell her more or the power to use even those he had.

But he had answered her question . . . as best he could. And somehow he had answered his own, as well. What does a man do when the one who was all that to him is gone? He remembers, and he goes on.

Crispin found a subtle change in the house when he came home at noon. Luther was around in back, splitting stove wood on the chopping block while Jonathan

297

collected the pieces and carried them to the cookshed for Hattie. Ellie was setting table for the midday meal while Michael fussed at her from his bar-pen—his bear-pen, Ellie called it—by the hearth. The windows were open and each room was bright with the fair day's sun.

Ring of axe and thump of pewter, lyric of many voices and the singing of birds in the meadow . . . he tipped his head, just listening. Come home soon, Nora, he thought. There's music in your house once more. He wiped his feet and went in.

The Gateway

XXVII

Some said they were a new breed, the people who pushed westward in those cauldron years of war and revolution while foreign empires bickered over lands they had already lost. A meld of those descended from the Scottish Highlands, the wild Irish moors and the hill pockets of Wales, they found fertile soil for their seed in America. Proud and cantankerous, volatile and steeped in lore that was entirely their own, they viewed the westward expanses as theirs to claim and they set their roots as the mountain pine that can crack granite in order to grow. They endured poverty, catastrophe, plague, and betrayal, and they added to their insatiable hunger for land a fierce restlessness and a capacity to endure.

In 1769 when John Finley led Daniel Boone from the Yadkin Valley through the Cumberland Gap, there were six white men in all of Kentucky. Four years later, when Jonathan Ferris died in his high field above the Ohio River, there were six thousand. By the end of the Red Knife Massacres the number might have been only half that. But in the spring of 1783 when Christopher Post led his Kentucky Militia out of Harrodsburg, there were nearly fifty thousand people in Kentucky, in settlements and on farms throughout the eastern half of it, and more coming in every day.

What Indians were in Kentucky might, on any given

day, have numbered as many as a thousand or as few as a hundred. Not since the time of the smokes had red men in great numbers roamed the wilderness land. They came to hunt—Cherokee from the south and Shawnee from the north, with a scattering of other tribes among them—or to travel through on their way to somewhere else. And they stayed far west of the onrushing edges of white settlement. With the red men as with the white, only the war-scarred, the addled or young males out for sport, actively sought conflict unless there was a purpose to it. And now, for the Indians, there was none.

Christopher Post had not been idle, either in Williamsburg and Richmond, or while he formed his militia in Kentucky. He knew the numbers and he knew the facts, and thus his expedition to sweep the "Red Menace" from Kentucky was mostly for show . . . that, and to give a reason to his volunteers for what was being done.

From the Ohio River to the Cumberland River was an average distance of a hundred miles, much of it forest, hills, and valleys, virtually all of it wilderness. For five companies of militia to sweep clean such an expanse was not within possibility. They would drive some ahead of them, possibly make them wary for a season, but many would slip through as the thin line of armed settlers passed. Such did not detract from the purpose of the "Boy Captain," as many called him. His purpose was to go west in force.

At the riverbank camp of Stephen Moliere, now a fortified and bustling operation reducing timber both above and below the falls for the construction of buildings and boats, Christopher Post spread his five companies in a fan to the south—foot companies in the broad center of the march, mounted companies on the flanks—and gave his sergeants their orders. Then he called on Moliere. "Should Spain gain land east of the Mississippi," he said, "she would control the river. There is nowhere that the Mississippi cannot be closed if gun

300

emplacements can be placed upon both banks."

"Spain held the river open for Americans through the war," Moliere pointed out.

"Spain was acting against England, not for the colonies. It was a test of empires then. Now it is a different thing. Spain never expected England to grant freedom to its colonies. Now that we have it, Spain will turn on us because she fears us."

"Yes." Moliere nodded. "I can see that. No monarch controls us now. We are a new sort of threat, aren't we?"

"If Spain closes the river, you will never send goods to New Orleans, Mr. Moliere."

"New Orleans *is* Spanish."

"And will be reached only by sea. Spain will strangle these colonies if she can."

"Then what do you propose?"

"The Articles of Peace between the Confederated States and England have been in effect for three months. Within six months, the last Loyalist will be gone from these lands. Negotiations are progressing in Paris and London to determine who has what sovereignty, and a treaty will be achieved. But sovereignty on paper means nothing. Presence is the stuff of sovereignty. How many boats will you have by end of summer?"

"Four at least. Possibly six."

"With cargoes?"

"If I had twenty boats, there would be cargoes and more."

"Then I ask two things of you. I ask that you put armed crews aboard your boats and take your cargoes downriver as you propose. And I ask that you coordinate your arrival at the mouth of the Ohio with me. Once and for all, we must make it clear that the Mississippi is not a Spanish river."

"Nor any lands this side of it Spanish lands," Moliere agreed. "Your commission . . . do you act on behalf of the Confederation of States?"

"I act entirely for the Commonwealth of Virginia. Let

301

us get our own house in order before we consign such matters to the people at Philadelphia."

Moliere grinned at him. "I like that. It is audacious. But will the Continental Congress appreciate it as well?"

Christopher shrugged. "What the Continental Congress likes or doesn't like is of no concern . . . even less so than whether the government of Virginia approves of people settling in its wilderness. The purpose of government is to accept established fact and document it."

"On that point also we agree. Very well, if Kentucky can have an army, then Kentucky can also have a navy. Possibly I can have six boats ready by summer's end. If I can conduct my business in a manner that serves both our purposes . . . why not?"

When the Kentucky Militia began its westward sweep, the mounted company on the left flank passed within a mile of where Awi-gadoga and his people lay hidden. Some of the young men among the Cherokee there wanted to follow after them and attack, but wiser heads dissuaded them. "They go to mark the land and make it their own," old Standing Deer said. "It is not our concern. Others may fight now over the Dark and Bloody Ground, but we have set our path. We will go to the river and cross it, and then we will go on north. If we must fight, let it be with the Shawnee who are between us and the Huron. Fighting the white man brings only tears."

Luther and Crispin had both objected to Julie's idea of going off into the woods with a surveyor. Luther, shocked at the notion, had reacted immediately: "What would Kate have thought?"

To which Julie responded, "Luther, Kate went off into the woods with you."

"Well, that was different, and you know it. I married Kate. You don't even know this—this Dodd."

"I most certainly do!" she snapped. "We're together

302

almost every day."

"But not all alone out in the woods . . ."

"We won't be all alone. He has a whole crew of surveyors. It will be a big group."

"Julie . . ." He took refuge in his last resort. "Well, it isn't seemly."

Crispin's reaction was a bit more thoughtful. "Seems to me it could be a mistake, lass. Those are yet wild lands yonder, an' wilder folks skulkin' about in 'em. A plain woman might not be threatened, but you're no plain woman."

"Are you saying I shouldn't go, Crispin?"

"Well . . ." He took refuge in higher authority. "Why don't we walk down yonder an' ask Nora what she thinks?"

"The way you asked her about her pockmarks? Crispin, I do think the world of you, but I don't think just everything is just everybody's business."

She made him stay home, and she went herself. She waved at the stockade gate, and after a time Nora came to the rampart. She seemed less tired than she had been before, more herself. The fevers inside were running their course, and in past days no one new had taken them and no more had died.

Standing close under the wall, Julie asked, "How is Seth now? Will he recover?"

"He'll recover," Nora said. "He will have scars, but maybe not deep ones. The sores are scabbing now and he has no new ones."

Then Julie told her—as quietly as possible—about Thomas Dodd inviting her to go along on his surveying expedition to the river and about the reactions of Luther and Crispin.

"Men," Nora said. "They try so hard to protect that sometimes they nigh can smother a body. It's your decision alone, Julie. What do you think you should do?"

"I haven't seen a place outside this settlement since I was Ellie's age," Julie said. "And, oh, sometimes I dream that there is so much out there to see. Thomas speaks of so many places, and so many things and—"

"Is it the journey, Julie? Or is it the young man?"

"I don't know. Why?"

Nora looked around. There was no one within earshot. "If it's just for the journey, then maybe Crispin could show you some of the wilderness around. If that's your only interest, it would be better that way. But if it's the young man, then Crispin would be no substitute . . . nor would anyone else."

"I've had thoughts about him," Julie admitted.

"Then there's no one but you can judge your own thoughts. And there's no one who should tell you go or stay, either."

"What would you do if it were you?"

Nora shrugged. "I went off to the wilderness with a young man once. I've never regretted it."

So Julie thought about it and wondered how one might know what was in one's own mind. Was it to see the wilderness, or was it to spend time with Thomas Dodd, to learn to know him better, to see him do that which he did and seemed to love so well? Or was it something else entirely? Dodd was here only for a time, then he would be gone—back to those places Julie had only heard about, places like Philadelphia and Trenton and Boston, or maybe on to other places where he would survey other new lands. She knew she would marry again. She would marry someone here or someone elsewhere . . . and the more she thought about it, the more exciting the elsewhere became.

When Thomas Dodd gathered up his crew and his equipment and rode north out of Harrodsburg, Julie Jackson rode with him. A dozen young men of the town, each with his own thoughts on the matter, watched them depart, and each felt that a dream had ended. Each separately, they had assumed that Leander Haynes had claim on Julie, and each had been reluctant to confront the quiet, pale-eyed woodsman. They sensed, as did others, something violent and frightening in him. Yet now someone not so timid had come along and snatched away the prize . . . the prettiest girl around.

West of a valley where smokes told of two cabins, carrion birds circled above the forest and settled among the trees. From a high place Goga the Crow saw them and noted where they were. Silent as the fall of night, he made his way toward them, to see what had died there. It was deep in a ravine, and the bodies had been covered with brush. But the birds had found them. Goga knelt above. They had been two men. Forest Shawnee from the north. One had died of a tomahawk cut. He could not tell how the other had fallen, but something in the way they lay said that he should look for sign upon the far shoulder of the ravine.

The prints were barely visible—moccasin prints where a man who knew how to leave no sign had been careless, just once. He had stepped on soft ground, two steps approaching the top of the ravine. He probably had been carrying a dead Shawnee, and he had stepped there, and there, and then beyond to throw the body into the ravine.

Two clear prints only, but they were enough. Goga knew the sign as he knew the face that went with it. *S'gohidihi* had been here, just that long before—more than a day, less than two. And smaller signs—signs one would not see at all except for knowing they were there to find—said where the Tenkiller had gone.

Goga the Crow returned to where the others were camped, watching birds rise in the distance ahead of a large party of armed white men moving westward. Beyond them was a second party, miles away, and beyond that another. For a time the four warriors watched in silence, then one said, "They drive the land. It is a game drive."

"More than game," another said. "They want to drive everything ahead of them. They want to drive people."

When the white men had passed and were distant, moving west, Goga said, "Tenkiller has been near here. He left two Shawnee dead, and I have seen where he went. His path leads northeast from there."

Without a word they picked up their weapons and followed him toward where he had found the sign.

A day later and thirty miles to the north, they found where Tenkiller had crouched, just hours earlier, to look at the many marks left by a large party of red people on the move. There had been warriors among them, but also old people and women and several children. They spread and circled, and one of them found trail sign. "Awi-gadoga passed here," he told the others. "He and his people go north in search of the Huron. They do not mean to return."

"Awi-gadoga was my father's friend," Goga the Crow said. "They took the Warrior's Road together when they were young and went to fight the Shawnee in their blood summer. They went all the way to the place of great waters and passed winter with the Huron. Awi-gadoga will be welcome there."

"Awi-gadoga may not live that long," another said, pointing. The track of Tenkiller lay upon the path of Awigadoga's people, leading away to the north.

XXVIII

Thomas Dodd had spared no effort in providing for Julie's comfort. One of the pack animals he had acquired carried a field tent, oilskins, wick lamps, a rug, goosedown quilts, a wicker chair, and a basket of bottled Madeira wines. The items would be invoiced to the commonwealth as "field equipment." However casual Thomas Dodd had kept his relationship with his pretty landlady, however light and breezy his presence when they were together, his intentions had become quite serious. Thomas Dodd had found in Kentucky, from the very day of his arrival at Harrod's old town, something quite beyond his expectations. He was in love. So, with characteristic thoroughness, he launched a campaign to win the lady.

The horse he selected for her to ride was a hand-gentled sorrel mare from the Post stock, fitted with a lady's saddle. The route he chose was dictated by the mission of his project—to establish a meridian northward from Harrod's original bench mark. But the schedule and pace of the outing he set for her comfort, planning the excursion with meticulous care. He intended that Julie enjoy the adventure and experience no discomfort in the slightest degree. He intended, by whatever means he could devise, for Julie McCarthy Jackson one day soon to become Julie Dodd.

Two previous trips with his assistants had established a line nearly twenty miles to the north, through mostly cleared and settled areas. They would pick up the line now at the final point they had established and push it on northward to the Ohio, and Dodd considered it a test of his skill to learn whether, indeed, the anchor mark at that river was opposite the mouth of the Greater Miami River. Cession of the Northwest Territories beyond to the Confederation of new states virtually guaranteed that extensive surveying would be required in those territories. It was his intention to cut himself a piece of that pie. Wilderness experience and the bench marks to show for it would stand well for him in seeking a contract with the Continental government—whatever form it took.

And so they rode out on a fine morning, Julie in her best travel clothes and bright bonnet, Thomas Dodd with eyes aglitter in the shadow of his cocked tricorn—both for the task ahead and for the lovely woman beside him. And they camped that night at a bluegrass glade above the Kentucky River, where deer peeped out from the shadows of the forest and flocks of pigeons beat whispering tattoos as they sought their roosts. Dodd instructed his men—two assistant geographers and six employed foresters—in camp routine and nightwatch, then had them get supper started while he walked with Julie to a sunset knoll to point out the next day's travel.

"Beyond that rise is our set point," he said. "When we came out before, we ran a true north line and then worked a grid back from it to place the starting point of each of the claims this side of Harrodsburg. Now, though, all we have to do is move straight north and set monuments each six miles. So we'll travel in a straight line . . . there." He pointed, taking the opportunity to lean close to her. She had removed her bonnet, and her hair smelled of sunshine.

"The land goes on and on," she said. "I've looked out from the stockade walls, but it never looked so big from there."

"It's big," he admitted. "More so than most know, even those who settle on it. They say there are fifty thousand people now, settled in Kentucky, and many talk of moving on because all the land is taken. Yet I'd wager that between here and the Ohio River, whose nearest bend is yonder fifty-seven miles—and for a dozen miles each side of the line—there aren't a dozen farmsteads. It's ignorance that says the land is full. It is empty, Julie, so empty that it cries out to be used."

"I've heard men talk in town. They say there's little enough land to be had where they can grow a crop. Others say everything is already claimed or owned, and there's no place for them to go."

"All that will change," he said. "It's normal, when no true boundaries are set, for those who have a piece of land to claim they have all that they can see. But fifty thousand settlers is nothing in a land that can hold a million and provide riches for them all. Look off there, now. You see the little patch where the wild peach grows? Someone will come along and find that before long and he'll claim it, because all he has to do is sprinkle some corn on the ground and it will grow and he'll think he's farming. And then once he has a cabin built, he'll decide all the rest of this around here is his, too, because all the rest that he can see is cedar groves and forest, and hills and meadows. It's the old way of looking at land: find a field that will farm itself and everything else goes with it. Boundaries will change all that, though, for a field that won't plant iself in corn will grow fine wheat if a man uses a tiller, and a cleared cedar brake will grow hemp for the market, and a managed woodlot will serve a good many farms . . . and a meadow that will fatten deer and buffalo will feed cattle and sheep and horses as well. With set boundaries each man will pull in his borders to what he can work, because he'll pay taxes whether he works an acre or not. And there will be room for plenty of new people here."

"Not the ones I've heard complain." Julie grinned.

"Some of them say that if a neighbor moves in within a mile, it's time to pack and move on."

"That's the other nature of the country, Julie. It breeds a restlessness in folks. It makes for movers. Kentucky . . . Tennessee . . . on the map the two together form a funnel. A long, pouring funnel piercing westward from the colonies toward the heart of the continent. It's a gateway, this land here. A place for the parting of kinds. There are movers and there are settlers. We are a stubborn race, Julie, lass. Some are too stubborn ever to be driven from a place of roots, and some are too stubborn ever to sink roots in the first place. Maybe Kentucky is where we weed ourselves out. Maybe this is where we sift the flour for what will someday be a nation's bread."

She tilted her head to look up at him, quizzically. Often he seemed to speak in riddles, but they were not the sort of riddles she heard from Crispin Blount. With Thomas Dodd it was as though he were constantly peering ahead somewhere, trying to see tomorrow and maybe catching glimpses just enough to make him hard to understand.

Yet she did enjoy the riddles, whatever kind they were.

"Which kind are you, Thomas? Are you a mover or a stayer?"

He smiled, his gaze lingering on her eyes. "I didn't say that there are *only* two kinds, my dear . . . friend. There are others, as well. Some of us simply glory in thrashing about among God's chaoses and trying to bring a bit of order to them."

"Like marking everything off in little squares?" she teased.

"Mayhap we get carried away sometimes, at that. I don't know whether range and township will ever happen here in Kentucky, dear little friend. Possibly metes and bounds will serve as well here. But yonder"—he pointed north again, and she noted that each time he did that he tended to lean close . . . closer than necessary for her to

310

follow the line of his point—"across that river over there, when these gateway lands have served their purpose, that's where the next funnel will be. And those will be ceded lands. There we will use the rectangles."

"We?"

"Well, those of us who get to do the surveying when it comes. If I am so fortunate, I will headquarter somewhere about Fort Pitt. There are towns there now, and they will grow."

"We saw Fort Pitt when we came to the Virginia territory," she said. "But that was so long ago, I barely recall it."

"You wouldn't recognize it now. Civilization has come to those lands. Towns and neighbors and stores and carriages rolling about on roads that ten years ago were trails in the wilderness . . . like this."

"I would like to see that," she told him. "Oh, and more than that. I would like to see Philadelphia. All I have heard about such places is . . . well, it's hard to imagine."

"Would you like to see them all, Julie? All those places you've never been? I go to those places. My trade takes me there. I wonder . . ."

He paused and she smiled. "You wonder what, Thomas?"

"I was just wondering what a man might have to do to earn the right to show such places to Julie McCarthy Jackson."

"I don't know, Thomas," she told him honestly. "But just at this moment, you seem to be doing it . . . or at least beginning to."

When they had eaten and sipped at a bit of his Madeira wine, he saw her to her tent and left her there with a proper and formal "Good night." And when he had gone off to find his own bed, she turned to face back toward Harrodsburg. It's a shame you can't be here at this moment, Luther, she thought. And you, Crispin, you fretting old rooster. Seemly, is it? Well, seemly it is.

The following day they entered hills and deeper

311

forests, and their passage was punctuated by periodic stops while Thomas and his assistants read their compasses, stepped off measurements, and entered copious notes into manuals. Julie watched, fascinated, seeing for the first time how he did the things he did. The land was huge and anomalous, yet he did in fact measure it and consign it to paper as he went. And each little x'd-in circle on his charts became in fact a corresponding fixed marker upon the land—a marker that would not disappear with the falling of a tree or move with the shifting of a stream, but that was fixed in place for others to locate exactly where Thomas Dodd had put it. In a way, what he did was like coming along after God had finished Creation and tidying up His work so it would be more useful for man.

And there was a fascination to it, she realized. The men worked as a team with their odd tools—bearing compass and astrolabe, plane table, chains and rods and lengths of iron. . . . There were always at least two afoot, coming along behind the foresters, one dragging the knotted rope that Thomas insisted upon calling a chain. "It is a chain," he explained, "because it is a chain-length. Sixty-six feet, exactly, from peg eye to peg eye. Four rods . . . no, not *rods* like those we drive into the ground, but rods of length. Sixteen and one half feet is a rod length. That times a half-mile makes an acre." Julie shook her head in puzzlement, but she did enjoy seeing them work.

Thomas would peg one end of his "chain" rope to the ground, and one of them would walk away with the other end, dragging it northward while Thomas directed him by reading his bearing compass and sighting across his plane table. Then when the rope was straight and its direction was what he wanted, he would loose the first end and move on, to start all over.

At intervals he would consult his astrolabe and compare his compass notes, then they would drive an iron rod into the ground and build a stone monument over it. Often these were accompanied by the notching of "witness trees" or the piling up of a cairn nearby, to make them easier to find. And always there were the copious field notes he kept, a record of every sighting, every monument, every feature of the terrain, as well as the interminable calculations he must make, calculations of the height of every hill, the elevation of every plain, sometimes even calculation of the height of witness trees. Julie's head spun at his explanations of the use of trigonometry for such purposes.

In places they waited while the foresters cleared a path with their axes, the American blades ringing and biting as they flashed in the sunlight. At one point he noted, "See how the axes punch through the wilds. Just a few years back I'd never seen such an axe. Yet now, one rarely ever sees the old curmudgeon blades. It's progress, my dear."

"What's strange to me is how many people bring American axes to Kentucky, when Kentucky is where they began."

"They did? I hadn't heard that."

"Of course they did. Crispin Blount and Jason Cook made the very first one." She paused, then giggled. "They chopped Squire Trelawney down to size with it."

She barely noticed that somewhere along the way he had stopped using the words "my dear friend." Now it was just "my dear."

On an afternoon they came into a meadow where cherry laurel still blossomed, and she wandered about, enjoying the varied colors of the wild lands while Thomas and his assistants did another reading. Enthralled and distracted, she didn't notice for a moment how quiet it had become, then she noticed it and looked around.

The men stood where they had been, bunched and frozen in the act of packing instruments. And all around were Indians . . . everywhere she looked.

Thomas snapped an order to his men, then set down the instrument he was holding—a theodolite, he called it—and raised his hands. Glancing over his shoulder, he called, "Julie, come to me. No, don't run. Just walk . . . directly to me."

Her eyes grown huge, Julie began to walk. Since coming to the overmountain lands, Indians had been a major part of her life. The deadly red menace, they were the ominous smokes that had hung above the horizons of her childhood, the fear in the eyes of people about her when they talked of life and death in the wilderness, the terrible presence always just beyond the clearings and the fields. Yet she had never seen an Indian. Now she gaped at them in terrified wonder as she walked slowly toward the gathered men. Tall and sinewy, hard muscles rippling beneath skin the color of bright copper, the warriors wore high moccasins like English buskins, together with fringed buckskin aprons, some brightly beaded in intricate designs. Most were bare-legged, although a few wore buckskin leggings. Most also were naked above the waist except for bits of ornamentation— here a necklace of gleaming bear claws, there beaded armbands, elsewhere little fans of bright shell dangling from earlobes. Some had shaven or plucked heads, tonsured like French clergy except for long crests of loose raven hair from brow to nape of neck. Here and there, among them, were some who wore three white-tipped feathers upright in their crests of hair. Others wore wrapped turbans of bright cloth with their dark hair falling below them. All of them were armed. One or two carried guns, rifles, or muskets, but more held bows with stone-tipped or steel-tipped arrows. What had she heard a man say once? . . . Indians generally preferred bows over guns because they were more efficient in forest lands.

Then she was beside Thomas and he whispered, "That's fine, Julie. Now stand very still. . . . No, don't look down. Look at them. Don't be afraid."

She lifted her head, chin high, and looked into one and then another pair of ebon eyes. Why were they so tall? They were as tall as white men. Then she realized, and a chill went up her spine. Cherokees.

314

Brush rustled and a man pushed forward from behind some of the warriors—a tall old Indian man. His hair, long beneath a bright turban, was streaked with gray, and his face reminded her of the drawing of God in Nora's illustrated Scriptures book. For a moment he gazed at them, impassive, then he said something she didn't understand and raised his hand, palm forward. Around him, warriors lowered their weapons—but only a little.

"I am Awi-gadoga," he said in slow English. "Standing Deer of the true people."

For the first time, Julie saw that there were others in the shadows beyond the warriors, women and children among them.

Thomas raised his hand as the old man had done. "I am Thomas Dodd," he said. "Surveyor to the Commonwealth of Virginia."

The old man looked at the other white men, then at Julie. His eye were dark again and she could feel the force of them upon her. "You have woman with you," he said. "You are not here to make war."

"Not today, at any rate," Thomas said. "We are measuring the land."

The old Indian pursed his lips and shook his head. "*Ani-yonega,*" he said. "White man measures everything."

"We go north to the river of white water. Ohio. May we go in peace?"

"Peace." The Indian shrugged. "The land is not ours anymore. If you think it is yours, then go upon it. We go north, too."

Some of the nearer warriors were eyeing their provisions curiously. Julie saw the avid glance of one of them and followed it. The Indian was looking at an axe. Thomas had seen the same thing. Turning carefully, he removed an axe from the hand of one of his wide-eyed assistants and held it up to be seen. Then holding it in both hands, he stepped forward. "For the people of Standing Deer," he said.

Awi-gadoga folded his arms and looked away, but one of the warriors strode forward, looked Thomas in the eye for a moment, then took the axe from his hands. He turned it over, seeing its shape and the curve of its haft, then said something to another in a sibilant, rhythmic tongue that sounded to Julie as though it were almost music. Only a few syllables could she catch. *"Galoya-s'di tsig"* . . . something, and *"a'sgoli . . . agadoli ale uwayi . . . tla-na tsiluga . . ."*

After a moment the old man nodded. *"Wa-do,"* he said. *"Tsisqua*—you would call him Bird—says it is a good axe. Good to the eye and to the hand, but not so good for killing."

"It wasn't meant for—" Julie spoke before she realized she was speaking, then bit her lip. Still, the old man was looking at her, waiting. "It wasn't meant for killing," she finished. "That axe is to help people live, not make them die."

Standing Deer gazed at her thoughtfully, saying nothing. She felt the blood rising in her face and took a deep, shaky breath. "The man who made that axe does not kill. He believes in life, not death."

"Few young men know the difference," the Indian said slowly.

"He isn't a young man," she said. "He is an old man . . . but only in years. He is a man who laughs and makes riddles and sings."

"What does he sing about?"

"All sorts of things. Everything. Sunshine and babies and winding roads . . . and about the little people, old legends and ballads and . . . ."

"Yunhwi-tsun'sdi?"

"What?"

"Little people . . . the wee people?"

"Yes. The wee folk, he says."

"Yunhwi-tsun'sdi. The wee ones." He turned away and said something to his people, then looked back at Thomas.

316

"You want to go north. Go north."

He walked away, and his warriors turned to follow him. One of them carried the gift axe. In shadows beyond the forest edge others, some of them women and children, ghosted away after them. In less than a minute they were gone, as though they had never come.

"Lady, you amaze me," Thomas said. "Who was that you were telling him about?"

"Crispin Blount."

"I thought so, yet I wondered. You make him sound a marvelous man."

She shrugged, smiling. "He is a marvelous man. Nora is a fortunate woman . . . more than she knows, I think."

"And that 'wee folks' thing? What was that about?"

"It's just an old song he sings sometimes . . . he and Luther, and sometimes others, too. I've heard it, but I don't know all of it. Ellie knows it."

"Would you sing it for me? The parts that you know?"

As they rode northward toward their early camp, Julie rode beside him and sang bits of the old song that she remembered. Sometimes Thomas nodded, recognizing a phrase or a verse. "I've heard it, too," he said. "I just don't remember when I did."

She thought for a bit, then sang, "So Belephon went before Old Rube himself . . . and he looked his . . . ah . . . oh! . . . his liege lord in the eye and said, 'Sire, lend an ear. There are no king's men here, only poor folk and likely to die.'"

"I remember that." He grinned. He raised his head and his voice. "'I have followed you, Sire, wherever you've led, and I've never been one to ask why. I have fought the king's soldiers and stood at your side and I will 'til the day that I die. But now I protest, Sire, for since time began . . .'"

"Sir!" One of the foresters hissed at him and pointed. In the brush, not far away, Indians were pacing them, glancing at them as though listening.

Julie glanced at the westering sun, then reined in her mount. "Is that a stream ahead, Thomas?"

He looked and nodded.

"If we stopped here to make camp, do you suppose they would stop, too?"

"I don't know. Why?"

"Well, we are all going the same way, aren't we?"

XXIX

They camped on the far side of a winding, laughing stream and the Indians made their own camp just across from them. Dodd and his men were nervous about that, but they lacked the deep hatred of red men that those longer in Kentucky often had. Dodd and his geographers were tidewater people, and his foresters were fresh down from eastern Pennsylvania. So they went about their tasks with no more than an occasional nervous glance at the people across the creek. Yet when they went for water and the Cherokee were there, too, they were only yards apart, dipping their water skins.

Julie stood on a cleared bank above the creek, watching those across the way, marveling at how like anyone else they were. They made their cook fires just as white people did, and they spread skins and shelters for the old people and the babies. They drew water from the stream and shared it among them, and those who wanted to relieve themselves went off into the brush to do so privately. Some of the women did not cover their breasts or covered only one, but the touch of nudity was not done in any provocative manner. It was only the way they dressed. And the warriors, among their own people, did not seem warriors at all, any more than did the young men who strutted about Harrodsburg with their rifles on their shoulders and their eyes on the ladies. Yet these were savages, she reminded herself. Her own sister—and so many others—had died at the hands of people just like those over there. At the thought of Kate a confusion grew in her. It had been impulsive of her to suggest a camp where these people also would camp. She could hate them, as others did . . . just as easily, she realized. She could despise them and want to see them die. She had reason enough to hate them. They—or ones like them—had killed so many decent people. The wars and the fighting went on and on. Why did she not feel the hatred that she could, just at the sight of them? Maybe it was one of those right over there, one of those tall red-skinned men with the tonsured scalp and flowing crest of raven hair? . . . Maybe that one with the cruel wide mouth and the three eagle feathers? . . . Maybe he himself had drawn the bow that flung the arrow that had put an end to Kate? . . . Maybe? . . . But then a child ran across his path—a little boy no larger than Jonathan and laughing in the very way that Jonathan sometimes laughed—and the warrior knelt to catch the child with a strong, gentle arm around his middle and swing him up as he stood, holding the boy above his upturned face, both of them laughing then. She had seen Luther do exactly the same thing with Jonathan. The sudden taste of hatred she had felt—had toyed with—collapsed in her throat, and she grinned at the sight of a tall, fierce red man and a small, fierce red boy being so like the pair that her sister had held so dear. She felt as though she would cry, just seeing the beauty of them. The tall warrior turned, saw her watching, and said something to the boy, still held high above his head. They both looked at her and she laughed and held out her arms, stepping down to the bank of the creek. The warrior said something else to the boy, then shifted him in his hand, and the child spread his arms as though he were a bird, flying. The warrior strode toward the creek, the boy flying above him, and Julie again held out her arms, aware that Thomas Dodd had come up behind her and was watching, entranced. If there was a thing the red people and the white had in common, above all else, it was their children. Here in the wilderness, encamped with savages, Julie reached for a child for all the world the way a doting aunt might reach for a favorite nephew, and the father responded just as any father would. He waded into the creek, mimicked birdcall for the boy, and lowered him toward the white woman's arms.

Then he stopped, shuddered, and the smile vanished from his face. His eyes rolled up past Julie to stare at Thomas Dodd—at him and beyond him into the sky— and the harsh crack of a rifle snapped through the forest. Julie screamed as the warrior went to his knees and dropped the child, head down. Lunging, she caught the boy and fell into the creek, rolling to hold him above water. Dodd took the bank at a leap, hit the creek, and went to his knees beside her, raising her as she clung to the child. He heard wild yells, the muted padding of feet on hard ground, the voices of his men at a distance, trying to control their animals. As he looked around the stricken warrior shuddered a last time and fell forward into the creek. His body splashed, rolled in the water, and lodged against Dodd's arm and knee. There was a neat small hole in the Indian's back, just between the shoulder blades.

Why was Julie there . . . there among those Indians? Even as he rolled behind screening brush, hoisting his powder horn to begin reloading, Leander's mind spun at the shock of seeing her there. For an instant he told himself he had imagined it, but he *had* seen her. Clearly, just in that moment as his finger tightened on the hair trigger of his rifle, she had stepped into view on the creek bank. Julie Jackson. It was her and there was no mistake. He had chosen the big warrior because he was at a distance, and his falling would create confusion among them. Maybe enough to give him time for a second shot.

He had fine-sighted twice on the warrior. The first time he had touched the trigger the man stooped to pick up a child. He had sighted again, the muzzle swinging slightly as the Indian moved toward the creek. Then, just at the moment of firing, there had been Julie. It made no sense. What was she doing, away out here and with Indians?

He poured powder and plugged the horn, his fingers working of their own will while his ears told him what was happening beyond the brush. The branches of a patch of dogwood had covered the smoke of his shot, and the sound had echoed here and there. He heard them shouting, calling, running around. But they didn't know yet where he was. It was what he had hoped for—time for two shots before he eased off into the forest behind him. Time to kill two Indians, then get away and come again when he was ready. But now everything had changed. Now he had to find out why Julie was here. Had they somehow taken her from Harrodsburg? He had to find out. If she was here, it was because the Indians had her. He must learn more. He had to get her away from them, to safety. It was the most important thing now.

He set a patched ball, rammed it home, and recharged the flare pan, freezing in place as a pair of warriors ran past, just yards away from him. They were circling the camp, looking for him. He could have killed them both, silently, and still had his second shot. But not now. He had to get to Julie.

Easing backward, he edged into shadows where the forest began above the creek, stood for a moment while his ears told him of the movements beyond, then turned and ran . . . the crouching, silent run of the forest hunter. Where his moccasins touched they made no sound and left no mark, and not a twig rustled or leaf turned as he passed.

Thomas Dodd got to his feet and lifted Julie from the water. The child in her arms sputtered and cried, and she clung to him, rubbing his chilled body, crooning to his fears. Dodd led her from the creek slowly, trying to see everywhere at once. There were Indians all around them, and the dark eyes that followed them said that a wrong move would mean death. Behind them, men pulled the body of the dead warrior from the water and crouched to see the bullet hole in his back. A woman came from somewhere, running, and pushed through them to kneel beside the fallen one. She ran gentle fingers over his face and lay her hand on his chest, then looked up at them with dark eyes that reflected shock, torment, and questions for which there were no answers. *"Tsani? Atsutsa Tsani?"*

The old man, Standing Dear, was beside her then, speaking softly. He pointed toward Dodd and Julie, then raised the woman to her feet and led her to them. When she saw that Julie was holding the little boy, she broke from him and ran. *"Tsani!"* she called, holding out her arms. Julie turned the child and handed him to the woman. "He's all right, I think. He's only frightened."

She didn't understand, but she cradled the child in her arms and sang soft words to him, soothing him.

"The child is her son," Standing Deer said. "The man—*Tsali Dali'sgi*—he was her husband." He took off his blanket robe and held it out to Julie, who was shivering from the cold. She stepped up to the Indian woman. "Here, let's wrap him in this." Between them, they got the child bundled into a cozy wrap.

Dodd looked at the dead Indian beside the creek, wishing someone would cover him with something before the woman looked that way again. "What happened? Was he shot?"

"He was shot." Standing Deer nodded. He paused, listening to shouts from a low crest beyond the Indians' camp. "The man shot him from there." He pointed. "But he isn't there now. He has gone."

"But . . . why? My God, why?"

There was no answer to that. Standing Deer turned to

323

say something to an old woman kneeling beside the fallen warrior. She repeated it to someone else, and people came with fur robes. One they spread over the dead man. Others they brought across to Julie and Dodd. He hadn't realized until that moment that he was as wet and cold as she was.

Standing Deer looked from one to another of them. "I think you are good people," he said simply. "I think not all white people are so bad. Only some. But you had better move your camp now. There is still a little light. Take your people and go on as far as you can from here. When we leave we will go another direction, so we do not meet again."

"But why?" Dodd was confused. "What have we? . . ."

"My people mourn for their dead just as your people do, Thomas Dodd. And when they grieve they become angry, just as with you. It is best for you not to be here when the warriors come back."

"The man who shot . . . ah . . . Chalee . . ."

"*Tsali. Tsali Dali'sgi.* Yes, a white man killed him. Now go. Make your little line northward, Thomas Dodd. Maybe little lines will hide the blood that stains this ground."

So, hurriedly, they struck camp and loaded their animals. But while the men worked Julie rummaged through her own luggage until she found the thing she sought—a little brass telescope her father had left so long ago, among his baker's implements. Then she crossed the creek once more and stood waiting until old Awi-Gadoga came to her.

She handed him the telescope. "For the boy," she said. "For *Tsani*. Tell him it is for looking forward, not for looking back."

The old man studied her. "Why do you give this?"

"I don't know." She lowered her head. "Only . . . well, maybe one day when he is a grown man . . . maybe the far-seeing glass will help him see . . . maybe it will

324

help him to remember that not all of . . . us . . . are his enemies."

"Can a far-seeing glass give wisdom, then?"

She raised her head and he saw the tears in her eyes. "I don't know," she said. "It just seems as though *something* must."

She waded back across the stream and Thomas helped her onto her horse. As they rode away in the evening shadows she looked back. There was no sign now of the woman who had lost her husband or of the little boy who had lost his father, but she knew where they were. Somewhere in the shadows the young woman sat alone, head down, rocking slowly back and forth, trying in whatever way she could find to contain her grief. Trying to understand what had happened . . . trying to grasp the reality that the man who had loved her was, abruptly and for no reason anyone could know, no longer there.

And maybe the little boy knelt beside her. . . . Julie took a deep breath and turned away, not to look back again. How could little Jonathan ever understand what had happened to the mother he had once had? How could that Indian child understand that his father was gone? How could any child ever understand?

The little boy's name was *Tsani*. Yet when his mother said the name, it sounded just like Johnny.

From a hiding place upstream, Leander watched the survey party move out, and questions swarmed about him. What were they doing out here? Why was Julie with them? Why had they been there, with those Indians? Didn't they know that Indians killed people? And why were they leaving now? Why were the Indians letting them go? It made no sense. None of it made sense. Yet they packed and rode away, and no Indians followed them. One old Indian even waved as they departed, and for a moment Leander lay his sights on that one, but no, to shoot now certainly would put Julie in jeopardy. It would be better to wait . . . to let them be far away before he killed again. The light was failing, and he decided he would return to where he had left his horse and packs. He would camp for the night, well away from here. Then he could decide what to do. His temptation was to circle around and go after Julie. Maybe then he could get some answers.

But not now, he decided. The woods were full of Indians, searching for him. And the memory of Luther's place was clear. He would not take the chance of again leading savages to where people he cared about were. The answers would wait.

He stayed hidden until the woods were dark and silent, and he was sure they had called off their search for the night. Then on silent feet he padded southward. He had gone a mile by the time moonlight touched his path, but it made no difference. He knew these forests as well in the dark as in the light. Just ahead was the thicket where he had left his horse. He would lead it another mile southward before he looked for a campsite for the night. It was a time to be cautious. Some of these Indians could follow a trail as well as he could. He had learned that.

Why was Julie out here with the surveyors? The question came back again and again. It tormented him. And with it came those feelings that always came when he thought of Julie—soft feelings that played around inside him, that tugged at the gentle parts of his heart. He should have gone to Julie long ago and tried to tell her how he felt. And suddenly he realized that it was time for him to quit . . . this thing he did. This thing he was so driven to do. Abruptly, he felt he had done enough. Julie was more important than the bad dreams that came to him, that made him go out into the wilderness and drown them in the blood of savages so that he didn't dream at all for a time. Walking silently through moonlit forest he realized, for the first time, that there was another way to halt the dreams. Julie could make them go away. He was sure she could. To have her, to be forever near her, that would be a better way.

In a quiet way, he felt that he was awakening from a long nightmare, a dream that went on and on and was painful but had no way out of the pain except to go out and kill Indians. Suddenly, he realized that he had done enough. Like warm sunlight searching out the dark places within him, new visions swarmed, visions that were Julie and were all that Julie could mean. He paused, looked around at the dappled moonglow striking through forest shadows, and took a deep breath. He felt free. He felt as though he had been released from a bondage. Julie was the answer. He didn't have to fight the dreams anymore. Julie would . . .

Shock and pain hit him like a sudden fist. Something was terribly wrong. Just a whisper of sudden sound and he felt things tearing inside him, going amiss. He looked down, wondering at what he saw there, the shaft of an arrow protruding from his chest. It looked all wrong there, and he reached to pull it away, and inside him more things tore and screamed. It was wrong . . . all wrong. There should be no arrow there. He should be going home now, going to find Julie. He should be getting his horse and going away to tell Julie how he felt . . . somehow to make her know what he had just now realized. Another whisper in the shadows and something hit him again. Now there were two arrows there, not just one. Why were there arrows? He staggered, trying to go on, trying to think and realizing that he couldn't think clearly. The moonlight seemed to blur and to fade, and shadows danced. He heard something hit the ground behind him and realized slowly that he had lost his rifle. But he didn't need it. He could come back for it later, after he told Julie, but the face before him now wasn't Julie's face. It was an Indian face, clear in the fading moonlight. It was a face he knew, and he smiled at the recognition. Round Eyes.

Like an old friend too long unseen, Round Eyes stood before him there, and he whispered. "There you are. I

327

thought I had lost you."

"*S'gohidihi*," Round Eyes said. Then like an old friend putting an end to suffering, he raised a bladed thing and brought down the darkness.

In moon-dappled forest they stood over the dead thing that had been Tenkiller, wondering at how gently, how quietly he had died. Then Goga the Crow told them, "Go get his horse and turn it loose. Leave him here where he has fallen. It is done." When one of them turned toward the dropped rifle, Goga said, "Leave that, too. We will take nothing that was his."

"Where will we go now?" one asked.

"The people of Awi-gadoga are ahead somewhere. We will go to them. If Awi-gadoga goes to join the Huron, then we will go, too." He looked around at the night forest. "This is not our land anymore. Too many ghosts walk here. It is a land of death and blood and winter. Awi-gadoga is a wise man. He seeks the summer places, if any such remain. We will seek them with him."

A Presence of Arms

XXX

Summer 1783

Lush summer lay upon the western territories when Christopher Post and the Kentucky Militia crossed the Tennessee River above its terminus on the Ohio and reached the Mississippi. One mounted company he placed atop a ridge there, with a view of both the Ohio and the Mississippi, and set them to building a pole stockade while he moved on southward with the rest. Eight miles along he found another vantage and assigned one of the foot companies to fortify it. The third fortification was ten miles farther south, and the fourth seven miles past that. With fifty mounted men at his back then he rode the remaining six miles on wooded trails, coming out of the forest on a high bank overlooking the river and the horseshoe bend beyond where the smoke of the village of New Madrid hung on the horizon.

He had traveled at a leisurely pace, sweeping first along the Ohio and then up the Green to the valley of the Cumberland, then back to the Ohio, and the red men where he had gone had moved either ahead of him or away to the north and south, out of his path. Only four times had there been an exchange of fire, and his only casualty was a youngster with an arrow puncture in his leg. Some Indians had gone to ground and let the militia

pass them by. Far more had simply picked up and left Kentucky for the time being. It was a hunting ground to them, not a home ground, and there were few in it who had anything to defend. And those who went westward told of his coming, so the Spanish were aware when he arrived. It was as he wanted it. Let them muster their troops—or their Indians—and feed them while he took his time in arriving at the river.

Through the final days of march he had kept scouts out in a long fan ahead, expecting and hoping for an attack in force. The attack, if it came, would not be Spanish troops. Several times a week riders reached him with dispatches, and Clayton Chase had an excellent system of intelligence. So Christopher knew that the entire complement at New Madrid was a single company of lancers. He knew also, though, that Vice Governor Jose Maria Navarro, commanding New Madrid, had given shelter to the renegade force of the Cherokee Nicolet and would not hesitate to throw Nicolet against him to avoid a Virginia presence in western Kentucky.

Still, though the militia moved at the alert from the Green River westward, no attack came. And when he began his fortifications along the river it was obvious that no force of warriors was in Kentucky at all. Nicolet had not crossed the Mississippi. He was still beyond, in New Spain.

Christopher sent scouts to the river, upstream and down, to scour its banks for evidence of hostiles. One trio of scouts rafted over to a large island that split the river upstream into two parts and learned from a French trader camped there that Nicolet would not be coming, now or ever. The chief who had molded the renegades of five tribes into a fighting force of more than a thousand braves was dead. He had died two weeks before, along with more than half of his people. An epidemic of smallpox had virtually wiped out his little nation.

By the end of August Christopher Post had five fortified points along the Mississippi, an hour's ride apart and each manned by fifty Kentucky woodsmen with long rifles. And only then did he do what he had waited seven years to do. With a company of mounted militia he rode downstream to the horseshoe bend, around its upstream curve, and directly across its expanse to the center bend. And there, a quarter of a mile away across the river, the flag of Spain flew above the cabins and the little fort of New Madrid.

Without invitation, welcome, or ceremony, the militiamen led their horses onto lashed rafts and crossed the Mississippi. It was a violation of every treaty presently in effect, as well as a violation of his orders, though not of their intent. Christopher Post had advised Clayton Chase that he would do whatever was necessary to assure that no Spanish claim could be made on American soil east of the Mississippi. His method was direct and efficient. Within the space of hours, the Kentucky Militia held all of New Madrid except the garrison stockade itself, and that was surrounded by mounted buckskinned woodsmen. Not a shot had been fired. The vice governor knew that muskets were no match in either range or accuracy for long rifles. Even with his pair of cannons, there would be no contest. The vice governor was a sane and cautious man.

For a time, then, Christopher Post rode leisurely along the paths of New Madrid. Tall and lithe in the saddle of a blooded black racer, spotless linen glistening between the lapels of his black coat, black tricorn square atop his head, he rode the ways of the village and savored the sound of his mount's hooves on the soil of the forbidden land. Somewhere out there, in the wilderness beyond, a long time before, soldiers of a foreign power had done insult to an adventurer. Two things had the Spanish taken from Matthew Post—the use of his leg and the fiber of his spirit. It was a display of will now, for Christopher Post to ride unchallenged through these streets while the Spanish hid within their stockade awaiting his pleasure.

When the sun stood above western hills he returned to the little fort and rode directly to its gate. To the nervous officer above, he called, "Respects to the Vice Governor. Captain Christopher Post requests to speak with him." He pointed to the ground in front of the gate. "Out here."

The guard turned to someone else, a civilian, who had appeared beside him. *"Que dice?"*

The civilian ignored him and leaned over the rampart to scowl at Christopher. "Señor," he said, "you have invaded a province of Spain. Is this an act of war?"

"Only if you choose to make it so," Christopher told him. "Otherwise, it is a courtesy call. Identify yourself, please."

The man drew himself up, stone-faced. "Jose Maria Navarro *de* Celestrón, *Gubernador Segundo de Nuevo España, a sus ordenes,* Señor."

"Most impressive. I am Christopher Post. Will you come out, *Señor,* to receive my compliments?"

"I will not, Señor. You are trespassing here. It is my duty to demand that you leave."

"As I intend to, when I am ready. But it is not my trespass I came to discuss. It is yours. As recently as three weeks ago, patrols from this garrison were on the other side of that river. That is not to happen again. Further, it is known that you yourself, *Señor,* have attempted to direct hostiles into western Kentucky. It is fortunate for you that we did not find them there upon our arrival."

"That is contested land," Navarro said.

"Not anymore, it isn't." Christopher smiled at him. "It is claimed by right of presence."

"What presence, Señor?"

"My presence, *Señor.* A presence of arms."

"Nonsense, Señor. A civil militia? A few backwoodsmen with rifles? I can call up troops . . ."

"Call all the troops you like, *Señor.* But if they cross that river, then it will be you who have committed an act of war, and there will indeed be contested land. But it will not be over there. It will be over here."

"Are you threatening me, Señor?"

"Let there be no question about it," Christopher assured him. Satisfied, then, he turned and rode away, his grinning militiamen grouping behind him.

Four days later the first flotilla of broad-horn boats from Stephen Moliere's new docks on the Ohio passed into the Mississippi and floated on downstream, escorted on shore by a company of Kentucky Militia. When they rounded the bend toward New Madrid, another company rode ahead to form in line on the bank across from the village with its little fort. The boats passed under Navarro's guns without incident, each flying a pennant of the Commonwealth of Virginia.

And on the third day of September, the day Benjamin Franklin, John Adams, and John Jay met at the Hague with British Commissioner Richard Oswald to agree upon conditions for the Articles of Peace—including cession of those lands east of the Mississippi to what the Earl of Shelburne called "the 13 U.S."—on that day Christopher Post held western Kentucky by presence of arms.

XXXI

Fall 1783

When the sycamores had shed their leaves and the oaks were gone to scarlet, Luther came up from the river leading Mystery behind him. Her packs were full of persimmons and sassafras root, her bells jangled merrily, and Jonathan sat perched atop her. Near a month they had been gone, harvesting Luther's crops with the help of Oban Calloway and his brood. The grain had gone by wagon road downriver to Stephen Moliere's docks, and the garden truck would see the Calloways through the winter until they could plant a crop of their own. A season's produce, they reckoned, would give them the means to pay Luther for the land.

"Old Rube's clan these were," Luther sang as they strode past the out-lots, "or the few that was left, for a many had died in the spring, yet still proud was each elf, for 'twas Old Rube himself who had spat on the foot of a king." His voice rolled out easily, sure and strong, and Mystery's bells kept rhythm.

"Many days had they fought," he sang, "there in—where was it, Jonathan? Where they fought?"

"Cave an' dish bog," the boy said. "You remember."

"Sure I remember. I just wanted to know if you did."

"I remember. Sing it some more."

"Many days had they fought, there in Cavendish Bog, and many a churl felt the sting of the wee deadly darts and the proud fighting hearts of a folk who would spit on a king."

"Those men that came by," Jonathan interrupted. "They said Christopher Post spat on somebody. Was that the king?"

"Christopher Post didn't spit on anybody, Jonathan. It was only a manner of speaking."

"Well, what did he do, then?"

"He told the Spanish to stay out of Kentucky."

"Is the Spanitch a king?"

"The Spanish are people. Like us, only different."

"Oh. Well, are any of them kings?"

"I guess one of them is. Why?"

"I bet Christopher Post would spit on his foot."

Luther grinned, glancing around. "I guess he might, at that. There's Harrodsburg, Jonathan. See? There's Granny's house."

"As ever was," Jonathan allowed. "How long are we going to stay, pa?"

"All winter, I guess. I told Mr. Calkins that I'd make pews for the church. That will take a while. And you have to start learning to read and write and cipher."

"Why?"

"Why? Because you have to, that's why. Do you want to be ignorant?"

"Is Michael going to learn, too?"

"When he's your age he will. Right now he's learning other things."

"Granny says Michael is a menace."

"If that's what she says, then that's what he is." He shook his head, marveling at the twists his son's mind could take. Trying to keep up with Jonathan's notions was like shooting at a flock of quail. They went all directions, all at once, and if a man couldn't pick out just one and sight on it, then he'd miss entirely.

Mystery's bells jangled in time to her tread and there

was lyric in the crisp air. "Yet the soldiers were many," Luther sang, "and the wee folk too few. Scythes and lances were launched on the land and each sunset bled for the blood of the dead tiny warriors, the last faerie clan."

"I don't much like that part," Jonathan told him.

"It wouldn't be the same song without it, Jonathan. You take the bad with the good. It's how life is." He rubbed at the stubble of whiskers on his cheeks. It's how life is, son, he thought. Maybe that's what the old song is all about. It's just how life is. "Then she showed them her heels," he sang, "set her course to the west and her bow sliced the sun-gilded sea, and the elves and the crew and the sixty-one, too, they all knew that one day they'd be free."

"Pa?"

"What, son?"

"You left out a whole mess of it, pa."

"I know, Jonathan. But songs are like that. A man can sing one part or another, and put them together any way he pleases. And it doesn't matter, because it's still a song . . . as long as you never stop singing."

He looked off to the west, to the distance beyond the far out-lots where the mists of change of season lay upon the wooded hills. Never stop singing. And always, because it's in the blood, with the singing comes the looking to the west. Forward, for us, means west. East is for those who look too much at the past. He remembered a chill evening—it seemed such a long time ago now—when each spoken word was a tiny cloud of mist in the blue shadows and Crispin Blount said, "See yonder star, Luther . . . the bright one, low down to the west . . . evening star some call it, though some have called it the western star. . . . I've stood atop a mountain ridge with men who went of evening to call on it for luck, an' I've wondered if it's in our blood to face the west when we seek good fortune."

Good fortune? The future, he thought. The future and

whatever it might bring. The swallows of morning, Crispin had said . . . they rise aspiral from the shadows to the sun . . . and had they threads to pull with them there'd be a brightness there.

A man might rise or he might fall. He glanced back at the pacing mule, at the bright-eyed, sturdy lad atop it. A man has threads to pull with him when he rises to meet the sun. And those threads are reason enough for the rising.

He had resumed the singing, and his mind was on those hills to the west . . . on the future and on his sons.

Ellie saw them coming from the roof of the church. She had climbed there to take a bit of honey-bread to Seth, who was setting shingles, then had stayed to watch him work. There was a pleasure in his rhythms as he drove the shingle nails, the ring of his hammer in the bright, chill air. Sometimes she found a comfort in being near him, in the concentration that was on his face when he worked. It was a comfortable face, the face of an old friend. The pox had left his cheeks dimpled, but she found no fault in that. It just made him look a little older . . . a bit more weathered.

She pointed. "Seth, look! Luther and Jonathan. Harvest must be done."

He paused, looking across the distance. "Then the Calloways stayed on. I guess they like his place."

"It's good land. Crispin says a tribe like theirs will need fine fields to feed them all, though Squire Trelawney can't understand why Luther doesn't want to keep the place anymore."

"I understand," he said, looking at her. "If it were me, I guess I wouldn't want to live there anymore either." He shifted on his foot-beam, corrected the alignment of another shingle, and drew a nail from his pouch to set it. The nails were bright and new, fresh from the draw-mill Crispin Blount and Jason Cook had installed in a shed behind the smithy. Samuel Calkins had traded a side of pork for twenty pounds of "punch-heads" to roof the

337

church. Crispin had grumbled about that—at the top of his lungs, as usual. Ellie grinned, remembering his words. "There goes th' first year's profit from th' draw-mill," he had said. "Samuel, your friendship is like to bankrupt us all ere long."

Calkins had adjusted his wire wig and glared up at the tall man sternly. "It's for the church," he reminded.

"Aye, for th' church. An' here by th' grace of God stands your best friends, full o' faith, hope, an' poverty!"

They had ignored him and made the trade, and Crispin himself had split the first bale of shingles.

Seth set another nail and Ellie noticed how strong his hands seemed, how sinewy the forearms beneath his rolled-up sleeves. She marveled at when he had grown so. She found she couldn't recall such changes happening, just that one day there they were—just as with the changes in herself. Strange it was, how things could change so and yet not seem to have changed at all. Seth was still Seth, and she was still just Ellie. All that either of them had been, they still were. Yet the differences were there as well, and in a way it saddened her, because the changing was not through. So much had changed, yet there was so much more that would, and she wondered where it would lead. Seth was her dearest friend. . . . Would he be more someday? She didn't know. The veils of change lifted so slowly, and still there were other veils beyond.

Still, for now, they were here. From across the distance now she could hear Luther's rich voice. He was singing as he approached the town, singing for himself, and for his sons, and for the changes yet to come, she suspected. She couldn't hear the words, but she heard the tune and words came to mind: *And there was one among them, the pixie Aella, who felt the old love of her race, and she listened . . .*

Seth's hammering stopped and she turned. He was gazing at her, smiling slightly. She hadn't realized that she was singing aloud. Pock-dimpled cheeks molded his smile, a tentative smile beneath eyes that reflected her own uncertainties. "Small and comely she was," he said softly, "just twelve inches tall, with dark eyes and a soul sorely tried."

She realized that he had learned the song from her, and it caught at her throat that he had. "And there was one who loved her," she murmured, "the stout Belephon."

"It near broke his heart if she cried," he added.

On the ground below the two mongrel puppies that Crispin had found barked and whined at the sound of their voices, impatient for Seth to come down from the roof and romp with them.

From the cutting-stump at the woodlot just down from the horse camp, Crispin Blount saw Luther and Jonathan coming into town. He set down his axe, wiped the sweat from his eyes, and pointed. "Look'ee yon, Mr. Sparrow, for there be a sight th' likes o' which one seldom sees. In a world bright an' cool goes a man with a mule an' a child wi' a gun on its knees."

Sparrow deposited an armload of stovewood in his barrow, looked where he was pointing, then pursed his lips and shook his head. "I wonder sometimes if the squire is right about you, Mr. Blount. He says you're the only man he knows whose tongue flaps loose at both ends."

"Trelawney's a jealous man," Crispin allowed. "Th' nearest to talent he knows is what he finds in others."

"Should I tell him you said that?"

"An' when didn't ye?" Crispin shrugged. "Were I to stop speakin' my mind and you to stop reportin' it, what would th' poor soul do for amusement?"

The barrow was nearly full, and he stepped to it and lifted its bars. "This should be aplenty to keep th' home fires burnin' a few days more," he decided. "I'm obliged for th' hand, Mr. Sparrow. Come around when yer belly growls. There'll be ham hocks an' beans awaitin', cooked wi' just a pinch o' clove."

At the dooryard gate Luther looped Mystery's lead,

retrieved his rifle from Jonathan, and set the boy on the ground. Inside the house a child's voice howled in abrupt outrage and Luther smiled. Yes, his mother was right. Michael was a menace. The door opened then and Nora was there, the toddler at her heel, peering from behind her skirts. "Luther," she welcomed him. "Oh, I so hoped you'd be home soon. Was the harvest good?"

"A fine harvest," he said as Jonathan raced past him, seeking a hug from his grandmother. "Sowing oats around the wheat kept the critters from it, and I got a good price on it from Mr. Moliere's drivers. Oh, I brought persimmons and sassafras root. I'll put the packs in the shed."

He stepped up on the porch, kissed his mother, and stooped to sweep up the toddler beside her. "Michael! You little nuisance, your pa has missed you despite your ways." He hugged the child to his chest, then held him away to look at him, feeling the same old twinge in his heart when he did. Every day, it seemed, the boy looked more like Kate.

"You missed Julie by a week," Nora was saying. "Thomas finished his first surveys and they've gone to Philadelphia. But they'll be back in the spring."

At the crossing of roads, where trails became a street, Crispin Blount set down his barrow and stood for a moment watching the little group there at his doorway. "An' what a sight for these old eyes," he told himself. "An' what blessin's be here at hand." He picked up his barrow and headed for home, singing for the world to hear, "An' ne'er was a winter but followed by spring, bringin' green for a summer land."

Afterword

Ballad of the Wee Folk

Now bring out a bench for this traveler's rest,
with some honest spring water to hand.
Then with me avail, for I'll tell you a tale
of the wee folk who came to this land.

'Twas the eve of St. Michael's, a gray bitter day,
when the fugitive *Harod* set sail.
From Land's End she crept and took spray on her bow
while her passengers prayed at the rail.

For these were no gentlefolk out for a lark,
nor stout merchantmen braving the gale,
but the poor folk of Land's End set out to be free,
and the quest it were death should it fail.

Sixty-one desperate souls and the crew were aboard
by head count entered down in the log.
And the fourteen below—of whom none must know—
were the wee folk from Cavendish Bog.

Old Rube's clan these were, or the few that was left,
for a many had died in the spring.
Yet still proud was each elf, for 'twas Old Rube himself
who had spat on the foot of a king.

Many days had they fought, there in Cavendish Bog,
and many a churl felt the sting
of the wee deadly darts and the brave, fighting hearts
of a folk who would spit on a king.

Yet the soldiers were many, the wee folk too few.
Scythes and lances were launched on the land
and each sunset bled for the blood of the dead
tiny warriors, the last faerie clan.

Then the magic and music was gone from the bog,
The wee folk had spent of their stock
to the last tragic trace. There were tears on his face
as Rube counted fourteen in his flock.

So to Land's End he led them by darkness of night
'neath a scarred moon that grieved at the madness
of kings in their glory who'd end such a story
and leave a whole world to its sadness.

Crossbow at his shoulder, Old Rube led them there
where the big folk were sorely oppressed,
and they crept aboard *Harod* and hid in her holds
to brave the dark seas to the west.

Not a wee soul was left in the whole of the realm . . .
only memories of magic they'd shared
with the self-same large race that had done bloody chase
until only fourteen boarded *Harod*.

Oh, a dark ship was *Harod*. Her crew was but wretches
escaped from the Land's End stockade,
and the folk the ship carried were poor souls long harried,
owning nought but the clothes they had made.

Dickie Quist, he was master aboard the sad ship.
A man of quick eye and dark mien,

he had stolen the ship when he'd given the slip
to the kin of a noble he'd slain.

On that dark howling day *Harod* took to the sea.
There was ice in the clouds hanging low
over captain and crew and the sixty-one, too . . .
and the fourteen wee folk down below.

Twenty days of foul winds, yet the old ship crept on,
avoiding the known lanes to drive
through the cold northern sea where no frigates would be.
Only thus could the *Harod* survive.

West they sailed, ever west. The supplies all ran low
and gaunt faces peered out to the sea,
for they'd heard that out there in the distance somewhere
was a land where poor folk could be free.

There were children among them and some took the chill.
There was hunger, and water ran low.
Yet still, in the hold, in their dark hidden fold,
the wee folk kept silence below.

"The big folk can never again be our friends,"
Old Rube told his sore-hearted band.
"It was their kind that fought us and drove us away.
Let them perish. I'll not raise a hand."

Now Rube, he was chief. They stayed hidden below,
though they grieved at the course they were plying.
They bent to his will, but it tore at them still
that, above, human babies were dying.

For these were no evil nor sorrowless folk—
warriors, true, but not heartless or prime.
No, these were the wee folk, and long friends of man,
who had cared for him since before time.

343

And there was one among them, the pixie Aella,
who felt the old love of her race,
and she listened adept as the human folk wept,
and found there were tears on her face.

Small and comely she was, barely twelve inches tall,
with dark eyes and a soul sorely tried.
And there was one who loved her, the stout Belephon.
Oh, it near broke his heart when she cried.

So Belephone went before Old Rube himself
and he looked his liege lord in the eye
and said, "Sire, lend an ear. There are no king's men here,
only poor folk and likely to die.

"I have followed you, Sire, wherever you've led,
and I've never been one to ask why.
I have fought the king's soldiers and stood at your side,
and I will 'til the day that I die.

"But now I protest, Sire, for since time began
our way's been to help humans in need.
We have lent them our lore and done deeds by the score
in the hope that one day they might heed
that the blindness and foolishness born to their race
are the stuff from which wisdom might grow.
Can we now turn aside after all that have tried
through all time, Sire, to help them to know?"

Old Rube stood in silence. His scowl and his scars
were a mask that could hide many things . . .
all the times and the tears, all the long lonely years
come to naught but the evil of kings.

Yet in Belephon now he could see himself then,
and he knew that the young elf was right.
There was no evil here, only sorrow and fear
and the poor folk who shared in their plight.

"You make me ashamed, Belephon," Old Rube said,
"For you show me what I could not see—
that the big folk up there have had as their fare
the same draught of betrayal as we.

"Now gather around me," Rube said to his tribe.
"We can help if we all lend a hand.
There are skills we must share with the big folk up there,
if we all are to reach a new land.
Marabit and Leropa, you'll tend to their ill.
You must reckon their stores, Homalind.
Pontigram and Grunvail, show them how to make sail
so this old craft can fly with the wind.
Take the helm, Belephon. Teach their steersmen the way
to play currents as one with the sea.
You there, Billit, and Gruns, lend a hand with their guns.
And their captain, well, leave him to me.
For this old ship is blind, just the way I have been,
but all that she needs is craft's hand,
then we'll show her sting to the ships of the king
and we'll sail to a bright summer land."

Then up from the hold came Old Rube and his tribe
to the decks where the fugitives huddled,
and they spread stern to tip through the groaning old
    ship
'midst a deck crew amazed and befuddled.

Belephon found the helmsman and made him kneel down
to learn to read rudder and fife,
and the deck crew all stared at the wee men who dared
set all sail. And the ship came to life.

Now she sang and she hummed and she clove through the
    waves
and she took the cold spray on her bow.
Belephone and the helmsman they hauled hard alee.
They would make for the shipping lanes now.

Dickie Quist was asleep, but he woke with a start,
for a tiny man stood on his chest.
There was frost on his whiskeres and fire in his eyes
and he carried a crossbow at rest.

"We go south," Old Rube told him. "We make for the
   lanes
where this *Harod* can run with the sea,
and if frigates await they shall find out too late
that oppressed folk can fight to be free."

The blockade was there, men of war three abreast
when old *Harod* drove out of the north.
The king wanted her dead. "Sink the *Harod*," they said,
and they loaded their guns and sailed forth.

Lightly armed was the old ship, and heavy with age,
yet she danced and she dodged and she blasted
until two were aground on the shoals of a sound
and the third man-of-war was dismasted.

Then she showed them her heels, set her course to the
   west
and her bow sliced the sun-gilded sea
and the elves and the crew and the sixty-one, too,
they all knew that one day they'd be free.

Dickie Quist and Old Rube plotted course by the wind,
Belephon and the helmsmen trimmed keen,
and the courses of men and the craft of their kin
brought to *Harod* a magic not seen
since the long-ago time in the age before kings
when the large and the small folk were one,
and Aella's eyes shone, for she saw reborn
what a king's whim had nearly undone.

For kings and their customs are born of decay,
when an old land has outlived its day

of freedom to all, both the large and the small.
It is then that folks must turn away.

For the world is far greater than any king's realm,
and with new lands abundantly blessed.
And many a king's found that among those he's bound
there are brave ones who'll look to the west
past the enemies lurking, the deserts and bogs,
past the cold night, the wintering sea,
and they may not know where but they know that out
    there
is a place where one day they'll be free.

Belephon at the helm had turned back to the rail,
knowing all that was back there was done,
but Aella went to him and she took his hand
and she turned his face back to the sun.

And Old Rube and the captain, they knew how it was,
and the folk aboard saw their sad glances,
but Dickie Quist said, "All that's back there is dead,
look ahead now, for there lie our chances.

"Then leave them behind, all the evils that were.
Let the old world inherit its woe.
For somewhere out there is a bright summer land,
and it's there that we're going to go."

And many a land would they see on their way,
and many times they would move on.
Yet each time and season would have its own reason
to remember them when they had gone.

For they went as two folks—the large and the small—
and as one left their mark on each thing
that they touched, for though poor, they had learned to
    endure,
and they knew how to spit on a king.

They would tame the wild forests and put in their crops.
In each place for a time they would stand.
Yet always out there—in the sunset somewhere—
they would know there's a bright summer land.

Song of the Yunhwi-Tsuns'di

From a place beyond the sea
the people once were driven.
In canoes they paddled west
with nothing left among them.
But small canoes followed behind,
though the people did not see them,
and in the small canoes were those
the people called the wee ones.
For while the people's land had shook,
and fires had smoked the heavens,
the wee folk also were cast out,
for they had fought the raven.
When the people lost all hope
and could no longer paddle,
and slept beneath the sea's dark sky
and thought they'd never waken,
the wee folk came upon them there
and saw that they were sleeping.
"These people are as lost as us,"
they said to he who led them.
"They are cast out, the same as us,
the ones who fought the raven."
So they tied thongs to their canoes,
and through the time of darkness
they paddled westward, pulling them,

the ones who did not know them.
And Man Above looked down at them
and saw where they were going,
and made the nighttime last until
a new land lay before them.
Then the people woke and went ashore
where new lands lay about them,
and saw a pathway leading north
to where the lands were wider. . . .

CATCH UP ON THE BEST IN CONTEMPORARY FICTION FROM ZEBRA BOOKS!

LOVE AFFAIR (2181, $4.50)
by Syrell Rogovin Leahy

A poignant, supremely romantic story of an innocent young woman with a tragic past on her own in New York, and the seasoned newspaper reporter who vows to protect her from the harsh truths of the big city with his experience — and his love.

ROOMMATES (2156, $4.50)
by Katherine Stone

No one could have prepared Carrie for the monumental changes she would face when she met her new circle of friends at Stanford University. For once their lives intertwined and became woven into the tapestry of the times, they would never be the same.

MARITAL AFFAIRS (2033, $4.50)
by Sharleen Cooper Cohen

Everything the golden couple Liza and Jason Greene touched was charmed — except their marriage. And when Jason's thirst for glory led him to infidelity, Liza struck back in the only way possible.

RICH IS BEST (1924, $4.50)
by Julie Ellis

From Palm Springs to Paris, from Monte Carlo to New York City, wealthy and powerful Diane Carstairs plays a ruthless game, living a life on the edge between danger and decadence. But when caught in a battle for the unobtainable, she gambles with the only thing she owns that she cannot control — her heart.

THE FLOWER GARDEN (1396, $3.95)
by Margaret Pemberton

Born and bred in the opulent world of political high society, Nancy Leigh flees from her politician husband to the exotic island of Madeira. Irresistibly drawn to the arms of Ramon Sanford, the son of her father's deadliest enemy, Nancy is forced to make a dangerous choice between her family's honor and her heart's most fervent desire!

Available wherever paperbacks are sold, or order direct from the Publisher. Send cover price plus 50¢ per copy for mailing and handling to Zebra Books, Dept. 2683, 475 Park Avenue South, New York, N.Y. 10016. Residents of New York, New Jersey and Pennsylvania must include sales tax. DO NOT SEND CASH.

**SADDLE UP FOR ADVENTURE
WITH G. CLIFTON WISLER'S
TEXAS BRAZOS!
A SAGA AS BIG AND BOLD AS TEXAS ITSELF,
FROM THE NUMBER-ONE PUBLISHER
OF WESTERN EXCITEMENT**

#1: TEXAS BRAZOS (1969, $3.95)
In the Spring of 1870, Charlie Justiss and his family follow
their dreams into an untamed and glorious new land — battling the worst of man and nature to forge the raw beginnings of what is destined to become the largest cattle
operation in West Texas.

#2: FORTUNE BEND (2069, $3.95)
The epic adventure continues! Progress comes to the raw
West Texas outpost of Palo Pinto, threatening the Justiss
family's blossoming cattle empire. But Charlie Justiss is
willing to fight to the death to defend his dreams in the wide
open terrain of America's frontier!

#3: PALO PINTO (2164, $3.95)
The small Texas town of Palo Pinto has grown by leaps and
bounds since the Justiss family first settled there a decade
earlier. For beautiful women like Emiline Justiss, the advent
of civilization promises fancy new houses and proper courting. But for strong men like Bret Pruett, it means new laws
to be upheld — with a shotgun if necessary!

#4: CADDO CREEK (2257, $3.95)
During the worst drought in memory, a bitter range war
erupts between the farmers and cattlemen of Palo Pinto for
the Brazos River's dwindling water supply. Peace must come
again to the territory, or everything the settlers had fought
and died for would be lost forever!

*Available wherever paperbacks are sold, or order direct from the
Publisher. Send cover price plus 50¢ per copy for mailing and handling to Zebra Books, Dept. 2683, 475 Park Avenue South, New
York, N.Y. 10016. Residents of New York, New Jersey and Pennsylvania must include sales tax. DO NOT SEND CASH.*